# The Jovian Run
## Sol Space Book One

James Ross Wilks

Cover design by The Cover Collection

# DEDICATION

This book is dedicated to my parents, Ted and Elaine, who gave me the tools and the drive to become the person I am.

It is also dedicated to those creators of science fiction who have provided such inspirational shoulders upon which to stand.

# CONTENTS

# PROLOGUE

It was one of the better restaurants on Mars. The Mars Needle, as its owner, a former Seattle resident, called it, towered over the surrounding smaller and larger buildings. From over three hundred feet in the thin Martian atmosphere the diners could enjoy a slowly rotating view of Tranquility, the surrounding city, and the Martian terrain that stretched for miles and miles beyond. The highlight of this gradual topographical survey was Olympos Mons, a volcano that dwarfed Everest and drew dozens of rich thrill seekers to its summit every year. Tranquility itself sprawled for over a mile in each direction, the lack of outside activity making it eerily deserving of its name. This was only the third time Brad Stave had found himself sitting down to dinner in the luxury restaurant, but each time the layout of the surrounding city reminded him of an ant farm made flat.

All of the modular homes, offices, warehouses, and other assorted buildings were connected by metal tubing. Some were painted according to the owners' whims, but paint was expensive and the process of applying it problematic, so most residents were content to leave their homes as they were constructed: base metal forged from the ore in the Martian soil. In addition to the other problems that accompanied external decoration, most private residences could not be seen except through a neighbor's window or one of the viewpoints like the Needle, so few people bothered. Brad's expected dinner companion had one of the most elegant houses on the planet. From the outside, it resembled nothing so much as a palatial mansion, the type that might have been found in the South of the United States in the eighteen hundreds. Brad marveled at its design from his table as the disc shaped restaurant rotated it into view.

The house sat at the edge of town, connected to a main thoroughfare by way of the same metallic tunnels that joined the rest of the buildings. The second floor of the domicile displayed a balcony, windows, and a door. The door was fake, of course, and the balcony would be useless without an EVA suit, but the windows were real. The appearance of the house was really just a façade placed over a particularly large modular Mars household constructed from the same reinforced steel as the rest of the houses, excepting the very cheapest. Brad reflected that Mr. Burr would in fact be able to see his house from here when he finally arrived. As the restaurant completed another turn, he tried to pick out his own house from the cluster of mid-sized metallic residences that made up the equivalent of the suburbs of Tranquility. He located the main avenue that his house was tethered to, then attempted to count twenty-three houses down. It was difficult due to the angle, distance, and the slow rotation of the restaurant. Eventually he gave up, deciding it didn't matter; they all looked the same anyway.

As the homes slowly spun out of view, Brad turned and surveyed the well dressed diners in the room. The majority of the fifty or so tables were occupied, though it was still early- about a quarter after five, standard Earth time. He caught sight of his boss standing next to the maitre d' and smiled in expectation. Owen Burr was one of the most affluent people on the planet, and it showed. He stood perhaps one and three-quarters of a meter tall, and was well proportioned. His suit, a black two-button piece both fashionable and timeless, was tailored to him perfectly. His olive skin showed few lines from his forty-five or so years, and his haircut was nearly perfect. He caught sight of Brad just as the man at the podium pointed his way and smiled. It was a rich smile framed by broad lips; it was a winner's smile.

"Brad, how are you?" the man said as he approached the table, extending a hand with perfectly manicured nails.

"Just fine," Brad replied as he rose, smiled, and offered his own hand. He mentally prepared himself for the handshake. Burr was one of those men with a vice-like grip that left all who shook his hand in pain for several seconds afterward. There was no twinkle of competition in his eye when he did this, seemingly no need to put people in their place or to show off. He was simply unaware of his potential to cause pain. They shook hands and Burr pulled the beautiful and expensive chair out from the table without looking at it. Brad returned the obligatory inquiry. "And you?"

"Oh fine, fine. I love this place. You know I can see my house from here." Burr smiled casually, perhaps a bit ironically at his turn of phrase. It was the kind of smile that made a silly thing charming simply through its self-awareness.

"I was just thinking the same thing." Brad ran his hand through black hair that was evidencing grey at the temples. A moment of silence passed while a waiter filled their water glasses and placed menus before them. By necessity, the majority of Martian cuisine was vegetarian, but some of the pricier dishes contained beef, pork, and poultry. Brad ignored the prices and looked forward to an extravagant meal. After all, he would not be paying.

After their drinks had been delivered and food had been ordered, the two men moved onto the pleasantries and updates that frame the opening of most conversations between people who have known each other for some time but don't speak more than once or twice a month.

"Yes, Cynthia is well, and the kids. Cassidy keeps bugging us for his first EVA walk. We told him that it would be a present for his eighth birthday, but he's not overly patient. We're obviously not going to buy him a suit; he's not going to stop growing any time soon, and Cynthia worries about the rental suits. I've got her mostly calmed down though, I think. Grace is… crazy." Brad laughed and shook his head. "Yeah, she's crazy I think."

Burr lounged in his chair somewhat, his half empty beer in his hand. "That's to be expected. She's… what, thirteen now?"

"Yes, thirteen." Brad nodded, taking a sip from his own light beer. He laughed again. "She screamed at us so loudly the other day I told her she was going to crack the window and kill us all. Know what she said? 'Good,' she said, 'then none of us would get to have a life.' All this because we said 'no' on cranial implants until fifteen. Were we that crazy when were teenagers? That…" he searched for the word, "histrionic?"

"Probably," his employer smiled. "I hear it goes with the territory. Teenagers, I mean. I think we block it out when we grow up, but I think all teenagers are crazy. They only pretend that they're sane and rational in movies to make us feel like bad parents."

"Mm." Brad shook his head. "Speaking of which, how are things between Victor and Junior? Any better?"

Burr's grin receded. "Afraid not, from what Victor tells me."

A serious and inquisitive look crept over Brad's face, and he leaned forward, dropping his voice a bit. "Do you really think Victor tells you everything?" He was immediately sorry he had asked, especially sorry that he had used the word *really*. The man across from him suddenly looked as if he had never been happy in his life. "I don't mean… I didn't mean to imply that you were fooling yourself into thinking that. I meant…"

Burr saved him from digging his hole any deeper. "Yes," he stated, quietly but with passion. "I *really* think he tells me everything."

"I'm sorry," Brad stated. He struggled to regain his composure and hoped that his simple apology would suffice.

The smile returned to the other man's face, rising like the sun after a thunderstorm. It was quite a welcome sight to Brad. "Of course, I could be wrong. No way to check. That's kind of the point, really."

Brad laughed through his nose, letting a tentative smile creep onto his face as well. Relief wound its way through him. "Yeah, I guess it is."

"Anyway, I'm glad you brought him up. I have the folder on the job. Are you still amenable?"

"I am."

Burr slid a small manila envelope from inside his left jacket lapel and placed it on the table. "This could actually be fun. She's really quite fetching."

"I don't care about that," Brad replied good-naturedly. "There's just one girl for me. But if this will help..." He let the sentence drift off.

"Oh, yes." The winning smile shone out from Burr's face again, the green eyes no less intense for the laugh lines around them. "It will help."

Brad broke the seal on the envelope and slid out a picture and several pieces of paper. The paper was unusual though not unheard of on the red planet. It was seen as an affectation among the rich, a luxury that somewhat recalled a bygone time. It also had the benefit of being easy to burn. He slipped the papers back inside the envelope, then regarded the picture. It was a printed photograph, clearly taken from a clandestine viewpoint and without the subject's knowledge. The woman who stared back at him from the picture was in her mid-thirties, quite beautiful, with strong cheekbones, a rounded, heart-shaped face, and straight red hair that fell past her shoulders. A smattering of freckles danced across her cheeks and dainty nose, and her well-sculpted eyebrows arched over chestnut-brown eyes.

"Hello," he said softly to the photo. "I wonder what you like to drink."

# CHAPTER 1

"Seriously? Are you still on this ship?" Don Templeton was standing in the doorway to Reactor Control, legs spread and hands on his hips. "You know if we get this job, we might leave tomorrow. You haven't taken any shore leave." His bushy eyebrows arched together in a mock scowl that nonetheless masked some real concern and disapproval. He was addressing a pair of legs that protruded from under a console. The legs were garbed in greasy grey cargo pants and sported combat boots at their ends.

"You're still here too." The woman's low voice found its way out from beneath the computer console.

"That's different. I was off ship for the last three days. Seriously, Portland is a really great town. There's this beautiful rose test garden, a mountain… Mount Hood… and a zoo. Actually, the zoo kind of sucks, but the roses are real pretty. Ever been?"

A long ebony colored hand appeared out from beneath the console, alighted upon a spool of solder, and snatched it back out of sight. "To a rose garden? Yes, sir." Templeton searched her voice for traces of irony and found none. Not for the first time, he wondered whether she was actually serious or a master of dead pan humor.

"No, to Portland. A jump ship could take you from the coast to town in just fifteen minutes. There's a huge park with trails and trees, even a big mansion up on a hill with a great view. Pitt Mansion or something." He walked forward several steps into the room and squatted down, wincing as his knees clicked and popped. "There's still plenty of time."

"Pittock. Pittock Mansion, it's called. I read about it. Built in 1914, opened to the public in 1958, most recent restoration done in 2109. Hand me that fifteen millimeter wrench since you're there, would you, sir?" The hand emerged again, palm open and expectant, a smudge of grease across the knuckles.

"You know reading about the place ain't the same as visiting it, right?" He cast about the small litter of tools for the wrench in question. Upon locating it, he lifted it from the metal grated floor and handed it to the woman. The hand disappeared again.

"Thank you. Yes, I know it's not the same. No, I haven't been to Portland before. Yes, I would like to go, but we work before we play. I've wanted to rewire this console since we left Phobos. It will make my life easier, sir, really." The hand emerged and deposited the spool of solder back, as near as he could tell, exactly where it had been before.

Templeton snorted laughter. "You didn't need me to find that wrench at all, did ya?"

"I like you to feel useful, sir." Again, no irony. "I

know it's your job to keep an eye on ship morale. I know the data shows that people who stay shipside and spaceside too long go section 8. I'm fine, sir. If I were in Portland smelling the roses and staring at mountains, I'd just be thinking about this console anyway. So I'm doing what makes me happy."

"Yeah, but Dinah…" He looked around the ReC room. It was no more than three meters deep and four across. Opposite the door he had entered, the only conventional door in the room, was a battery of control consoles arranged under a set of windows. In the floor to his left, the trap door that led down into the reactor room was closed, flush with the floor. He stood up, shaking the pains out of his knees, and looked through the windows down on the silent and still reactor. "This room is so small. There's so much space out there, and if this job takes us to a Jovian planet, this could be your last chance for weeks - even months."

There was silence for several seconds and the moment stretched. Finally, a grunt issued from under the console, the sound of someone completing a job to satisfaction. A second later, the rest of the lithe woman he had been talking to slid out from under the console. Dinah Hazra wore a jet black tank top only a few shades darker than her skin. Her hair was shaved close to her skull, and her sharp cheekbones lent her a gaunt air despite her wide nose and full lips. She looked up into the man's ruddy and lightly freckled face as he extended a hand down to her.

"Okay." She cracked a light smile. She took the proffered hand, using the larger man's weight to spring to her right foot, lowering her left a second after she was vertical. She looked him in the eye. Regardless of the fact that he was taller and heavier than her, Templeton always felt a bit intimidated when she turned her full gaze on him. "I'll go walk the shoreline, maybe go for a swim. Would that make you happy, sir?"

"It'd make me feel very useful. Is that good enough?" He arched his eyebrows. "But don't think about swimming. The ocean's way too cold this far north." She looked at him, her face unchanging. "You know that. You read that too." He shook his head. "You know, of the sixteen people on this crew, you make me feel the least useful."

She broke her gaze away and began collecting her tools. "Sixteen? Did we fill those security spots, sir?"

"Yeah, both of 'em," he said, somewhat unnecessarily. "Not the best resumes I've ever seen, but the captain decided to take a chance on them. They know how to bust heads and put on an EVA suit. Beggars and choosers and all that. Temporary contract. We'll have to see how they work out."

"What did Kojo think of them?" She placed the wrench back in its place in the toolbox, and there was a click as the magnets secured it.

"He hasn't met them yet. He's visiting family in Kenya, not expected back till late tonight."

She looked at him and raised an eyebrow. "You hired two new security crew without the security chief's okay? Without him even meeting them, sir?"

"It's not like we had a choice. Kenya's a five hour flight, and he didn't want to be disturbed." He drew himself up. "'Sides, when my crew is on leave, they're on leave. The captain and I are more than up for hiring new crew." He looked at her with some mock indignation.

"Hired most of you, didn't I?" Dinah finished replacing her tools, but did not respond. Templeton cleared his throat, and then added, "That said, I'd be curious for your take on 'em if you don't mind."

"I can't right now, sir. I'm on leave," she stated matter-of-factly and walked out of the room.

The couple sat in their metal and fabric lounge chairs looking out at the mushroom rocks that dotted the Oregon coastline. Most of them were a mixture of deep grey and green, growing mosses and plants. Gulls turned lazy orbits around them, squawking to each other in a language all their own. From the top of the ship, they could see miles and miles in each direction. To the south, other ships rested along the water line, and the layered pattern of waves was mathematical in its regularity. To the north, the slowly eroding dune of Cape Kiwanda rose, looking deceptively small until one spied the people climbing it like ants on the world's largest anthill.

Squinting at the coastal sun despite the parasol over her head and the sunglasses covering her eyes, the woman turned to her husband. "Told you it'd be pretty up here."

"I never doubted you, dearest," replied the man, continuing to gaze north to the sand dune and beyond. "I just thought we might spend our last night here in Astoria. It's only a few minutes up the coast by ship. Apparently they filmed some old movie there. It's supposed to be beautiful. Authentic."

She smiled at him. Pieces of her blonde hair held their light curves as they waved in the strong breeze. "For someone who chooses to make their living on a spaceship, you sure do have a soft spot for old Earth towns and history. You know if you lived there, you'd go crazy in a month."

"That I would, that I would," he assented, sighing. After a moment, he added, "Earth is a nice place to visit, but I wouldn't want to live here."

She chuckled. "Besides, Jabir will be back with Gwen soon, and then we'd have to clean her up, pack her up, and get two rooms for the night."

"She could stay on the ship," he replied, finally looking at his wife. "I think she's ready for that now. Eight is old enough to spend the night without us."

"You're probably right. Maybe it's me that's just not ready."

The man, John, suspected that she disagreed with him about their daughter being ready to stay alone in her cabin on the ship, but appreciated his wife's willingness to hide her disagreement behind a mask of her own attachment to their child. Understandings and small compromises like this, he thought, made marriages work.

"Maybe next time we come back, we can get away for a few nights, just the two of us," he offered.

She favored him with a grin of understanding. "Yeah, that sounds great." As she finished speaking, they heard the ring of footsteps on the ladder, and the dorsal maintenance hatch they had used to access the top of the ship opened. Their first mate, Donovan Templeton, appeared and blinked in the bright sun. He was breathing a bit heavily from the climb up the ladder. As he emerged from the portal and lowered the door back, he regarded the two of them.

"Hey, you two. How's it going up here?"

John Park, the vice engineer and Dinah's right hand

man, turned his Asiatic features to him, a pleasant look on his face. His dark hair was cut short to make it more manageable in zero G, and he possessed a wide thin mouth and a small nose. His slim frame was wrapped in a towel from the waist down, and his bare, hairless chest and shoulders were shaded by the parasol attached to his beach chair. Despite the near eighty degree weather, the shade and constant breeze at this height regularly brought out gooseflesh on his arms and chest. Charis, John's wife, sat to his left on her own chair, also wrapped in a towel and sporting a faded white tee shirt. Her dyed blonde hair was put up in a bun, strands blowing about her rounded face, and her fair features found protection under her own umbrella.

"Going great, Don," John replied.

"Nice and private," Charis added.

Templeton offered an apologetic wince. "Sorry." He looked around. "Where's Gwen?"

John opened his mouth to reply, but Charis spoke first. "Jabir took her on a hike in the gorge outside Portland. Said he could use the exercise. Nice of him to give us the afternoon off, especially if we're casting off tomorrow." She tilted her head inquisitively. "*Are* we casting off tomorrow?"

Templeton put his hands on his hips and looked southward down the coast at the tide and the other spaceships moored at docking ramps along the beach, each about a hundred yards apart from one another. He could see three, but knew there were more out of sight behind a large bluff. His grey jacket, left unzipped, flapped in the breeze. "Don't know. Captain's not back yet. Should be soon, though." A bit of his unease at being the senior officer on the ship crept into his voice. "Should have brought my sunglasses," he added, raising a hand to shade his eyes. "Beautiful up here though."

A moment passed while the couple regarded him. The breeze swelled and waned, never stopping altogether, and the gulls continued their conversations round the rocks.

"Was there something you wanted, Don?" Charis ventured as kindly as she could.

Templeton, seeming reluctant, took several seconds to answer. Finally he dropped his hand and turned to her. "Yeah, I wanted to see if you had completed the synch with local servers to update our astrogation charts. You know that can take hours to do, and I want to make sure we're ready to go if we gotta go quick."

Charis stifled her sigh in the back of her throat. "Not yet," she admitted. "You know we can do that from space, right? I mean, we don't start losing netlink strength until we're over a thousand clicks from the atmosphere."

Templeton's *we've had this conversation before* expression took up residence on his features, his smile fading and his expression turning business-like. "Yeah, I know, but you know that can get unreliable, and if the update is a big one… well, the last thing you want to be telling the captain is to slow down so you can finish synching the astrogation charts because netlink picked this day to turn turtle." Templeton's watch beeped faintly as if to emphasize his point.

Charis hoped her sunglasses hid her eye roll, but she did not object.

"Tell you what. Take another hour up here if you like, but I want that synch completed by sundown. Alright?"

Charis nodded. "Yes, sir," she said without ire.

The first mate looked down at his watch. "Well, looks like the captain's back. I've gotta go. You kids enjoy." As he turned back towards the hatch, he cast his eyes down the hundred feet or so to the water below. He could just make out a small dark shape swimming a few dozen feet out in the water *sans* wetsuit. He laughed and shook his head as he reached down for the dorsal maintenance hatch.

From the scrubby hillock that overlooked the beach and berths, Captain Staples admired her ship. *Her* ship. She spent far more time on board looking out than she did regarding it from the outside, and it still gave her a thrill to see it parked, hovering four meters above the swelling tides. She let her eyes trace the smooth contours of the craft carved in gunmetal grey, the roughly conical shape that tapered to a broad cockpit in front. From her perspective, the craft swelled out and back, the large engines at the aft barely discernible. She could just make out the name *Gringolet* in green paint on the side. The electromagnets submerged in the surf beneath her ship kept it aloft and in place, allowing the reactor to be taken offline for maintenance. The atmospheric wings were currently retracted, and the VTOL engines were pointed at the sea.

"Hey there, boy. It's good to see you again," she said aloud. As she spoke, her eyes drifted down and spied her friend and first mate walking down the loading ramp and onto the sand. Rather than moving to meet him, she waited for him, looking back up at her ship. Her chin-length blonde hair whipped about, unsecured in the wind, and brown eyes squinted from a broad pale face at the sun's reflection gleaming on her vessel. After a few minutes, Templeton reached her. He was, she thought not for the first time, looking a little tired. Though he was only a few years past fifty, his sandy hair was greyer, he walked a bit more slowly than he did when she first met him a few years ago, and he breathed somewhat harder. He was breathing a bit hard now.

"Welcome back, Captain." He turned and looked up at the ship with her. "Never get tired of looking at it, do you?" he asked rhetorically, knowing well his captain's love of her ship. This was not the first nor third time they had stood like this and gazed up at the instrument of their livelihood.

"Indeed." The captain's high clear voice carried over the wind. "It seems she hangs upon the cheek of night."

Templeton raised an eyebrow. "It's still daytime." She didn't reply. "Lemme guess. Hamlet?"

His captain turned to him, shaking her head. "Romeo and Juliet."

"Would've been my next guess. Seriously," he replied, turning back to her from the ship. "So don't keep me in suspense. I'm dyin' here."

She allowed some satisfaction to creep into her voice. "We got the job."

"Great!" he almost shouted, and for a minute she thought he was going to take her by the shoulders or hug her, but instead he simply rocked up on his toes and back down again. "Am I going to like it?"

"Probably not, but it pays a ton, and it should be easy enough. Shall we?" She gestured towards the ship, and together they began walking back over his footprints in the sand, heads bowed a bit against the wind which had been picking up as the day progressed. "It's a delivery job. Our first port of call is Mars for a pickup. We'll be there for a few days, and then we head all the way out to Cronos Station at Saturn for a drop off."

Templeton grunted. "Something told me it would be a Jovian run. You know Mars is on the other side of the sun right now. That will turn what should be a two day journey into a week."

"If we thrust all the way, yes."

"And," he continued, "I could be wrong, but I think that Saturn is pretty much the complete opposite direction right now."

"I'll need to check with Charis, assuming she updated the astrogation charts, but I believe you're right."

"It doesn't make a whole lotta sense. Why not wait until the planets are closer? Why not hire a ship already on Mars to bring whatever they want transported here, and then we could take it on to Saturn? Did they say?" They reached the ramp and began ascending into the cargo bay of the ship. Templeton's breathing became a bit more labored.

"Maybe there are no ships available on Mars, or no appropriate ships, or no good ships with our record. As for waiting, they seem to be in a rush, which will make sense once you hear the full details. They're paying well for a chartered flight." She shrugged. "They didn't say why, and I didn't try to talk them out of it."

"What's the cargo?" he asked as the shadow of the vessel fell over them.

"Two passengers, their effects, and a few cargo crates. That's all. For that we get six hundred and eighteen thousand."

"They're paying us all that to run just two people and some crates all the way to Saturn? It seems like a waste to me." He held up his hands, adding, "Not complaining." They reached the shuttle bay and headed across, past the shuttles and jump ships, to the elevator at the back of the cavernous space.

"Well, it's a relocation move." She paused to organize her thoughts, and then began. "The meeting was with a couple of executives from Libom Pangalactic. You know how paranoid those types are about corporate espionage and the like. That, I assume, is why they wanted me to come alone. I had to sign a waiver saying that I wouldn't tell anyone about the job if I decided to turn it down before they would even *tell* me what the job was." She pressed the button in the elevator for deck two.

"It *seems*," and the way she stressed the word made it clear that her faith in the stories of corporate energy executives was somewhat lacking, "that the key computer engineer on Cronos Station died in an EVA accident." Templeton displayed the frown of those who hear of a tragic death that holds no personal meaning for them. "They need to replace the man who died, and since this accident has slowed production, they want some redundancy. So they've hired two new computer techs, a scientist and an engineer. Both are top dogs in their field, and Libom is paying through the nose to relocate them. First class all the way." The elevator came to a smooth stop and the doors slid open quietly. Staples led them, a half a step ahead, towards the mess hall.

"By first class, do you mean…" Her first mate let his question drift.

"Yes. They're not to lose any time, so that means stasis tubes."

Templeton shook his head. "You know we don't have any stasis tubes on board." Staples stopped and turned to him, looking up at the taller man with a nearly expressionless face that communicated quite effectively. "Okay, that was stupid. Of course you know that."

"It's true we don't have any tubes on board at present," she said, continuing, "but we have the reception bays for them in CB4. Libom is paying for the tubes, and we will get to keep them when we're done. I made it part of the deal." Again, self-satisfaction edged into her voice. "I'm a bit peckish," she added as they entered the mess hall. Templeton eased himself down at one of the benches while his captain rooted through one of the refrigeration units. "So we head for Mars and spend two days there. We'll meet the engineers and give them a tour of the ship. Not much point, I suppose, as they'll be unconscious the whole trip, but I don't like to let anyone aboard my ship I haven't met. Plus, it need hardly be said that the ethics of transporting people who begin and end a journey in stasis are sticky at best." She emerged with a raspberry yogurt, plucked a spoon from a nearby magnetic tray, and settled down across from her friend.

The man shrugged slightly. "Naturally. Gotta be sure that the people *want* to go where they're goin'."

"Indeed. After the tour, the technicians in Tranquility freeze them, we bring them aboard, and we're off to Cronos Station."

"Mm." He grunted.

"After we deliver the stasis tubes and they're revived, we're done. And because I know you're wondering, we will be paid forty percent before we depart Mars and the rest upon delivery. I trust that you'll handle informing the crew and dispensing pay?"

He nodded his graying head. "Sounds easy enough."

She smiled wryly and said, "It always does."

# CHAPTER 2

The next day, Clea Staples sat in her seat in the ship's cockpit, the seatbelt snug around her waist and shoulders. Her hair was held back from her face by two small colorless metal barrettes, one on each side. The chair itself was scuffed metal and partially covered in well-worn and comfortable black leather. From it she had a slightly raised view of the room and the sleepy Oregon coastline towns beyond the windows. Bethany, the pilot, sat directly in front of her, her small frame nearly swallowed by the chair. Only her coffee colored hands were visible as they flew over the controls, running final system checks.

"Yegor, do we have final clearance from berth control?"

"We do, Captain," the Russian replied with little trace of an accent. He sat to Bethany's right and somewhat back along the curve of the front of the cockpit. "Are you set, Bethany? You have EM control?"

The pilot's high thin voice was barely detectable over the sounds of the ship as it throttled up. "Yes, Captain."

Staples turned to her left and addressed Templeton, who was seated next to her. "Final check. Is everything in order?"

He scanned down his surface, verifying the check list. "All cargo secured, double checked. All crew on board. Go from control. Mmmm... yep. All set." He looked up and nodded, then turned to the console on his left side and depressed a coms button. "*Gringolet* ready to depart. Everybody check your belt." His loud voice rang out through the cockpit and the rest of the ship as he spoke. He shifted his finger to a side console and typed in a three-digit code. "John? Is Gwen belted?" Charis, sitting to Bethany's left, shot him a look of gratitude.

"Yes, all set." John Park's voice came through the speaker over the first mate's console scratchy but loudly. "Thanks."

"Yah hum," Templeton intoned, and then turned back to his captain. "Set."

"Bethany, the ship is yours," Staples said. Her voice carried the air of a task that has been completed often enough to become routine, but whose potential for disaster should never be forgotten.

There was no response from the small young woman, but as she manipulated the controls in front of her, the ship began to rise steadily. The electromagnets increased their power output, pushing the vessel upwards. As they did so, Bethany gently allowed thrust to creep out from the VTOL engines. The thrust provided by the magnets waned, and the pilot increased the thrust proportionately, keeping the upward velocity almost perfectly constant. The goal of any good pilot was to transfer the thrust from the magnets to the engines without too many jolts, and preferably without the downward facing engines disrupting the tides below. Particularly bad pilots could earn fines for their ships by bringing up the thrust too early. Staples thought that she had rarely seen a pilot, especially one only twenty-one years old, able to strike that balance as well as Bethany Miller. Eventually the ship began to tilt skyward. There was a hum as the atmospheric wings extended. The crew felt the ground move from beneath them to behind them, and the moon came into view in the early morning blue sky. Bethany continued her manual ballet, and the ship slowly picked up speed, accelerating towards escape velocity with barely a shudder.

Ten minutes later, Bethany's long black hair began to drift away from her head and shoulders. She brushed it lightly out of her face, her heavily shadowed eyes intent on the gauges in front of her. It rippled back like an eel and rallied for its return. Her hands continued to push it away, the actions seemingly part of her work. Eventually, her manipulations slowed as she restricted herself to the odd attitude correction. "Wings retracted, low orbit established. We are atmosphere free, Captain," she said, her voice just audible against the quiet hum of the computers and the deeper rumble of the engines.

"Excellent work as always, Bethany." Staples found herself hoping that her young pilot would become more emboldened as a result of the confidence she placed in her, but it had yet to happen.

Bethany took the compliment in silence, tilting her head down as she smiled a bit and allowing her hair to drift in front of her face for a moment.

"Captain, berth control reports no problems and,

naturally, no fines. Total bill for docking is four hundred, thirty-two fifty," Yegor said, reading off his communications console. "Okay to pay?"

"Please do." Now that they were in space again, the takeoff having been among the smoothest she had experienced, Clea Staples sighed and relaxed. She missed Earth when she was away, but not as much as she missed her ship when she was anywhere else. She undid her safety harness and pushed off lightly from the base of her chair, stopping herself easily with a hand when she reached the forward observation window. "Mind giving me a roll, Bethany?" She looked down at the girl next to her, dressed head to toe in black. Not for the first time, she wondered what strange events had landed this quiet but amazingly talented girl on her ship.

As Bethany reached for the control sticks, Templeton turned to his control console and depressed the shipwide coms button again. "Prep for a roll," he stated out of consideration for the vertigo-prone crew members like himself, and then fastened his eyes on the floor.

*Gringolet* rotated along its Z axis to the left, spinning the blue and white world in front of them. It moved from below to above, and as it did so, Staples pushed up and back from the front console. She grabbed the grip bars on either side of the skylight and surveyed the planet of her birth. The clouds and storms swirled over the surface, and as she watched and the ship gained some distance, the islands of Nippon crept into view off to her left. She smiled, and her breath fogged the window, obscuring the view. As Bethany continued the roll, Staples allowed herself to drift away from the glass, pushing off at the last second to send herself back to her chair.

"Don, you'd better check on our new recruits. This is their first time under thrust on a starship, didn't you say? We'll get under way at…" she looked at her watch, "noon."

"Had that same thought myself, Captain," Templeton replied as he undid his seatbelt and maneuvered himself towards the door at the back of the cockpit.

After making his way down to the crew deck, Templeton expertly pushed his way forward from handhold to handhold, allowing his fingers to drift over the walls from time to time. Finally he arrived at the last doors of the hallway, and he paused for a second to listen. Two male voices issued from within, both heated, and he heard more than one impolite word. He knocked on the door of the cabin. A moment later the door opened, and he was looking at Dean Parsells, one of his new hires.

"Hey there, Dean. I thought I'd come down and check on you two." The man, though the smaller of two new crew members, was nonetheless large. He floated at close to two meters tall, and his weight was approaching one hundred kilograms, at least on Earth. He had short, dark hair, and his chin was too small and his eyes set too close together to be considered handsome. Templeton looked over Dean's shoulder as a table drifted by. A second later there was a loud bang as the errant furniture ricocheted off the wall. Parsells regarded him and smiled.

"Yeah, come in. We're having some trouble, I think." His voice was heavy. He moved aside and Templeton pushed himself into the room. Instantly, he had to duck as a chair came drifting towards his head.

"Whoa," he declared, and reached out a hand to catch

another chair spinning in place on his right. The room was a mess. At least they hadn't unfastened the beds. "So, I know you boys have been in space plenty. Wouldn't've hired you if you hadn't." He looked over at Harrison Quinn. Templeton reasoned that he was well over one hundred kilos. He had the face of a boxer, of a man who had been in plenty of fights. That he had scars on his fists and not his face indicated that he had won most of them. "But this is different from mining ore in zero G on an asteroid. See, the floor is the floor when we're planetside, but that," he pointed at the wall to his right and the general aft of the ship, "is the floor when we're under thrust, which will be most of the time." The two men looked at the wall, at him, and at each other. The marauding table drifted quietly past them again, pinging off a chair and taking on a new trajectory.

"We use this time in zero G to reorient the ship. That's what most of the crew is doing right now: rearranging their rooms. That's why all of your furniture comes unclamped from the floor. You need to clamp it to that wall there. That'll be your floor in," he looked at his watch, "about two hours. And it'll stay that way till we reach Mars, most like." The larger man looked at him and shook his head, not in confusion but in exasperation. It was a look that said *this is so freaking weird*. "It takes a bit to get used to."

"Wait," Parsells said, considering. "So if that wall becomes the floor," he pointed at the same wall that Templeton had indicated, "how do we get out of here?"

"See how the door is wide and located at the left side of the room? It's designed to convert. And see this switch?" He pushed himself over to the wall and indicated a light switch covered with a hinged piece of plastic. "Watch this." He lifted the plastic and flipped the switch. There was a distinct *thunk* as ten centimeter wide panels in the floor and ceiling retracted. Each was about a half a meter across. Suddenly there were ladders in the room, built into both the floor and ceiling. "There ya go. There's another one in the hall; they're all over the ship. You'd better get comfy with climbing around while we're under thrust. If you need to go from aft to fore, well… the ship's two hundred fifty-two meters long. Thrusting, that makes it over two hundred meters tall."

Understanding was dawning on Parsells' face, but Quinn still seemed to be struggling with the concept. "Look, think of it this way. When you got on board, the ship was on its belly, right? So this," he pointed to what the men currently thought of as down, "was the ground. But when we're thrusting, which we normally do at about point six Gs, it's like the ship is sitting on earth, but on its butt, nose to the sky. Getting around means literally climbing the walls." He grinned at his own joke.

"But what about the bridge, um, sir?" Quinn inquired, consternation still plaguing his face. "Do they have to climb up to their seats? And if they do, isn't that like lying in a bed all the time?"

Templeton pushed off from the wall and intercepted the floating table as it drifted back his way. "They can do that if they want, but the whole cockpit tilts. We call it the cockpit. It tilts ninety degrees. The whole nose of the ship does. The upside of that is that you get to sit normally when we're thrusting. The downside is that, well, you gotta look up through the skylight to see where you're going. Doesn't matter much; we don't steer by sight too often."

He expertly pushed off the far wall and grabbed a handbar on the aft wall, swinging the table into place with his other hand. "Here, one of you help me clamp this down. Parsells?" Parsells moved over to him somewhat awkwardly. Their resumes said that the men had a few years of zero G experience, but it also said that it had been a few years since they had been in space. It was evidently a bit more difficult for Parsells than hopping back on a bike. "Quinn, you grab that chair and bring it over here. Look," he said to Parsells, "see that thumb latch on the table leg? Just press it against the wall and hit it like this." He flipped the switch to demonstrate. "It doesn't matter where. Once we're thrusting, you can rearrange it wherever you want."

Still yawning, Captain Staples walked into the mess hall in search of some light breakfast before the morning shift. The room was occupied by two burly men who sat next to each other, each with a plate of eggs and potatoes about half-eaten in front of them. They looked up at their new captain, and the smaller of the two smiled awkwardly.

After a moment, Parsells spoke up. "Good to be aboard, Captain." Quinn nodded at her.

Staples smiled in welcome. "It's good to have you both aboard. Do you have any questions that I can answer?" She began rummaging through a refrigeration unit.

Quinn looked at his friend, who faced her in turn. "Yeah, actually. We wanted to have a real beer with dinner last night, to celebrate our new jobs and all. Can't drink a toast with lemonade." He gestured towards his cup.

"I don't allow alcohol on my ship, Mr. Parsells." This news clearly did not sit well with the two men, who looked at each other as if the horse they had chosen to bet on had just broken a leg. She carried her yogurt and a spoon over to the table and sat down. "Travelling between planets is not dissimilar to how many describe war: long periods of boredom punctuated by brief moments of terror. In my experience, boredom and alcohol mix poorly, and terror and alcohol even worse. We have movie nights, poker nights, a plethora of board games, a small gymnasium, and somewhere between two and four billion stars to count in this galaxy. The day-to-day running of the ship will take some of your time as well." She tried for a genuine smile and suspected that she had pulled it off.

If Parsells had further thoughts about the dry spaceship, he did not share them. Instead, he said, "If you're here, who's running the ship right now?"

"No one, actually." Parsells' eyes grew wide with concern.

"But someone's steering, right?"

She took a bite and shook her head.

"What if we hit something? What if we go off course?" Quinn was beginning to look alarmed as well.

Her voice was reassuring. "There's not much to hit. The average density of space is about one atom per cubic centimeter." She held the thumb and forefinger of her right hand about a centimeter apart to demonstrate. "Most of space is just that: space. It's aptly named," Staples offered. "As for course corrections," she continued, "we're pointed at Mars. The computer can handle things for a bit while we eat and sleep. All it has to do is not turn. There's almost always someone in the cockpit to keep an eye on things. And if we did somehow get off course, well, we've got thirteen more days to Mars. What's one hour one way or the other?"

Parsells grunted, clearly a bit embarrassed. He turned back to his food.

A minute later, a well-structured, slightly gaunt man with deep black skin and a bald head entered the mess hall. He wore a tight grey shirt buttoned down the front that left little of his well maintained physique to the imagination. Where the short sleeves, which looked close to bursting, ended at his biceps, muscular tattooed arms extended and ended in powerful hands. Staples read the situation and decided to let her security chief have his moment with his new recruits. She stood up and smiled at the men, taking the remains of her breakfast with her.

"I have some work to do. I'm sure I'll see more of you in the coming weeks."

As the captain exited, the new entrant crossed to the food that the ship's cook had left in warmers on the counter. He quickly and efficiently spooned the eggs and potatoes onto a plate, plucked a container of orange juice, and finally sat across from the two men with his breakfast.

Fork in hand, he looked at them and said, "This is probably as good a time as any to introduce myself. I am Kojo Jang, and you work for me." His voice was deep, and though his English was impeccable, it carried traces of a Swahili accent.

"I thought we worked for the captain," the normally laconic Quinn responded. His friend looked at him in surprise and tapped him with his elbow. Parsells smiled in apology for his friend.

Jang did not smile back. "No. I work for the captain. You work for me, though you should always listen to her. I must apologize for not meeting you earlier, but I returned to the ship only shortly before takeoff, and there was much to do." He took a bite of potatoes, perhaps to give them a chance to reply. Neither said anything, so Jang swallowed and continued. "I will need to show you around the ship. You must study the blueprints until you can find your way in the dark. This may seem excessive. It is not. If the ship ever loses power, you will be grateful for the knowledge. We will need to go over firearms procedures; I was told you both have firearms training. Is this correct?"

Parsells answered quickly, perhaps before his friend could. "Yeah. We were both security guards at a prison; we carried pistols, trained with them, all that."

"Good." It was clear from Jang's quick response that Parsells had offered more of an answer than he wanted. The two men ate and listened silently as Jang spoke. "We will continue to train. We will need to go over ship procedures. You must learn what to do when we both arrive at and depart a planet or moon so that your first mate does not have to move your furniture for you." The men had the decency to look sheepish. "We must train in hand-to-hand combat."

Parsells laughed. "On a spaceship? I mean, I know Templeton told me that we'd have to know how to fight, and we do, but really, what are we gonna do, throw a knife out a window at another ship?"

Jang regarded him silently, and his smile died. Finally, he responded. "No. We will not be throwing knives at other ships. Not all operations that this crew performs happen aboard this ship. If the captain needs to meet a contact in a disreputable bar, you may need to provide security for her. If Mr. Burbank and Mrs. Trujillo, two of the work crew, are loading valuable and desperately needed medical supplies into the cargo bay destined for Phobos and they are attacked by criminals hoping to sell said supplies on the black market, you will need to provide security for them." The new hires looked suspiciously like teenagers being given a lecture. Jang was clearly not finished. "And if pirates attack and board this ship in an attempt to take our fuel, our food, our cargo, and our personnel, you most certainly will fight to defend this ship."

At this, Parsells spoke up. "Pirates, really? I mean, we've heard stories, but does that really happen?"

Jang drew himself up and looked down at the two men as much as was possible while they were sitting. "There is not a scenario I have described that I have not experienced." He paused for dramatic effect. "You must be prepared for these and many other possibilities. Everyone on this ship does their part and helps where they can. If that means helping Mr. Park to work on the reactor, then that is what you will do. There are no responsibilities outside your job description, only those you have not yet learned. The men who previously held your positions found me a harsh task master. I don't doubt that is part of why they chose to leave this ship, but I do not take chances with the lives of my crew. Security," he added as if speaking some great aphorism, "is like insurance. One pays for it and, if everything goes well, one never needs it, but one would never wish to be caught without it when things do *not* go well." With that, he stood and headed back to the buffet for more food. Parsells rolled his eyes at his friend, and they both went back to finishing their breakfasts.

# CHAPTER 3

The ship had been at six-tenths of a G of thrust for just over a day when Yegor Durin spoke up. "Captain, I'm getting some noise." He tilted his head to the side and pressed the earpiece into his right ear. Staples, regarding the back of his head, his short ponytail, and his tanned profile, waited patiently for his report. The two of them and Charis MacDonnell were the only people in the cockpit. It was the beginning of first shift, and most of them were still waking up. A long minute passed, then two more while the coms officer listened and ran numbers on his console. Possible identifications flashed up on his screen, and he sorted and dismissed them almost as quickly. Finally, he turned to her.

"I think it's a satellite, Captain. I make it a Yoo-lin mark VII. It's still got enough power to transmit; the signal is pretty strong. General distress. It's damaged-"

"I'll say," Charis interjected.

"-and it knows it," he finished.

"We're way past the green line out here, Captain,"

Charis offered. "Could be good salvage?"

"Maybe," Staples assented. "How far?"

Charis and her compatriot both turned to their consoles, firing numbers back and forth and exchanging data verbally. After a minute of this, Charis reported: "If we turn and slow down at…" she winced as she said it, "two-point-seven Gs for three hours, we can stop in time to salvage it. It will cost us the better part of a day, depending on how hard we thrust back up to speed. We would still have time to make our appointment on Mars if we stopped."

"Three hours. That's going to be uncomfortable. Yegor, I'm going to call the staff to the cockpit. Be ready to give us a rundown of that satellite in five minutes."

"*Da, Kapitan.*" The man muttered, unconsciously reverting to his native language as he concentrated on the signal and pulled up data from the ship's computer.

Four-and-a-half minutes later, the chairs in the cockpit were filled just as they were during the ship's departure from Oregon the day before. One of the four guest chairs lining the back wall was also occupied by a swarthy man with a strong nose, dark eyes, short-cropped hair, and an excellent profile.

"Decided to join us, Doctor?" Staples asked as she spun around in her seat. Though medical was a fifty-meter climb down the ship, the man wasn't winded in the least. He was in his mid-thirties and in excellent physical shape.

Jabir Iqbal smiled charmingly. "You know I love to watch you work, Captain." The smile broadened. Perhaps coming from Templeton or Durin, the comment would have seemed inappropriate, but the doctor seemed to pull it off, and Staples found herself close to blushing. She gave a curt nod and spun her chair back round to face the rest of the staff, as much to hide the spots of color in her cheeks as to do her job.

"Dinah, are you patched in?" Staples addressed the air.

From down in the ReC, Dinah's bold voice issued from the speakers. "I'm here, sir."

"Yegor?" she said, indicating that he should start.

"Captain," he nodded back at her, and then looked around at his fellow shipmates. "The satellite is a Yoo-lin mark VII. It's a communications satellite. I repaired one once in high orbit. Best guess is, given how far out it is, that it collided with a meteor or another satellite and spun off out here. Lucky us.

"The Mark VII is nuclear powered, and judging by the strength of the distress signal, the reactor is still online. That means uranium, which we can adapt to our reactor. The Mark VII reactors were rated for at least a hundred years before replacement, and they were put up mostly around 2105. It should still be about eighty percent fueled, which will be more than enough to cover what we'll burn slowing down. Circuit boards and electronics will be resalable, but not for too much. The wiring should be worth something. The Yoo-lins were designed to provide military and spacewatch eyes as a way for the company to make money from government contracts, and that means the lenses are valuable. Some of the mechanisms use soft metals, including gold. Most valuable, though, is the communications suite itself. It may be twenty-five years old, but I should be able to adapt it to our systems and provide some versatility and horsepower to our coms. Summary:" he glanced down at his surface, then back up at the captain, "about one hundred thousand dollars worth of materials, fuel, and an upgrade to the ship."

Templeton whistled through his teeth. "That's a nice little bonus for the crew. I assume we'll have to slow down in a hurry?"

Staples replied. "Yes. Charis says three hours at close to three Gs, and every minute we spend deciding makes that thrust more uncomfortable, so we need to make the call now. I'm inclined to stop and pick it up, unless there are any objections." A moment of silence passed. "Dinah, are you ready for a turn and burn? Charis will send down the exact data."

"I think so, sir," the head engineer's answer was nearly instantaneous. "All readouts show green. A sustained three G thrust should be a strain, but not a problem."

"Excellent." The captain turned to her left, shooting her first mate a look.

Without words, he turned and opened the shipwide coms. "Heads up, people." His voice issued from every speaker on every deck. "We're going to turn and burn for a nice little salvage stop. We'll be pulling two-point-eight Gs for about three hours. Strap in, grab something to do, and try to ride it out. We begin burn in…" he paused and looked at Charis. The blonde navigator held up four fingers, "…four minutes." He released the coms button and looked at Charis again. "Where's Gwen?"

Without looking up from her control panel, she answered, "She's with her father. It's math lessons this hour. He'll take care of her."

As he finished, Charis cut the engine thrust, and a moment later, the sense of weightlessness became apparent. The navigator continued her work on the controls, and Bethany took the ship through a gentle one-hundred-and-eighty-degree pitch. After two minutes or so, an Earth much smaller than the one Staples had regarded the day before crept back into the window, finally settling above them in the skylight and somewhat to their right. Staples spent a few precious seconds gazing at it through the skylight above her chair, and then said, "Do it."

Charis' voice came through the speakers this time, counting down the time to thrust. "Prep for bedsores in five, four, three, two, one…"

One-and-a-half grueling hours later, Yegor spoke up again. "Captain, I've got chatter coming in from another ship… and it's close."

Staples leaned forward in her seat and almost immediately regretted it. Under the weight of the intense gravity incurred by the deceleration, her normal sixty kilograms became over one-hundred-and-fifty, a weight her medium frame was not used to. She had experienced high-G conditions before, of course, most of them had, and the body could be conditioned to deal with them through time and exposure, but it was never enjoyable.

Charis frowned, looking down at her instruments and readouts. "I'm not getting anything," the navigator commented, making adjustments and looking over her data. "Is it far out or right behind us?"

"Right behind us, I'd say." Yegor replied. "They're warning us off the find; say they've got the prior claim." The captain looked back at her navigator.

"No way," Charis countered. "No way. I scanned far enough before our turn. Nothing was close enough to get there before us unless it was moving fast to begin with *and* willing to pull six Gs of deceleration. Even with gravity couches, that's dangerous."

"Hold on," Yegor interjected, his attention clearly divided between the headset in his ear and what Charis was telling him. After a few seconds passed, he added, "They say they're not there yet, but they have tagged the satellite with a claim beacon and will be there shortly."

A bad feeling crept into Staples' gut.

"That don't fly," Templeton stated emphatically. "Salvage code says 'first come, first serve.' They can't just fly around space tagging debris and calling it theirs. So what if they've got a rail gun that can shoot transponders at .25c? If they don't get there 'fore we do, it's ours. That's what the code says." He nodded at his own assessment of the situation.

Staples' jaw tensed. "Not everyone respects the code as much as we do, Don."

"But it ain't legal. What are they gonna do, shoot us?"

Every set of eyes on in the cockpit was on them. Even Bethany, her hair hanging straight down about her face like icicles, her dark eyes wide, had leaned around her seat to watch the two of them converse.

"No, I don't think anyone out here would risk that." The captain tried to assuage her crew's concerns. "The lanes between Mars and Earth are a little too well monitored. They'd never get away with that. But if we go to the police and tell them some rival crew stole our salvage, well… half of them see salvage as theft anyway, green line or no." She looked pointedly at Charis. "Is there any way to tell how far out they are?"

Charis shook her head. "Not if they're coming at our

ass." She thought for a moment. "Unless we could power down the engines for five or ten minutes, then I could get a clean radar sweep. But then we'd shoot past the satellite, which kind of defeats the point. Unless of course…"

"…We resume deceleration at three Gs or so." The captain finished her thought. The moment stretched. The harder they pushed the engines, the more painful the ride became. Three Gs was generally considered the safety limit; no captain was happy to push their ship or their crew up to three, and certainly no one in the cockpit liked the idea, but it was difficult to plan without knowing how far away the other ship was. If the other crew had a reading on them and knew their engines were burning in their direction, they'd know the Gringolet wouldn't be able to ascertain their position. "Five minutes to get a fix?" Staples asked.

The navigator frowned and shook her head. "I can't promise it'll be that short. The further out they are, the longer the wait for the radar return."

Staples tapped her fingers on her armrest for a second while she considered, then said, "Okay, let's do it. We need the information, and we've wasted too much time and fuel on this to come away with nothing. Don, let everyone know what we're doing." As Templeton leaned back to his shipwide coms button, Staples added, "Wait. Yegor, did that transmission contain an ID?"

"*Da*, Captain. It's the *Doris Day.*"

Captain Logan Vey's deep voice flowed clearly from the speakers and through the cockpit. "So it's clear, Clea, that we've got the prior claim. We saw it first. We tagged it first. Our *property* is currently attached to it. You wouldn't steal from another crew, would you?" Vey was speaking to her as if she were a rebellious teenager, one who had been caught shoplifting and who would regret their decision if only they could be made to see the error of their ways.

"If by property, you mean that three centimeter transponder, you can have it," Staples retorted evenly. She allowed a trace of contrition to enter her voice. "And not that laying eyes on something matters, but what makes you think you saw this thing first, *Logan*?"

Due to the distance between the two ships, the response took a few seconds to come through. "The fact that I know exactly what kind of radar suite you have on that old ship of yours, and that mine is twice as powerful. I've got a Narda G223. Ask your Russkie or Missus MacDonnell over there; they'll confirm that." Staples looked at Yegor, who thought for a second then regretfully nodded in confirmation. His face changed to a shrug, which his shoulders tried to match, though the movement clearly pained him. She couldn't blame him; the man weighed about two-hundred-and-seventy kilograms at present. The expression was clear, however: *if he's telling the truth*. She suspected he was. Logan Vey's vessel was newer, faster, and more expensive than hers.

"Well, it doesn't matter. Some kid with a high-powered telescope on earth might have seen this thing before either of us. I don't plan on leaving it there until he comes to pick it up either. If we beat you to it, that's it." The captain hoped she sounded certain and flinty, but her buttocks and legs were paining her dreadfully under the strain of the engines, and she just wanted it to end.

Vey continued, undeterred. "Look, Clea, I like you. I like your ship. Don't make me-" Staples tapped a button on the surface inlaid in her armrest and the transmission cut off. Templeton smiled over at her. He tried to project approval, but his face was tinged with concern.

"It seems," Staples spoke over her right shoulder without turning the chair around, "that you chose a very interesting day to visit us up here, Doctor."

"Indeed," the doctor replied in his richly accented voice. "As fascinating as this is, I cannot help but feel that I should be in the medical bay, especially if this *ibn il-Homaar* intends to make good on his bluster."

"Oh, I don't know about that, Doc." Templeton interjected, turning in his chair. "Medical's twenty meters down ladder from here, and you weigh, what, two-hundred-and-twenty kilos right now? I know you like to keep in shape and all, but if you got hurt, who'd patch you up?"

"I'll overlook your well intentioned comments about my weight, Mr. Templeton, and simply say that I can go and get ready to receive casualties once we stop," he rolled his R's subtly and unconsciously, "though I have the utmost faith that our captain will bring us through without a scratch."

"If anyone can. What's that mean, anyway?"

Iqbal raised his eyebrows. "What, '*ibn il-Homaar*?'"

"Yeah."

"Son of a donkey."

"Nice," Templeton said, and swiveled back around.

Twenty minutes after the captain patched herself into the shipwide coms to outline her plan to the crew, but still thirty minutes out from the satellite, *Gringolet's* thrust diminished. Had anyone been looking, the satellite itself would be clearly visible through the aft observation windows that peeked up above and below the engine housing at the back of the ship.

When they were only four minutes from the satellite, the already depressurized shuttle bay door opened and a utility vehicle the size of a 20th-century minivan was launched violently out of the portal. The UteV, as they were commonly called, was fired from a jury-rigged launcher that pushed it up to nearly three Gs of thrust in the opposite direction. This was enough to counteract the speed it acquired from the larger ship, which meant that, relatively speaking, it was not moving. Almost immediately Dinah Hazra, the UteV's sole occupant, began thrusting the small vehicle towards the satellite. Manipulator arms unfolded from the front of the craft, which was comprised primarily of a hemispherical glass viewport.

An additional two minutes later, *Gringolet's* engines flared significantly brighter, pushing well over three Gs for fifty-two seconds, and the ship came to a full stop. As it did, Bethany immediately took over attitude control from Charis, and the vessel pitched one hundred and eighty degrees, nose over end, to face the oncoming rival ship. As it did so, the cockpit realigned, tilting up ninety degrees and recreating the characteristic conical shape that her captain had recently admired on the beach. The doctor hastily flung away his safety belt and pushed himself off the bridge and down towards medical. The *Doris Day* was now plainly visible to the crew in the cockpit, as well as anyone else who cared to look from a forward viewing port.

Captain Vey's *Doris Day* had been top-of-the-line when he acquired her, and that was none too long ago.

The ship shared the roughly cone shaped outline with *Gringolet*, but it was a bit smaller. Because it was newer, its engines were also smaller, giving the ship an overall slimmer profile from the rear, which was exactly the view that the crew was treated to as they watched the other ship approach. Bethany made some slight adjustments based on her data readouts and visual stimuli, and *Gringolet* placed itself rather precisely between the oncoming ship and the satellite. The hair tie normally found round her wrist was holding her hair back, and though it floated freely, not a strand of it strayed in front of her face.

"How long until she reaches us, Charis?" Staples inquired tensely.

"At current thrust... twelve minutes. She's coming in awfully fast, Captain. My numbers show she'll stop before she hits us, but not more than a thousand kilometers." Charis did not try to disguise the fear in her voice.

Templeton's hands tightened on his armrests. "That's real close. All she has to do is let off thrust for a few seconds and-"

"She won't." His captain cut him off. "Vey won't do that. He could burn us, but getting that close would risk his pretty new ship. He's just trying to show off and intimidate us."

"It might be working," Yegor muttered.

"You're sure, Captain?" Templeton asked.

"If this be error and upon me proved..." she replied distractedly, leaning forward, her eyes pinned to the approaching engine flair in the window. Her first mate, well familiar with his captain's proclivity for quoting classics, especially in tense situations, took that to mean that she was sure.

Instead of questioning her further, he turned to his panel and spoke into his microphone. "Dinah, how you doing out there?"

Dinah's slightly broken voice came through almost immediately. "Just fine, sir. How are you?"

"Nervous. How close are you?"

"About eleven minutes away from the satellite. That was a tricky maneuver, launching me while under thrust, but you put me in a good position, sir." She neglected to mention that the UteV launching mechanism was both her idea and invention.

"I don't suppose you could speed things up?" Templeton asked.

"I promise not to get there any sooner or later than I can get there, sir." In spite of himself, he smiled at her response, knowing he should leave her alone. The woman was an expert.

Ten minutes later, as the *Doris Day* was approaching zero speed, a dark disc came flying up and around its engines. The drone immediately began moving under its own thrust towards the ventral side of *Gringolet*. Charis picked it up right away. Rather than report to her captain, she patched herself through to Dinah in the UteV. "Dinah, I've got something headed towards us. Looks like a probe or a drone. Probably a drone. It's using the 'Day's' speed to fly past us. Suspect it's coming right to you."

"I can try to block it," Bethany said in her reedy voice, "but then we'll be out of position to block the *Doris Day*." She sounded regretful, as if the physics of the situation were her fault.

"Hold position," Templeton ordered.

"Can we shoot it?" Charis asked.

The first mate shook his head. "It's too maneuverable for slugs at this range. It'd just move out of the way. A tac missile could catch it-"

"No," Staples interrupted him. "No weapons. I don't want this to escalate, and I certainly don't want to give Vey the opportunity to say he opened fire on us to defend his property. Whether the satellite is his is debatable at this point. That the drone is his isn't. Let it go. Dinah will have to handle it."

As if to put their fears to rest, the chief engineer's voice came through the speakers. "I've got it. Locked on." Templeton blew out a breath of relief, and Yegor's face lit up.

Once she had grabbed two support bars on the satellite with the UteV's capture arms, Dinah began to thrust backwards towards the ship. The four small jets that surrounded the rounded viewing port in front of her propelled her steadily. The EVA gloves made her hands no less dexterous on the controls, and she maneuvered the craft with deft confidence. A few seconds after she had begun to gain speed, she looked up through the top viewing port and saw the sun reflect off the shiny black drone as it came flying around *Gringolet*, changed vectors, and headed straight for her. Its capture claws extended menacingly. She was sure the drone was being controlled by someone aboard the other ship. Not putting a person in it gave it distinct advantages; it was capable of thrusts and vector alterations that would pulp a human occupant. The drone was the kind of high-tech luxury her crew couldn't afford. *It isn't fair*, she thought for a second, and then shook her head to clear it. Fair was irrelevant; the situation was as it was.

Back in the cockpit of her ship, Templeton tensed. "That thing'll tear her UteV apart." His voice was little more than a strained mutter.

"No," came Staples' quiet but tense reply. "He won't risk killing her. He'll figure she's wearing a suit, but still, something could go wrong. He won't risk it."

"Then what's he planning?"

"We're about to find out, I think."

The drone descended on Dinah's UteV like a hawk on a rabbit. At the last minute, it fired retro thrusters and stopped short of colliding with her. Its capture claws grabbed hold of the two support bars on the opposite side of the distressed satellite, and it began to pull. Dinah looked at the thing, a jet black disc that resembled nothing so much as a giant metallic Go piece with a single red sensor eye facing her. It was a scant five meters from her craft, silently blowing thrust in the face of her vehicle, and winning the tug-of-war. She increased the thrust of the UteV to maximum, and the drone responded in kind. The support bars warped under the strain, and emergency lights on her console began to flash, but nothing had given way yet.

Dinah began to fire her dorsal jets, rotating the three connected objects in space. Then she spoke through the open com channel. "Bethany, listen to me…"

On board the *Doris Day*, Captain Vey looked across his bridge expectantly at his Second Mate. Beyond the window in front of them, *Gringolet* faced them nose-to-nose, maneuvering to keep itself between their ship and the satellite. Vey was a large man, once a very intimidating physical specimen, and though his stomach had grown in recent years and his muscle had lessened, he still possessed a formidable physique. He had fair skin and close cropped curly hair, which he ran his hands through often as if to retard its recession.

"Well?" he asked; his deep voice carried, as it often did, a hint of threat.

The second mate, a dark-skinned woman in her early thirties, was wearing a VR helmet and haptic control gloves. Her hands were clamped firmly around an invisible object, and she was gesturing towards herself with them. "She's not letting go, but that UteV doesn't have the thrust the drone does. If she doesn't want to let go, I'll just bring her along."

The captain replied irritably, "That's like to take more time than I'd-"

Suddenly his pilot, who had been trying and failing to outmaneuver Bethany and get around the other vessel, interrupted him with a loud exclamation. "What the hell?" *Gringolet's* VTOL thrusters had turned to face them, and the ship was thrusting violently away.

Just as the structure of the Yoo-lin mark VII satellite was starting to buckle from the opposing forces, and just as the drone was achieving maximum thrust, Dinah let go.

The drone rocketed away at what she estimated must be six Gs of thrust. At the same time, the *Gringolet* grew immeasurably closer in her forward view, blotting out the stars as Bethany brought it thrusting back. Just as they had planned, the drone flew squarely into the rear of the ship before the drone's pilot on the Doris Day knew what was happening. The drone was crushed between the satellite and the engine housing, and small pieces of it and the satellite itself broke off and floated in various directions. Dinah worked the controls to reverse her movement away from the ship and her prize.

She allowed herself a dignified grin, and said, "Exactly as planned, sir. The drone looks to be non-functional and the package is mostly intact. If you could move free of the area, I'll reacquire in just a few minutes. And please thank Bethany for not crushing me too."

"Copy that," her captain's voice came through her EVA earpiece. "We're moving." Dinah began pushing the UteV back towards the satellite, using the capture claws to push aside the larger stray pieces of debris.

Suddenly, Templeton's voice came through the earpiece. "Dinah, we've got two more drones headed your way! We can't stop them. Tell me you have another amazing plan."

She considered for a moment before replying. "Will a crazy one do, sir?"

A minute later, the two drones flew silently around *Gringolet*, one above, one below, and barreled towards her small metal can. She had just secured another hold on the satellite, but the safety of her home ship was now two hundred kilometers away. There was no way she would make it before the drones pried the satellite away from her. Dinah double-checked her craft's hold on the target and looked quickly up and down at the incoming drones. She doubted they would play as nice this time. She looked over her calculations on the screen in front of her and the flashing execute button. She shook her head to clear it, wishing she could wipe sweat off her brow in an EVA suit, and then took a deep breath. Her eyes closed for a second, then opened.

"Now, sir," she said, and pressed the button. Responding exactly as programmed, the UteV redirected all of its available thrust through the forward ventral and rear dorsal thrusters. Safety lights immediately blazed and klaxons sounded, but she silenced them with the flip of a switch. The craft quickly began spinning end over end like a runaway Ferris wheel, and Dinah Hazra was subjected to upwards of seven Gs. The sensation was one of falling forward and down, perhaps curving unceasingly around the outside loop of a roller coaster, but much, much more unpleasant.

Black motes flooded her vision and the sounds in the craft grew distant. She knew that she was close to passing out. The UteV was spinning end over end, taking the satellite with it. The drones paused, their retro jets firing and their pilots unsure of what to do with the situation they faced. At the precise moment she had programmed the computer to do so, knowing that she was incapable of the split-second timing necessary to aim precisely, the capture claws released and the satellite went careening off towards her home ship. The drones, once their pilots had finally grasped what had happened, gave pursuit, but it was too late. Bethany was already bringing the ship around, and Templeton was opening the shuttle bay door. The small pilot, her eyes darting back and forth from her control panel to the window, aligned the ship, and the satellite flew into the bay and crunched against the back wall.

"Dinah, are you okay?" Templeton asked, the alarm in his voice quite clear.

After a few seconds, her voice came through the speakers. "Bit dizzy, sir. Otherwise okay."

"That was a hell of a move. Christ. Nice throw."

"Nice catch, sir."

"Yeah, thank Bethany for that. You'd better-"

"Missile!" Charis shouted. "There's a tac missile following the same trajectory as the first drone. It's looking to pass us!" The desperation in Charis' voice was infectious. Templeton turned to launch intercept chaff, even as he knew that it wouldn't help if the missile wasn't targeted on them. Bethany fought the urge to put the ship between the missile and the woman in the UteV.

"Open coms to the '*Day*!'" the captain said, her voice nearly a shout. "Now!"

Yegor tapped a few buttons and nodded quickly, indicating that he had opened a channel to the other vessel.

"Logan, what the hell do you think you're doing? You lost. You don't need to hurt my crew."

There was an agonizing moment of silence while Vey took his time replying. When he did, his voice dripped with condescension. "You need to learn what happens when you keep me from my toys, Clea."

Templeton's communications ceased abruptly. As the small craft stabilized and her vision cleared, Dinah looked through the window towards the ship. She breathed deeply and sighed, smiling despite her pounding headache, content to wait for the first mate to reestablish contact.

Her hands were trembling from the experience and she was sweating more than ever, but she was all right. She watched the two drones move off and back to their home vessel; there was no point in them troubling her now. Suddenly she spied the telltale glow of an incoming hostile projectile. She squinted at the missile, trying to identify its make and tonnage, another part of her mind calmly trying to tell her how irrelevant that information was.

It took her about two seconds to run through all of her options. There weren't any. *Gringolet* couldn't save her, not at this point, and the small craft she currently inhabited was incapable of outrunning or outmaneuvering a tac missile. She could eject; the EVA suit would sustain her for several hours in space, but the shrapnel from the explosion would undoubtedly kill her. She had no jetpack to gain distance she would need to have a chance of survival anyway.

"Huh," she said. There was nothing to do but wait; she estimated perhaps four seconds. The missile flew straight and true, descending towards the aft dorsal section of the utility vehicle. With an audible thunk, it bounced off the back of her little metal can, sending it into a lazy spin. Realization of her survival dawned. She immediately dismissed the possibility of a malfunction as too remote to consider. After snorting laughter for a second or two, she breathed a sigh of deep relief and hit the coms button.

"It wasn't armed, sir. Warning shot, I make it." A mixture of cheers and sighs floated to her across the vacuum of space. She closed her eyes and let the craft drift for a few minutes more.

"Or what *can* happen," Vey's voice mocked the crew

from the cockpit speakers. "Let's not do this again."

"Logan, you're a son of a bitch," Staples replied, and cut coms.

# CHAPTER 4

Once the UteV was secured in the shuttle bay and the bay was safely repressurized, Dinah climbed out of the vehicle. She pushed her way across the back of the cavernous room, floating over to the elevator. The lift carried her up to the EVA prep room, and along the way she removed her helmet. As she exited, she found several members of the crew waiting for her, the captain in front. Behind her floated Donovan Templeton, navigator Charis MacDonnell, Charis' husband and Dinah's right-hand man, John Park, communications expert Yegor Durin, Doctor Jabir Iqbal, and even the cook, Piotr Kondratyev.

"Hey!" shouted Templeton. "The lady of the hour!" He clapped twice in excitement and appreciation.

"I would think that would buy me at least the day, sir," Dinah responded, pulling off her thick-fingered gloves. Templeton pushed off a wall handle and came forward to help her disengage the back piece from the suit. She allowed him to render his assistance.

"Really fantastic work, Dinah," Staples stated,

pushing herself forward and offering her hand. The chief engineer shook it and nodded somewhat gravely at the compliment.

"Just doing my job, sir."

"Nonsense," Staples replied immediately. "You did outstanding work," her tone turned somewhat scolding, "but you were less careful with your life than I like my crew to be, especially my one-of-a-kind, jack-of-all-trades engineer. We could have just let them have it."

At this point the crew members had surrounded her in a rough half circle, floating somewhat awkwardly and touching each others' shoulders to stay in place and upright. Dinah looked her captain in the eye as she released her hand and casually said, "I never judged myself to be in any real danger, sir. I hope this doesn't mean you're losing faith in my abilities."

Staples broke into a wide and toothy grin, many of the surrounding people laughed, and even Dinah smiled briefly.

"She'd be a fool to!" Templeton declared loudly. The statement fell flat, and Staples shot him a sideways glance. He shrugged awkwardly and apologetically, still laughing.

After the other crew had congratulated her and the back patting had subsided, the doctor addressed her in his rich voice. "I'd like to see you in Medical once you get changed, Ms. Hazra. You subjected your body to, what did they tell me, seven gravities? How do you feel?" His eyes moved over her face, assessing, looking for signs of stress, pain, or discomfort.

"It was barely six," she responded, "and I feel fine."

"Nonetheless. Doctor's orders," Iqbal replied with some flair. "Shall we say Medical, twenty minutes?"

The captain spoke up before Dinah could reply. "My orders too. I want you checked out and with a clean bill of health. You went through quite an ordeal out there, whether you admit it or not."

"I'll choose 'not,' sir," she replied, "but I'll be there."

Staples nodded. "Good. I think we can have a family dinner after all that, once we get under way. I don't know about you all, but I'd rather have gravity when I eat."

There was a general chorus of agreements.

Nineteen minutes later, the ship was moving towards Mars again under a single G of thrust. John was manning the ReC. Dinah Hazra opened the door into the Medical bay. The bay was a high ceilinged rectangular room over fifteen meters in length. It was half again as wide, and one wall was layered with hinged, pull-down beds. Stretchers stood in storage, strapped into wall cradles next to the door, and magnetic medical trays sat at strategic positions along the wall opposite the beds. At the far end, Dinah could see the doctor's private office, the windows currently transparent to the rest of the bay. While the majority of the ship was stark, gunmetal grey, the walls and ceiling of the Medical bay were tinged blue, adding to its general air of sterility. The floors were different from the usual deck grating. Medical was the only room in the ship that had been outfitted with the recently invented, cutting edge, and highly expensive artificial gravity floor panels.

As Dinah poked her head through the door, the doctor looked up from his surface and smiled at her in welcome. From her perspective, the man appeared to be standing on the wall. The effect was disconcerting to most of the crew members, but they all appreciated their captain's extravagant expenditure on the artificial gravity. Altering the Medical bay whenever they entered atmosphere would be work intensive and problematic, and a shift from gravity to weightlessness or vice versa could be deadly if it came in the middle of a delicate medical procedure. Feeling for all the world like Fred Astaire, she climbed through the door, somewhat awkwardly altering her orientation to the doctor's version of *up*.

"Dinah Hazra, reporting as ordered, sir," she said, finding her footing.

"*Ahlan wa sahlan*, Lieutenant," the doctor replied. Dinah blinked several times, taken aback. "If one is going to act like they are still in the military, one should not be surprised when they are addressed as such. I am not a *sir*," he continued, not unkindly.

"I'm not *in* the military anymore. And I don't particularly like being reminded that I was, Doctor." She took several steps towards one of the hinged beds on the wall, her voice demonstrating slight irritation.

"That is fair," he replied, "but I hope you don't think you're fooling anyone aboard this ship about how you spent your formative years."

She sighed and cast her eyes downward. "No, I suppose not, but it's also not something I like to advertise." A thought occurred to her, and she looked up sharply at him.

As if reading her mind, he raised his hands, palms outward, in a gesture of peace. "As your doctor, I may have read your rather lengthy and impressive military record, Ms. Hazra, but as your doctor, I am also obliged to maintain confidentiality." He gestured to the table she had approached, and the woman turned and hopped up on it, her legs dangling a few inches off the flooring. He was wearing pale blue scrubs and a white lab coat, and when he hung a stethoscope around his neck, the stereotypical image was complete. He came around in front of her and added, "And as your friend, Dinah, I am honor bound to keep your secrets." She looked at him steadily and without comment, but he could detect gratitude in her eyes.

"So," he said, a little too loudly and dramatically, signaling the transition from friend to physician. "How are you feeling?"

"Just fine," she said for what she felt was the tenth time since she had tossed the satellite at the ship.

He proceeded with his check up, exploring the glands in her neck with his firm fingers, prodding her back, measuring her breath with the stethoscope, and testing her reflexes. He asked her to hold out her hands, and they exhibited a slight tremor despite her efforts to hold them still.

"That's not unusual," he commented somewhat dismissively after regarding them for several seconds. "Did you lose consciousness?"

"Almost," she answered reluctantly.

He sat back against the lowered bed opposite her and nodded. "Other common side effects of exposure to high G acceleration include black motes, temporary loss of vision, tunnel hearing, temporary loss of hearing, changes in blood pressure, muscle cramping, damage to vision, even brain damage if the brain is robbed of blood, and consequently oxygen for long enough. Tell me, how long were you putting your body under the strain of 'barely six' gravities?"

"Less than thirty seconds," she replied.

"Ah. I think we can rule out brain damage, then, though I'm going to have a careful look at your eyes." He took up the ophthalmoscope next to him from one of the magnetic trays and then paused. "Cervical acceleration-deceleration, also known as whiplash, can also be common, depending on the direction which the body is accelerated. Tell me, which direction *were* you accelerating?"

Dinah leaned forward, putting her head nearly between her knees for a moment. "Like this."

"Ah, counted on your headrest to save your neck, did you? Very clever, especially considering the stresses of your situation." He smiled in approval.

She shrugged. "If I remember my training correctly, 'eyes-in' is also the least likely to be damaging to the retinas."

"Yes, well, let's see if those drill instructors had it right, shall we?" He leaned forward and brought the ophthalmoscope to bear on her right eye.

Once her eyes were checked, her blood pressure taken, and even her blood sugar measured, Iqbal leaned back against the opposing bed again. "It seems you came through, as you said, 'just fine.' You may experience some light-headedness and trembling for the next few days, but that should pass. Your eyes are fine. Seven gravities of acceleration is rarely permanently damaging to people in short doses, especially those with prior exposure to its effects, but there is no harm in being cautious. An ounce of prevention, as they say." He paused a moment and took a breath. "Tell me, how is the prosthesis treating you? Would you mind if I examined it?"

After a few seconds, Dinah nodded and replied, "Yes,

that's fine."

"It's the left, correct?" She was tempted to be annoyed with him. She didn't quite walk with a limp, but her slightly irregular gait betrayed the existence of the prosthetic to anyone looking. She decided to let it pass; he was just trying to be polite, even if she felt as if he were coddling her. She nodded again.

The doctor knelt down in front of her and gently rolled up her left pant leg. The combat boot ended where her mid-calf would have been, and from out of the boot the artificial leg rose up to cup her flesh and blood knee. Two small black cords, one emerging from either side of the prosthesis, connected to nodes imbedded in the flesh on the sides of her knee. He unlaced her boot and pulled it off. The haptic sensors in the artificial foot and calf sent signals to the nodes which sent signals to the nerves in her knee which sent signals to her brain telling her that someone was taking off her shoe. The sensation was oddly distant, however, not unlike people's descriptions of their limbs when under the effects of morphine or hallucinogens.

With the boot off and placed on the gravity flooring, the doctor regarded the prosthetic, a mechanical device encased in plastic that mimicked the shape of her other leg almost precisely. "Can you arch your foot for me?" She did so, suppressing her objection to the possessive. It was only as much her foot as her boot was. "Rotate your ankle." She complied. He produced his reflex hammer and ran it under the arch of the foot, and she shivered. "How does that feel?" The sensation her brain received told her that it should be ticklish, but she had not been ticklish since childhood, and so the conflicting information left her feeling confused and uneasy.

"Unpleasant," she stated flatly.

"Sorry," he said, as a matter of reflex, continuing his evaluation. Finally he stood and handed her the boot. "How is running with it?"

"Hurts a little bit."

He took this to mean that it hurt a fair amount. "If you want, I can disable the limb's haptic feedback."

"No thanks. It's worse wearing it when I can't feel anything." She set about lacing up her boot.

"As you wish. Tell me, do you sleep with it on?" He leaned back on his table again.

"No," she admitted.

"It's okay," he assured her, "it's only recommended, not required. The idea is that constant feedback will trick the brain into forgetting that the limb is artificial."

Dinah looked at him and said, "That is not something I want to happen, sir."

Later that afternoon, Charis sat down at the multi-function table across from her eight-year-old daughter, Gwen. They were in their room, one of the larger cabins on the ship usually reserved for passengers. It was about as wide as it was tall, three meters in each direction, though it was more than twice that deep. Its depth ran perpendicular to the long axis of the ship, allowing for the maximum use of space. Whether the vessel was in atmosphere or in space under thrust, whether the current floor was a floor or a wall, the room retained the same dimensions. As with the majority of the other rooms on the ship, its furniture was clamped to the floor but could be easily moved to correspond to *up* during atmospheric transition. There was an access door to a restroom on the back wall, and Gwen's room lay beyond that. Her small bedroom had the benefit of a window.

"Mom, what happened before?" Gwen asked. She was short for her age, and her chin-length brown hair was held back from her face in two pigtails on either side of her head. Her eyes carried some of her father's sharpness, and were a deep, inquisitive chocolate color, though they sometimes showed a hint of hazel. Her nose and chin were angled and her cheeks rounded, still carrying some baby fat, though she was fairly thin overall. Despite her father's Korean heritage, her skin was very fair, nearly translucent, and delicate blue veins showed lightly at her temples. She wore simple drab olive cargo pants, but her tee shirt was bright pink and slightly worn, a much loved recent purchase from a second hand clothing shop in Portland, their last port of call. At the moment, her hands rested on top of one another on the cool metal of the table, and her face hovered a few inches above them as she leaned forward, all of her concentration on her mother.

"You mean before when the ship was moving around?" Charis asked, leaning back in her chair and sipping a carbonated beverage.

"Yeah. After we stopped being heavy," the girl responded, nodding.

"You were such a good girl through that," Charis said and smiled. "I was very proud of you. Your dad said you were very good. I know that was a long time to sit still and be heavy."

Gwen perked up, grinning, reveling in the compliment. "I tried really hard to be good. Dad and I told stories together. We told one about a girl who had a monster for a pet, and that monster was hungry and wanted to eat, but the girl didn't have any food, so the monster ran away and the girl had to chase him in her spaceship, and…"

As the girl paused to take a breath and continue, her mother seized her opportunity and interjected. "You two tell some great stories! But I want to answer your question from before, about what happened with the moving ship."

Gwen paused a second, her mind refocusing, then said, "Oh, yeah. You may continue."

Charis couldn't help but laugh. "Well thank you, my lady," she said in her best gracious courtier voice. After taking a moment to collect her thoughts, she began. "Well, you know how I told you we're flying from Earth to Mars?" The girl nodded emphatically. "Well, we saw something valuable on our way, so the captain decided to stop so we could pick it up."

"Captain Clea?" Gwen's face glowed with the light of idolization.

The woman leaned forward and smiled, shaking her head a little bit. "Yes, Captain Clea, the one who reads to you. You know we only have one captain on this ship, silly." She reached across the table to grab the child's nose, and she buried her face in her hands, giggling. "Anyway, the captain decided to stop to pick it up. We had to stop really fast; that's why we had to be heavy for so long. Do you remember what I taught you about being heavy and thrust?"

Gwen's voice took on the aspect of one reciting an important historical document. "The greater the ac-cellery-ation or de-celery-ation, the greater the effects of gravity."

"Deceleration. Very good. And do you know what

that means?"

Gwen screwed up her face and raised her shoulders and hands up in the air in a histrionic shrug.

Charis smiled and rolled her eyes a bit. "It means that the faster we have to start or stop, the heavier you get."

"I knew that. I knew it all along," Gwen asserted, looking quite sincere.

"Mmm. So once we stopped, Dinah went out in a UteV to get it. The valuable thing, I mean. It was a satellite." Gwen blanched a slightly paler shade of pale, but she didn't say anything. Charis knew her daughter was a little bit afraid of the chief engineer. They had tried to teach her to hide it out of politeness when she encountered the woman, but it had been a struggle. "Unfortunately, another ship wanted the satellite too, and we had to race them to it."

"They wanted to steal it?"

"Yes they did."

Gwen processed this, then asked, "Was it theirs?"

"Nope."

"Was it ours?" The questions were coming fast now.

"Well, it's ours now. It wasn't really anybody's at that point."

"So it never belonged to anybody before us?"

Charis grappled with the question for a moment. "Well, it belonged to a company who made it once, and they put it up in space around Earth, but then it floated away."

"It didn't want to be in space?"

Charis despaired for a moment that her daughter would ever run out of questions, but then reminded herself that apathy, that most constant of teenaged traits, was probably only a few years away. Not for the first time, she resolved to appreciate her daughter's inquisitiveness while it lasted. "The satellite doesn't *want* anything. It's just some computers and metal. Computers aren't alive, so they don't want anything. It was broken, so it drifted away or maybe it got knocked away by another satellite or an asteroid or something. There's this thing called the 'green line' around Earth. It's an imaginary line that we pretend exists around the planet."

"I bet you can find that line on your mastrogration charts, right mom?" Gwen interjected, her eyes widening.

"Astrogation, yes I can. Very good!" She beamed. "You actually know what your mommy does for a living." Gwen's smile was so wide that nearly all of her teeth showed. "Anyway, anything that drifts past the green line is fair game." When no look of recognition showed on the small girl's face, she added, "It belongs to anyone who gets it. Finders keepers."

"Finders keepers," Gwen echoed. "And we found it?"

"Yes we did. But not everyone follows those rules. A bad ship called the *Doris Day* came along and tried to take it from us, even though we were first. So we had to wrestle them for it a little, and that meant we had to move all round." She shook and rotated her head and shoulders to illustrate her point to her daughter. "They were tough, but we beat 'em in the end."

"Cool," Gwen said, her interest waning. "Who's Doris Day?"

"You know, baby," Charis looked at her and shook her head. "I have no idea."

A little while later, as Charis was reading from her

surface and Gwen was lying prone on the floor, reading a book on her own version of the same, the door opened and John walked in. Charis looked up in surprise and said, "Hey. I thought you were in the ReC until dinner?" Once they had gotten under way to Mars again, the captain had given everyone who had been on duty during their confrontation with the *Doris Day* the afternoon off to wind down. That meant that John had to cover Dinah's shift in the ReC until the planned family dinner that night.

"I was supposed to be, but Dinah insisted on finishing out her shift once Jabir cleared her for duty. You know how she is." He closed the door behind him and took off his jacket, securing it to the wall with a fastener strap. He took a beverage from its secured plastic ring in the small refrigeration unit built into the wall and sat down at the table across from his wife. "Besides, I wanted to catch up with you." Something in his voice told her that the conversation would not be cheery.

Charis glanced over at her daughter. "Gwen, honey, would you mind going into your room and looking at your book there?"

Gwen looked up, her legs bent at the knee, her feet scissoring back and forth. "Why?"

"Mom and Dad need to have a little time to talk." When Gwen didn't move, she stood up and gestured in a herding motion with her hands towards the back of the room and Gwen's space beyond. "Come on. Just give us a little bit of time and we can watch a video together before dinner, how's that?" John looked on and smiled.

"Fiiiine," Gwen grudgingly agreed, standing up and frowning her deepest frown. She stalked towards the door, doing her very best to look as though her mother had just kicked her out of an orphanage and into a blizzard. They heard both the doors to the bathroom and to Gwen's room close a little too loudly, and then their daughter was safely ensconced and they could speak.

Charis sat down at the table again and, hoping to keep the tone light, said, "What's on your mind, oh husband o' mine?"

"Well, first, are you okay? I mean, I know I asked you earlier, but it's been a few hours now, and that was a really tense situation. Are you okay?" John's brow wrinkled with concern as he looked at her.

She sighed deeply before answering, not in frustration, but to center herself. "Yes, I'm okay. It doesn't feel quite real, you know? That's not the first time we've been through something like that. Not the second either, I guess. But I feel all right." She laughed a bit. "It was really tense for a bit there. I thought they were really going to kill Dinah." She sighed again. "Thank you for your concern. Really, I appreciate it."

John nodded, his lips pursed a bit. He had shaved that morning, and though his beard growth was starting to show on his cheeks, not one of the short dark hairs on his head was astray. Just as handsome, Charis thought, as on the day they met. She worried sometimes that the extra few kilograms she had put on when she carried Gwen, the lines that had formed on her face, from age, the pressures of her job, or the joys of motherhood she knew not which, would trouble him. He seemed to her not to age at all, but he had never shown any indication of looking elsewhere or being any less attracted to her. Just as good a man, she thought, as on the day they met.

"Of course," he said. "Of course." He let a few

seconds of silence pass, and then added, "How much danger do you think we were in?"

Realization dawned on her. "Ah. This again."

"Look," he continued hastily, "I'm not saying that we should talk about getting off the ship again. We talked about all that and we decided to stay. I just… I don't know. I just wanted to see how you felt."

A slightly sardonic look crossed her face. "About?"

He leaned forward in his chair and his voice gained an edge. "About raising a child on a ship that people shoot missiles at."

"No one shot any missiles at us." His face ably communicated his thought: *come on.* "I mean it. No one shot at us. They shot at Dinah."

"And Dinah is not part of 'us' now?" he pressed.

"Well, she wasn't on the ship at the time. And they didn't *really* shoot at her."

"They didn't shoot a missile at her." The tone in his voice said he and she both knew that wasn't true.

"Well, not a real missile. It wasn't armed. They never intended to really hurt her."

"Do you know that for sure? How do you know that the missile didn't just malfunction?"

"I was in the cockpit. I heard what Vey said. He was just trying to scare us. It was very clear that he meant it to be a warning." She kept her voice at the same volume, but it was difficult to keep it from building in intensity as they argued.

"Or it malfunctioned and he played it off that way. You can't trust what that man says." He tried and failed not to sound scolding as he said it.

"Of *course* I can't trust him, but do you know what the

chances are of a warhead not detonating on impact? It's like…" she searched her memory for the data, "ten thousand to one."

"Are those odds you'd gamble our lives on?" He pointed towards the door. "Would you gamble Gwen's life on those odds?"

"Of course not," she replied instantly. "But first, that's not the same thing. Secondly, the chances of us crashing on takeoff or landing are greater than that."

He looked at her incredulously. "This is supposed to help your argument?"

"No." She sighed and paused, re-centering herself. "All I'm saying is, we all take risks. If we were in some office job and suburban house on Earth, there'd be a chance of danger every time we put Gwen in the car, or let her play soccer, or… I don't know, try out for cheerleading!" Against her best efforts, her voice had risen nearly to a shout.

John regarded her gravely for a second, and then a smile spread on his face. She looked at him darkly. "I hope you're not laughing at me."

He chuckled briefly. "No…" he grinned, "I was just picturing Gwen in a cheerleader uniform standing at the top of a pyramid of girls shouting *Gimme an A!*" He gesticulated with his arms as he delivered her mock lines. Charis' anger broke, and she began to smile as well.

"*What's that spell?*" she added, her voice rising. "*Astrogation!*"

They both grinned at the thought and at each other for a moment, and the tension between them dropped several levels. It became easier to remember that they loved each other, that they were partners and not adversaries. Finally, John assumed a more serious face and his voice found an air of contrition. "Look, you're right, I know. Things could happen to her, to us, anywhere. Some occupations are more dangerous than others, but of course there are no guarantees. I just worry that we're screwing up our kid."

Charis opened her mouth to reply, but John stopped her with a raised palm. "I know, I know, everybody screws up their kids. Your parents did. Mine *certainly* did. And we turned out all right. I just worry. There are no other parents here to talk with, to get advice from. No kids to play with. And space *is* dangerous; not as dangerous as it was fifty years ago, but it's still dangerous."

Charis nodded sagely, happy that the argument had taken on the quest for common ground. "It is." She raised her finger to make a point. "Don has kids, you know," she hastened to finish her sentence before he could object, "but they're not on this ship. They're grown, they weren't raised on a ship, and it's awkward to ask your boss for advice on how to change diapers." He nodded as she made his points for him. "All true."

"I'm not saying we should get off. Staples is the best boss I've ever had, and the best captain you've ever had, and while I can be an engineer on any planet, a navigator pretty much has to be on a ship. I guess I just needed to talk through this, say that I was scared for us and for Gwen, and maybe say," he raised his hands in the gesture of a shrug, "maybe we keep our options open. Maybe we can find a home on a big transport liner someday, something that has other kids, something with a school where we don't have to beg our friends to tutor our daughter because we're both math nerds. You know," and he risked, smiling, "something that people don't shoot missiles at."

"Okay. We can keep our options open. Who knows, right? Maybe this job will just make us rich and we'll retire. Buy our own island."

"Well, it's sure been great so far."

Bethany Miller moved between the rows of leafy plants, a waifish shade easily lost in the misty humidity of the starboard hydroponics bay. Her tiny, coffee-colored hands reached out as she walked to brush a leaf here or caress a stalk there. The majority of the plants were grown in nutrient rich water contained in pots and jars of various sizes, depending on the needs of their roots. Excepting where the plant emerged from them, the containers themselves were covered as well as possible with plastic wrap to stop the solution from escaping when the ship was not under the effects of gravity. Even so, the room remained humid, and it made Bethany's usually straight dark hair curl at the ends. The containers were suspended in the air by metal dowels that allowed the containers to rotate, much like the plastic players in a foosball table. Weights at the bottoms of the jars kept the plants upright.

Like most of the living units, the hydroponics bays were long rectangular rooms running perpendicular to the long axis of the ship. They were also located along the dorsal hull, which allowed panels to be opened so that sunlight could be admitted to the rooms when the ship was in atmosphere. The panels were open now, but as *Gringolet* was headed away from the core of the system, the sun was mostly behind them, and only a few diffused rays made their way into the room. Bethany had turned on the

UV lamps when she entered the room to supplement the natural light, and now she made her use of her afternoon off to check on the condition of her plants.

They weren't her plants, of course. A hydroponics bay was not necessary for a ship of *Gringolet's* size, but there were a number of advantages to having one. The plants helped recycle the air that the crew was constantly polluting with carbon dioxide. The rooms provided a therapeutic and peaceful space for the crew, though Bethany spent more time in the bays than the rest of the crew combined. The biggest advantage the bay provided, however, was also Bethany's main reason for being here now. She walked over to the tomato plants on their hinged trellises, looking for the ripest of the fruits, and touched each gently before selecting three to pluck and contribute to tonight's family dinner. She slid them into the canvas satchel slung over her shoulder.

She heard the door to the bay open and instinctively ducked behind the tomato plant to hide.

"Bethany?" She heard a woman's voice call: Dinah's. The chief engineer held a certain fascination for the petite pilot. She looked up to the older woman, marveling at her confidence, her abilities, her character, and her occasional demonstrations of whip-crack wit, and yet Bethany was intimidated by her in equal parts and avoided direct contact with her whenever possible.

She glided down the row of edible plants and peeked her head around the celery. "Yes?" she asked, her voice even higher and lighter than usual.

When Dinah saw the large eyes with their heavy mascara, she stepped fully into the room and closed the door behind her. She checked her usually purposeful stride and instead sidled, a bit awkwardly, down the row of plants and towards Bethany.

"I was looking for you," she said. Bethany did not reply, looking instead at the floor. She did, however, step the rest of the way out from behind the celery to face her would-be interlocutor. "I wanted to talk to you about that conflict with the *Doris Day* today." Dinah stood in front of her, several inches taller, but Bethany's silence continued. "You did really well. I mean *really* well." The dark eyes remained on the floor, and the automated misting spray clicked on as if to fill the silence.

"Hey, look at me, girl," Dinah finally said, not unkindly. Bethany looked up and somewhat tremulously met her eyes. "You're a damn good pilot. I've seen pilots with twenty years of experience that are no better than you." Bethany cast her eyes downward again, but this time she smiled at the compliment. Dinah put her fists on her hips. "That move where you backed up into the drone, right on cue: perfect timing. And that catch... not too many pilots could have done that. I don't know where you learned or who taught you, but you have a really amazing ability, and I wanted thank you. You might have saved my life out there today." Dinah knew that she was probably exaggerating, but she was determined to communicate with the reclusive pilot.

Another few seconds of silence passed, and finally Dinah nodded, turned around, and headed for the door. When she was nearly there, she heard Bethany's reedy voice over the spray mechanism. "My dad."

"What's that?" Dinah asked encouragingly, stopping and turning around.

"My dad taught me," the young woman said, a little

louder, stepping forward.

"Was he a pilot?"

"Yes." She paused for a moment. "He flew a transport ship between the Earth and the Moon when I was a teenager, and I did it with him." She began moving down the row of plants as she spoke. "From when I was thirteen to seventeen, anytime I wasn't in school, I was on the ship with him." She stopped in front of a patch of herbs and plucked a sprig of spearmint, tucking it into her shoulder bag.

"What about your mom?" Dinah asked, following her at the distance of a few paces.

Bethany just shook her head, and Dinah thought for a moment that she wouldn't continue speaking, but then she pressed on. "He drank a lot and did drugs. Sometimes he couldn't fly the ship, so I had to do it."

"Weren't there any other crew members who could fly the ship?"

Bethany shook her head again, continuing to the next section of herbs and selecting two basil leaves that made their way into the bag. "No."

"What sort of ship was it?" Dinah feared that she was pressing her luck, but she didn't want to lose the opportunity to get something out of the young woman. As far as she knew, apart perhaps from the captain and the doctor, this was the most Bethany had shared with anyone on the ship.

"Boeing Light Courier, B-233."

Dinah was shocked. "Bethany, that's a tiny, two person ship, and a bitch to handle besides. You were flying that by *yourself* at the age of thirteen?"

Again, the pilot nodded and moved onto the dill. Her

fingers began exploring the herb's tender leaves, plucking what she wanted from the small plant. "I was actually nine the first time I had to fly it. He kind of showed me how, 'cause he was drunk and he wanted to sleep. I knew if we didn't make the deliveries, we wouldn't have any money." Her voice had been steadily approaching a normal speaking volume, unconsciously Dinah thought, as she collected the herbs that Kondratyev had no doubt requested to prepare the evening's repast. "It was just letters, private letters from companies and stuff, and it didn't pay that much, but the ship and the apartment was all we had. I missed so much school they wanted to hold me back." She looked up at Dinah for the first time in several minutes, and her eyes were full of anger. "And I could do the work! I'm really good at math." Again, her gaze returned to the plants and she seemed to deflate. "But I just wasn't there to get the notes, and sometimes… sometimes I was just too sad and I didn't want to go. I never got to finish."

A second after she stopped speaking, she looked up at Dinah with shock and fear, realizing what she had given away. Dinah considered letting it pass, but instead she pressed the moment. "If you didn't finish high school, how did you get into pilot school? How did you get your license?"

Bethany neither moved nor spoke. The misting spray clicked off, and the silence deafened. Bethany's shoulders rose up and every muscle in her seemed to tense, then suddenly they released and the energy went out of her. "I never went to pilot's school. I faked my graduation certificate when I took the test." She looked at the other woman, her eyes wide and defiant. "I passed the test! I passed the license test with a perfect score."

Dinah laughed. "I don't doubt it."

"I *have* my flight license," Bethany muttered, despondent.

"But you lied to get it." It wasn't a question. Bethany nodded, doing a fair impression of a criminal just sentenced to the gallows. Dinah closed the distance to her and stopped when she was about a pace away. "Let me tell you something, Bethany. I don't care how you got your license." The dark eyes looked up at her in surprise. "I don't even care *if* you have your license. After what you did today, I trust you with my life. And trust me, I don't say that lightly. You've been on this ship for nearly a year now, and I have always been impressed with you." Bethany smiled perhaps the biggest smile she had since she first came on board.

"And don't worry, no one will hear about this from me. I've got my own secrets, my own past, you know."

Bethany impulsively asked, "From when you were in the military?" Dinah stiffened slightly. The smaller woman seemed to retreat into herself, her shoulders hunched and her head down, as if in anticipation of a blow. The engineer wondered what other terrible experiences the girl had been subjected to beyond being forced to fly a rusty old courier ship, but she didn't want to push too far.

"Yes, from my time in the military," she finally responded. "It's not a part of my past I like to talk about."

"I understand," she said, and Dinah thought she did, too.

Another moment passed. "See you at dinner," Dinah said abruptly but kindly, and walked out of the room.

"Yes, sir," Bethany murmured, smiling, and turned

back to her plants.

At about eighteen hundred hours standard Earth time, the crew drifted into the mess hall from all corners of the ship. The dinner that Piotr Kondratyev had prepared sat buffet-style in magnetic bowls on the countertop against one wall. The main course consisted of seasoned chicken in a mushroom and wine sauce, pasta salad, buttered and peppered green beans, and fried potatoes. There was an appetizer of *svekolnik*, one of the cook's specialties, and even a leafy green salad. Piotr encouraged everyone to eat the salad, as the greens would not keep.

Like the rest of the ship, the mess hall was designed to alter depending on whether the ship was in atmosphere or in space. It was wider than most of the other rooms to accommodate the whole crew and guests if necessary. As a result, its ceiling was over four meters high. The entrance was on deck two, but the room actually stretched up to encompass part of the deck above, and it had the same retractable skylight slats as the hydroponics bay. When in atmosphere, these allowed sunlight in through the ceiling, though right now they were located on the wall. The eating area consisted of several long tables with benches attached, much like those that might be found in a school cafeteria. In cases where the room was needed for other purposes, the tables could be folded up and pushed to the far wall or even attached to the ceiling if there was no gravity.

By ones and twos, the sixteen crew members served themselves food and sat down at the table to eat. As was traditional, Templeton sat near Staples near the head of the table. The rest of the crew sat where they pleased or where they found room. They did not eat together often enough for people to develop favorite places, though Bethany invariably sat in a corner seat near the end of the table. As the tables filled and the meal progressed, the noise of the individual conversations grew, people talking in groups of two or three, a few eating quietly.

As dinner was winding down and a few scattered crew members were finishing their seconds, Templeton did his fork and cup routine to garner the attention of the others. The talk ceased and all eyes turned towards him. "We've got a bit of a tradition on this ship, something we do when we all get together like this, which ain't that often, admittedly. The tradition is storytelling."

At this, Staples took over. "As many of you know, I am a fan of medieval literature, of literature in general, really. One of my favorite stories is *Sir Gawain and the Green Knight*. It's about one of King Arthur's greatest knights: Gawain. In part one of the poem, the narrator notes that Arthur doesn't like to have a meal until someone's entertained him with a story or some heroics. Now we've obviously already sat down and had our dinner. I wouldn't make anyone listen to a story before eating this great meal. Thank you, Piotr." She said, turning to the ship's cook who was sitting several seats down from her.

At this, various people spoke up to thank the large bald man with a heavy brown goatee flecked with grey. He muttered *spasibo* several times and raised his hand in acknowledgment.

"But now that we've finished eating, I'd like to hear a story. If possible, please make it full of adventures, marvels, princes, battles, or some combination thereof," Staples finished.

Several of the seated personnel looked at each other. Some murmured, and a few looked as if they were considering volunteering. Templeton looked expectantly from face to face. The three members of the security team, who were seated together, were quiet as a graveyard. Charis' arm rested around her daughter. Gwen was leaning against her mother, and her eyes were beginning to droop. Finally, Yegor, the communications expert who had first found the satellite, raised his hand.

Templeton nodded at him, faced turned his way, and he began. "I used to work for a telecom company: Global Telecom Systems," Yegor began in his lightly accented voice, his elbows on the table and his hands folded in front of him. "I was part of a team of people who did satellite maintenance and repair. We used these one-person, short-range space skiffs to gain orbit and clamp onto our satellites. Sometimes we had to install hardware upgrades, sometimes replace antennae or solar panels, sometimes even do reactor maintenance. It was an okay job, sometimes tedious.

"Well, I used to work with this man named Felix. He was a small, kind of rat-like man. Greasy dark hair, beady eyes," he squinted for effect, "even bucked teeth a little bit. And he always complained about the jobs. 'Too much work,' he said. 'Not enough money,' he said. 'No promotions,' he said. And he was mostly right. Occasionally people got promoted, but only if they were really good at their job. 'Why not me?' he was always asking.

"So one day, Felix gets this idea in his head. He thinks *what if I pull off a big heroic adventure?*' As he said the word adventure, Yegor tipped a wink at his captain, but didn't miss a beat of his story. "*Then* I *would get promoted*, he thinks. We are basically repair men. Adventures for us... are not that common. So he decides to make one. This is what he does.

"Felix spends two weeks learning how to reprogram a satellite to do exactly what he wants. Next time he services satellite B66, he uploads his program. Next week, when he is up near B66 doing maintenance on another satellite, B66 suddenly, marvelously, tragically, starts to fall out of orbit. Felix is ready for this, of course. He flies his space skiff away from other satellite and starts to chase B66, yelling into radio the whole way, telling about how the satellite will 'crash into city and kill millions of people if he can't stop it,' and 'don't worry, he will put his own life at risk to save the poor defenseless people.'" A smattering of laughter flowed up and down the table. Gwen's eyelids were in danger of meeting each other in the middle.

"So there he is, rocketing into lower orbit to catch deadly B66. He extends his capture claws, steers in close, eases right up to the satellite..." Yegor had leaned forward as he spoke, and here he paused for dramatic effect. "And he catches it, perfectly. So, now all he has to do is thrust out of atmosphere and he is a big hero, he figures. So, he pulls up on the stick and..." Another pause. "Nothing happens. He checks his engines. Nothing. He tries to restart. Nothing." The table was rapt, and Yegor was threading out the story expertly.

"The weight of satellite overloads the engines, and they are malfunctioning. He is good as dead, he thinks. So now he gets on radio again, only this time it is 'Help! Help! Mayday!' Fortunately for him, there is another space skiff doing maintenance near him. Mine. So I push burn all the way and head for him. He is in low orbit now and starting to heat up. Five minutes later, I get to him and he still has hold of this stupid satellite. I tell him 'Felix, let go of this satellite! I can't pull you both up.' But he won't. He has worked so hard on this programming, and he wants to be a hero very badly. Finally I tell him 'Felix, if you don't let go of satellite, I will leave you here!'" Yegor nearly yelled, and Gwen's eyes opened wide for a moment before slowly closing again. Every other pair of eyes was on the storyteller. "So… he lets go of the satellite.

"I grab his skiff with my capture claws and I push for higher orbit. Poor Felix watches this multi-million dollar satellite and his one chance at promotion and riches fall away to Earth below. We manage to get into stable orbit, I bring him aboard my ship, and we radio for a tug to get his skiff."

Yegor paused to take several swallows of his lemonade. In the pause that followed, Charis asked, "Did it actually hurt anyone?"

Yegor shook his head, his ponytail swaying back and forth. "*Nyet*. It landed in the ocean, in shallow water. Solar panels and antennae burn away in reentry, but it is well made. GTS retrieves it and does an investigation. They find Felix's program and instead of big promotion and big raise, he gets fired. But me," Yegor smiled and puffed out his chest, "I get promotion and raise for saving Felix!" Laughter and cheering rippled up and down the table, and there was scattered applause.

After it had calmed down, Templeton asked, "What ever happened to Felix?"

Yegor grinned, his big teeth showing. "He got hired by a satellite programming company. He makes more money than ever now!" This was followed by an even bigger chorus of laughs and applause.

"Excellent story." The captain stated. "Thank you, Mr. Durin. And I believe that concludes dinner."

"Yeah, don't you all have jobs to do?" Templeton asked.

# CHAPTER 5

Six days later, *Gringolet* was berthed at Tranquility space port on Mars. Planet fall had been routine, and now the crew had three days to resupply and pick up their charges before beginning the long part of the journey: the trip to Saturn. The spaceport had berths for over two dozen vessels, and more were being added all the time. Tourism was a large part of the burgeoning city's business, and so public works made every effort to make visitors welcome. Vacationers could take rovers out to explore the planet's surface, climb around, up, or camp on Olympus Mons, or engage in other more questionable activities. The Martian cities had all been founded in joint ventures by Earth governments, but as time passed they began to desire self-governance. There had been a bloodless rebellion fought in congress and through broadcasts and netlink, and the various countries such as the US, China, Brazil, and Europa that had helped to fund and populate the colonies had agreed to relinquish governmental control. Now the cities, ostensibly democratic, had their own governors and small senates. There was even an elected Martian parliament, but the constitution the cities had ratified left them so powerless as to be mostly decorative. The difficulties of travel between the cities combined with the limited available living space tended to make each city insular. There was an intercity rail network connecting the various cities, and a small intercity tourism industry had cropped up, but interaction between the cities was cumbersome and limited.

The draw of visiting the red planet aside, many of the Martian cities also encouraged tourism though their lax legal system. By adopting soft laws on some of the most controversial issues of the day, the Martian cities could attract those looking for illegal genetic modification, advanced Artificial Intelligence research, questionable cloning practices, and a variety of other services that were illegal or heavily regulated on Earth and the Moon. The laws governing these were system-wide and beyond the power of individual cities to set aside, but enforcement was a grey area, and punishments were less severe as a matter of course on Mars. Tranquility also served as a rest stop, providing fuel, food, and parts to ships heading out to or returning from Jovian space. It was a port where, provided one had the money, one could hire new crew members, buy and sell exotic goods, or simply indulge in hedonism. It was in fact the ideal stop for the job that the crew of the Gringolet now had before them.

Once the ship was settled on its landing gear and the receiving tube was attached to allow the crew to enter and depart without the need for EVA suits, various members of the crew departed for errands both personal and professional. The receiving area, which extended tubing to seven ships currently berthed, provided a variety of delights. The concourse was filled with data shops featuring movies and books, boutiques with authentic Martian clothing made from imported materials, massage parlors for weary space travelers, restaurants promising authentic Martian cuisine, bars with robotic bartenders, and mini casinos with generous one-armed bandits. Holographic advertisements glowed and rotated over storefronts. Robotic automatons roughly approximating the human form gave directions, suggested places of interest, and otherwise answered questions as needed. Well-dressed men and women offered to introduce space-faring travelers to someone who might ease their long periods of loneliness, though they steered clear of families. Keeping up appearances for the tourist trade was in everyone's best interest.

Templeton navigated this bustle with the determination of a man on a mission. He passed the barkers, the more subtle offers of companionship, and looked for a relatively honest and hungry looking rickshaw driver. The majority of main tubes that connected the various parts of Tranquility were pedestrian only, and while most citizens could afford the hydrogen cell trikes that were street legal on the few tubeways large enough to allow for motorized transport, few bothered. Parking was outrageously expensive, and movement from one quadrant of the city to another was easily achieved through a small underground light rail system.

Finally, Templeton found a young man who struck him the right way. He was not yelling for a fare, only standing quietly by his rickshaw. When he approached, the youth, probably only fifteen or sixteen, simply said, "Take you somewhere, mister?" He was thin and well muscled, short for his age, but he looked as if he could run for hours without becoming winded. He had dirty brown hair reaching to the collar of his ratty white tee shirt and running shorts covering half of his skinny legs. His sneakers, however, looked brand new. His features were sharp, and a slight fuzz shaded his upper lip and chin.

"Shouldn't you be in school?" Templeton inquired.

"It's Sunday, mister," the youth replied.

Templeton realized the boy was right. "Well, then. I need to go to Beeftown. How much?"

"Fifty dollars," he replied instantly. Evidently the request was not out of the ordinary.

"Deal." The older man produced his wallet, pulled out a creased fifty-dollar note, and handed it over. Then he climbed into the back of the rickshaw, the young man climbed onto the bicycle seat in front, and they were off, the bike moving easily in the light Martian gravity.

The rickshaw took him on a familiar route, though there were more tubes branching off the main thoroughfares than Templeton remembered from his previous visit several years earlier. People strolled here and there through the tubing near the walls, the human forms punctuated by the occasional automaton on some errand for its owner, and the rickshaws used the middle, always keeping to the right. Several similar carriages passed him going the other way, a few drawn by two people and seating larger numbers of passengers with luggage. Twice the tubing let out into cavernous rooms with high ceilings that accommodated shops on either side, the Martian version of strip malls, and then the ceilings came back down and they were in the tubes again, always headed vaguely left as they circled near the outside rim of Tranquility. As they travelled away from the spaceport, Templeton noticed that the roads, such as they were, became dirtier and the shops seedier. After roughly ten minutes of steady travel, they entered Beeftown.

Public works on Mars were a different animal. Because every house, every building, every street needed to be protected from the lifeless Martian atmosphere, it became necessary for the government body of each city to keep a steady stream of revenue in order to expand. This revenue came in part from income taxes, property taxes, and tourism, but it also came from import taxes. Vast covered hydroponics bays and even soil farms surrounded most cities, but livestock was still a problematic industry on a planet with no arable soil to provide sustenance. Thus, most meat was imported from Earth, which drove up the prices considerably. Any city, even one on Mars, produces both grey and black markets, and Tranquility's permissive laws and lax enforcement only encouraged them. The section of town that Templeton was now entering had a mirror in most every major city throughout history. It was the place one could go to *get things*. One of those things was lower-priced beef, often of questionable quality. It was this industry that had given Beeftown its appellation, though the industries it housed had become far more varied over the years.

Templeton's driver applied the brakes and looked over his shoulder. "This good?" he asked. Templeton nodded and climbed out of the vehicle, handing over another five as a tip.

"Thanks kid," he said, and strode off, enjoying the ease of walking when he weighed thirty-five kilos or so. As he began his peregrination, he transferred his wallet to the inside pocket of his grey flight jacket and zipped it up. The ceiling rose perhaps seven meters above him, and fans, strategically placed in the ductwork that latticed the roof to provide fresh air to the denizens below, rotated slowly. The room was large, nearly a hundred yards in length, and there were people everywhere. Some stood and spoke, but most walked on some errand or another. There were fewer of the expensive privately owned automatons here; they tended to disappear, victims of the Martian equivalent of chop shops. On his right, a line of butchers hocked their meat, either attempting to accost passers-by or haggling with buyers in front of them. On his left, a vivid holographic neon sign advertised live girls and boys, available for dancing and, Templeton suspected, other rhythm-based activities. He strolled down the center of the room, eyeing the stores, turning sideways here and there to slide by some individual or a group of people.

The store coming up on his left was called *Imagina*, and it was one of several shops in Tranquility to offer quasi-legal or, for the right price, illegal body modifications. Plastic surgery was of course legal, and one could alter one's appearance as one chose quite legally on Mars or anywhere else in the solar system. There were some modifications, however, that remained illegal and were frowned upon by most of polite society. Most of these concerned turning the human body into a weapon. Templeton had known someone who had known someone, allegedly, who had poison sacs surgically installed in his cheeks. The man could, if Templeton's source could be believed, spit corrosive acid that would blind and paralyze another person, possibly worse, at a range of ten feet. Other examples included brain implants that secreted outlawed mind altering drugs and retractable sub dermal blades or projectiles. The blades or projectiles themselves weren't the problem; those were ordinarily legal, but if the person in question had them attached surgically, they could never be effectively disarmed without invasive surgery. The police unions had done their best to ensure that modifications of that kind remained illegal.

On his right, past another thinly veiled brothel, was a shop purporting to sell real, Turing Compliant AIs. This Templeton seriously doubted. The programmers ensconced in the shop no doubt created impressive simulacra, perhaps even halfway decent robotic servants, but not true sentience. Artificial Intelligence research had come a long way since electronic computers had eclipsed their analog antecedents nearly two hundred years before, but there was currently a system-wide ban on Turing Compliant machines. That law even Tranquility upheld. Ever since Mary Shelley's *magnum opus* of 1823, literature had been filled with tales of man's inventions coming back to haunt him. The genre had done its work well, and though it was still a hotly contested issue, the majority of people believed that the benefits of truly sentient AIs were not worth the risks involved. He walked on.

Near the end of the street, Gringolet's first mate found the shop he wanted right where it had been on his last visit. It was called *Ping's Garage.* The storefront showed any number of electrical and mechanical parts in its windows. The bell over the door rang as Templeton entered, and the man behind the far desk looked up. Everywhere around him hung metal racking supporting lengths of wire, machine parts, tools, and other assorted mechanical parts. The store was close, dark, and smelled of grease and metal. The man was of medium build and wore a greasy blue Hawaiian shirt that was in the process of moving from a deep ultramarine to a lighter sky blue patterned with similarly faded flowers. A small pot-belly pushed against the counter in front of him. He had sharp Asiatic features and laugh lines were scored deep into his tanned skin. His short hair was graying, and he was clean shaven.

For a moment he squinted at the new arrival, and then his face brightened. "Don! How are you?" He came around the corner, holding his arms out for an embrace and waving Templeton towards it with his hands.

"Fine, fine. Good to see you!" Templeton strode forward as he answered and embraced the man. They withdrew and looked at each other. "How's your wife?"

"Mm. The same. Hates me, loves our grandkids." He smiled good-naturedly and shrugged.

"I sure hope so," he replied, "seems a shame to move to another planet for grandkids you hate."

"Oh, she loves them. Spoils them rotten, I say." He moved back around the counter and Templeton approached from the other side. "Wait until they become teenagers and turn into little demons, I say. Hah! We'll see then."

"Oh, those are fun years, let me tell ya," Templeton said, nodding gravely.

"Yeah, how are your kids? Talk to them much?" the man inquired, putting away some open notebooks and pushing an unidentified engine piece off to the side.

He smiled grimly. "Not too much, I'm afraid. I don't think they really blame me for leaving Karen, but she's still angry, and that makes it hard for them. She's just so involved in their lives, and I'm not around much, you know, so I think it's just easier for them to keep me at arm's length. They're good though, they're real good. Roger's working at the bank still. Up for a promotion, I think. And Martin is teaching fifth and sixth grade science. Yeah, they're good."

"Good, good," Ping offered. After the exchange ended, an awkward moment passed, and then Ping added, "You just in town for a few days, or…"

"Yeah, just for a few days." Templeton sighed, pushing through the moment and examining some of the hardware hanging on a rack beside him. "Listen, I came across something out past the green line and I stopped to pick it up." He deliberately used the first person to avoid implicating any of his crew. "It's a satellite, a damaged Yoo-lin mark VII. The coms suite has been stripped, but the rest of it is more or less intact, and I'm looking to unload it. Never found a better man for giving me a fair deal on salvage than you, Ping."

The potential for profit gave the other man's eyes a glassy sheen, and he wrung his hands together unconsciously for a moment. "Oh, yes, yes. Yoo-lins are good. Lots of copper and gold in there. Are the lenses intact? You have specs?"

Templeton produced his surface, typed in his pass code, and pulled up all of the data and pictures he had on the recovered satellite. Ping queued up his own surface, and Templeton flicked the file over to him with a gesture on the screen.

"Yes, yes, I think this will be good. You have it with you?"

"Nah, it's on the ship. I didn't want to bring it out here if you didn't want it, and no use declaring it if I can't get a good price for it."

"I think we can work something out," the man replied. "Just let me run up some numbers. Can you bring it by tomorrow?"

"Shouldn't be a problem."

Several minutes later, after their business was concluded and they had exchanged a few more pleasantries, Templeton left *Ping's Garage* and walked back the way he had come. After twenty paces or so, he turned and walked into one of the shops he had previously passed.

John and Charis walked through an entirely different part of Tranquility, and Gwen walked between them. She held her father's hand, her other hand pointing at various sights and shops around them. The Martian Mall, as it was called, was a decidedly family friendly space for tourists, though the dimensions were roughly analogous to those of Beeftown. Gwen had been asking for a Martian tee shirt and a new pair of sneakers, and so they had decided to do some family shopping. Now they strolled from storefront to storefront, and the people milled about them, passing, entering, and leaving, punctuated by automatons that drew the young girl's attention without fail.

"What about that one?" Gwen pointed, not for the first time, at a child's shirt on a mannequin in the front window of a small shop.

"I thought you wanted a purple shirt, honey," her father replied. Gwen had been obsessive about purple lately, and there was scant little of it on the ship.

"I do, but that one's really pretty. Maybe we can get that one *and* a purple one?"

"Gwen, we talked about this." Charis buttressed her husband's defense. "If you want that one, then we can't get shoes too, and you've nearly outgrown your sneakers."

"I know." The girl was momentarily downcast, but then she spied another clothing shop two doors down, and she was dragging them both by the hands to go inside. The shop was cramped, like most of the stores on the planet, space being at a premium, but the clothing was well made. Gwen eventually settled on a purple tee shirt a half a size too large that said "The Red Planet" in orange lettering. The letters were surrounded by glitter that Charis could already picture on her pants after a load of laundry. She couldn't decide whether the fact that there was no actual red on the shirt was ironic or simply inaccurate.

Gwen was jumping up and down in excitement and enjoyment of the light Martian gravity as they approached the counter to pay. Before they could reach it, John turned to Charis. "Hey, can you handle the shoe shopping? Dinah asked me to pick up a few parts for the ship."

"Why can't Dinah pick those up herself?" she asked inquisitively.

John chuckled a bit. "You know her. I'm not even sure she plans to leave the ship while we're here. Something about overhauling the reactor gauges."

Charis nodded, perhaps a bit reluctantly. "Yes, sure. I'll meet you back on the ship?"

"Sure, babe." He kissed her quickly, and when they had paid and walked out, he gave his daughter a kiss on the cheek and strode away quickly.

Clea Staples walked into a bar. It was one of the older watering holes in Tranquility, called *The God of War*, and it did its very best to imitate the hole-in-the-wall run down biker bars that wheezed through life in every small town in North America. In truth, there were very few bikers on Mars. The planet's vehicle restrictions made the pastime impractical at best, but the throwback decor made for a familiar place for locals looking to spend some of their paycheck, people hoping to forget their lives for a time, and tourists on a budget. Grungy guitar music from some prior decade invaded the street outside, reminding passers-by that some things never change, regardless of the planet. Inside was a sparsely lit collection of garish beer-sign neon, cheap furniture, and video entertainment. Some wall-mounted surfaces displayed various broadcasts, and a holo-stage at the back was tuned to some sports match transmission from Earth.

As her eyes adjusted to the light, Staples surveyed the room. It was just past noon, and only a few regulars sat on stools near the bar watching the game. A group of young men and women, probably tourists, were eating pub lunches and drinking overpriced imported beer. Some bars on the red planet purported to brew their own beers from grains grown on-planet, but *The God of War* was certainly not one of them. After another few seconds of scanning the room, she found the person she was looking for.

The woman looked different than she had the last time Staples had seen her. Her eyes were blue now, her nose smaller and wider, and her mouth was more puckered. The hair was almost blue-black, now standing in short spikes on her head. There was an unmistakable look in the woman's expression, however, that Staples felt she would have recognized anywhere. The woman raised a hand in greeting, and the captain walked over and took a seat opposite her at the remote table.

"Clea." Her voice was husky, deeper than her build and face would have suggested. "Long time."

"I almost didn't recognize you."

The other woman smiled politely. "That is precisely the point, my friend. It's Jordan now, by the way. Jordan Fecks. How long has it been?"

Staples had no doubts that the other woman knew exactly how long it had been, but she answered anyway. "Nearly a year now. How are you adjusting to Mars? Keeping yourself busy?"

The woman waved her hand airily. "Oh, the details of my personal life would bore you to tears, I'm sure, but I'm just peachy." Staples expected that the details of "Jordan's" personal life would actually terrify her, and she was glad that she hadn't answered honestly, but she had expected as much. "How is that ship of yours? What brings you to Mars?"

"*Gringolet's* holding together quite nicely. Work brings us here. A transport job. I'm not supposed to talk about it. I signed a waiver and everything." Her tone was ironically self-important. The waitress lazily made way over to the table and took their orders. Staples ordered a mid-range import beer. Jordan asked for a refresh of her water. Once she had sauntered away, Jordan spoke.

"Let me guess. You're transporting two engineers to Saturn." She studied her nails as she said it.

Staples shook her head. "Should I even ask how you know that?"

The woman called Jordan laughed a bit. "No, I don't

think so. No." After another moment passed, she added, "I assume there is a reason you wanted to meet? I do love seeing you, darling, but I had to take two trains halfway around the planet to get to Tranquility. I do hope that this is more than a social visit."

"I'd like to hire you. You are still a Private Investigator?" She raised her eyebrows.

"Was I ever? You know, if I remember correctly, the last time you hired a Private Eye, it cost you your job." Jordan continued to regard her nails with her blue eyes, picking lightly at her thumb with her index finger.

"True," Staples assented, "but it bought me my ship. I think I came out ahead."

Jordan shrugged. "If you say so. What's the job?"

Staples sighed and looked around the room. The regulars hadn't moved, the score hadn't changed, and the vacationers were just ordering another round. With the music playing, no one was in earshot of them. "I've got two new crew members that I'd like more information on." She produced a manila envelope from her flight jacket and set it on the table. "There's something off about them. I don't trust them."

The blue eyes flashed up at her, the brows raised. "Then why did you hire them?"

"I was in a rush, and Don pushed for them."

"Ah, Templeton. Still the softie. I know you like to keep someone on your right hand who actually likes people more than books, Clea, but don't you think you would be better off with someone who displayed some guile? Some subtlety?"

"I've had enough of guile. If I wanted to be surrounded by backstabbing vipers, I would have stayed at my old job. Don is a friend, and even better, what you see is what you get with him." She felt herself blush a little bit as she defended her first mate.

Jordan seemed unfazed by her response. "Suit yourself." She took a sip of her water, and Staples drank several swallows of her beer, which was not nearly as cold as she would have liked. "So anyway, you and Don hired these new crew members, you don't like them, and you want me to look into them. That should be easy enough."

Staples pushed the envelope over to her friend. "Harrison Quinn and Dean Parsells. They were friends before the hire, came as a pair, and apparently they were security guards at a prison up until two months ago. Their résumés are in the envelope along with pictures and background check information. Their references are good and their records are clear."

Jordan nearly spoke over her last word. "But you don't like them. So fire them. What did you hire them for?"

"Security."

"So fire them. Clea, there are plenty of security personnel on Mars hungry for work." She sat back and smiled a bit. "I could even recommend a few."

Staples smiled a bit nervously in response. "I don't think I want to hire anyone who has worked with you."

Her interlocutor feigned righteous indignation. "Why Clea Staples! Are you implying that I keep unsavory company? I'll remind you who I am sitting across from at the moment."

"No offense," Staples responded, not quite sure whether the woman was genuinely offended under her somewhat comic veneer. "Most of the people you've introduced me to have frightened me."

The woman's response was a thin-lipped grin. "I always thought you were smart, Clea. But you still haven't answered the question. Why not just fire them?"

Staples leaned forward, her chin jutting out a bit. "Because they haven't done anything wrong. Because I can hardly hire them on Earth and fire them on Mars. Because I could be wrong, and I don't want to fire good men just because they rub me the wrong way."

Jordan sighed through her small nose. "Oh Clea. That need to do the right thing is going to get you in trouble one of these days. Again."

"I don't doubt it. Anyway, please look into it. We're leaving in two days."

"It's unlikely I can turn anything up by then. If I can't, I'll just transmit the report to you once you're en route. Along with my bill, of course."

Staples drained the last few sips of her beer. "I'd appreciate that."

"Grand. Anything else?"

"Yes, actually. Have you ever found a paper bag with one hundred thousand dollars on the sidewalk in front of you?"

Jordan considered for a minute, as if perhaps the situation had come up a time or two. "I can't say that I have. One does live in hope, however."

"Neither have I. There's a serial number off a satellite on a slip of paper in there. See what you can find out about it?"

"As you wish. If there's nothing else, I need to get going. I have an appointment with a man I am dying to meet, and I don't want to be late."

"No, that's all. Thank you, Jordan." She made herself say the name.

As she left the bar alone, Staples suppressed a shudder, wondering what sorry man had made himself deserving of the attentions of the woman now known as Jordan Fecks.

In another bar in an entirely different part of Tranquility, a small man sat by himself. He was young, scarcely into his third decade, and he had greasy dark hair that fell uncombed and unkempt around his face. Several years of personal neglect and the low Martian gravity had left him thin and under-muscled, and though his appearance was disheveled, his eyes were sharp and bright. He wore a long black duster over his everyday street clothes, and he slouched in the dimmest corner of the darkest bar he could find. This establishment, *The Redbar*, was not far from Beeftown, and no small part of its profits came from the sale of things that were not on the menu. However, the man was interested in the bar for its seclusion, not its illegal drug selection. There was no mid-afternoon rush, and people did not come here to eat.

The man produced his surface, logged into a secure server using a password, thumb print, and retinal scan, and began to type.

*Received your last update.* Gringolet *has arrived a day later than expected. It is set to depart in two days. Read over files of crew you provided. Tried contacting crew member you specified. Success. Crew member will meet me here at* Redbar. *Price is still to be negotiated, but if money is good, subject has agreed to our terms. I have the virus drive to give the subject as well as the ampoule if necessary. Wish me luck.*

Once the message was sent, the man slouched down again to wait. He ordered another soda to be polite and, he hoped, to avoid attracting attention. The soda came, and he took a sip. He thought about passing the time by watching a broadcast on his surface, but then decided against it; it might look as if he wasn't serious about the negotiation. He fidgeted nervously. A shadow fell across him, and he looked up, smiling to see exactly whom he had hoped to see.

# CHAPTER 6

Martian days were just over twenty-four hours and thirty minutes long, though the years were nearly twice the length as Earth's. Communication and commerce were so regular between the burgeoning cities and Earth that the Martian citizens had decided to keep Earth hours, lest scheduling, and especially calendar reconciliation, become a problem. From the perspective of Martian residents and visitors, day was the hours when stores were open and people worked, and night was when partying, clandestine meetings, and sleep occurred. They had decided on Greenwich Mean Time, and sometimes this matched up to the actual cycle of light and dark on their smaller red world and sometimes it did not. For most inhabitants, it did not matter. The vast majority of people lived, worked, slept, ate, and died in metal housing with a few windows. No one stood in the sun of the Martian noon without an EVA suit on.

Captain Staples and her first mate stood side by side at the entrance to the tubeway that led to their ship. The digital clocks placed at regular intervals over the stretch of the concourse indicated that it was nearly seventeen hundred hours. Their passengers, the two computer engineers who had been hired and paid considerable amounts of money to move out to a mining station orbiting Saturn, were due at five for a tour of the ship. Staples and Templeton both wore their flight jackets and slacks. The crew had no uniforms per se, but they had matching jackets, and it was unofficial ship policy to wear them when meeting potential clients, passengers, and the like. Staples' blonde hair was parted on the left, and it hung to her chin, covering a bit of her right cheek. Templeton's graying dirty blonde hair was mostly tucked under a cap with a bill, which made him look a bit older than his fifty-four years.

"Do you know what they look like?" Templeton asked.

"No I do not," Staples replied without looking at him. Her brown eyes scanned the crowds moving back and forth, alighting briefly on any group of two if it consisted of a man and a woman, and finally relinquishing her expectations the pair when said couple walked by them without a glance. "If they're late, they're late."

Seventeen came and went. At five minutes past the hour, Staples spied a likely pair. The man was large, about two meters tall, and looked to be in his mid-thirties. The short brown hair on his head became shorter as it approached his ears and neck. He had a strong, broad nose, blue eyes, and a wide cleft chin. A fairly traditional light grey suit and blue tie covered what was evidently a robust physique. He would have been an intimidating specimen had he not carried himself with a light positivity, perhaps due to the Martian gravity, that made him seem to be in a very good mood. Next to him walked a shorter woman, perhaps in her early thirties and only a few centimeters taller than Staples, with long red hair that flowed past her shoulders. Her eyes were a rich brown, and her heart-shaped face was accented by a smattering of freckles that climbed from one cheek to the other via her nose. Her lips were full and sumptuous, and her body was lithe and appealing in a light maroon chemise sweater and black business slacks. The man was good-looking, but the woman was gorgeous.

As they weaved through the crowd, it became evident by their behavior that they were looking for a particular docking tubeway. Staples looked over at Templeton and saw that his mouth was hanging slightly open. She nudged him lightly with her elbow, and he shook his head and clamped his jaw shut. Finally, they approached, each wearing a welcoming smile. Staples did her best to return it; it did not always come as easily to her as it did to her friend.

Templeton was the first to speak. He held out his hand to the man, grinning broadly. "I'm Donovan Templeton. I'm first mate on Gringolet. You must be Doctor Henry Bauer."

The tall man shook his hand with some enthusiasm and said, "Henry, please. Herc, actually."

"Herc. Don." He turned his attention, not reluctantly, to the woman. "Don," he said again, extending his hand to her.

"Evelyn," she replied in a slightly deeper voice than Staples had expected.

"This," Don said with obvious pride, turning to his

employer, "is Captain Clea Staples. *Gringolet*," he gestured back to the tubeway and the ship beyond, "is hers."

"I'm very glad to meet both of you." She shook hands with the pair of them, noting the way the man's hand dwarfed hers and the woman's was soft and uncalloused. Staples suddenly felt a bit like a frumpy country bumpkin in her flight clothes next to the well-educated woman in front of her. A brief pause helped her restore her composure, and she continued. "It's my pleasure to show you around my ship today. Though you won't be awake for it, you'll be spending three weeks on him, and I insist on all stasis passengers getting a tour."

"Him?" Evelyn asked. "Aren't ships traditionally female?"

"Aren't captains traditionally male?" Staples countered in what she hoped was a friendly tone.

The woman laughed briefly, a charming and husky affair. "True, true. If I had a ship, I'd want him to be a boy as well." She raised her eyebrows as she said it, and Staples actually found herself thinking that the woman's smile was sexy.

"Well I've been excited for this all week," Herc Bauer cut in. "I love spaceships. If I hadn't gotten into computers, I think I might have liked to be a pilot. Is the pilot on board?"

Templeton answered. "Yup. You can meet her if you like, though she's a trifle shy. We got a few crew members on board, but most are out enjoying the city. There's a long trip ahead of us, and we don't get to sleep through it." He spoke with a twinge of good-natured jealousy.

"'Scuse us!" A voice sounded from behind the crew members, and they looked behind them. Parsells and

Quinn were wheeling a flatbed cart burdened with a large item covered in a tarp down the tubeway and out into the concourse. Parsells was guiding from the front, and Quinn was pushing from the rear.

"Fellas!" Templeton nearly yelled, his agitation showing. "I said that we'd take that over later."

The two men stopped, and the cart squeaked to a halt. "You said at seventeen," Parsells objected.

Templeton tried to keep his voice diplomatic for the sake of appearances. "I said we had an appointment at seventeen, and that we'd take it over *after* that."

Parsells looked petulant, perhaps even hurt. Quinn's face was expressionless. "You want us to take it back?"

Templeton looked at their two guests. Herc was politely attempting to look elsewhere while they conducted ship business, but Evelyn looked on, seemingly rapt. He looked over at Staples.

She made the decision. "No, it's fine. Don, why don't you go with them. Take it now, that way it's done. I can certainly handle the tour." In truth, she was a bit nervous about talking with two strangers on her ship, but that was no reason to make things more difficult than they had to be.

"You sure?"

"Absolutely." They all stood aside as Parsells and Quinn manhandled the cart through the tubeway and into the main hall. The captain indicated the now-vacant metal tube that led to her ship, and said, "Shall we, doctors?"

"This is Reactor Control," the captain said as they walked into the room that overlooked the nuclear reactor nestled in the back of the ship. "We call it the ReC for short." The room was currently empty, and Staples and her two attendees crossed the room to the control panels on the wall. Bauer leaned over the controls and looked down through the angled windows onto the reactor. The large engine which drove the ship and supplied power took up the majority of the room below, stretching five meters across, four deep, and over three high.

"Nuclear power, huh? Fusion?"

"So they tell me," Staples replied. "I'm not the expert. I'm sorry that Dinah couldn't be here, but she and much of the crew are off ship on shore leave. She's our resident engineer," she looked down into the reactor room herself, then added, "and tactical officer. I'm actually less sure of what she *can't* do. She could tell you about this reactor all day."

"I'd like that," Herc replied with some enthusiasm, his eyes pouring over the reactor. "I wish we could wait to go into stasis until a few days into the journey."

"I've no doubt that our crew could show you a good time around the ship, but I'm afraid we just aren't qualified to handle the procedure of putting people under and waking them up. We actually don't have any stasis tubes of our own on the ship." She stepped away from the window and looked at the pair. Evelyn was standing near the door regarding her with some trepidation. "Don't worry," she tried to reassure her, "we've got lots of experience transporting them. We've got a cargo bay that's been specifically set up to house them. Think of it like this: we've got a safe car with a well-made back seat… we just don't own any infant car seats ourselves." Evelyn's look of ease returned, and her concerns seemed somewhat assuaged.

Herc either hadn't been concerned or had been so intent on the nuclear engine that he hadn't noticed the shift in topic at all. "I'm surprised you don't have holographic controls here." He was looking at the control panel. "This ship is only, what… thirty years old?"

Staples nodded. "About that. I did get him used. There were actually holographic controls in here when I bought the ship, but Dinah removed them when she came onboard." Herc looked at her quizzically. "Dinah has…" she paused, searching for the right words, "been on ships for a long time, and in some delicate, even dangerous situations. She's a big proponent of Murphy's Law: if something can go wrong, it probably will. With machinery, that translates to: the more complex it is, the more things that can go wrong with it. Holographics don't work if the power's on the fritz, but switches, buttons, and knobs? Analog has its advantages. There are surfaces, of course," she gestured with an open palm to the blank black screens set into the control panels, "but when you're in space, redundancy and safety are the name of the game."

Herc nodded, seeming to understand. "It's like this reactor." He said. "Nuclear power is over a hundred and fifty years old, but it still works, and we've nearly perfected it at this point. Cars used some form of the combustion engine for nearly that long. Sure, we refined it over the years, but at the end of day, it's still a combustion engine. *If it ain't broke…*" He let the platitude trail off.

Staples laughed. "You sound like my first mate."

"Don. Seemed like a good man. Honest. I can see why you'd want someone like that working with you."

"He is," Staples ruminated as she spoke, staring at nothing. "He is a good man. I'm lucky to have him."

"Well, we've just met," the other woman interjected, "but I think he admires you a lot. It might not be luck. You might deserve him." There was a hint of provocation in her voice, but also the warmth of a well-intended compliment.

The captain demurred. "I can only…" she broke off as Evelyn's eyes fluttered up in her head and her knees seemed to grow weak. She stumbled a step to the side, putting her hand against the wall, and it looked as though she would collapse to the ground. Bauer rushed forward and did his best to catch her and support her head at the same time. Unsure of how to help, Staples looked on anxiously.

"Are you all right?" she asked instinctively, though it was obvious that the woman was not. The large man had no problem holding her up, but her head was lolling to the side, and her eyelids were fluttering fiercely. Staples moved forward to help Herc support her on the other side, pinging her watch as she did so. "Doctor, are you aboard?" she spoke into the device on her wrist, then said, "Should we lay her down?" She looked with some concern at the cold metallic floor.

"I am here, Captain." Jabir Iqbal's accented voice emanated from the captain's watch as she placed one of Evelyn's arms around her shoulders. The woman's eyes were beginning to open, and they could feel strength returning to her limbs.

"We need you in ReC. One of our guests has fainted," she said after awkwardly tapping her watch again.

Just as his reply, "I'll be right there," came, Evelyn murmured, "No, I'm all right." She was finding her balance again, placing her feet flatly on the floor and taking her own weight. Staples and Herc slowly released her, but he kept his hands out, prepared to steady or catch her if necessary.

She blinked in the light and looked at both of them. "I'm all right, really. I just got dizzy for a moment. Please tell the doctor I'm alright. He doesn't need to come."

"Do you feel like you can walk?" Staples asked.

"Yes," she said delicately in her husky voice. "Yes," she said again, this time with more conviction.

"Good, then you can walk to Medical." The redheaded woman opened her mouth to object, but Staples spoke over her and with authority. "No discussion. My ship, my rules." She hoped her smile made her seem less like the dictator she felt like whenever she said something like that. "I insist on my passengers being well taken care of."

Bauer immediately supported her. "You weren't just dizzy; you just about passed out there. You really should see the doctor." She looked back and forth between them, still a little unsteady, and finally nodded sheepishly.

The doctor was waiting at the door when they arrived at Medical. As the ship was in the Martian atmosphere, such as it was, and consequently on its belly, there was no odd gravitational transition as the three entered the long bluish room. Iqbal had prepared the nearest bed, and he guided the woman to it as he introduced himself. Evelyn was attempting to placate them as she walked to the bed under her own power.

"I'm fine now, really." She turned around, sat down on the bed, and faced the three of them.

"Ms. Schilling," he began. "It is Ms. Schilling?" She

nodded and smiled. "Ms. Schilling, if I had a dollar for every sick patient who told me they were 'fine,' I would be a good deal wealthier than I am." He looked briefly at Staples. "Please don't take that as a remonstration, Captain. I am quite content with the current state of my remuneration." He turned back to his patient. "Now please tell me, do you still feel faint?"

She shook her head.

"Light headed at all?"

She looked at him and winced a bit, looking as sheepish she had looked in the ReC. She held out her fingers a centimeter apart.

"Just a bit, I see. Are you comfortable enough to sit up, or would you rather lie down?" As ever, Staples was impressed at the doctor's soothing and authoritative voice and its ability to engender trust and confidence.

"I'm all right to sit." She was leaning forward a bit with her hands gripping the edge of the metal bed, her pale and lightly freckled wrists just visible below the sleeves of her sweater.

"Very well. Captain, Doctor, I'll have to ask you to wait outside. Doctor-client confidentiality, you know."

Staples and Herc turned to go, but Evelyn quickly interjected, "No, it's fine. They can stay."

Iqbal raised an eyebrow, but said, "As you wish." Once he had picked up his stethoscope, he added, "I'll need you to take off your sweater please." Once she was down to her tee shirt, he began his examination, checking her breathing, pulse, blood pressure, and other minutiae. "Your pulse is fast, your breathing a bit quick and shallow, and your blood pressure seems high, though it is difficult to tell without a baseline from your medical records.

Frankly, you seem to be suffering from a light case of nervous exhaustion. Tell me, have you experienced anything lately that might account for these symptoms? An illness perhaps, or some other physically trying incident?"

"I…" she groped for the right words, "had a particularly fun weekend." She blushed as she spoke, though it seemed to be more from a flood of pleasant memories than from embarrassment. "I met someone in a bar, we hit it off, and we spent the next twenty-four hours or so drinking and, well, indulging ourselves." Her chin lifted slightly as she divulged her one-night stand to perfect strangers, as if to challenge them to comment or judge. No one did.

"Hm. Twenty-four hours is a long time for one to remain intoxicated. Tell me, did you perchance partake of any other mind or physiologically altering substances?"

The woman shook her head.

"You're sure? You didn't lose any time during this period of drunkenness?" His questions came without a hint of judgment, only evidencing a desire for information.

"No." She smiled a somewhat coy and satisfied smile. "I remember it quite well."

"Well, I am pleased for you," he said reflexively. The other two looked on, Staples leaning against another table behind Iqbal. "Lightheadedness and dizziness certainly can be aftereffects of the consumption of alcohol, though it is unusual that you should feel it more than a day later, even if you really overdid it. When was the last drink you had?"

"Mmm," she thought, looking up at the ceiling. "Saturday night with dinner. Say about nineteen? Then I took a rickshaw home and slept all night. I actually didn't wake up until about noon on Sunday."

"I see," the doctor responded, looking levelly in her chestnut brown eyes. "Tell me, were you hung over when you awoke? Exhaustion, headache, the like?"

"Um," she thought for another second, squinting a bit as she did so. "Exhaustion: yes. Headache: no. Just groggy, very groggy."

"Unusual, but not unheard of." He drew himself up to his full height and stepped to the metal tray beside him, putting down his stethoscope and picking up his ophthalmoscope. "If you don't mind, I'd like to keep you here for a full examination."

She was shaking her head before he had finished speaking. "No way, Doc. I really am fine now. I'm sure I just overdid it, and anyway, this silly business has taken up enough of your captain's and your time." She looked over at Staples, who returned, the best she could, a look that said *don't worry about it.*

"Well, I can hardly make you stay, but I really recommend that you undergo a thorough examination, if not by me, then by another licensed physician." He put down the ophthalmoscope with a slight air of defeat.

"I will," she said unconvincingly. "I've got to be at the stasis center in a few hours, and I'm sure they'll do a full check up before they put me under. I'm fine, really." She winced as she realized that she had earned Iqbal another phantom dollar.

As the three of them were walking out of the Medical bay, Evelyn stopped suddenly and said, "I forgot my sweater! I'll be right back." Staples nodded, and she and Herc continued down the hall as she turned around and ducked energetically back through the door, all traces of her prior faintness seemingly gone. Iqbal was standing by the bed she had sat upon, holding out her maroon sweater to her with his left hand.

She did not walk so much as saunter up to him, stopping closer than she needed to, and took the sweater from him. She looked up at him.

"You know, it's too bad I won't be awake for this journey, Doctor. You seem really interesting."

He looked down at her just as steadily. "Now that the examination is finished, our interactions need not be governed by formality or in a professional manner. Please call me Jabir. And may I say, Ms. Schilling, that it would be a pleasure to get to know you as well. One doctor to another."

She raised her eyebrows, shamelessly suggestive, then tipped him a wink and was gone through the door, the sweater bobbing over her shoulder. He let out a long sigh of appreciation, and then turned and walked back to his office.

"If you don't mind me asking a personal question," Staples said as she sat across from her two soon-to-be passengers, "what exactly is the difference between a Computer Engineer," she looked at Bauer, "and a Computer Scientist?" She shifted her gaze to Schilling. They were seated in the mess hall at one end of the long tables, cold plastic-wrapped sandwiches on plates in front of them and beverages nearby.

Evelyn's laugh sounded, and Herc grinned. "That's a personal question?" she asked.

"We get that all the time, actually. Well, I do," Herc added. "Simply put, a Computer Engineer focuses more on the building aspect of computers." He pawed at his sandwich with his large but dexterous hands, excavating it from the plastic wrap and setting it down on the metal plate. "It's really where computers and Electrical Engineering meet. We deal with the construction of integrated systems, power flow, wiring, and hardware in general. That's a broad definition, you understand." He took a bite of his sandwich and seemed somewhat surprised at being pleased with it.

"We have a great cook named Piotr," Staples offered by way of explanation. "He's in charge of food purchases, meals, keeping the pantries and refrigeration units stocked, that sort of thing. I'm sorry he's not here right now to make us something warm. He's off ship buying supplies for our journey; it's obviously critical that we have an abundance of food when we make long trips like this."

"Doesn't he get shore leave too?" Evelyn asked between bites of her own sandwich.

Staples nodded somewhat regretfully. "He does, but not as much as some. Some things need doing while we're in port, and that means some crew members have more time off than others when we are berthed. It's just a reality of the job, but Piotr doesn't mind. Still," she looked over at the door to the mess hall as if expecting the burly cook to walk through it, "I'm surprised that he's not back yet. Maybe he *is* taking a bit of shore leave out there. But you were saying about Computer Science?" She looked at Evelyn, and then began work on her own well-made turkey sandwich.

"Ah, yes." She put down her food and wiped her mouth with her napkin. "Computer Science is, well, there's a lot of overlap really, but comp sci has more to do with data, how instructions are processed by computers, data protection and security, and programming languages. It's a lot of data."

"So if I wanted someone to write me an AI program, that would be you." Staples said, pointing at Evelyn.

She nodded in response. "Yes, though that is way beyond me. And illegal, I might add."

"Do you ever think that will change?"

"Mmm," Evelyn equivocated.

"Yes, but not anytime soon," Herc cut in. "AI is the future. It's where we're going, but I think people are too scared. Too many movies and books about evil computers destroying mankind, too much human arrogance. You know how long it took people to accept that we're descended from apes? We don't like competition; we're…" he thought for a moment, "in love with our own uniqueness. We're not ready for another group of creatures that think too. That's really what Turing Compliant AI would be: another species. People don't know enough about it, so they're scared. People keep trying to pass that vote, but I don't think it'll happen anytime soon."

Staples put down the crust of her sandwich and considered. "You know enough about it. Are you scared of AI?"

"Absolutely," he said, and took another bite.

Early the next morning, shore leave was over and nearly every member of the crew was back on board. Templeton and Staples were back at the tubeway entrance to the ship, and this time Dinah Hazra was standing with them. They were waiting on the official delivery of their passengers who had evidently been put into stasis the night before. The stasis process had of course been theorized as a means to deal with the daunting amounts of time required to cross the vast reaches of space between planets long before it had become possible. And despite its invention and subsequent minimizing of accidents and fatalities, it remained somewhat impractical for the average traveler. People and other creatures such as pets could be placed in cold stasis, which effectively slowed the aging process to the point where it was negligible, and though it was common, it was not quite routine. A team of skilled experts oversaw the process of both submersion into and emersion from stasis, which was completed in a special lab, and it often took several hours. Even after stasis was achieved, it was considered common prudence for the team to monitor the subject for the following eight hours or so in case anything went wrong. Finally, the stasis tubes were transferred to the ship in question and hooked into the requisite reception bays. The tubes came with their own power supply, but the bays supplied redundancy in case of a power failure as well as other chemical needs, such as coolant, from storage tanks. It was this delivery that the three crew members were waiting for now.

"Have you ever been frozen?" Templeton asked conversationally to neither of them in particular.

"No," his captain replied, shaking her head lightly. She was looking for their expected guests again. She suspected that she would have more luck seeing them coming this time.

"Yes, sir," Dinah replied, also keeping her eyes on the people walking by. There were far fewer this morning than the night before, and many staggered more than they walked as they sought some reanimating magic from their cups of coffee.

Templeton turned to look at her. "Really? When?" Dinah neither looked at him nor answered. Her eyes remained on the crowd.

Templeton abruptly became aware of his faux pas, and changed his question. "What was it like?"

The dark-skinned engineer looked at him, her hands clasped behind her back, her feet slightly spread. "Disconcerting. The process lowers your core body temperature to all but halt aging, the need for food or drink, or brain activity. No brain activity means no dreaming."

"You sleep for weeks, or even months, but you don't dream?" Templeton shook his head.

"No, sir. Dreams result from the brain processing the activities of the day, that sort of thing. There is no activity. It feels like someone just turned off your brain, and then turned it back on. It's not even restful. I usually woke up tired."

"Huh," Templeton mused. "'Usually'? You been in stasis more than once?" Again silence greeted him. Staples spied her opportunity to save them from the awkward moment.

"Here they come." Four technicians were wheeling two large metallic boxes down the concourse towards them. The boxes were as wide as a bookshelf and three times as thick. The technicians had them on trolleys slanted back at a thirty-five degree angle. The stasis tubes would probably have been too heavy for them to handle if not for the light Martian gravity. The technicians were accompanied by Parsells and Quinn, whom Templeton had sent to meet them at their vehicle to provide security. It was really just a formality, but he figured that it was better to be safe than sorry. The two men looked as dour as ever to be up early. The entourage was rounded out by a man in a blue lab coat and scrubs; the lab coat listed his name on the lapel, Pelzer, as well as the name of his company, Stasis Solutions, across the back. Greetings were exchanged, digital documents shown, fingerprints given, authorization granted, and finally they were ready to push the tubes one at a time down the tubeway and up the ramp to the ship.

As tube A went by her, Staples looked down at the signed transfer documents on her surface that assured Stasis Solutions that she and her crew took full responsibility for the man and woman in the tubes. "A is Evelyn," she said, imagining the lovely woman unconscious in the huge metal coffin. There were no windows in the devices. She felt a touch of nervousness as she realized that there was no way for her to be sure that it was in fact Evelyn in the tube. Perhaps Doctor Pelzer and Stasis Solutions had made a mistake and sent Evelyn off to Venus like a lost suitcase. She tried to put it out of her mind; they were professionals, and anyway, there was nothing she could do about it at this point.

"B is for Bauer," she said as the second tube passed her. Once everyone had walked down the tubeway, Staples took one last look around the concourse. People still milled about, walked to work. A shop keeper was opening his store for business on the other side of the large room. A good-looking man in his mid thirties with black hair graying at the temples leaned casually against another closed storefront. A woman spoke in heated tones to a child who looked as though she was on the verge of tears. A man with a black duster and greasy black hair stood further away, looking in her general direction, shifting somewhat nervously from foot to foot. Clea Staples took one last look at Tranquility and walked towards her ship.

# CHAPTER 7

Day two.

"Do we really gotta do this?" Parsells asked, sweat dripping from his face. He and Quinn were both standing, their feet spread, bent over, their hands on their knees. They wore weighted vests over their sweat-damp workout shirts. The tall, bald, dark form of Kojo Jang stood near them, his hands on his hips. He seemed unaffected by his weight vest, and he was barely sweating. His breath came easily, while Parsells and Quinn both gasped. Jang had just had them run ten sprints, from the base of the back wall of the cargo bay up to where the elevator disappeared into the ceiling when the ship was horizontal. Parsells stood up and put his hands behind his head, desperately trying to catch his breath. "Can't we at least take the weight vests off?"

"Then what would be the point of this? We are currently accelerating at about six tenths of normal Earth gravity. Quinn, your file says you normally weigh one hundred and nine kilograms under normal Earth gravity.

Right now, you weigh about sixty-five kilograms. That makes exercise easy, and it's a good way to get soft. People who spend a great deal of time in space tend to lose muscle mass."

Parsells looked at Quinn and tried not to roll his eyes at his friend. "But we used to live in zero G, and we didn't work out that much then."

"You were also, if memory serves, spending ten hours a day mining asteroids. Here, it is easy to spend days or even weeks without encountering physical exercise. It is important to stay in shape."

"But," Parsells groped for another objection that might put off the next set of sprints another minute, "if we gotta fight, it'll be on Mars, or the space station around Saturn. That's light gravity or no gravity! Why should we-"

"Get used to being heavier than you normally are?" Jang finished his sentence, pointing to his forty kilogram weight vest. "Do you remember, just over a week ago, when we were decelerating at nearly three times normal gravity?" The looks both Quinn and Parsells wore on their faces said that they did. "What if you were called upon to fight, or to run, or to climb under those conditions? Adrenaline can only be counted on to do so much. You must be ready. Now," he pointed to the far end of the cargo bay, "ten more sprints."

"Drill instructor from hell," Parsells muttered under his breath. It came out louder than he intended.

Jang did not reply, except to shout, "Go!"

Five minutes and ten trips across the cargo bay later found Jang breathing a bit more than he had previously and Parsells and Quinn lying flat on their backs, gasping like stranded fish on a lakeshore. Their lungs burned, their legs hurt, and Quinn had a stitch in his side that he might have traded for stomach cancer had he been given the option.

Jang let them rest for a minute before beginning on his next lecture. "There are advantages to working in a variable gravity environment; one of them is training. Few ships accelerate at greater than sixty or seventy percent of Earth gravity, though most are capable of more. It is comfortable for the crew, and the faster one thrusts, the greater the fuel consumption becomes. Most crews allow themselves to become soft, their muscles to atrophy. They do not understand the advantages that can come from training for high gravity environments, especially when operating in a low one." He looked down at the two men. Parsells was working to get himself into a sitting position, but Quinn remained prone. The security chief removed his vest, letting it drop heavily to the floor, and indicated that the men might do the same. They did so gratefully, Quinn struggling up as he did so.

"Observe," Jang said, and then took off running towards the elevator shaft which bisected the back wall of the cargo bay currently serving as the floor. After a few meters, he leapt into the air and landed a seemingly impossible ten meters distant on the far side, having easily cleared the three meter tall elevator shaft. Quinn and Parsells looked at each other in disbelief. A few seconds later, Jang jumped up on top of the elevator shaft and into view again. He put his hands on his hips in a manner that Parsells was quickly beginning to hate.

"The effects of light gravity make feats possible that would have been considered superhuman only a hundred years ago." His deep voice echoed around the large chamber, bouncing off the UteVs and jump ships arrayed above them. Far above them, currently acting as their ceiling, the cargo bay doors stood closed and sealed. It made the two men nervous knowing that empty space and instant death were on the other side of those doors, but their new boss seemed to be quite comfortable with the setting.

"What if someone bumps the wrong button on the bridge - the cockpit," Parsells corrected himself, "and accidently opens those doors?" He pointed up as he spoke.

"As I am sure was true when you were mining asteroids, there are a dozen safety protocols in place to prevent that from happening," Jang replied as he lightly leapt down from the elevator shaft, making it look like no more than a one meter drop.

Parsells snorted laughter. "Probably not as many 'safety protocols' in place as you think, but yeah, they were careful with us."

"Just so." Jang walked up to them. "Next is weapons training."

Quinn smiled, and Parsells nodded. "Sounds a lot better than running sprints. Where do we do that?"

Jang began walking over to a metal case that stood two meters tall with gripbars arrayed around it. The case was nestled on the floor against the wall next to the elevator. "In here."

"In here?" the usually quiet Quinn asked. The worried look had appeared on Parsells' face as well. "With live ammo? Isn't that dangerous?"

Jang leaned over and typed a six-digit code into the keypad on the weapons locker. "It is, but only if we shoot each other." He pulled open a locker and removed a projectile rifle. "The hull of this ship is twenty-five centimeters thick. It is designed to deflect small asteroids if necessary, provided we are not going too fast. You wouldn't get through the hull with one of these in a hundred years."

"But there are weapons that cut through hulls," Parsells said, bringing himself to his feet, his wet shirt clinging to his chest.

"Yes. We have a few, and I want you to be familiar with them, but we do not train to attack other ships. We train to defend ours."

Day four.

Clea Staples stood in the dorsal observation lounge, looking somewhat down towards her home planet. The viewing window stood at a forty-five degree angle, extending over a meter up to meet the wall in front of her. When the ship was horizontal, the window acted like the rear windscreen of a car. Now she stood at the base of it, looking backwards to the constantly shrinking red planet and the tiny blue world beyond. She couldn't see it, but she knew it was there, somewhere beyond the sun. The stars blazed as always. She considered the facts that any burgeoning astronomer understood: that the light of the stars she was observing consisted of photons that had been born in the heart of a star and sent on their way thousands, perhaps tens of thousands of years before. The tiny particles had travelled for centuries to find their home, finally, in her retinas. It was old knowledge, but it still amazed her.

The engines were not visible from the viewport, but the blue iridescence that they created obscured her view to a small degree. Here, in one of the aft-most rooms on the ship, their noise punctured the bulkheads and filled the chamber. A metal table and chair hung clamped to the wall behind her; no one had come through this room to reorient the furniture the last time they had been in zero G, and the effect was somewhat disconcerting. Rearranging the furniture did much to alleviate the feeling that the crew was standing on the walls when under thrust, but there was no need and no desire to change every room each time the ship entered and left atmosphere. Staples suspected that this observation lounge had last been used on Earth, perhaps for a game of cards or a private luncheon.

There was a knock at the door. Staples frowned and waited. The knock came again, and she sighed and said loudly, "Enter!"

The door, in the ceiling from her perspective, opened outwards and Yegor Durin's head poked through. He was squatting on the bulkhead wall that held the door, and his mop of unsecured dark hair hung down around his face. From his perspective, the door was a trapdoor in the floor.

"You don't have to knock, Yegor. This isn't my bedroom. The lounges are public places, unless they've been reserved."

"I... alright. Mind if I join you?" he asked a bit hesitantly.

Staples shook her head broadly. "Come on in."

The panels in the floor had been left retracted from the captain's climb down to where she stood. Yegor swung himself around and began clambering down the ladder. He wore a black tee shirt and well-worn jeans, an outfit she had seen him wear many times when off duty. His hair was wet as though he had just showered; the tips of it brushed against his shoulders.

"The door," Staples reminded him. It was important to keep the heavy doors secured when they were not in use. If the ship had to cease thrust or take evasive action, heavy doors swinging loose could be a serious danger.

"*Da, Kapitan.*" He took a few steps back up, leaned over, grabbed the door, and swung it into place as he descended again, being sure to latch it closed securely. He then made his way down the rest of the ladder and walked over to stand next to his captain, gazing down through the window as he approached her. She turned back and regarded it with him silently. A minute or two passed.

"Amazing, yes?" he asked finally.

"Always," she responded. Another moment of silence.

"You know, I grew up in Vladivostok," he said suddenly, apropos of seemingly nothing.

"I think I remember that, yes," she replied, still looking through the window but curious as to his intention.

"I grew up in a generation of young men sold on the idea of spreading the city into the ocean. The water had risen to cover some of city at that point, and we knew it wouldn't stop." He puffed his chest out and threw his shoulders back some as if touting some glorious plan. "So the new plan was to expand into the ocean." His shoulders dropped. "Everyone was looking down. I kept looking up. I wanted to go into space, but they kept saying, 'no, Yegor, we need you to be part of bold new expansion of Russia!'" He chuckled lightly. "I didn't even like swimming. When I was sixteen, my parents made me take underwater welding classes. I was so angry, I ran away from home." He was silent for a while, and they both looked down through the portal as if hypnotized.

Finally, Staples, smiling a bit, prompted him. "Did you go join the space circus?"

He looked at her quizzically. "Space... circus?"

She shook her head and turned back to the window. "Never mind. It's a thing, a common joke. Running away to join... never mind. You were saying?"

He chuckled again. "I returned home two days later, mugged, beaten, and ready for class. Decided that space wasn't for me. So I worked hard in school, studied communications. I went to college, got job in underwater communications strategies."

"Were your parents proud?"

"Very proud. Then I started looking for other jobs. Figured I was going to work underwater for the rest of my life, but at least I could do it somewhere not Vladivostok. I found the job opening at GTS working in space. I applied, got the job."

"What did your parents say?" she asked, turning back to her coms officer.

He pursed his lips together speculatively. "Don't know. Never told them. They went to bed one night. When they woke up the next morning, I was gone." He was silent for a few more moments, and then he looked at her. "Not their life to live."

She nodded. "I've been thinking lately. We all have these ideas about how people should live their lives. 'This idea is terrible,' or 'that opportunity was wasted.' I think the truth is that people have the right to spend their lives anyway they wish."

Yegor nodded in agreement. "I think so too." He turned back to the window at their feet and regarded the stars.

She continued to look at him. "Yegor, was there something that you wanted to talk to me about?" she inquired.

"I don't want to bother you while you're off duty."

It was her turn to chuckle. "Well, I think you've blown that."

He turned to her, appearing suddenly apologetic.

"Relax," she soothed. "I've quite enjoyed our talk. Besides, I'm the captain. I'm never really off duty. What can I do for you?"

"Well, I wanted to ask you about the new coms suite we got from the satellite. If I tie it into the existing coms hardware, it will extend broadcast sorting, strength, and clarity."

"Would you have to take coms offline?" she asked.

"Oh yes, for a few days I think."

She arched her eyebrows somewhat disapprovingly.

The man shrugged and raised his hands apologetically. "It is what it is. I can get them back up in two days as long as everything goes well."

Staples mused for a minute. "Okay. I want the upgrade, no question, but I'm going to ask you to wait. I'm expecting to hear from a friend of mine on Mars about an inquiry I made. I was actually hoping to have received it by now. I'd like to wait until I get that message before we go coms dark. Once I do, I'll give you the go-ahead. Sound good?"

"Sounds good," he replied, and headed for the ladder.

Day five.

"Your move," Yegor said in Russian, a smile on his lips.

Piotr looked at him in a way that clearly communicated that he was aware of the fact. His dark eyes surveyed the board for another minute in silence, and Yegor took another sip of his bourbon. Finally the bald cook moved the magnetic rook across the board and positioned it to threaten his opponent's bishop.

"You can't rush greatness, my friend," Piotr said, much more comfortable and fluent in his native tongue. "How goes your grand project?" He reached for his own metal cup of the Kentucky bourbon that he had smuggled onboard the ship back on Earth.

"Slowly," Yegor replied as he surveyed the chessboard's new and more threatening configuration. Piotr's move was not one he had failed to anticipate, but he did not expect such a bold move from his fellow countryman. "There are a dozen connection points that need to be tested, each with its own passkeys, and once that's done-"

"Mm hm," Piotr interrupted, ably communicating his interest in chess over the complexities of integrating communications suites built by different manufacturers.

Yegor looked at him. "That's really why I invite you here, Piotr. You're such a great listener."

"If only you talked as well as I listen," he rejoined, and Yegor smiled and bent back to the game. Piotr looked around the coms officer's quarters, spare as they were, his eyes eventually settling on the small bookshelf his friend maintained. The books were held in place by a piece of twine across their spines. There were the classics he expected from their shared country of birth of course, but he had found that Yegor had a curious love for American literature as well. Mark Twain was hiding between Anton Chekov and Leo Tolstoy, and William Faulkner had cozied right up to Fyodor Dostoyevsky. As far as he was concerned, the best thing to come out of the American south was currently warming his belly. He took another sip.

Yegor slid a magnetic pawn into place to protect his bishop. "Then you talk and let me listen." His face grew more serious. "How is your sister? The children?"

Piotr shook his head. "The same. Poor. I'd like to find that bastard."

"Then you'd be in jail and she really would have no one to help her." His face was sympathetic. "How's the motherland?"

Piotr snorted derisively. "You watch the news." His bishop slid out from the back row to threaten the offending pawn. Pieces were quickly piling up on this one exchange, and the scent of blood was in the air.

"I try not to, actually. Home isn't home anymore."

Piotr nodded. He had known of his friend's familial trouble for some time. "Then why ask me?"

"So…" he reached out to touch a piece, then withdrew his hand as he reconsidered. "I can show you what a good listener I am." He smiled absently as he focused on the board.

"Well, the lines have been stable around Moscow for some time. The hardliners won't give up the capital, and the rest of the country doesn't want a bloody battle. The whole reason they began fighting against Moscow was their totalitarian rule, their intolerant views, and their bloody tactics. It doesn't make much sense to kill them all for their beliefs, even if those beliefs are terrible. Anti-Semitic, anti-gay, anti-freedom… they're like some relic of the 20th century, and they just can't accept that the world has moved on."

Yegor was silent a moment longer, then brought a knight to bear, further increasing the potential casualties should a battle ensue. "Seems like there's always someone digging in their heels and trying to hold back progress. I'm just embarrassed that it's us… well, our country, anyway."

Piotr shrugged. "I say fight." At first, Yegor didn't know whether he was referring to the situation in Russia or the chessboard in front of them, but then he continued. "Some people you can reason with. Some people you can't. It's like the Nazis. You can't talk them out of their idiocy."

Yegor sighed. "Maybe you're right. Too bad." He took another sip, reached for a piece, and girded himself for battle.

Day seven.

As she made her way to the mess hall, Staples heard two voices. John Park and Don Templeton, she thought, and wondered what they were doing up at this hour. It was nearly midnight ship time, and after an hour reading Kyd's *The Spanish Tragedy*, she had just given up on sleep for the time being and decided to rummage a raspberry yogurt from the galley. The two men seemed to be arguing by the tones of their voices, but they stopped abruptly as she padded into the room in her slippers and robe. Park was wearing a pair of sweatpants and a ratty tee shirt, and Templeton was dressed in his usual flight jacket and slacks.

Staples wondered idly whether he washed them frequently or simply had seven sets of the same outfit. They were both looking at her. Beyond them, at the other end of the table, Piotr sat quietly regarding them like a member of a crowd at a tennis match.

She gave a lopsided grin and continued walking over to one of the refrigeration units. "Don't stop on my account." She fished around inside, unclasped a yogurt from its plastic holder, and lifted a metal spoon out of the magnetic silverware tray. The men did not continue. Staples sat down at the table near Don, placed her spoon and plastic cup on the surface, and rubbed her eyes tiredly. When she had finished, she looked back and forth at the two of them. "No, really. What's the subject of discussion?"

Templeton regarded a spot on the table pointedly, but John said, "The AI research bill. They're voting on it – again - in a few months. We've been having a little debate."

"I see." She opened her midnight snack, spooned out a bit, and leaned forward eagerly as if about to watch two champion poker players begin a game.

Templeton still seemed reluctant to discuss the matter in front of his captain, but Park had no such reservations.

"My first mate here believes that we should stop progressing as a species."

The gross oversimplification did its job, and Templeton rose to the bait. "I didn't say that at all, and you know it. I just said that in some areas, there should be limits. Look, take weapons. Let's say some scientist says he can build a weapon that will blow up a planet. Do you fund that? What if he says that he's going to spread the research all over netlink? Do you try and stop him? 'Cause you know some kook out there is gonna use it."

"Fair point," was Park's tame rejoinder, "for weapons. But Artificial Intelligence isn't a weapon."

"It could be."

"So can this ship. Do you know how much damage this ship could cause to a city? To a planet? If we ran at one G of thrust for six weeks, we'd be going twelve percent the speed of light. Can you imagine if we plowed into New York City going that fast?"

"There's safety protocols to stop that," Templeton said weakly.

"Anything that can be invented can be circumvented. There's a counter for everything."

"Maybe. But ships ain't what we were talking about either. You're talkin' about creating something just as smart as a human. We get smarter as we get older, learn more and more, 'cept there's a limit on that. We grow old and die. Machines don't die. They just get older and smarter and pretty soon some AI is at three hundred IQ and what if it decides it don't like humans so much?"

"Oh, the old 'what if' argument. You say 'what if it's evil.' I say 'what if it's good?' Imagine the problems it could solve, the technology it could create, the diseases it could cure."

"Why should it give a crap about us? It's not like it'll be human."

Park gestured at the table with his index finger as he spoke. "But if we *teach* it to be good."

Templeton guffawed. "Teach it?" He asked incredulously. "It's a damn machine. Do you know how naïve you sound? You're gonna teach it right from wrong? Who says it'll even acknowledge those concepts? I'm not even sure *I* acknowledge those concepts. And if it's really AI, then won't it get to choose what to do with its lessons like any other intelligent person?"

Suddenly John seemed to be on the defensive. "Well, it would have to be monitored, safeguarded, have a kill switch, that sort of thing."

Templeton leaned forward, savoring the moment. "'Anything that can be invented can be circumvented.'"

John rolled his eyes. "Okay, yeah, but this would be different."

"How so?"

"Well, the scientists who are programming the AI would have total control; they could monitor programming, brain functions if you will, and if things stray into the danger zone, they flip the switch."

"I'm afraid," Staples interjected, putting her spoon down, "that this opens up an entirely new can of worms. You're talking about terminating a sentient intelligence because you don't like what it's thinking. Once you've created life, do you have the right to destroy it?"

John and Templeton looked at her. "Well, it's not life," Templeton answered. "It's just programmed to act like it."

"Can you prove the difference, Don? A Turing Compliant computer is indistinguishable from a human being. That's what Turing Compliant means. The problem isn't how do we create artificially intelligent life. The question is: what do we do with it once we have?" She placed both of her hands on the table, one over the other, and looked back and forth to the two men as she spoke.

"What you use AI for?" Piotr's heavily accented voice came from the end of the table, startling them. They had nearly forgotten he was there.

John, still championing his cause, replied, "Whatever else you use a computer for, but better. Imagine a computer able to make decisions, weigh moral consequences, on a battlefield. It could stop the loss of human life."

"Great. Then there'd be *no* reason not to go to war," Staples muttered.

"Okay, bad example. Imagine a self-aware machine performing surgery, or exploring outer space, or babysitting your children, or... I don't know, running a space station. This whole journey we're taking could be avoided; instead of having to fly highly trained specialists to the far side of Saturn, which is, I've heard, not a really fun to place to live, we could just transmit a computer program or launch a computer out there, and... done!"

"Nice job, John," Templeton said smugly. "You just talked yourself out of a job. See you at the unemployment office."

"Look, I'm not talking about replacing *people*, just about the possibility of us growing as a species with the help of a new tool, the way we always have," John replied. It was becoming clear to Staples that his theoretical points outstripped his ideas about practical application.

"I have question." Piotr's deep voice came again from the end of the table. "What if AI doesn't want to be explorer, or babysitter, or tool?"

Staples nodded in agreement. "In many ways, that's the crux of the matter. Most people are concentrating on all the bad things that could happen if full AI research gets the go-ahead and it goes bad. The truth is, some kids go bad too. We don't stop having children because they might turn out to be serial killers or thieves. The real problem here is rights. If you're going to create sentient life…" Templeton looked at her in objection. "… fine, just call it sentience. If you're going to create sentience, truly self-aware machines, then you have to grant them the same rights you grant every other person. Life, liberty, all of that. If you don't, it's slavery, a very ugly thing that we've worked very hard to stamp out as a species."

"But if you *program* them to do a certain job…" Park ventured.

She looked at him. "Does Gwen always do what you ask her to?" She didn't bother to wait for an answer before continuing. "Does every child raised in a given religion choose to follow that religion in their adult years? The essence of sentience is choice. We are currently the only sentient species that we know of. Plenty of animals will die to defend their homes, or their young, or their mates, but we're the only ones that will die to defend an ideal. The rational part of our brain can suppress the animalistic part, our survival instinct… our programming, if you will. We can choose to ignore millions of years of evolutionary programming. You have to grant that if we create a sentient machine, it will have that choice as well. If it doesn't, then we haven't created sentience. When you're talking about inventing AI, you're talking about inventing another species, and as someone pointed out to me recently, we're not very good at sharing the spotlight."

The two men mused on this for a minute. Templeton finally spoke up. "So I don't get it. Are you for or against the AI research bill?"

"Oh, I'm against it," she replied without hesitation. "I don't think we should pursue AI at this point." Templeton smiled in triumph and John frowned. "But not because I'm afraid of what they would do to us. I'm afraid of what we would do to them." And with that, she stood up, dropped her spoon in the sink, placed her cup in the recycler, and went back to Thomas Kyd.

Day nine.

In the captain's chair of the cockpit, Clea Staples was brooding. Charis sat at her astrogation console. To her right sat Bethany, though as usual, the back of the pilot's chair hid her from view. To Bethany's right sat Yegor, and he was looking expectantly at his captain. Staples' short blonde hair was pinned down with her barrettes in anticipation of weightlessness, and her slightly cleft chin sat in the palm of her hand, her elbow resting on the armrest of the chair. She wasn't happy.

"Are you absolutely sure we haven't received any personal transmissions from Mars since we've left, Yegor?" Staples inquired, though she knew the answer already.

"Afraid not, Captain. I checked the log three times. No message from Jordan Fecks, no message from anyone for you, or for anyone for that matter." Yegor continued to regard her, and she continued to gaze through the window at nothing in particular.

She tapped the fingers of her other hand several times, as if she were expecting the message to come through any minute. Finally, she spoke. "Okay. If I were going to hear from her, I would have heard by now. We're due to stop thrusting and to drift for a few days in zero G.

It's as good a time as any to go dark. I assume the lack of gravity will be a help and not a hindrance to your work?"

"*Da, Kapitan.* Some components of the coms system are heavy. It's easier to get the new coms suite around the ship in zero G too. Besides, I'm used to working in zero G from my days with GTS." Yegor sounded rather like a child eager for a new toy.

"And there is no way to install the new suite without losing both coms and local radar?"

Yegor shook his head. "Sorry, Captain. We'll still be able to use our watches and shipboard coms, but nothing outside the ship will work."

"That's all right. It's not like anyone is talking to us anyway." She sighed and looked out the window at the stars again. "And it's not like there's anything out here to see either. Let's prep to cut thrust and then make our turn. We'll resume thrust in… how long, Charis?"

Charis' fingers ran over her controls, and then she looked up. "We should start deceleration at point six G in three days. Best window is to start between ten and eleven. That should put us at the same orbital speed and altitude as Cronos Station in twelve days. With any luck, we can dock in time for dinner."

Day eleven.

Staples floated down two decks in the elevator. It was always an odd sensation, feeling the metal box move around her. If she hadn't tucked her toes under a conveniently placed strap, she would have found herself pressed to the ceiling. Once out, she pushed herself with the various grab-bars situated in the hallway to the closed door of the ReC. Upon reaching it, she reoriented herself, taking hold of one of the nearby wall-mounted bars, turned the latch, and opened the heavy metal door. It swung open on well-oiled hinges, and the captain expertly slipped inside and used the wall as leverage to pull and secure the hatch behind her. Dinah was standing, more or less, at one of the control panels situated under the glass windows that overlooked the reactor, her feet wedged under the currently extended brace bars to keep her from floating away. She had a steadying hand on the control panel and was turned half around to regard her visitor. As was her custom, Dinah was wearing a grey tank top, dirty cargo pants, and leather combat boots. One eyebrow was arched in expectation.

"Welcome to the ReC, sir," she said. It was clear from her body language that she would prefer to continue with her work, but a well-instilled sense of protocol kept her facing her employer.

"Hello, Dinah. Please," she gestured at the panel, "continue. I wanted to see how things are with the engines."

Dinah turned her back to her, monitoring numbers on the surface built into the console and making minor adjustments to various sliders and knobs as the information in front of her changed. "You could just read my reports, sir."

"You know you are the only person on this ship who writes me reports, don't you?" Staples asked. She pushed off from the wall and drifted over to a neighboring control panel, not too close to the engineer, and looked down through the window. "Everybody else just comes to talk to me in person."

Dinah replied without looking up from her work.

"Would you like me to deliver my reports in person, sir?"

Staples shook her head and a few stray blonde hairs waved back and forth as she did so. She considered, not for the first time, the other woman's choice in hairstyles. "No, I want you to do it your way. But since I'm here, why don't you tell me anyway?"

Dinah let out a breath that might have been a sigh, gathered her thoughts, and then spoke. "We thrust consistently for seven days between Earth and Mars, including a fairly large strain when we went up to three Gs for a few hours. We didn't have time to do anything but the most cursory of maintenance checks on Mars." There was a pause as she entered some data. "Then we were under thrust for another nine days. The engines, the reactor, they're rated for it, but then this ship isn't brand new either. So now that we're drifting for three days, I'm taking all of the reactor chambers but one offline to run diagnostics. There's not enough time to clean them all, but three is a bit dirty, so John and I will be doing a wipe tomorrow before we begin thrust again."

"I appreciate that. I also think you're being overly cautious. We've been under thrust, more or less constantly, for over a month at a time without going through all that."

"Better safe than sorry, sir."

"You could take the evening off," she ventured. "It's dinner shift now, but we've got a movie night planned in the mess hall." She regarded the woman as she spoke. Her face made her glad she wasn't inviting her to poker night.

"Thank you, sir. I'll consider it." There was still no eye contact.

A few moments passed while Dinah continued to work. Finally, Staples said, "Dinah." She did so in such a way to cause the engineer to look up at her. "What are you doing here?"

Dinah gestured back at her console. "As I said, sir, I am running a diagnostic on the reaction chambers and prepping them for…"

Staples interrupted her. "That's not what I meant and you know it. You're one of the most talented engineers I've ever seen or heard of. You handled that dust up over the satellite masterfully. You're a creative problem solver, a hard worker, and you've gotten us out of more than a few scrapes over the past two years." The captain did not expect her deluge of compliments to move the woman any more than her invite to movie night had, and she was not disappointed, but that was not her intention. She pressed on. "You could easily land a larger commission on another ship. We both know I can't afford to pay you what you're worth."

Dinah finally did her the honor of pausing in her work and looking her full in the face. "Money is not the only reason people do things, sir. In fact, in my experience, it is one of the worst reasons people do things."

"Oh, I don't know. The drive for profit has brought about some amazing inventions. We are currently living on one of them. Space ships are freedom incarnate, but they didn't give this one to me for free."

"Space ships," Dinah mused. "You can add to that list of profit-based inventions weapons, slavery, subjugation of the poor, armed occupations, and exploitation of countries. Shall I continue, sir?" She became more heated as she spoke, and it was clear to Staples that she had stepped into something she had not intended.

"Fair points all." She attempted to backpedal a bit. "Some would say that money is not evil; it's what people do with it that defines them."

"Mostly rich people say that. Are you trying to fire me, sir?" Dinah raised her eyebrows.

Staples tried and failed to stifle a laugh. "Certainly not. But I was in business long enough to know that when I've got an asset that I can't afford, I should be planning to be without it sooner rather than later."

"And what business was that, sir?" Dinah was looking back at her panel, but she wasn't working. It was surprising to hear her ask a personal question, but Staples guessed she couldn't pass up the opportunity. Few of the crew knew what she had done before buying a space ship and heading out to Sol space, though she knew that they conjectured and traded rumors.

"Sorry, with what battalion did you say you served, Ms. Hazra?" Staples countered. Her tone was playful, but she knew that she was treading on shaky ground.

There was a moment of flat silence, and then the engineer grunted. "You don't have to worry about me, sir. I'm not planning on going anywhere. If you want an answer as to why, then I'll say this: you don't care about money either, and that's more than I can say about anyone else who ever gave me orders." She resumed her work.

Staples looked taken aback. "You don't think I care about money?"

"No, sir, I don't."

"Then what *do* you think I care about?" she asked, quite curious for the answer.

"If you're going to compound chief engineer and tactical officer with duties as a psychologist, sir, I really may ask for a raise."

Staples smiled broadly. "I guess I asked for that. Whatever I'm doing right, I am glad to hear it keeps you here. Everyone on this ship is better for it. Maybe we can bear our souls and pasts to each other some other time."

"I'll look forward to that, sir." The ironic tone of her reply was uncharacteristically devoid of equivocation.

The captain pushed off from the control panel back to the door and let herself out of the ReC. She glided along the corridor, correcting herself with little pushes here and there, and turned right at the next junction. As she reached the hull of the ship, she kicked herself left again and began the push to the elevator that would carry her up to deck two and the mess hall beyond. She drifted past a porthole, and a hole in the stars caught her eye. She turned her head to look, but she was already past the window. She halted at the next one, grabbing on with her hands as her legs swung past her, and gazed out. There were no stars. It took her eyes a few seconds to adjust and her brain another second to process what she was seeing: another ship, painted jet black, right next to hers.

# CHAPTER 8

There was only one type of crew that Staples knew of that would paint their ship black. She keyed her watch for simultaneous shipwide broadcast and nearly yelled into it.

"Pirates!" Her voice rung out from the speakers and reverberated through the hall. "Pirates starboard side! Security teams arm up, senior staff to the cockpit, everyone else get in your quarters and stay there." She took a precious second to rekey her watch to the cockpit coms alone. "Bethany, evasive action! Pull us away port side." Without waiting for a reply, she began pushing herself down the hallway as fast as she dared. Out of the corner of her eye she saw the dark shape grow even more in the portholes she passed. She wondered for a second how the hell they had managed to pull right up alongside *Gringolet* without them knowing when she suddenly remembered Yegor's maintenance. She cursed loudly.

As she reached the elevator, a voice came through the speaker of her watch. It was Yegor's. "No one's here but me, Captain. Everyone went to dinner." He sounded panicked and upset.

"Dammit," she swore again as she maneuvered herself into the elevator. "Okay, Bethany and the others will be on the way. Can you pull the ship away?" She jammed her finger on the button for the appropriate deck and held it there impatiently. The elevator doors lazily slid closed.

"I don't think… I used to fly small ships, Captain. I don't know…"

"Try!" Staples shouted. Suddenly there was a jarring thunk that she felt in her bones. The entire ship seemed to shake for a moment around her. Fortunately, the elevator mechanism continued to rise smoothly. "Okay, Yegor? Don't touch the controls. Either they're throwing things at us, or they've just made a magnetic junction, probably with a boarding tube. If you pull away now, you're likely to rip a hole in the side of the ship."

Yegor's voice came through again. "*Da, Kapitan,* but wouldn't that be better than pirates on the ship? Pressure doors would seal, yes?"

"In theory, yes." The elevator neared the end of its ponderous climb. "And we may have to do that, but we're not there yet. I'll be in the cockpit in one minute." The doors slid open and she pushed off with her legs, moving rapidly down corridors to the spine of the ship and the cockpit beyond.

As the other ship's boarding tube magnetically sealed to the side of *Gringolet*, Dinah was closing and latching the door to the ReC. She pushed and pulled her way down the corridor, moving much faster than Staples had scarcely a minute before. She made the same turns, then brought herself to an abrupt halt at the first porthole she came to. By craning her neck, she was able to see where the boarding tube was attached, one deck down and several yards towards the stern of the ship. Upon reaching the elevator a few seconds later, she produced a screwdriver and struck the safety latch hidden at the top of the door, which promptly slid open. Grabbing the upper lip of the elevator portal, she swung her legs up and in, aimed herself down the shaft, relatively speaking, and fired herself off at the door below her. From inside the elevator shaft, it was a simple matter to trigger the door release mechanism and to propel herself out onto the lower deck.

Another few twists and turns brought her face to face with Kojo Jang and his two new security personnel. Jang had evidently been near a weapons locker, because he was armed with a rifle, several clips of ammunition, and a pistol. Parsells and Quinn, rifles slung, were moving awkwardly behind him when Dinah came around the corner. When Jang stopped short, they nearly ran into him.

"Corridor B17," she said without preamble. "That's where they'll be coming through." Jang only nodded silently and tossed her the pistol from his holster. It floated straight at her, and she caught it as she moved towards a branching hallway that would take them in the direction they needed to go. Jang and Dinah led, and the two other men followed, a small flotilla of armed crew members.

Dinah allowed Jang to surge ahead as they neared the door that led to the corridor where she had estimated the boarders would be cutting through. The large bald man grabbed the door handle roughly with his ebony hand and eased it open. They could immediately hear and smell the cutting, though they could not yet see it. The air was acrid with the scent of a focused laser cutting metal. The hallway in front of them branched left and right, and it was from the left that the sounds of hull breach were coming. Once the door was open, Jang eased his head around the corner and gazed down the hall.

The wall of the ship was perhaps six meters away, and another hallway that led towards the aftmost compartments of the ship branched off after half of that distance. The smoke and choking gasses released by the laser cutting through the hull were becoming worse, and it was clear that the pirates' circular entryway was nearly finished. Jang checked his rifle, cocked it, and removed the safety. Dinah readied her pistol and gestured to Quinn to move up. Quinn did his best to push past the woman and placed himself in a sitting position by using his legs and back to brace himself against either side of the corridor they occupied. Jang floated above him, leaning out the best he could and training his rifle on the hole. It was a poor place for cover, but shooting a semi-automatic rifle in zero G was problematic at best. If the shooter was not secured, they could easily send themselves spinning out into the line of fire or accidentally aim a weapon at a friend.

Dinah tapped her watch and spoke into it. "Captain, I'm with Jang, Parsells, and Quinn. We're at B17. They're cutting through into the ship. We're armed and ready to repel, but it's not a very defensible position."

Staples voice came through immediately. "Roger. They may just want fuel or cargo. Don't put yourselves at risk for-" And then there was no time to talk because the circular disc of the hull had come loose. It moved purposefully into the corridor; someone was behind it, pushing it forward, using it as cover. Jang opened fire, and the sound was deafening in the enclosed space. Quinn was shooting as well, but there was very little of the aggressors to see. It was easy to hide behind cover when one could travel horizontally. Bullets thudded against the large metal disc, its sides still orange and glowing from the heat of the laser.

After a few moments of fire, Jang realized that it was pointless until he could find a clear shot. He ceased and yelled for Quinn to do the same. The large man fired a few more rounds, then complied with the order. Jang shook his head in dismay.

"How are they steering that thing?" Quinn asked.

"I don't know. Probably magnetic grips on the other side," Jang conjectured.

Dinah nodded. "If they've got jetpacks, they can push that piece of the hull all the way up here."

Jang leaned out again to look. "They're not firing back. Perhaps we should approach and try-" his sentence cut off as his head snapped back and he was thrown violently across the narrow hallway and into Quinn, who swore and tried to move out of the way. Dinah and Parsells both braced a hand in the open doorway and pulled the limp body of the security chief back through the door. Quinn regained his bearings and leveled his rifle.

"They're shooting now!" he yelled, and fired off several shots which pinged harmlessly against the disc. This time he saw it: a hand with a weapon extended around the disc and fired. He jerked his head back just in time, and some large, slow moving projectile bounced off of the wall where his head had been half a second earlier.

Dinah was holding the unmoving and unresponsive Jang in one arm, her other hand drum-tight around a grab bar on the wall. Parsells and Quinn's features showed a mix of stress and fear as they stared at him. His eyes were closed. She examined the wound to his head and then noticed the blood on her hand. She looked up, wide eyed, at the two men, and then back down at her bloody hand.

"Lock this door, now!" she barked. "Don't open it for anyone or anything." The woman did not wait for a reply, but swung herself around and launched herself back down the hall the way they had come, looking for all the world like a mouse scurrying away from a hungry cat.

When the captain reached the cockpit, it was empty. Staples suffered a stunned moment of silence, then moved into action. She pushed herself over to the starboard cockpit window and was just able to make out the boarding tube latched onto her ship like the proboscis of some venomous insect. Even at only a few meters away, the other ship was difficult to see because of its black finish. She judged that it was smaller and faster than her vessel; perhaps an old style military interceptor. There had been little in the way of large scale space combat since space ships had become a fixture in the inner system, but that didn't stop governments and corporations from preparing for it. This was just the type of vessel that was designed to do exactly what it was doing: board a larger, slower ship and steal cargo, take hostages, or commandeer the vessel.

"Captain!" Charis shouted as she soared into the cockpit, accidently sending herself past the doorway and into the consoles at the front of the room. She worked to reorient herself in the air, and managed to save herself from anything more than a bruised shoulder. Though her blonde hair was in a ponytail, it threatened to obscure her vision as she righted herself.

"I'm here, Charis," Staples said as she turned herself around and pushed off for her captain's chair.

A minute later, Bethany and Templeton had joined them in the room.

"What do we know?" Templeton asked as he clipped himself into his seat with his safety harness.

"First, did anyone see Yegor? He was up here a minute ago," Staples inquired.

"I passed him," came Bethany's reedy voice.

"Where was he going?" Staples struggled to retain control of her voice. She knew from experience that yelling at the girl would only cause her to shut down.

"I don't know. The back of the ship, I think. He didn't say." The pilot's eyes were large with fear.

"Okay, we'll deal with that in a minute."

Charis said desperately, "Captain, can't we just pull away?"

Staples opened her mouth to answer, but then Dinah's voice came out of the watch on her wrist. "Captain, I'm with Jang, Parsells, and Quinn. We're at B17. They're cutting through into the ship. We're armed and ready to repel, but it's not a very defensible position."

She tapped her watch to reply. "Roger. They may just want fuel or cargo. Don't put yourselves at risk for-" Suddenly there was the sound of gunfire and the line went dead. A half a second of silence followed. She forced herself to answer her navigator's question. "Once they form a magnetic junction, that bond is tougher than steel. It has to be, or this wouldn't work. If we pull away, we could well rip a hole in the side of the ship. We may have to do that, but we've got a security team down there fighting, and I don't want to take the risk of blowing them out into space."

"Can we shoot them?" Charis asked. Staples was reminded of her similar question two and a half weeks prior during their conflict with the *Doris Day*.

"We can," Templeton said suggestively, though he knew what his captain's answer would be.

"We're too close. At this range, shrapnel and debris could tear us apart. Besides, they haven't shot at us." Templeton looked at her with wide-eyed frustration, though he would not contradict her in a crisis situation. She addressed his objection anyway. "I'm not saying they're friendly. What I mean is this: they got the drop on us. Completely. If they wanted to destroy the ship and sift through the remains, they had every opportunity. They don't want to kill us."

"You mean they don't want to destroy the ship," Templeton countered.

"You're right. It is very possible they want to kill us and take the ship. If it becomes clear that that is their intention, then we'll do what we have to. I'll tear this ship to pieces myself before I let them have it." Charis and Bethany both looked at their captain. "But," she said to calm them. "But, they may just be here for a smash and grab. Maybe they want fuel, maybe cargo, maybe parts. If that's the case, I'm inclined to let them have them."

"But Captain, if they take all of our fuel…" Charis' question did not need finishing.

"Then we'll drift here until a rescue ship comes for us. I can live with that, but I won't trade lives for gas."

"Well how do we know what they're here for? Wait

until they kill one of us?" Templeton inquired desperately.

"If Jang and Dinah and the others have them pinned at B17, the only areas they have access to are the engines and rear storage. As far as I know, no one is back there. Except…" Her voice drifted off. She punched another button on her watch. "Dinah, come in." There was no response. Precious seconds ticked away. "Dinah!" Nothing. She hit another button. "Jang, are you there?" Silence. "Jang?"

A second later, Parsells' voice came through loudly. "Jang is hit!" No sounds of gunfire or fighting echoed in the background. Parsells' voice was oddly surrounded by silence.

"Is he dead?" Templeton asked.

"No, stunned. They hit him in the head with a stunner. He's bleeding, but he's just out cold." Parsells' reply was abrupt and tinged with doubt.

"What's your status, man?" Templeton's voice was insistent.

"Engineer ordered us to close the door, so we did. They're not trying to come through here. Don't know what they're doing." Staples unbuckled herself from her seat and swung herself around her chair.

"Stand by, Parsells," Templeton said, and then looked at her. "Captain, what are you doing?"

"They're after the stasis tubes," she replied flatly. She pushed herself off the back of her chair and towards the locked weapons locker on the back wall of the cockpit.

"What?" Templeton rasped. "The stasis tubes? How could they know? How do you know?"

Staples stopped herself and began typing the code into the keypad. "They're using stun rounds. They've boarded on the same floor as CB4. They're not trying to take the rest of the ship. This isn't some random pirate raid." Wrenching the door open revealed a row of seven rifles and one empty slot. She pulled out a rifle. "This is a contracted hit. We should assume they have blueprints of our ship, details of the crew, everything." She pulled out a pistol and strapped it to her hip. Charis had unclipped herself from her seat to watch, but she made no move towards the guns. Bethany sunk lower in her chair. The first mate shed his seatbelt and launched himself towards his captain.

"What are you doing, Clea?" Templeton asked, though it was plainly obvious to the first mate.

Staples strapped the rifle to her back. "We are responsible for those people, Don. I am responsible. We took money; we said we would deliver them, safely, to Cronos Station."

"Well, you'd better hand me one of those then," he replied, reaching out his hand as he halted himself with his other on the bulkhead.

"When was the last time you practiced with one of these?"

Templeton shrugged. "Probably about the last time you did: a few months ago now. Does it matter?"

"No, I don't suppose it does," she replied as she passed him a rifle. "Bethany, Charis, I want you to say here. You have the ship. Try to find Dinah. We may need to break away after all, and I want you here."

Yegor Durin shoved himself violently down the various metal hallways of Gringolet, a rifle strapped to his back. As he approached the last juncture that would take him to B17, he heard the voice of one of the new men, he thought it was Parsells, say "…know what they're doing." He rounded the corner and saw the battle, such as it was. The door into B17 was closed, and Quinn was holding onto a bar on the wall. His other beefy arm was wrapped around Jang, who was unconscious. A few droplets of blood floated free in the zero-gravity environment. Parsells was braced against the opposite wall and holding up Jang's arm. He had just finished speaking into the unmoving man's watch. Both of them had rifles slung on their backs, and a third rifle, presumably Jang's, floated lightly from its strap where someone had tethered it to a grip bar.

As he pushed himself down the hall to the three men, he heard Templeton's voice come through a communicator watch. "Stand by, Parsells."

Parsells and Quinn looked up at him as he approached. He seized the grip handle just short of their position and braced himself to stop his momentum. "Is he all right?" He nodded at Jang.

"Just stunned," Parsells responded.

"What are you doing here?" Yegor asked, a hint of accusation in his voice.

Parsells immediately looked defensive. "Engineer lady told us to close the door and not open it for anything."

"Dinah? Where is she?" Parsells shrugged. "What are the pirates doing?" Parsells shrugged again. Yegor grunted with frustration and shook his head.

"Look, we're just following orders here. Figure we got 'em contained in the back of the ship." Yegor did not reply, but he unslung his rifle and reached for the door. Parsells raised a hand as if to restrain him. "Whoa there, man. She said to keep this door closed to everyone, no matter what."

The communications officer stopped and looked at the two men. "We are under attack. This ship is under attack. We cannot just float here like fools. Now move!" There was a moment where it looked as though Parsells would put up a fight, then he reluctantly swung himself out of the way. "You want to stay here, fine," Yegor said. He wrenched the door open and leveled his rifle. He inched forward, peering around the corner. The large circular section of hull had been braced on the near side of the adjoining hallway to act as a shield, and it covered nearly all of his view between that hallway and the boarding tube magnetically locked to the ship beyond the freshly cut hole. In the small window of space between the disc and the wall, Yegor could see two men in body armor pushing a large, metal, coffin-like box towards the boarding tube and the pirate ship beyond.

"Get back here!" Parsells hissed. "They'll see you! We got to close the door!"

"You have to the close the door, close the door," he said and pushed off towards the waiting pirates and the stasis tube beyond.

Not viewscreens, not windows, not portholes: nothing compared to seeing the stars from inside an EVA suit when floating in naked space. Dinah had admired them many times before though a thin piece of polycarbonate, but she was in too great of a rush to do so now. She pushed herself out of the small airlock chamber and into an untethered drift. The smaller black ship loomed above her, and she could clearly see the metal boarding tube that it had extended perpendicular to the long axis of both ships. From the bottom, they somewhat resembled the spires of a bridge, one larger and gunmetal grey, the other smaller and jet black, with a thin strip of roadway between them. Dinah gripped the controls of her jetpack and aimed herself towards the portion of the enemy ship from where the boarding tube extended.

It only took a minute of thrusting to cross the one hundred meters of space. Hard-won experience had taught her to keep her eyes on the ships in question and not to look around, tempted as she might be by the stars. It was entirely too easy for one to lose one's sense of direction. The human mind evolved over the course of millions of years, always with a solid concept of *up*. It could be extremely taxing to be in an environment where there was no true up.

Once she reached the base of the long cylindrical shaft, she used the jetpack to push herself over to the ship. "Come on… come on…" she muttered as she searched. "There." She was halfway around the tube when she found the access panel. A screwdriver and a focused minute of work later, the access panel cover was removed, and Dinah carelessly tossed it over her shoulder. Under it lay a thick black electrical cord. She gripped it with her left hand, bracing herself, and reached with her right hand for the cutting torch tethered to her belt. Like the screwdriver, it was attached to a wire which unspooled as she pulled so that it could not get away from her if she let go of it. She flicked the safety off and ignited it. The torch began to glow, and a second later a short white-hot flame emerged. It was the matter of only a minute's work to cut power to the electromagnets holding the ships together. As she completed the job, she looked over and saw the two ships separate.

There was a silent expulsion of air from the hole in *Gringolet*, and she allowed herself a moment of satisfaction when she saw three bodies fly out of the gaping wound and into the hard vacuum of space. That satisfaction evaporated when she recognized one of them. Then she saw the stasis tube fly out of the ship as well. She pushed off the now useless boarding tube and began to pilot her way towards the floating member of her crew. Her training told her that a human could survive perhaps fifteen seconds in space, but that there was nothing, absolutely nothing that she could do to get Yegor Durin back in atmosphere in that time, or even in the next two minutes. Regardless, she could at least recover his body. She was nearly halfway there when she spotted the telltale glow of two incoming missiles.

Templeton and Staples were nearing the elevator that would take them down to the deck that housed, among other things, Cargo Bay 4 when the depressurization alarms went off. Their sound, a deep whine that rose in pitch then broke off before repeating, was unlike any other alarm on the ship. It was one that crews very rarely heard, and one that instantly invoked terror.

The captain stopped short by bracing herself on a wall, immediately tapped her watch, and yelled to be heard over the alarm. "Charis, report!" Templeton scrambled to avoid floating into her.

"We're free, Captain!" Charis was shouting as well. "Hold on!" A second later, the alarm ceased. Charis' voice returned, this time at a normal volume. "I don't know how, but it looks like they lost their hold on us. Bethany is pulling us away." As she said it, Templeton and Staples could see and feel the effects of the ship's movement as they both drifted towards the wall. She was comforted to know that Bethany would be gentle; a ship with an unsecured crew undertaking extreme maneuvers could easily injure or kill its passengers.

"What do we do?" Templeton asked, wide eyed.

Staples thought for a second. "Back. We go back." They turned around and pushed themselves towards the cockpit. Templeton arrived first, and Staples swung in behind him and pushed herself over to the window facing the other ship. It seemed to be moving up and away from her as Bethany banked the vessel away. Just as Staples was beginning to wonder how they had gotten so lucky, the other vessel exploded.

# CHAPTER 9

The gout of flame that the explosion produced was brief, gone as soon as it burned through all of the dispersing air. The destruction was absolute, and anyone looking at it would have no doubt as to the possibility of survivors. It was an odd sensation to watch a ship burn and disintegrate in space; it happened in total silence.

Staples was unable to tear her eyes away from the spectacle. It was the first time she had ever seen a ship of that size destroyed. The results were spectacular and horrifying. Thousands of pieces of debris spun off in every direction. She thought, though it was difficult to tell, that there were bodies in that mess of burnt and rapidly cooling metal. Without looking away, she raised her arm to her mouth, feeling as though she were caught in a fever dream. She pinged the shipwide coms button on her watch and said, "Brace for impact from debris." Her voice, flat and featureless, echoed immediately through the speakers of the cockpit and the rest of the ship.

There was a tapping sound, as if of a polite knock at

the door. Then it came again, and suddenly there were dozens, then hundreds. It was as though she were under a tin roof in a hailstorm. The debris pummeled the side of her ship; some pieces were the size of a fingernail, others were as big as a car. The larger hits shook the ship, and Staples felt herself pushed into the window as Bethany increased the acceleration of *Gringolet* away from the explosion. She braced herself to hear the depressurization alarm again, but it did not sound. The pieces of the destroyed ship continued to fly apart, a beautiful and hideous ballet of twisted composites and polymers, and eventually the rain of detritus on the side of the ship slowed and then ceased altogether.

She finally turned away from the remains of the disintegrated vessel to look at the others in the cockpit with her. Templeton and Charis were both gazing out the window as well, fascinated by the scene. Her first mate was hanging onto her chair to steady himself, and Charis half sat in her seat with one arm around the headrest. Bethany was stealing looks over her right shoulder, but her mind was clearly on piloting the ship.

"Is everyone all right?" Staples' voice sounded distant to her, bizarrely loud in the silence that followed the buffeting of the hull by the pieces, and in all likelihood, the people who only a minute ago were crew members of the other vessel. Seeing the pirate ship destroyed had made her feel vulnerable, barely protected from the vast gulfs of space which surrounded her. She thought of her ship as her home, a world unto itself; that world suddenly seemed very small and very fragile, a tin can afloat in a deadly ocean.

No one answered. She cleared her throat and

swallowed. "Is everyone okay?" she said with some insistence.

Bethany's answer came first, light and soft. "Yes, Captain." Templeton echoed her remark, but Charis just stared through the window.

Staples tapped her watch again for shipwide coms. "I want everyone to report in to Templeton. I want to know where everyone is and what their condition is." She looked at him pointedly, then pushed off from the window and drifted to her seat opposite him. "Don, are you with me?"

With a start, the man seemed to come to his senses. "Yes. Yes, I'll get right on it." He dragged himself into his seat, strapped himself in, and began to work the console next to him. Voices began coming through, the computer sorting them so that they did not speak over each other. One of the first was John's.

"Gwen and I are okay. We're in our quarters. Is my wife up there? Is she okay, Don?"

Templeton took a moment to pause the incoming calls and answer. "She's fine, John. We're all fine here in the cockpit. A little shaken up, but fine. Be with you in a minute." Belatedly, as the shock began to clear, he remembered that Yegor was not there, and that he had no idea where the man was or if indeed he was all right. The rest of the reports rolled in, and finally Templeton looked up. "I've got confirmation from everyone on the ship except Yegor and Dinah. Parsells and Quinn say that he went through the door into B17 right before the depressurization alarms went off." He paused for a moment as they considered the implications of that. "No one can find Dinah." Another pause. "Jesus, what happened?"

"I don't know," was all Staples could say. "Goddammit, I wish coms were up. We need to report this."

"Yegor picked a hell of a time to tear things apart, didn't he? Do you think he's…?" He left the sentence drift off.

"I don't know that either." She heaved a great sigh. "All right. All right." She thought for a moment. "We need to gather, to inform people, to check on people. Tell everyone to gather in the mess hall in five minutes. Tell them…" she searched for the right words. "Tell them that the attack is over and that we are safe."

Templeton did as he was instructed, relating his captain's orders to the crew. When he had finished, he unbuckled himself and Charis did the same. Staples pushed herself towards the back of the cockpit and stopped to return her rifle. She took Templeton's from him and placed it back in its cradle. She had noticed the missing rifle the first time, but now the full meaning of it struck her.

"Yegor must have taken it, headed down to fight."

"Why would he do that?" Charis asked. "He should have stayed here. You told everyone to get to the cockpit."

"Maybe he felt responsible," Templeton ventured. "He must have realized that the only reason they were able to sneak up on us was because our coms and radar were down."

The captain closed the locker slowly, grateful to be rid of the firearm, but the situation bothered her. "Maybe. Maybe he went down there to help. But maybe not."

"Well, you know he went to fight." Templeton's voice was insistent. "That's at least one thing we can be sure of. That's what Parsells said: that he was down there and charged into B17." Charis was holding onto a bar by the doorway and watching them. Bethany had unstrapped herself and was maneuvering herself around her chair.

Staples looked at the other two crew members, reluctant to share what she was thinking. She lowered her voice conspiratorially. "Why would they attempt a stealth approach, Don? They would have to know we'd see them coming. How could they know that our coms and radar were down?"

Templeton's face was a mask of puzzlement for a second, then he scowled at her doubtfully. "That's a hell of an accusation to make of a man who's been on the ship for almost two years, Clea."

She ignored his anger, but shook her head dismissively. "I'm not accusing anyone of anything. I'm just thinking. We'll talk about it later. Right now, we need to get moving." She pushed herself to the door and was about to exit the room when Bethany uttered a noise somewhere between a scream and a gasp. Staples turned around and looked at her, but she was gazing over, wide eyed, at the window. There was a person in an EVA suit, one of their EVA suits, floating outside and tapping on the window. Through the glass and the polycarbonate helmet, the face of Dinah Hazra was plainly visible, and she was not smiling.

It took nearly five minutes for Charis to get down to the starboard airlock and depressurize it. Once she had, she hit the red button on the control panel that unlocked the outside door. Several seconds later, she watched the door open slowly and Dinah wormed herself into the small room, the maneuver made more difficult by the jetpack on the back of her EVA suit. Dinah closed and locked the door, and Charis repressurized the room. The green lights came on, and the chief engineer removed her helmet with a sigh of relief that Charis saw but did not hear. Finally, the inner door was opened, and Charis surprised herself by propelling herself forward and hugging Dinah as she discarded the gloves of her EVA suit. The dark skinned woman awkwardly embraced the fair skinned one with one arm, the other attached to a handle, and then pulled away to arm's length.

Charis looked abashed, and said by way of explanation, "Sorry, sorry. It's just; it's been terrifying." She looked the other woman in the eye. "What were you doing *outside the ship*?" She stressed the last three words, as if the engineer had voluntarily stepped into a burning building and had just returned.

"It's complicated. I need to report to the captain, now." She was climbing out of the suit as she spoke.

Charis wiped at a moist eye. "Of course, of course. She's in the mess hall. Everyone is, except Yegor. We can't find him." The tear detached itself from her finger and floated across the small airlock room.

"He's dead," Dinah replied flatly, and gently pushed past her, leaving her EVA suit floating in the chamber.

"What?" The last two years spent in the cockpit across from Yegor came back to her in a flood, and she found herself refusing to believe the other woman. "How? How do you know? Are you sure?" She followed along behind her, spewing questions.

"I saw him outside the ship." She began moving rapidly down the corridor, and Charis had trouble keeping up. "I need to talk to the captain, now." With a few more pushes, she left the navigator behind.

Charis shouted one more question at her as she sped off like a torpedo. "What happened to the other ship?" Dinah did not answer.

It only took the engineer a few minutes to reach the mess hall. The entire crew, fifteen people in all, was gathered, some belted to the dining benches, others holding stabilization bars on the walls. They seemed almost to a person to be in silent shock. Even Gwen floated wide-eyed and mute beside her father, his arm protectively curled around her shoulders. Yoli, one of the ship's cargo roadies, was having her arm examined by the doctor. Staples and Templeton were at the far end of the room, each gripping a bar, and Templeton was speaking.

"We're not exactly sure what they were after. They got the drop on us 'cause of some coms and radar work we were doing. They used stunners, so they weren't trying to kill anyone." He looked at Staples for a second. "We think they were just trying to rob us, a smash and grab."

Dinah took this moment to interject from the back of the crowd, and everyone turned to look at her. "I am sorry to interrupt, sir, but there is a situation that needs immediate attention."

"Dinah!" Templeton nearly yelled her name. "Thank God you're okay. What situation?"

"There's a stasis tube floating free out there. It was in B17 when I cut the magnetic junction, and it flew out into space, sir. It should be able to keep the person inside alive, but we need to retrieve it with a UteV as soon as possible."

There was a moment full of murmurs and surprised discussion as the crew processed the rather stunning revelation that Dinah had been outside the ship cutting power cords. As Staples and Templeton digested the situation, they realized that it did indeed require immediate attention.

"John, can you take out a UteV and try to find the stasis tube?" Staples asked, though it was clear that she was not really asking. Park slowly nodded, plainly reluctant to leave his daughter.

"I'll help get you out there," Charis added from the back of the crowd where she had appeared a few moments earlier. She looked over at Jabir, who was already motioning Gwen over to him with a smile on his face. There were quick hugs given, and then the couple moved off rapidly towards the cargo and shuttle bay. Not for the first time, Staples was grateful that she had good people she could count on.

Once they had left, Staples cleared her throat and the murmurs and discussions tapered off. "Dinah, what happened? How did you get outside? Why didn't you tell us what you were doing?"

Dinah pushed her way through the people near the door. She noticed Jang strapped into a seat near the doctor. He was conscious, though he held his head with one hand, and there was a bright white bandage near his temple. She resisted the urge to snap to attention, an absurd concept in zero G anyway. Instead, she took hold of the table end and began her report.

"Once the aggressors made their magnetic junction, I headed down to B17 to see what I could do. I ran into the security detail on the way, and they provided me with a firearm." She looked over at Jang again, who nodded at her, and then over at Parsells and Quinn, who sat at the table on the opposite side of the room. "It became clear from the situation that the aggressors were here for a specific reason. When I realized that Mr. Jang was stunned, I surmised that they were attempting an extraction of an item or items. I knew that we could not pull the ship away without significant damage, so I instructed Mr. Parsells and Mr. Quinn to lock the airtight bulkhead and not to open it for any reason." This time she glared at the two men, and Parsells shifted uncomfortably.

"I assessed that the only way to detach the aggressor's ship was at the source. I exited the ship in an EVA suit and proceeded to cross the gap between the two ships with a rocket pack." At this, the silence in the room was broken by gasps and whispers. She proceeded as though only she, Templeton, and Staples were in the room. "Once there, I cut power to the electromagnets. If," again she looked at Parsells, "my directions had been followed, no crew member would have been hurt."

Templeton broke in. "Why didn't you tell us what you were doing, Dinah? We could have helped!"

"With all due respect, sir, I don't believe you could have. I did not tell you because I was in a rush to put on the EVA suit and exit the ship. I planned to tell you when I was outside, but I forgot that the coms were down. By the time I remembered, I was unable to communicate with you."

Templeton scoffed at this and looked at Staples, but she merely nodded and said, "Continue."

"Once I cut the power, the two ships began to drift apart. I saw three bodies and a stasis tube exit from the breach in B17." She paused for a moment. "I believe one of them was Mr. Yegor Durin." At this, there were gasps all around and general consternation. Gwen looked tearful and confused, and Jabir took her by the shoulders and lifted her to hug her. There was a loud bang as Piotr, Yegor's fellow countryman, slammed his fist on the metal counter behind him. It came again and again, and the cutlery bounced and shook in its magnetic tray until Declan Burbank, another of the ship's cargo roadies and a friend of the cook's, put his hand on Piotr's arm and he stopped.

"Then what happened?" the captain prompted. The noise died down again, though it was punctuated here and there by sounds of grief and shock.

Dinah's face was impassive as ever. "I judged that I could not retrieve the stasis tube. I also judged that it would survive in vacuum for the time being, so I began moving to collect... our crew member. As I was moving, I saw two incoming missiles headed for the enemy ship."

Templeton and Staples looked sharply at each other. "Missiles? You're sure?" Templeton asked, rather pointlessly.

"Yes, sir. I only saw two, but from the damage to the other ship, I believe there were at least four."

"We didn't fire them." He looked around at his assembled crew. "Does anyone in here know anything about these missiles?" There was only quiet whispering as each crew member looked at their colleagues and waited for someone to speak up. Quinn and Parsells were passive observers, and Bethany was tucked in a corner behind the doctor and his temporary ward.

"I don't believe they came from our ship, sir." The whispers subsided as the engineer spoke.

"What?" Templeton asked. "Are you saying they fired

at themselves?"

Dinah considered only a moment. "I don't believe they did, sir. I believe there's another ship out there." There was no stemming the tide now, and the room erupted in raised conversations. Conjecture, concern, and fear flew about, and Staples let it ride for a moment before nodding at Templeton to get control.

"Hey! Hey!" he shouted, and the noise abated, though it did not cease altogether. Piotr slammed his fist on the table again, and while it was unclear whether he did so out of frustration or to quiet the rest of the crew, it had an effect all the same. "Finish your report, Dinah."

"Yes, sir. I judged that I had only a few seconds to remove myself from harm. I used the jetpack to maneuver around *Gringolet* as fast as I could and used the ship as a shield. I regret that I was unable to retrieve Yegor before I did this, but there just wasn't time, and I judged him beyond saving at that point anyway. The rest you know, sir."

The concerned voices rose again, and Gwen was crying into the doctor's chest now. Jabir caught Staples' eye with a beseeching look. She nodded, and he glided silently out of the room, still holding the girl to his chest. The captain knew she had to say something to defuse the situation, but she was unsure what.

Templeton's voice rang out loud and clear over the room. "Okay, listen. Listen." The voices diminished. "We were attacked by pirates. They didn't want us, or to hurt us. They wanted our passengers. They didn't get 'em, thanks to our chief engineer here. Someone or something blew up that other ship. I don't know what it was, and yes, that scares me too, but it's clear that if they wanted to blow *us* up, they could. They didn't fire at us. They helped us, and I take that as a good sign. We will get to the bottom of this." He looked around the room for a dramatic moment to drive his next point home. "In the mean time, we've got a lot of work to do. We need a damage assessment. The ship needs to be checked, nose to tail. We need engine diagnostics. If you're in a department, get there. The rest of you: I want this ship checked. Every room, every window, every corner. Parsells, Quinn," his eyes passed over Jang for the moment, "Ian, Declan, Piotr, and Yoli – if you're feeling up to it -" he nodded at the Hispanic woman holding her arm gingerly, "that means you." There was a moment of silence. "Now! Let's do it!"

Men and women began to push off from wall bars or unbuckle belts and to work their way out the door. As Jang headed for the exit, Staples addressed him. "Kojo, you'd better get back to Medical."

"If I may, Captain, I would like to join the search. You have my word that I am feeling well enough."

The man looked anything but well, but Staples sensed that perhaps he needed to prove something after being knocked unconscious in the attack. She nodded, and he left. Only Dinah remained with her captain and first mate.

"You know, sir, that if there were any hull breaches, depressurization alarms would sound." It wasn't a question.

"He knows," Staples answered. "Probably they all do too. But what they need right now is reassurance that we are okay and that the ship is okay. This will help, and it gives them something constructive to do. A goal." Dinah pulled her way along the distance of the table, grabbing the far edge and coming to rest a meter from the other two.

The captain continued, "And while we're on the subject of things left unsaid: you said you forgot that coms were down due to Yegor's retrofit of the satellite suite. I've never known you to forget something like that."
Templeton looked at her, expecting an answer, but Dinah did not provide one. Instead, Staples turned to him and said, "She didn't tell us what she was doing because she knew we'd order her not to." She turned back to her engineer. "I know the old axiom about it being easier to ask for forgiveness than permission, but don't think that I won't get angry at you for disobeying orders you bloody-well know I would give if you gave me the chance to." She heaved a deep sigh, more out of relief than anything else. "Sometime when you haven't saved the ship."

Dinah fixed her eyes on a place past Staple's head and said, "I didn't save everyone, sir."

"Yegor was an accident."

The engineer pursed her lips in anger. "It wouldn't have been an accident if Parsells and Quinn had done what I told them. I told them no one through."

"Did you tell them why?" she countered.

For the first time since she had entered the room, the other woman looked at a loss for words. "I... didn't. There wasn't time."

"These aren't military officers, Dinah. You can't expect them to follow orders without reason. They had no idea what you were planning. I'll talk with them and see what they have to say about what happened, but if Yegor told them to move aside and let him through, well... they're the new guys. *Everyone* outranks them. I might have done the same."

Templeton spoke up. "I feel like we're forgetting

something here. What about the other stasis tube? Did they get it? Is it still in CB4? We need to check."

"I want to know that very badly as well, Don, but we need to handle one problem at a time. The only way into CB4 is through B17, and that's hard vacuum at the moment. What are our options, Dinah?"

Dinah's eyes refocused on those of her captain as she spoke. "I see three ways in, sir. One: we can use an EVA suit and fly outside the ship to the hole, climb in, and proceed to CB4. Two: we can use the hallway leading into B17, B23 I believe, as a makeshift airlock. Someone goes into the corridor in an EVA suit, closes the doors, then opens the door to B17."

"I don't like that option," Templeton said.

"Neither do I," added Staples. "Those doors are designed as emergency depressurization control, not airlocks. Besides, I don't want to depressurize any more of the ship than we already have."

"I agree, sir. Both of these options come with an added problem. It is safe to assume that the pressure door into CB4 closed automatically in response to the depressurization alarm. If that is true, it is likely that the stasis tube is intact and that the room still has atmosphere. If we enter from vacuum, we vent the atmosphere, which is dangerous to both the stasis tube and the person in the EVA suit."

"Agreed. Option three it is then. We repair the hole and repressurize B17. How long will that take?" Staples inquired.

"It might not take long at all if the circular hull piece can function as a patch. I'll need to get out there with Mr. Park and a UteV and see what I can do."

Templeton shook his head. "This is going to be made doubly tough without coms. Jesus, the fun never ends."

"Ordinarily, even EVA suit-to-suit coms are routed through the ship's coms suite, but I can probably rig up something using the guts of some watches." Dinah spoke with confidence about the operation.

"Looks like we've got our work cut out for us, eh?" Templeton's voice was heavy.

Staples shook her head. "God, I wish Yegor was here."

# CHAPTER 10

Without communications, the retrieval of the errant stasis tube was an agonizing wait. There was no way to know how the search was going aside from looking through a window. John's UteV buzzed through the ever expanding wreckage that floated away from the ship in all directions. Though not under thrust, Gringolet was still moving at over 5000 kilometers per second. The pirate ship had matched their speed, and so the debris was mostly moving in a dissipating cloud at roughly the same speed. Charis was waiting down by the cargo and shuttle bay, manning the controls required to open the already depressurized bay for her husband when he returned. Templeton, Jang, and Gwen held themselves to the starboard control panel on the bridge and tried to follow the UteV's movements as it weaved in and out of the wreckage. Several other crew members were stationed at strategic portholes along the starboard side of the ship watching, and Yoli and Declan were in the rear observation lounge to help as well. After more than a half hour of watching the small craft maneuver deftly around the wreckage of their attackers, Templeton was beginning to lose hope. It was quite possible that they would never find the stasis tube, or that it had been destroyed in the explosion. The idea of leaving someone, alive but asleep, to float in vacuum until the power supply on the stasis tube depleted and they slowly froze to death was horrifying, but he also knew that each passing minute lowered the chances of their passenger's survival. The stasis tubes were capable of using their batteries to provide heat in cases such as this, but they were certainly not designed for prolonged exposure to space.

It was Gwen who spotted it first. "He got it! He got it!" Staples and Templeton squinted through the window, and they could just see the UteV closing in on a piece of debris that looked about the right size and shape. As the small craft slowed, the capture claws extended, and John did his best to manhandle the stasis tube in their direction.

"Bethany, can you close the distance?" Templeton asked, and was answered by a slight pull away from the window as *Gringolet* banked towards its second engineer. The movement was gentle, only about two degrees, but it was enough to close the distance to half. John seemed to have grasped two of the grip bars on the side of the tube designed to help people maneuver it in zero G environments. The small engines on the craft glowed lightly and briefly, and it began to cross the remaining gap to its mother ship.

"Gwen, do you want to tell your mother that your dad is on his way back?" Templeton smiled over at the crew's youngest member.

Gwen nodded, her dark hair spilling out of her

ponytail and swaying back and forth as she moved her head. She pinged her watch to talk to Charis, then spoke into it, sounding as official as she could. "Navigator Mom, this is Gwen speaking. You-tee-vee is returning to the ship. He found it!"

"Thank you, honey." There was more than a little relief in Charis' voice.

Staples smiled, then immediately felt guilty. One of her crew, a friend, was dead, and one of her passengers might well be too. She found, however, that she was also very glad to be alive. She had put on the bravest face that she could, but she had considered it a real possibility that the pirates were going to kill them all. Even once it became clear that they were after their cargo and not the crew, she was not sure that the other ship would not attack them once they were clear. Of course, Gringolet was armed as well, but it had still been a very dangerous situation. All of this and more ran through her head, but all she said was, "We should head down to the cargo bay."

Several minutes later, the bay was repressurized, and John, Templeton, Jabir, and Staples, their hands on grips, floated near the stasis tube by the back wall of the cargo bay. The UteV was docked nearby, and John still wore his entire EVA suit except the helmet, which he had clamped to a hook on the wall. The tube itself had been hastily secured to the deck with some cargo straps from a supply closet. Gwen was outside in the hall with Charis. Templeton had asked her to take the girl out when they saw the condition of the tube. It had clearly taken damage in the explosion, and it seemed to be ruptured in several places. More concerning was the lack of electrical activity.

There was, in their immediate assessment, no way the occupant could be alive. A large letter A was stamped on the front of the device.

"Who is it?" Templeton asked morosely.

"Evelyn," his captain replied. "Evelyn Schilling."

"God, she was so young and smart." He looked over the damage, shaking his head. "I'm afraid we're going to need to open it, Doc."

"Indeed." The doctor's voice was grave. "We'll need to preserve the body for the rest of the trip, if that is your wish Captain."

"It is." She sighed heavily. "I... we should still deliver her to Cronos station. I failed to protect her, but we can at least take her the rest of the way."

Her first mate turned to her, shifted his grip, and put a hand on her arm. "You didn't fail, Clea. There was nothing you, or me, or any of us could have done."

"We could have let them take her. She'd still be alive."

John spoke up. "You don't know that at all, Captain, no offense. Pirates aren't known for taking prisoners."

"They're not known for stunning people either," she replied sharply, rounding on him, her eyes moist. "They might not have killed her. If they wanted her dead, they could have just shot her in the tube."

Park's head dropped, defeated, but Templeton continued the line of thought. "Then they wanted her alive, maybe to repair their ships or computers. She was smart, after all. From what I hear about people who live out here picking off ships... she might be better off here." He gestured down at the tube that had become a casket.

"That's an awfully big *might*, Don."

"It does not actually matter, Captain," Jabir weighed in. "You did not make this choice. Your ship was under attack, and you were ready to die defending it and your passengers, if what I hear is true." He glanced at Templeton, who nodded. "You could not have known what Dinah was doing, and she could not have known that another ship would fire missiles at our assailants. She may have gambled by detaching the boarding tube, but I believe she had every reason to think that this stasis tube would survive in vacuum. It would have, I suspect, had it not been lacerated with shrapnel. And that is assuming that the tube would be in a vulnerable position when she cut the power to the magnets. There were many variables, and as much as you like to think that this is your world here on this ship," Staples looked at him angrily, but he continued unperturbed, "you cannot control everything. This," he regarded the inert device, "was tragic, but it was not anyone's fault."

"No one on this ship, anyway," Templeton corrected angrily, though it was clear his ire was directed not at the doctor but at the other vessels.

"That is what I meant, of course."

Staples hung her head. She could find no fault in their logic, but after the two years she had spent on the ship with the crew, she naturally thought, as many captains did, that everything that happened on her ship was her responsibility. "You may be right," was all she was ready to grant them at the moment. It was a step, she knew. "Anyway, let's get to it. We have a long to-do list, and another passenger we need to get to."

The doctor and John moved forward, transferred their grips to the handles of the stasis tube, and began the process of opening it manually. As they did so, John said, "Captain, I'd like permission to continue searching for Yegor's body when we're done here."

Staples thought for a minute, then shook her head. "I want him back. I do; he should be with us, but we've got a ship to repair. We need to get B17 repressurized. Then you can look. You know," and she paused until he looked up and met her eyes, "it's very unlikely that you will find him."

John nodded reluctantly. Finally, he undid the last manual lock with his screwdriver and placed the tool back in its sheath on his belt. He and Jabir lifted the lid away from rest of the case, and though she wanted to avert her eyes, Staples forced herself to look into the open chamber at the occupant, expecting to see the comely features of Evelyn Schilling. Instead, she saw the body of Herc Bauer, frozen and pallid, a plaster cast about his wrist.

"How does it look out there?" Templeton's voice came in broken and full of static through the jury-rigged watch fastened to the inside of Dinah's helmet. She had set the line to transmit constantly, but the watches weren't designed to transmit through the hull of a ship or through space, and the reception was spotty at best. Templeton, Park, and Ian Inboden were all on an open frequency with her. The first mate was in the cockpit pressed against the window to minimize the distortion from the much thicker hull. Park was manning a UteV which Inboden, the ship's reclusive mechanic, was tethered to. Dinah was tethered to it as well, and as they moved through vacuum towards the breach in the ship's hull, they inspected the damage that the explosion has caused to the starboard side of the vessel in the light of the spots John was targeting.

"Not terrible, not great. I don't see any other breaches, but some sections of the hull are going to have to be replaced in dry dock. The damage looks to be worse towards the stern, sir." Dents, scrapes, and buckles could be seen along the side of the ship. In some places, pieces of shrapnel remained protruding from the hull, and Dinah made note of their locations to check from inside the ship. No depressurization had been detected by the ship's automated systems, but a knife wound in a body might not start to bleed until the knife was removed. She gave quiet thanks that none of the debris had struck the comparatively weaker portholes; the impact might have been enough to crack them.

"Sounds expensive but survivable. Anything that will stop us from firing up the engines and decelerating?" Templeton inquired.

"I can't tell from here. I still need to get into the ReC and run diagnostics on the engines. It is possible they took a hit, or that some of the main circuits are damaged. Stand by, sir."

They were nearing the rear of the ship, and the damage was worse here. Not only was there the obvious roughly cut hole that their attackers had made, but there were several large dents from strong impacts in the rearmost thirty meters of the vessel. Bethany had been pulling *Gringolet* away from the other ship when it had exploded, turning to put the engines at the rear in their face. The result was that the stern had taken the brunt of the damage. Two of the craters in the hull looked large enough to hide a car in, and she noted that one of them was just above CB4, the location of the other stasis tube. It was unlikely, she thought, that the tube had taken damage, but it wasn't impossible.

"Let's get closer, Park," she instructed her second engineer, and the UteV moved in towards the circular breach. "Ian, I want you to come through with me. We'll try to get the disc back into place and reseal it. I'll stay inside, you stay outside. Park, you keep him in position."

John maneuvered the small craft right up to the hole, giving a small blast of rearward thrust to stabilize himself when they were about two meters away. Dinah and Ian untethered themselves. Dinah was first through, expertly using her jetpack to turn herself horizontal and to drive through, rotating back around when she was inside the ship. She pressed herself up against the side of the hull and extended an arm. Inboden, a mechanic first and astronaut second, fought the controls to move himself towards the hole. He threw out his hand when he was close, and the chief engineer managed to grab it and drag him inside. It was eerie to be in the ship and still be in vacuum. It felt to her as if she were standing in the living room of her house - when she had owned a house - with the entire front wall of the room missing. The lines between inside and outside, normally of vital importance in space, were blurred. She didn't like it.

The disc that had been cut out of the hull was nestled against the side of the corridor, blocking the hallway that the pirates had used to access CB4. The piece of hull should have weighed over a thousand pounds under the effects of normal gravity. There were a variety of tasks that zero G made more difficult; fortunately, moving heavy objects was rendered quite the opposite. The two of them, through light applications of thrust, moved down the corridor and to what she hoped was their readymade patch. She gave a sigh of relief when she saw that the pirates had cut at an angle, aiming their cutting torches slightly out as they had carved their circle. The result was not a perfectly squat cylinder, but something that more closely resembled a large metallic peanut butter cup. The logic behind this was simple. Their attackers had planned to use it as a shield as they moved into the ship, and by cutting it in this shape it could only drift in, not out, of the hole they had made. It also had the benefit of making it very easy to hold in place while they welded it back into place.

The effects of gravity might have been negated, but the rules of inertia remained, and it took both of them several minutes of pushing, pulling, and grunting to get the thing moving. The magnetic handles that the pirates had used to steer it had been left attached, and they were able to use these in conjunction with their jetpacks to drag the piece of hull back whence it had come. As they approached the hole, Dinah moved around to the back of the disc and pushed as best she could without a handle while Inboden pulled. As the makeshift bandage closed the last meter to the wound in the ship, the UteV's lights were blocked and the hallway designated B17 on some designer's schematic decades earlier became a bit darker. The conventional lights had blown when the air was sucked out of the hallway, but the emergency lights had kicked in, and they were designed to work in vacuum.

It was the matter of another minute's work to rotate the hull disc round until they could match it up perfectly to its original orientation, thus providing a tight seal. The cutters had carved the hole by hand, and though they clearly had been skilled, the disc was not a perfect circle. Once it was in place, Dinah slapped adhesive patches on the seams in various places to hold it. Outside, the mechanic did the same. John had come up behind him in the UteV, and he gently placed a capture claw around the handle on the back of Ian's jetpack. Finally, it was time to begin the welding process. Dinah set her jetpack on .1 G constant thrust to keep her pressed to the wall, and used her arm and feet to brace and move herself. On the other side of the hull, Park was moving Inboden in a slow circle as he welded.

"I feel like a paintbrush out here," he muttered. Park and Templeton laughed audibly, and Dinah smiled.

It took nearly fifteen minutes for them to melt the metal into a seal all around the disc, and when that was completed, the mechanic set about applying hull patches over the newly welded seam. Park used the craft's other capture claw to pull them from the outboard storage crate and to hand them to him one by one. Finally, it was done.

"Sir, are you there?" Dinah asked, glancing at the watch plastered to the inside of her helmet near her left ear.

"Yep. You must be inside; I can hear you better."

"The seal is completed. You can try repressurizing B17."

"Roger that."

"Keep an eye out for leaks out there," Dinah said to the repair crew on the other side of the freshly repaired hull.

A few seconds later, the air level in the hallway started to rise. Dinah could neither hear nor see it, but the atmosphere gauge on her wrist told her it was increasing.

As the air pressure grew, she held her breath, hoping the seal would hold. There was no reason it shouldn't; they had been more than thorough, but then, it had not been a good day. The hallway, though not very large, took several minutes to repressurize. This was far more time than the cargo bay, but the cargo bay was designed to be depressurized and repressurized rapidly and regularly. The ship's hallways were not.

Once her gauge indicated that the atmosphere in the corridor was as normal as the rest of the ship, she spoke. "It looks like its holding in here. Do you see any atmosphere venting outside?" The question was a formality. The men would have told her if they had seen anything amiss.

"Looks fine out here, chief," Inboden said, his voice slightly laced with static.

"All right then. You can come back inside now."

"Templeton?" It was Park's voice.

"Yeah, John. After you drop Ian off, you can go look for Yegor, but I don't want you more than 2000 kilometers from the ship. You understand me?"

"Loud and clear, Don."

Dinah looked once more at the gauge on her wrist, then reached up to undo the safety clamps and remove her helmet. The air filled her lungs easily, but it was bitterly cold. Her breath showed briefly in front of her face as she breathed out. The heaters were going to take a little while to warm the hallway, and she was glad that she was still in her suit. A light tap on the controls of her jetpack sent her back down the corridor to the door that she had ordered Parsells and Quinn to seal. It was odd seeing it from this side. She imagined Jang leaning out to shoot a rifle, imagined being the attacker pointing a stun pistol at him and shooting him in the head. Once she reached the branching hallway with the sealed door, she gripped a support bar and stopped herself. She reached down and opened the door. On the other side were Staples and the doctor.

The captain shivered as the blast of cold air hit her in the face, and the doctor's teeth chattered for a moment until he got them under control.

"It is very cold in here, sir." Dinah's breath continued to mist as she spoke. "We can wait a few minutes if you'd like."

"No," she shook her head, "we need to see to our passenger." She produced a pair of gloves to protect her hands and slid them on, and the doctor did the same.

A frigid minute later, they were in front of the door to CB4. It had auto-sealed when the hallway had depressurized, and it took Dinah only a few seconds to get it open. When the door swung in, there was no rush of air. The room might have been without air briefly, but once the door had closed, the air circulators had refilled it. Dinah moved in first, her captain and Jabir close behind. CB4 was a fairly large room, and like most on the ship, it was rectangular and ran perpendicular to the spine of the ship. The ventral and rear walls were covered in submerged hooks designed to hold cargo in place with the help of straps. Right now the room contained only two medium sized containers, each a meter square, and the stasis tube, a large letter B showing on the front. The docking node that had housed the other tube stood empty. None of this, however, demanded the three crew members' attention so much as the massive convex dent in the top left corner of the room. It had evidently not caused a breach, but the hull was clearly quite damaged, and various electrical cables and even a support strut hung down brokenly.

The stasis tube itself seemed undamaged, but there were several red lights blinking on its interface that had not been there when it had been wheeled past Staples on Mars. Dinah was already cruising over to it, having pushed herself off the doorway, and the captain and the doctor were right behind her. Dinah scanned the readout, then pulled off the gloves of her EVA suit and began typing on the screen.

"It's been damaged," she said as she worked.

"It doesn't look damaged." Staples countered, though as she said it, she knew it was absurd to contradict the woman.

"It's electrical damage. The supply sources were compromised. There was a power surge, and the tube was subjected to maybe a minute of vacuum." Jabir approached and looked over Dinah's shoulder, nodding as he read the display.

"So what does that mean? Is the person," she assumed it was Evelyn Schilling, but she was no longer certain, "in there alive? Are they all right?"

"Yes, sir." Dinah's reply was immediate. "But I don't know if they will continue to be. The tube needs repairs. I might be able to do it, but I really don't want to operate on a stasis tube while someone is inside.

"I concur," the doctor added.

"So what do we do?"

"The way I see it, we have two options, sir. We either leave it closed and hope for the best, or we open it and make up the guest room."

Staples looked at her overpriced and overqualified doctor. "Can you do that?"

"Yes," he nodded and continued in his richly accented voice. "There are procedures to follow, and while it is not something that I have done before, the procedure is fairly simple. Waking people from stasis is not nearly as complex as putting them into it. Tell me, does this constitute a breach of contract?"

"I don't much care at this point. Besides, I want answers. Herc was supposed to be in this tube. I don't know what that means. I don't know if Evelyn is in here or not. This job has turned into a real mess, and whoever is in there, I'm hoping they can clear some things up."

"Very well," he replied. "I could open the stasis tube here, but I prefer to do so in Medical."

"All right," Staples said. "I'll have Declan and Yoli move the tube down to Medical." She shifted her focus to her chief engineer. "Can we detach the tube without causing any further damage?" Dinah nodded.

"I'm afraid that Ms. Trujilo bruised her arm on a bulkhead in her attempt to rush to her quarters. Speed and zero-gravity travel rarely mix well." The doctor's tone made it clear that asking Yoli to help was out of the question.

"I can do it, sir," the other woman offered.

"No, now that this is done, I want you in the ReC looking at the engines." She thought for a minute. "Ian will just be getting back on the ship. You know what? Get Parsells and Quinn back here to help."

"As you wish, Captain. I'll prepare Medical." He pushed himself off from the tube and back towards the door.

# CHAPTER 11

"All right, Captain, you can come in, but please keep the conversation light. I have informed Ms. Schilling of the broad details of the situation and of the death of Mr. Bauer. She is feeling somewhat fragile, as one would expect." Doctor Iqbal stood in the doorway to Medical, quite decidedly in his captain's path, until he was done speaking. She nodded her assent, and only after another moment did he reluctantly step aside and let her in. Setting foot in Medical after several days of weightlessness was both a relief and a burden. Her brain told her that things were normal again under the effects of the gravity plating she had paid a great deal to have installed, but her body almost immediately felt like a prison as her 135 pounds returned. The plating could be set to lower or higher percentages of gravity, but the doctor kept it at Earth normal: 9.81 meters per second per second. He maintained that it was necessary to not only help keep him healthy, but also to properly gauge his patients' health. The human body had evolved to function at homeostasis under normal

Earth gravity, and that was how he felt it should be evaluated. Staples secretly suspected him of cranking up the gravity when no one was around in order to use the space as a private workout room, but she had never caught him at it, nor would she blame him for doing so if she did.

As she entered, she saw Evelyn Schilling lying on the same bed the doctor had put her on back on Mars. She was wearing a green hospital gown, and a pale blue sheet was pulled up to her waist. She had pinned her long flame colored hair back from her face. Though her eyes were puffy and somewhat reddened, she was not crying.

Staples was again struck by the beauty of the woman, and wondered if she had had surgery. Plastic surgery to alter one's appearance, more specifically to make oneself more attractive, was hardly uncommon, and if one had the money, the possible alterations were remarkable. Amongst the upper class, astounding transformations could be achieved. Of course, there was no accounting for taste, but over a hundred years of study of the science underlying attraction had shown that certain facial shapes, certain contours, and above all, symmetry were most universally appealing. If in fact the fair skinned woman in front of her had undergone surgery, the captain thought that her surgeon was to be commended.

Staples, slightly unsteady on her heavy feet and trying her best to wear a sympathetic smile, walked across the room. She stopped a few feet short of the bed. "Evelyn. How are you?"

Evelyn took a deep breath and then released it as a shuddering sigh, and for a second her lip trembled and Staples thought she was going to cry, but she didn't. "I'm okay. I won't say I'm fine," her eyes flicked to the doctor, "but I'll manage. I just can't believe this. I can't believe your ship was attacked." Her brows furrowed and her eyes glistened. "And I can't believe you lost a crew member. Is it true that he died trying to save Herc?" Her husky voice was higher pitched than normal.

Staples searched for an answer that was honest and that did not belie her doubts on the matter. "He was a very brave man."

"Poor Herc. I didn't know him - I mean - not well, but he was a good man." She nodded at her own statement as she spoke.

"I only met him the once, but I thought he was too. Evelyn, I need to ask you some questions. Is that all right?" She closed the rest of the distance to the bed, unconsciously crossing her arms across her chest. The woman on the bed nodded. Jabir had walked around and was standing on the other side of his patient, ready to warn his captain off with a look if necessary. "My manifest said that you were in tube A, but we found you in tube B. Do you know why?"

She nodded immediately. "Herc hurt his wrist after dinner. It was stupid, really. Some guy bumped into him and walked off, and then Herc realized that his wallet was missing. He chased after the guy and gave him a good tackle. He's… he was a big guy. He got his wallet back, but he sprained his wrist. When we got to Stasis Solutions, they gave us a full examination," she looked at the doctor a bit slyly, "and they decided to put a cast on it before they put him in stasis." She finished her statement as though it had cleared everything up, but the look on Staples' face said she clearly hadn't.

"Sorry. They had tube B all ready to go for him, but

then it was going to take them a bit to put the cast on, so they said they would just put me in B and him in A. They said they'd change it in the manifest. I guess they forgot."

The blonde woman searched the engineer's eyes, and though she was far from an expert, she saw nothing but open-faced honesty. She decided to accept it for now. "All right. Do you have any idea why someone would hire a crew of pirates to kidnap you?"

"Me?" The lovely brown eyes widened incredulously. "You think they were after me?"

Staples allowed some steel to creep into her voice. "I am absolutely sure of it." She wasn't one hundred percent sure this was true, but she wanted to push the woman to give any explanation she might have. Iqbal gave her a withering glance, but he did not interfere.

"I…" she looked around the room as if for answers. "I have no idea. I mean, I'm a talented computer scientist. Maybe they needed one, but there have to be easier ways."

"Absolutely. I don't know what your salary is, but I suspect that they could hire you ten times over for what that crew was likely paid to abduct you."

"I don't hire myself out to pirates, not even for ten times regular pay, but I take your point. Okay. So it wasn't about money." Evelyn had taken on the look of a person attempting to solve a puzzle. "I was just hired by Libom Pangalactic; I'm certainly not party to any corporate secrets as yet. I've been head programmer at a few small firms, but nothing that I can imagine warranting abduction by pirates." She smiled slightly, showing perfectly straight teeth. "It would sound exciting and romantic if the results hadn't been so horrible."

"Maybe someone didn't want you working for

Libom. Maybe they were trying to keep Cronos Station from getting up to speed. I heard that the loss of their previous computer engineer was hurting production. Perhaps a rival energy company?"

"I suppose that could be it," Evelyn ruminated, then frowned. "But then why just me? Or why try to take just me? Herc and I weren't in exactly the same fields, but given what they told me about their issues, I think he would have done a fair job on his own." She paused a moment, then added. "It should have been me. If Herc hadn't hurt his wrist, I would be dead and he would be alive."

"You can't drive yourself crazy with *what ifs*, Evelyn. This was nothing you did. *They* did it." She gestured with her head towards the starboard side of the ship and the cloud of debris beyond.

"Maybe they were going to take both tubes?" the doctor interjected in an effort to steer his patient away from survivor's guilt.

Staples shook her head. "If they had wanted both tubes, they would have taken them at the same time. They were smart and well planned. It would have made no sense to take one and then go back for the other. Too inefficient, too much time. No. They wanted you and you specifically. The question is why." There was a moment of silence as they all pondered the question. "Is it possible that there's something on you, maybe in you?"

"What, like Stasis Solutions implanted some sub-dermal data chip carrying secret messages in my skin?" When she said it aloud, it did sound rather ridiculous, but the doctor was shaking his head.

"Believe it or not, I checked. I scanned her body for

anything non-organic when I brought her out of stasis."
Both women looked at him, surprised. He shrugged. "I
read a lot of spy novels," he offered by way of explanation.

"Maybe it's not you. Maybe it's the tube," Staples
conjectured. "I'll have Dinah have a look at both of the
stasis tubes once she's finished with the engines."

"You know, Captain, Ms. Hazra is not a skeleton key
for all of the ship's problems."

Staples narrowed her eyes at the doctor briefly, but
did not answer. After another few seconds of thought, she
sighed deeply. "We've got over a week before we reach
Saturn. Depending on the condition of the engines, that
might increase. I'm tempted to keep you confined to
Medical, Evelyn, for your own safety." The woman's
expression ably conveyed that she was not amenable to
that. "But you're not a prisoner; you're a passenger. In fact,
you're a guest. I'll have some quarters prepared for you.
You can come and go as you please. Actually, if you don't
mind, I have some work for you."

Evelyn's face lit up.

"The loss of our communications officer, Yegor
Durin, has hurt us in more ways than one. He was in the
middle of refitting the communications suite with one we
salvaged from a derelict satellite. Coms and radar are
down, and I suspect that you might be the best person to
finish the job. Charis and Dinah could probably do it
between the two of them, but they're already busy, Dinah
especially, and it's hardly their area of expertise." She shot
a look at Iqbal, as if to say: *see, Dinah doesn't do everything.*

"Sure, I'd be happy to. Might help keep my mind off
things." She swung the sheet off of her legs, revealing a
tantalizing view of one thigh, and made to jump down

from the bed.

Jabir put a hand on her shoulder to restrain her. "Just a minute, Doctor. I would like to dot a few more i's and cross a few more t's before you go gallivanting off around the ship."

Evelyn looked over her should at him, and her eyes were large and plaintive. "Give it to me straight, Doctor. You're just trying to keep me in bed, aren't you?"

It was exceedingly odd, Staples thought, to see Evelyn sitting in Yegor's seat on the bridge. She was sure that she wasn't the only one. Jabir had given the woman a clean bill of health to work, but he had restricted her to, by his definition, light duty. That meant no more than a few hours at a time, and certainly no more than six hours a day. She took to the work with a great deal of enthusiasm which seemed, as far as the captain could tell, to be how she took to most things. Staples found it difficult to pin her down exactly. She had a fun, flirtatious, sometimes irreverent manner, yet she was unquestionably intelligent and capable, and she addressed her work with a great deal of seriousness. Evelyn had been out of the stasis tube and moving about the ship for only a day and a half, but it seemed that more than a few members of the crew had taken an interest in her. Staples couldn't blame them. The woman was lovely, and it was well known that grief and arousal were old friends.

At the moment, she was wearing a pair of khaki slacks and a black tank top, much like the sort that Dinah preferred, and her red hair was twisted into two braids at the back of her skull to keep it out of her face. Her pale arms carried a smattering of freckles that increased in density as they fell to her hands, which were themselves strong and marked by dry skin. The majority of the time she had spent working was in the communications room, a small, chamber dense with computer equipment at the bow of the ship. It was tucked beneath the cockpit but above the cargo bay. There had been a learning curve, she explained to the captain, but her understanding of the communications hardware and software was growing rapidly. If everything went to plan, the hope was to have the coms and radar restored within another two days of work, though she had intimated that she might have to bend her physician's orders to accomplish this feat. Some of her work required adjustments from the primary coms panel in the cockpit, and so here she was, bent over the surfaces in Yegor's chair.

Charis was working quietly at her station, and Bethany huddled in her chair, her eyes moving between the stars and the new woman on her right. Don, meanwhile, sat next to his captain, staring absently at Evelyn as well, though Staples was fairly sure it was Yegor's chair and not the woman that was the source of his pensiveness. The loss of their crewmember had been difficult for the majority of the crew. John had searched as long as the captain had allowed him, and even a bit longer, but he was unable to find Yegor's body in the wreckage of the pirate ship. They had decided to hold a funeral service for him, and Don had spoken; he had said some very touching words to the crew about the man. The entire thing had been awful and odd, and it all seemed to lack closure without his body. This was amplified by the tension that seemed to infect the crew. Fear of another attack hung heavy in the atmosphere. There were wild theories about where the missiles had come from. There were also, despite the first mate's efforts to quash them when he encountered them, rumors that Yegor had been paid to disable the coms.

A muted debate on whether to hold a funeral for Herc Bauer had arisen as well. No one on the ship had really known him. Evelyn had met him a few days before *Gringolet* had arrived on Mars, though she had heard of him by reputation before that, and Staples had only spoken to him for about an hour. In the end, Don and Clea decided to postpone the funeral. Once coms were back up, assuming Evelyn's work proceeded apace, they could find out where the Computer Engineer had family. They had every expectation that they would be stopping at Mars on the way back to the core planets, and perhaps he could be given a proper funeral by people who had known him there.

"Captain, are you there?" Dinah's voice came through the speaker on her watch. Staples shook her head to clear it of her reverie and tapped it to reply.

"Go ahead."

"I've completed my diagnostics of the engines, sir. They took minor damage from the debris in the explosion of the other ship. We can slow down, but I'm not comfortable pushing them above point four Gs."

Charis turned around with a grim look, blonde wisps of hair floating about her face. She needed to dye her roots, Staples thought absently. "That's a bit of a problem, Captain. Our original flight plan was to turn around and start decelerating at point six Gs by now. At that speed, we won't be able to stop in time; we'll fly right past Cronos Station."

"But you've got another option for us, right?" Don asked.

Charis thought for only a second. "We could take a contoured approach, curving out and then back in to generate more distance between us and the station. The greater distance will buy us more time to slow down."

Templeton nodded. "How much time would that add to our trip?"

Her eyes flicked up as she thought. "About three days. We'd be late."

"Well, this job is already fairly well ruined," Staples chimed in. Templeton opened his mouth to reply, but she pressed on. "I'm not saying it's our fault. We're a charter flight, not a military escort, but they may not care much about that. We'll explain the situation to them when coms are back up."

Evelyn looked up over her shoulder and smiled, then went back to work.

Staples pinged her watch again. "Okay, Dinah, let's make our turn and prepare to decelerate."

"Copy that, sir. Engines ready on your command."

"Charis, plot our new course. Don, tell the crew that we're going to start deceleration in forty minutes. Bethany, if you would be so kind as to give us a gentle over?"

Bethany's dark eyes appeared for a moment around the corner of her chair and she said, "Yes, sir," then turned back around. Templeton cocked an eyebrow at his captain. She had noticed the Dinah-ism as well, but decided not to address it, at least not now. Charis was already working on their newly projected, roundabout course to Saturn, and as Templeton began his shipwide address to the crew, *Gringolet* began to turn end over end, facing towards the increasingly distant sun.

The ship had been under the thrust of deceleration for five hours when Evelyn Schilling paid a visit to Medical. She made the odd transition from floor to wall as she entered, the gravity plating holding her solidly while the plating built into the wall on her right worked only half as hard to repel her. It was an unfortunate reality of ships that had invested in the new technology that they had to not only pay to install the panels in the floor to create gravity on which to stand, they also had to install them in the stern-ward wall. Otherwise, the people in the room would be subjected to two sources of gravity when the ship's engines were firing. The stern-ward wall panels were working to repel her at point four Gs, just enough to cancel the gravity created by the thrust of the ship.

After nearly two days of weightlessness, the Computer Scientist had decided to celebrate the reintroduction of gravity by literally letting her hair down. It flowed behind her luxuriously in the light gravity as she moved about the ship, but it fell as it would on Earth as she took a few steps into the Medical bay. Its usual denizen was not immediately visible, but the windows to his office were darkened. After a moment's hesitation, she walked briskly down to the office and knocked on the door. It opened, and Jabir Iqbal stood in front of her. He wore a black collared shirt, a deep blue tie, and black slacks. A temporarily discarded surface rested on his chair behind him. His smile was broad and welcoming. The two faced each other in the doorway to the office.

"Doctor Schilling. Tell me, how are you feeling?"

"What time is it, Doctor?" she countered quite

quickly.

Without looking at his watch, he answered, "About ten minutes after twenty. Why?"

"I thought you were off duty at eighteen?" It was clear that she had planned this conversation, but he was more than willing to play his part.

"I am, actually, but how would you know that?"

"I asked." Her manner was direct, and she stood not half a meter from the man and looked up into his eyes. "So what are you still doing here?"

"I spend a great deal of time here. I find the gravity comforting. Why are you asking about my schedule, Doctor?"

"Call me Evelyn. I asked because I wanted to know." She moved closer to him, and he could feel her warm breath on his face. When her lips were a scant ten centimeters from his, she turned to her left and looked through one of the office windows at the rest of Medical. The windows were opaque from the outside, but transparent from the inside of the office. "You saw me enter, but didn't come out to greet me." A slightly mocking pout touched her lips as she looked back at him. "Why?"

If he was thrown off by her teasing, he did not show it. His answer came quickly and easily. "It was an opportunity to observe your balance under the effects of altering gravity."

"I thought you said you were off duty?" she scolded.

His reply was immediate. "I did. It was out of personal curiosity, not professional." Their mouths were closer than ever, and their eyes were locked, but he did not incline so much as a centimeter to meet her.

The moment stretched for several seconds, and suddenly she laughed, a throaty, rich sound, and turned away from him. She walked out into the Medical bay proper, then turned around and leaned against the wall. He took a step out of the office and faced her. "You're good. Usually men are slobbering all over me by now."

"Please, do not misconstrue my lack of visible salivation as a lack of interest, Evelyn." He stood easily, his hands in his pockets. "I usually attempt a bit more decorum, especially around impressive women such as you."

She laughed again. "Oh, I'll bet you've seduced women all over this solar system, haven't you Doctor? You seem about as used to getting your way as I am."

"Since I am off duty, as we have unequivocally established, I would prefer you call me Jabir. I would also prefer to not discuss the finer points of my sordid past. It is hardly the reason you came in here. Tell me, how do you like our little ship?"

She moved away from him, just a bit, to see if he would follow as she spoke. "Oh, a subject change? You *are* mister cool. I like it. The ship I mean." She turned and took a few steps away, then turned back around, her long hair flying around behind her and coming to rest against her shoulders. "Or I should say, I *also* like the ship. The captain gave me some quarters all my own, Piotr cooked me a fabulous meal, and Bethany gave me a plant for my room. It's a lilac. She's an odd one, that girl. Quiet."

"I believe she's quite taken with you." Jabir halved the distance between them, then stopped, hands still in his trouser pockets.

"Am I her type?" She broke eye contact as she

contemplated this for a second. "Huh. I hadn't guessed."

"Doctor Schilling, I believe you may be in danger of being everyone's type, as I am sure you know."

She shrugged lightly. "What's the point of making lots of money as a Computer Scientist if you can't enjoy the benefits of it?" Her face became serious for a moment. "Thank you, by the way, for not telling the captain about my surgeries. There's nothing metal in me, but I'm sure the augmentations to my cheek bones and the like showed on your scan."

He inclined his head in a gracious nod. "Doctor-patient confidentiality is a watchword of the trade. There was no need to mention such things. Few of us are created as we would wish to be. Some exercise to modify their bodies, some pierce their ears, others have their faces altered. Should we not seek to become who we wish to be, both inside and out?"

She stopped her dance away from him and closed the distance rapidly, smiling warmly. Again, she halted less than half a meter from him. "So, we're both attractive, well educated, intelligent, and open minded people. Is there a reason we're not having sex right now?" Her eyebrows raised dramatically.

"I must confess," he adopted a slight look of mock regret, "I cannot think of a single one." Finally he inclined his head towards her, and the dance ended in a kiss. The kiss increased in intensity, and they embraced tightly. Several passionate minutes progressed, and just as his hands found her hips, he felt her lean back from him. Her lips broke contact, and he thought for a moment that she was dancing away again, but the movement increased, and all of a sudden she was falling away and down from him.

He clutched at her and managed to grab her round the small of her back. Her head tilted back and her eyelids fluttered fiercely. As her knees went out from under her, he shifted around to pick her up and place her on a nearby medical bed.

"I… feel…" she muttered, "I… feel sick."

Jabir leaned her head gently back on the bed, pulling its back half up so that she was reclining rather than horizontal, and he put a hand on either side of her face. Her eyelids were continuing to flutter, and from what he could see, her pupils were dilated and her gaze was unfocused. She was flushed and shaky, and a light cold sweat had broken out on her brow.

"Evelyn, can you hear me?"

She moaned briefly, and her eyes opened and came into focus. She looked at him with a glazed expression, but there was recognition in her gaze. "Yes, I can hear you." Then she leaned over the bed and vomited on his shoes.

An hour later, Evelyn was back on her feet. Though the doctor had been reluctant to release her from Medical, she had convinced him that she was much recovered, and he could find nothing physically wrong with her. He had attributed her episode to the aftereffects of being in stasis, perhaps due in part to the damage the stasis tube had taken. He was, he admitted, no expert in cryogenics, and though he had read up on the subject, he could not also be sure that Stasis Solutions had done their job entirely well. They had, after all, failed to update the tube assignments in their computer system.

For her part, Evelyn had been eager to get out of Jabir's presence. Though the sickness had obviously been out of her control, the attendant embarrassment still made her cheeks burn. She had never had an intended seduction end with such mortification, and even once she had begun to feel better, there was an uneasiness that crept over her. The doctor's strong, swarthy features and well-proportioned physique had seemed so alluring a few minutes before, but she now found herself uncomfortable around the man and desirous to leave his presence. So she had done her best to assuage him with many more "fines" and nearly ran out of the room. She intended to do some more work, late as it was.

After stopping by her room to brush her teeth and pour some water on her already wilting lilac, she decided to go to the mess hall to refill her recently emptied stomach. She climbed up three decks, a task that strained her not at all given the near Martian gravity the engines were currently providing, and made her way down a hallway. She paused along the way to scan a ship schematic on the watch Don Templeton had given her. She turned right and a minute later saw the door to the mess hall in front of her. Inside, Piotr was finishing up some dishes. Several trays of food from the evening meal stood on the counter in sealed containers. It had been a pasta and shrimp concoction that she had enjoyed far more on the way down than on its return. The cook was a large man, bald-headed and darkly bearded, who looked up at her as she entered. She smiled at him, but he returned to his washing. Evelyn remembered Templeton saying that he had been quite upset at the man Yegor's death, and so she decided not to take it personally. The other two occupants of the mess hall were the security men, Parsells and Quinn she thought their names were. They sat across from one another in quiet conversation, their dinners long finished and cleared, and they sipped from their magnetic cups.

She was going to send a smile their way as well, but the way that Quinn leered at her made her uncomfortable, so instead she headed over to the refrigeration units. It was regrettable, she thought, that she had become somewhat used to the look; she had learned to ignore it the best she could.

"You want I should fix something for you?" the man at the sink asked without looking up from his work.

"Mmm." She didn't think she could handle the shrimp again, delicious as she had found it. "No, I'll just get a snack if that's okay."

"Sit." He gestured to the table. "I make you something."

"Yeah, come join us," Parsells said, and he waved a hand to her, his other hand gripping his cup. He patted the seat next to him. Quinn was looking at her quite wantonly, and she suddenly wanted to be there even less than she had wanted to be in Medical. When she didn't respond, he cajoled her further. "Come on, come here." His voice was projecting friendliness, but there was an edge behind it that she didn't like, and she thought that she smelled alcohol in the air.

"You know, I have some work to do, so I think I'm just going to take it with me," she addressed the cook, trying to keep from turning her eyes back to the men at the table. "I don't want to give you any trouble." She opened the nearest unit and fished around until she found a prepackaged cheese and crackers kit. She plucked it out along with a bottled water. "Okay if I take this?" She held them up for the cook's inspection. Piotr looked at her, then nodded and turned back to the sink. She decided that this was the unfriendliest room she had been in on the ship thus far and made a hasty exit.

Several hours later Evelyn was finishing up in the small communications room. She had nearly completed the work that Yegor had begun - the installation of the coms suite from the satellite. It was a bizarre feeling, knowing that the man whose job she was working to finish had died. Though she was not a coms expert by any means, the interfacing of the two modules was not overly complex, only a bit tedious and time-consuming. First, she had had to puzzle out what Yegor had been doing. Once she had accomplished that, she was able to extrapolate his overall plan. Now that the new suite was installed, a job she morosely thought that would have been better suited to Herc, she would have to work to get the new and older systems talking. That would involve writing some programming code, but that was far more her specialty than the heavy lifting of replacing data cards, swapping components, and running wires.

After extricating herself from the machinery in the room, she gave it one more examination, double-checking her work. There were no errors as far as she could see, but it would be impossible to tell until she got the system fully up and running. She packed the scattered tools she had borrowed from the ship's engineer back into the bag she had been given, wiped her slightly greasy hands on a rag which she bagged as well, and made her way out of the cramped and warm room.

Parsells and Quinn stood side by side outside the door, Quinn looming even larger than Parsells, and both wore plain blue flight jackets. The two men had been waiting for her, she judged as she stepped into the hallway, for a little while. As far as Evelyn could see, they didn't appear to be armed, but she could detect the strong scent of alcohol in the corridor. A second's assessment told her that she was in real danger. She considered trying to talk them out of it. She could appeal to their better natures, if indeed they had them. She could also attempt to explain that they would never get away with it, though she couldn't think of a book or movie where that threat had ever worked. She might even be able pretend to be playful and flirtatious. If they thought she wanted them, perhaps it would allow her to slip past them. Unfortunately, doing so would only lead her to a ladder she would need to descend carefully lest she fall half the length of the ship.

In the end the look in their eyes settled things. It was all over their faces; there was no doubt what these men had in mind. They weren't trying to decide what to do. They had decided.

Evelyn took a step back, swung the toolbag behind her, and threw it right at Quinn's face. Under ordinary circumstances a bag of heavy tools might have been too much for her to hurl successfully across a meter and a half of distance at a man's face, but the lighter gravity made it quite possible for her. Unfortunately, the reduced gravity that made the bag easier to throw also lessened its impact significantly. Instead of ten kilograms of toolbag hitting Quinn's face, a hit that might well have broken his nose or jaw, four kilos of assorted wrenches, screwdrivers, and small power tools surrounded by canvas like a pillowcase merely knocked him back. He gave a surprised grunt, but that was all. As soon as the bag left her hand, she reached for her watch. She wasn't familiar enough with the device to activate it without looking at it. She hit the coms button with a shaky finger and was about to press a name when Parsells, faster than he looked, lunged forward and caught her left arm. He clamped his meaty fingers around the watch and ripped it from her wrist. It clattered against the far wall, and Quinn, his balance regained, stomped his foot on it, then slid it back with his foot.

Evelyn tried to wrench her arm away from the man, but his grip was like a vice, and now he was reaching for her other hand. She brought her leg up in a savage arc to knee him in the groin. He saw it coming and rotated his hips quickly. As a consequence, she dealt him a swift kick in the thigh, and it seemed to do him no harm. His movement, however, had given her a moment of opening, and she tore her wrist free and backed up a step. Both men advanced on her. Parsells' face showed anger, and Quinn wore the same leer he had given her in the mess hall.

From behind her attackers, she saw a shadow appear, and a voice said, "Mind if I join in, boys?"

# CHAPTER 12

Dinah Hazra crept up the ladder formed by the retracted slats in the corridor. She had learned the trick of moving silently a long time ago, and though every instinct in her told her to rush, she knew she must not. She was nearly at the top when she heard the struggle begin. A crash sounded, which she suspected was her toolbag dropping to the floor, and a grunt followed. *Slowly, silently*, she told herself. She climbed up into the corridor, putting first one foot down, then the other. In front of her, Parsells had one hand clamped on the woman's wrist, and he was prying her watch off. Quinn was regaining his balance, the canvas toolbag already forgotten at his feet. Parsells tore the watch off and tossed it against the wall. Quinn's foot crashed down on it, then sent it flying back. It slid along the thick hull metal, passing right between Dinah's legs and stopping before the drop.

The element of surprise was probably not necessary for her to take these men down. She suspected that they knew how to handle themselves in a fight. Templeton would not have hired them if they had not, but they were not trained, not like she was. Even so, combined, they outweighed her by close to a factor of four. The corridor was not wide, and that would limit their mobility, but there was no reason not to give herself every advantage. One did not seek to create a fair fight; one did everything one could to ensure that the odds were in one's favor. That was how to win a fight. Even so, she couldn't help herself. She wanted to see the looks on their faces.

"Mind if I join in, boys?" she asked.

She didn't wait for an answer. As Parsells' head snapped around, shock dawning on his face, she was already kicking him in the knee, taking care to use her actual foot. Quinn was the larger of the two, but she judged Parsells to be the faster, and that made him the greater threat. Parsells cried out as his leg buckled. He staggered, but did not fall. Quinn's face as he turned his head to look at her wore a frighteningly vacant leer. She had judged him a sadist, but there was something more in his face, a detached expression that spoke of casual brutality and indifference to suffering. She would have bet money that he had killed before. No matter; he was not the only one.

She struck Quinn with a straight jab to the nose, and his head rocked back, but only for a second. The punch had not had much behind it. Force equals mass times acceleration, and her fist had less than half its usual mass at the moment. Fighting at lower gravity called for different tactics. The large man's eyes had closed instinctively when she punched him, and as he brought his head forward and his eyes opened, his boxer's nose not even bleeding, she grabbed a handful of his sandy hair and yanked him down and forwards. He had been prepared for another blow meant to drive him back, but not to be pulled forward. He staggered and nearly lost his footing. He was momentarily bent over as far as his friend, but he did not fall until Dinah dealt him a follow up heel kick in his kneecap. She sidestepped, and over he went, his stomach hitting the ground first. He managed to break the fall somewhat by splaying out his hands in a pushup position. This did not help him when Dinah stomped on the back of his head, driving his chin and nose into the metal beneath him. Now his nose was bleeding copiously.

Parsells, meanwhile, had gathered himself enough to throw a punch at her. It came quickly, a practiced roundhouse from his right hand, and she was barely able to duck beneath it. Predictably, he followed up with a left, but this time she was ready. She stepped inside his guard, twisting as she did so, careful not to trip on the man at her feet, and his fist sailed through air. As he was resetting, she brought her right elbow up into his throat, a blow that pushed him back against the corridor wall. She hit him again, in the nose this time, with the same elbow. Before she could do so again, he brought his fists and forearms up in a boxer's guard to protect his face. Striking his large stomach was a fool's game in this environment. Experience told her that men often thought that their opponents would follow the same rules they saw when people fought on broadcasts. She was not the least restricted.

Dinah lifted her heel and slammed it into Parsells' already wounded knee, and it buckled again. He didn't go down this time either, but he backed off a step, which gave Dinah a moment to slam her foot down on the back of

Quinn's head and grind his nose and face into the floor again. He moaned and tried to rise, but then she repeated the process, and instead he slithered to the side in an attempt to escape her.

Meanwhile, Parsells was preparing himself for a more drawn-out fight. His fists were up and his elbows were in. He had shifted stances to protect his wounded leg, and he would be weaker for it. Every fighter had a favored side, but despite the fact that Dinah had made his untenable, he was no less strong and ready and large. Dinah took a step back and regarded him for a moment. No words passed between them; she saw no point in talking. Had he been sober, he might have realized that he was outclassed. His opponent was as yet undamaged. He might also have given it up; there was no endgame here, no way out of the trouble he was in one way or the other. But he was drunk and angry, and he came on like a bull. She kicked Quinn sharply one more time in the face, then dropped into a fighter's stance and backed away, giving ground, acutely aware that the end of the corridor and a severe drop was only a few meters behind her. He closed the distance, limping as he came, but still with plenty of fight in him. He glanced only briefly at his friend, who was drooling blood on the floor and holding his ruin of a face.

Suddenly he feinted right, and then jabbed with his left. Dinah was ready, and turned the hit aside with a forearm. A flurry of blows followed from the man. Alcohol had done far less damage to his reflexes than to his reason, but she blocked or dodged every swing. It was just dawning on him that she was playing possum when a heavy wrench hit him in the back of the head. He staggered forward and reached his hands behind his head to protect his skull. The protective gesture perhaps saved his skull but did little for his fingers as Evelyn swung the wrench into the back of his head again, this time breaking a finger. He tumbled forward onto flooring, crying out and snatching his hand away from his head. Evelyn stepped forward, straddling his back, and hit him once more on the top of the skull with the wrench, though this time some of the fight seemed to go out of her. As Parsells slowly dragged himself into a fetal position and his hands moved up to cradle his head again, Evelyn lowered the wrench.

Dinah looked at her pointedly. "Are you all right?"

The redheaded woman was shaky and breathing fast. The wrench hung loosely in her hand at her side. She raised it again as if to hit the two men, then let it to the floor with a bang. "I think so. Jesus. Thank you."

Dinah only nodded once. She looked down at Quinn and Parsells, both still conscious but seriously injured. "Do you want to hit them some more?"

"What?" Her eyes moved back and forth between the pair. "No." Her breathing was beginning to slow. "I mean, yes, but no."

"All right then." Dinah tapped her watch without looking at it, keeping her eyes on the downed men, and then raised it to her mouth. "Sir, we have a situation in D27, the corridor next to the coms room."

"What kind of situation?" Templeton's voice was wary and concerned.

"Parsells and Quinn are in need of medical attention, sir."

"What? Why?"

"They attempted to assault Ms. Schilling, sir. I prevented them."

There was a distinct pause. "Are they still alive?"

"They would hardly need medical attention if they weren't, sir."

"All right, I'm on my way. I'll have Doc, Jang, and the captain meet us. It's going to be a pain to get them out of that hallway if they can't walk."

"Feel free to keep them here indefinitely, sir." She lowered her wrist and finally looked away from her incapacitated adversaries to the woman standing in front of her. "Nice choice." She nodded at the wrench on the floor.

Evelyn looked at it. "Oh, thanks. Actually, I meant to grab a screwdriver." She leaned against the wall, then slid down it into a sitting position. Her head hung between her knees, and one of her boots rested in a small pool of Quinn's blood. It was clear to Dinah that she was in shock.

"Doctor Iqbal will be here in a minute. He'll look you over." Dinah attempted to sound reassuring, but her voice came out in its usual flat tone.

"I feel like I just *came* from Medical." She looked up at Dinah, her eyes wide. "This is not my best trip ever." The dark-skinned woman did not reply.

The next two minutes that passed were filled only with Evelyn's breathing, the moans of Parsells, and the bubbling gasps of Quinn. Neither man made an attempt to do anything but lie still. From below, the sounds of climbing came to them as several others clambered up the length of the ship.

"Thank you. Again. Thank you for helping me, and thank you for letting me hit him."

Dinah nodded again. "I wouldn't have let you if you'd had the screwdriver."

Don Templeton knocked on his captain's door. A few moments later, the handle turned and the door opened. Staples stood on the doorway, looking up at him, her brown eyes intense. It was near to three, but she wore slacks and a white tee shirt, and there was no trace of sleep on her face.

"You asked me to come by when everything was sorted out with Parsells and Quinn," he said simply. She nodded and stepped aside to allow him in.

Staples' room was the same size and layout as his. Indeed, it was only a few doors down from his, though hers was quite different in appearance. Like most of the rooms on the ship, it was long and rectangular, and at the far end there were two doors, one a closet, the other a bathroom. That was the extent of the similarities. While his room was sparse with items but thick with pictures of his family, Staples' was packed with books. The variations of gravity on the ship made conventional bookcases impractical, but there were cases of books stacked against nearly every wall. This was the sign of a true bibliophile, as nearly every book a person could want was available digitally. There was no need to keep paper books, especially on a space ship, but the captain did just the same. One was left open on her bed now, and he was just able to read the cover.

"This can't be the first time you've read *The Odyssey*," he said, indicating the book.

She did not turn, but instead sat at one of the two chairs clamped to the floor next to a writing desk. "No, but it's an old favorite. I'm reminding myself that hardship and journeys go together." She sighed deeply, clearly not wanting to discuss the matter at hand, but unable to avoid it. "What did Jabir say?"

Templeton moved past her and took the other seat, putting his arms on the table as he leaned forward. "Doc says they'll be okay. No life-threatening injuries. He stopped the bleeding and stitched them up, but they'll both need surgery in the long run. Parsells' knee is a mess. Busted ligaments, dislocated kneecap. He's also got a bad concussion from Evelyn's wrench. Quinn is worse. His nose and jaw aren't just broken; they're shattered. He's going to need reconstructive surgery on his face. We're lucky Dinah didn't kill them."

She narrowed her eyes. "You know as well as I do that luck has nothing to do with it. If she wanted them dead, they would be."

"Yeah," he assented. "Yeah, I suppose you're right. Anyway, I did what you said. Once Doc stopped the bleeding and made sure they won't die if we stick them in a room, that's exactly what we did. I had Jang escort them to open quarters we have on deck 5, well away from the rest of the crew. They've got food, and water from the sink, obviously. Jang removed their cuffs and locked them in there. You should have seen Jang; he looked ready to finish the job Dinah started. Putting them in there is as much for their safety as anyone else's. They can rot there until we figure out what to do with them."

Staples mused on the information for a few seconds, then said, "Thank you for taking care of that."

"It's my job." He let another few seconds pass. "What *are* we going to do with them?"

She stared absently at the open book on her bed. "What do you think we should do with them?"

"It ain't my decision, Captain. It's yours."

"Of that I am well aware. I didn't ask you to make the decision, Don." She dragged her eyes away from the book and met his gaze. "I asked you what you thought."

"I… I might let Evelyn decide. Or take a vote from the crew. Or I might just beat the hell out of them myself."

"Don, listen to me." She leaned forward, her own arms on the table, and they were less than half a meter apart. "It's impossible to be unbiased about this. We hired them, we trusted them, and they betrayed us. It's not our fault. It's not your fault."

Templeton did not reply, but the look on his face made it clear that he thought otherwise.

"Did you check their references?"

He sighed. "Yes," he admitted with reluctance.

"Did you conduct the background checks?"

"Yes."

"Then it is not your fault. You might have recommended them, but I made the final call to hire them. Either these men have avoided trouble through luck, or… I don't know what, but they were bad before we ever met them. I need you to accept that. 'There is no art to find the mind's construction in the face.' You couldn't have known."

"I feel like we just had this conversation an hour ago, but in reverse." He shook his head, still holding onto the idea. "They rubbed people the wrong way from the moment they came on board. Looking back, it seems pretty obvious."

"They're hardly the first people to rub people the wrong way on this ship. Remember when Dinah first came aboard?" She smiled a bit, hoping it would be infectious, but his face remained stoic.

"Still," he persisted. "I should have... I don't know, should have kept a closer eye. If Dinah hadn't happened by... I just don't want to think about it." His eyes were fixated on his hands in front of him. There was a small fleck of blood, either Parsells' or Quinn's, stuck under a fingernail despite the fact that he had washed his hands three times. Once the doctor had stabilized them, he and Jang had moved them one at a time to Medical and then finally to the makeshift cell.

"You know, just as well as you know that Dinah didn't leave them alive by accident, that Dinah didn't 'happen by.' But we'll come to that when I talk with her." She gathered herself and took a deep breath. "We're not going to perform any 'ship justice.' We're not barbarians. When we get to Cronos Station, we'll turn them over to the authorities and present our evidence. We'll stay as long as we have to in order to testify. Let's hope the wheels turn faster than they do on Earth."

Templeton didn't say anything for a minute as he thought this over. "All right. Will this make you rethink converting a few of the empty crew quarters into a permanent brig?"

She shook her head. "No. I don't run a prison, and I don't want cells on my ship. If we need to make due by converting a room from time to time, then we do, but no cells. In my experience, people rise to the expectations you set for them. If we expect criminals, that's what we'll get."

"We didn't expect these guys."

"No we didn't, but there it is." A few moments passed. "I know you want more, Don. I know you're angry. I am too. These men, members of my crew, attacked a passenger on my ship. A guest." She gestured towards a stack of cased books on her wall. "You know, a number of ancient texts have a lot to say about the importance of hospitality. I don't think we're doing a very good job. In fact, I'm beginning to wonder if anyone will ever hire us again." He opened his mouth to object, but she held up a hand to silence him. "Let's just get through this job first. We'll see what comes after that. After all, we're still ten days out."

"Hey Bethany?" Evelyn called out as she entered the hydroponics bay. "Are you in here?" She scanned the room, the long rectangular space nearly overgrown with various flowers, vines, and vegetable plants. The misting spray had recently ended, and the haze that hung throughout the room gave it even more of an impression of a jungle in a can. A few seconds passed without a response. Just as she was turning to go, a voice issued from some corner of the captive forest.

"I'm here." It was unmistakably Bethany's high thin voice, and Evelyn wondered if the young woman had answered when she first asked and she simply hadn't heard it.

"Where?" the redheaded woman asked. She wandered into the room and pushed aside several leaves with her left hand as she moved.

"Here." Bethany's small frame and jet black hair came into view as she stepped out of the foliage.

"Hey, there you are," Evelyn said cheerily. "Listen, I think you gave me a dud." She held out the object in her right hand. It was the lilac Bethany had given her a few days before. The purple flowers had faded to brown, and the entire plant was bent over as if made of rubber. Bethany seemed to forget her shyness for a moment and took several strides forward to look at the plant. She touched it gingerly, stroking it lightly as the other woman held the potted plant out in front of her; a few petals drifted away from their home and down to the floor.

"It's only been two days!" Bethany's voice was raised. "What did you do?" She voice carried a hit of accusation as she looked up to meet Evelyn's brown eyes with her own.

"I didn't do anything. I just watered it like you told me." Evelyn's voice was devoid of defense.

Suddenly, Bethany appeared to become aware of how close she was standing to her, and she looked back down at the dead flower, blushing fiercely. She gently took the plastic wrapped planter from Evelyn, being careful not to touch her sparsely freckled hands, and carried it away. "I'm sorry," she said, though Evelyn couldn't be sure whether she was apologizing for her accusatory tone, the death of the plant, or just as a matter of reflex. "I'll get you another one."

"I'm worried I'll just kill that one too. I usually do pretty well with plants, but maybe lilacs aren't my thing." Hands on her hips, she inquired, "Have anything else?" in the manner of a curious shopper.

Bethany nodded. "I have a few roses." She put the lilac down on a small table bolted to the wall, then moved into another row and was lost in the green again. "I heard what happened. Are you okay?"

Evelyn heaved a sigh. She was getting that question a lot, of course, but it was nice to know everyone cared so much. "I am. It was scary, but I didn't get hurt. Thank

God for Dinah."

"Dinah's amazing." The reverence in the pilot's voice was clear. A moment later, she emerged again with a miniature purple rose bush suspended in a plastic sealed pot. "They're really pretty." She handed it over to Evelyn, then added, color burning her cheeks, "It's perfect for you." Then she beat a hasty retreat to the jungle, and Evelyn smiled an adoring smile and headed for the door.

Later that evening, Staples sat in the captain's chair looking out at the still-receding sun. It was hard to believe that after everything that had happened, they were still on their way out. She looked forward to the moment when they would enter Earth's atmosphere again and be able to breathe unprocessed air. Charis was monitoring the trajectory of their new course to Cronos, and Evelyn had assured her that coms would be functional shortly. The matter of Yegor still plagued her. After nearly two years on the ship, she did not want to believe the man had betrayed them, had betrayed her. Even so, the pirates had attacked when they were most vulnerable, and that was difficult to ignore.

Evelyn's energy level had been increasing over the last ten to twenty minutes as she had been working, her movements changing from steady to abrupt. Staples hoped that her increased excitement meant that she was close to finishing. It was hard not to watch her. Even if, as she suspected, the woman had had surgery to make herself more attractive, that did not change the fact that she was gorgeous. Of course, as plastic surgery had become more prevalent, safer, and cheaper, it was not unusual to see perfectly symmetrical faces that conformed to all the textbook definitions of beauty, but there was an openness, an approachability about the computer scientist's looks and manner that was impossible to deny.

Finally, Evelyn detached her surface from the main console, turned around, and spoke. "Captain, can I speak to you privately?" Charis looked up from her work, but didn't say anything. Staples considered telling her it was fine to speak in front of the other woman in the room. She certainly trusted her navigator, but she decided to indulge her guest.

"Sure. We can retire to my quarters if you like."

Evelyn stood up and tucked the surface into a holster on her belt to free her hands for the climb down ship.

A few minutes later, Evelyn followed Staples into her quarters and closed the door behind her.

"What's up, Evelyn? Were you able to get coms working?"

"I did that half an hour ago." Her eyes were wide, and Staples frowned but said nothing as she waited for the explanation. "Since then, I've been examining an anomaly I found in the coms and radar data."

"Well, it's been offline for days. That's to be expected."

"No." She shook her head and produced the surface from her belt. She woke the screen to show the captain a great deal of data and charts that meant very little to her. "It's from before Yegor took down the coms system to install the new suite from the satellite."

Staples' eyes narrowed and she inclined her head. "Explain."

The redheaded woman drew in a breath, searching for layman's terms. "So I was looking at the data that the radar and coms were recording. I wanted to review everything that the ship had monitored and recorded since we left Mars. I was using it as a baseline to measure against the upgraded systems. I was looking through it in condensed form, just at a glance. Nine days of data in about two minutes. That's why I noticed it."

"What?" She stood a few paces from the other woman, and though the chair was next to her, she had no desire to sit. That sinking feeling had entered her gut, the same one that had come over her when they had most recently faced off with the *Doris Day*.

Evelyn looked at her levelly, hoping to convey the gravity of what she was about to say. "Minute to minute, even hour to hour, everything looked normal, but when I looked at it all together, it was obvious: your radar data was has been faked since sometime in your - our- seventh day out. It's like a business that lies about their income to get around paying taxes. From year to year, it all looks legitimate, but when you look at the big picture, patterns emerge. Once I noticed that, I looked more carefully at the coms data. That's been faked too, and almost from day one."

Staples' stomach dropped another few inches. "How is that possible?"

"My current theory? You have two different problems here, and two different causes. I think the false coms are coming from another ship, one that's been following you and rebroadcasting an edited version of Martian chatter."

Staples nodded slowly as understanding began to dawn. "We've suspected that there's another ship out there. The missiles that destroyed the pirate ship, as we told you, were not fired by us. If they were right behind us and far enough back, we wouldn't have seen them. That also explains Jordan."

"Jordan?"

"I was expecting a message from a friend on Mars within a few days of leaving for Cronos. I never heard from her. I suspected that something might have happened to her, but then, she's a tough cookie, so that didn't make much sense." She pursed her lips in frustration. "Whoever is following us must have intercepted the message and kept it out of the rebroadcast they sent on to us."

"Could they have read it?"

"Maybe. It would have been encrypted, but any encryption can be broken given enough time, or so I'm told. What about the radar on day seven?"

"I hate to say it, but this is the more disturbing part. The radar went down because of a computer virus in your mainframe. Someone on this ship uploaded it sometime during the seventh day after we left Mars."

Staples sat down in the chair. "You're saying that even if Yegor hadn't taken the coms and radar offline, we still wouldn't have seen the pirates coming."

Evelyn nodded and sat down across from her. "That was exactly what the virus was designed to do. It was feeding false data to the radar systems, showing them empty space. Like the coms jamming, I only noticed it because of the regularity of its reporting. It's actually an amazing virus. I've worked with them before, but I've never seen anything like this. It's highly advanced. It slipped past your firewalls without them even noticing."

"You sound impressed," Staples said despairingly.

"I am."

"If it was so impressive, why didn't it do more damage?" She was leaning forward now, her hands on the sides of her head.

"Because it wasn't programmed to. It could have taken out your engines, your navigation, probably even life support. This virus could have left *Gringolet* a floating hunk of metal, one full of frozen and suffocated bodies, I might add. If it didn't do it, it's because whoever wrote it didn't want to hurt you."

Staples understood. "It's the same reason that the pirates used stunners. Whoever wanted you off this ship was determined to do it without killing anyone." She paused and took a breath. "So let's go through this. There are, by my count, two parties at work here. One is following us and blocking coms from Mars. The other hired, or blackmailed, or threatened someone on my crew to install a virus in our mainframe, a non-lethal virus, so that non-lethal pirates could sneak up on us and abduct you. And when those pirates tried, the first party, our mysterious ship, fired missiles at them and destroyed them. I suppose it need not be said that they don't share our second party's concern for the sanctity of life."

"This brings back to our earlier question. Why me? Why do I matter?" Evelyn's brown eyes were wider than ever, and she looked quite frightened.

"I don't know, but I mean to see you safely to Cronos station. It may be that the other ship, the one that's tailing us, will also make an attempt to abduct you." She spoke clearly and slowly for emphasis. "I am not going to let that happen, Evelyn."

"Thank you. Plenty of people might use me as a

bargaining chip, if they thought that's what I was. I suppose I should offer to give myself up and all that to save the ship."

"No." She sat back and regarded her gravely. "We don't do that. No one is going to be handed over."

"Thanks." She sniffed a bit and her voice shook. "I didn't want to go. I'm not much for the martyr bit. This is… this has been pretty terrible, but you've been great to me."

Staples was aghast. "Evelyn, two of my crew members tried to rape you."

"Dinah told me you didn't know them. You just hired them."

"That's true; we did." She paused for a moment while she pondered. "And that makes me think that perhaps we should have a little chat with them about computer viruses and pirate attacks."

The other woman nodded, and they stood up to go.

Staples, Evelyn, Templeton, and Kojo Jang climbed down the ladder built into the corridor floor to the hallway at the bottom of the ship. Jang reached the floor first, and he was the first to hear the sound. As the others joined him in standing near the ventral stern of the ship, he looked at them quizzically.

"Do you hear that noise?"

"What?" Templeton asked.

The dominant sounds were those of the engines and reactor, especially this close to the rear of the ship, but Staples thought she could detect a lighter, higher engine sound. "I hear it." She squinted with concentration. "It sounds like a motor." Suddenly, her eyes widened and she took off at a run down the corridor. Jang sprinted after her, and Evelyn and Templeton brought up the rear.

The captain rounded the corner and the end of the hallway that contained the door to the quarters where they had locked Quinn and Parsells came into view. She could see the source of the sound. A small vacuum pump was set up beside the room, and a hose snaked out of it and to the door. The hose, she could just see, was held in place by heavy duct tape.

"Call Jabir!" Staples shouted as she dashed forward. Jang was right behind her, and Templeton jabbed his watch to put the call through to the doctor.

When she got to the door, she frantically seized the hose and tried to yank it away from the door, but the tape and the negative pressure of vacuum inside it held it firm. Jang had the presence of mind to kneel down quickly and turn off the small pump, but still the hose would not come free. Jang and his captain gripped the sectioned blue hose and together they pulled hard.

The tape came away from the door and there was the sound of a miniature windstorm as air flooded back into the room. Staples struggled with the lock while Jang peered through the two centimeter hole that had been crudely cut in the door.

"They're unconscious," he stated matter-of-factly, "but they're both breathing." He stood up and moved away as Staples ripped the door open, the air having equalized enough to provide only a small bit of resistance.

Breathing hard, Templeton jogged up to them and looked around the security chief's form and at the two unconscious and bandaged men in the room. "Doc's on his way."

The four of them stood still for a minute. "First rule of sabotage?" ventured Templeton.

"As the first rule in assassination? Kill the saboteurs?" Jang questioned.

Staples did not answer. Evelyn stared at the two unconscious bodies, not entirely sure how to feel.

# CHAPTER 13

"It's long past time for another ship meeting," the captain said as she faced the crew. They were in the mess hall again, and people were lined up against the walls or sitting at the tables. Templeton and his captain stood next to one another at the far end. As she surveyed the crowd, she saw a crew of faces she knew well. Charis and John stood off to the right, a sleepy Gwen in her father's arms. Dinah stood at parade rest nearby. Bethany lurked in a corner, peeking out from behind the doctor. Piotr sat at the table with an uneaten sandwich in front of him. Next to him were seated Ian and Declan. Yoli sat as well, resting her injured arm on the table. Jang, the ever grim security chief, leaned against the wall near the door, eyes sweeping the room. Evelyn Schilling, the seeming source of all their trouble and a person the captain felt duty-bound to protect, stood her hands behind her back near the bald and gaunt man. *One of these people*, Staples thought, *has betrayed us*.

"I want to be very clear about what is going on. I

want you to know that I considered not telling you everything. There's a good chance that this will upset and disturb you, but I believe that you deserve the truth." She took a deep breath, then plunged ahead. "You all know that the coms and radar were down when the pirates attacked. That was because of Yegor's work with the new coms suite. We have since discovered that someone planted a computer virus in the mainframe since we left Mars. That means it has to be someone on this ship."

She expected murmurs, questions, maybe even outrage, but there was only silence. The crew looked around at one another, but no one spoke. "We have also learned that the other ship out there has been blocking our coms and feeding us false chatter from Mars. Evelyn, would you like to add to this?" She looked pointedly at the woman, and all eyes turned to her.

Evelyn stepped forward and spoke, gesticulating as she did so. "I looked through your past coms traffic to see if I could isolate the transmission signature that was broadcasting, still is broadcasting, the faked chatter. It's complex enough that it carries a signature, and I found a match in your ship's archives. It's a ship called the *Doris Day*."

This time there was a good deal of murmuring. Ian cursed loudly, then looked apologetically at Charis and John. Gwen looked around, seemingly somewhat confused, and John tried to pacify her.

Staples raised her voice to be heard. "We believe," she began, and the discussion subsided, "we believe that the pirate ship was attempting to abduct Herc and Evelyn, our two passengers." The slight smudging of the truth came easily. The captain saw no reason to place all the weight on the woman's shoulders, and from where she stood next to Jang, she looked grateful for it. "Whoever hired the pirates is also responsible for our mole, for the person who uploaded the virus into our mainframe. Now there is no further threat from this virus. Evelyn has assured us that the virus completed its task and then shut itself down. Our mainframe is clean."

There was more muttering at this. Staples distinctly heard the words *relief* and *traitor*.

"Furthermore," she pressed on, "we believe, against all expectation, that it was the *Doris Day* that saved us from the pirates by destroying their ship."

"Why?" Yoli asked. "Why help us? Vey has always been a bastard. He'd never help us."

"We don't know that either, but I suspect that he'd do whatever was required if he were being paid. It is possible that Vey will attempt to abduct Evelyn as well."

"Wait," John spoke up, shifting Gwen away from his face so that he could speak more loudly. "If they want her too, why take the risk with missiles? Couldn't they have killed the people they wanted?"

Dinah caught her captain's eye, and Staples nodded for her to speak.

"Thank you, sir." She turned and addressed John. "I believe I can answer that. The captain asked me to check the stasis tubes. They were each carrying a transponder." She walked forward and placed a small blue disc with a sharp point, about the size and shape of a large thumbtack, on the table next to Piotr's sandwich. "That's the transponder I found attached to the satellite we picked up right after we left Earth." She placed two more seemingly identical discs on the table. "Those are the transponders I found buried in the machinery of the stasis tubes." Before people could begin speaking, she continued. "The missiles that destroyed our attackers were already in motion when I saw them, but that doesn't mean they were accelerating from their origin point. In fact, if they had been, I suspect that I never would have had time to get away. I believe they had been launched by Vey's ship, then powered down when they reached us, waiting for the right circumstances."

"Which were?" Charis asked.

"One: the ability to destroy the pirate ship without destroying us, and two: the condition that they still read that the stasis tubes were on board our ship. The fact that Bauer's tube was so close to the hull breach that it was pulled out into vacuum and destroyed by the explosion is not something that could have been anticipated."

Staples waited a minute to let all of this sink in. There were voices and discussion, but mostly, the crew was silent as they processed. Finally, she continued. "I'm afraid there's more. As all of you know, Parsells and Quinn attempted to attack our passenger." She knew her chief engineer well enough not to compliment her on her role in the prevention of that attack in front of the crew. "We... I decided to incarcerate them until we could bring them to trial on Cronos. Since then, someone has attempted to murder them."

Except for Jang, Jabir, and Evelyn, those standing traded looks and gasps, and those sitting made similar noises. Staples heard Yoli say "good" and saw Ian nod in agreement. She had not expected any sympathy for the men, and indeed she had little herself. "Doctor, would you like to report on their condition?"

"Yes." Jabir took a step forward and leveled his gaze

across the room. "The effects of the hypoxia are more extreme in Mr. Quinn's case than in Mr. Parsells. I expect that patient Parsells will fully recover in time, though his lungs and eyes will need surgery and prolonged therapy if they are ever to be as they were. Patient Quinn has suffered permanent brain damage. He is conscious, but I estimate his IQ to be somewhere around forty-five. I do not think he remembers much of his former life, and many of his day-to-day abilities are gone. He can no longer read or write, and it is quite likely that he will forget his own name from time to time. Make no mistake. Mr. Quinn may be alive, but his life is over."

The discussion that came from this was confused and varied, and Staples did not blame them. Quinn and Parsells' intended crime was a heinous one, but she was not convinced it was one that warranted near brain death.

"Do you think that those assholes are the ones who infected the mainframe with the virus? Could they be the traitors?" It was Yoli again, her dark eyes staring at her captain intensely.

Staples nodded. "They could be. We were on our way to ask them that when we discovered the vacuum pump attached to their cell. I still intend to have that conversation with Parsells when he is recovered enough to do so. In the meantime, we have some problems. We may have a saboteur on board. We definitely have a murderer on board. The fact that they did not succeed, or fully succeed, does not change their intention. I know that some of you think that those men got what they deserved. Frankly, I am inclined to agree with you, but that is not for us to decide. We are none of us judges. Mr. Templeton will be conducting an investigation. This is not," she paused for effect and tried to meet the eyes of every one of her crew members before she finished, "how we solve problems on this ship."

"What about our other problem?" It was Ian this time. "What about that other ship out there that's keeping us cut off?"

"That," Staples replied, "I am happy to report, is one problem we do have a solution to."

"So how exactly is this going to work?" Templeton asked. He sat in his customary seat next to his captain in the cockpit, and the other three chairs, astrogation, pilot, and coms were occupied by Charis, Bethany, and Evelyn respectively.

The befreckled woman sitting in Yegor's old chair swung around, her safety belt keeping her snug in her seat. "I don't know how far your rival ship is behind us, but they can't be too far because they've been making course corrections to stay in our wake since we left Mars. Otherwise you would have seen them. Now that we're turned around, facing in-system, they must have dropped back to keep off our radar. The improved coms suite won't help us with that. It's a lot easier for them to follow us than for us to see them following us."

"Ships leave all sorts of radiation trails through space if the engines are thrusting," Charis expanded without looking up from her console.

Templeton nodded. That he knew. "But, now that we're facing them and our coms and radar are up, we'll see them coming if they try to make a move. They ain't going to sneak up on us."

"No, they can't," agreed Evelyn. "The good news is

that they're far enough back that it takes them a while to detect our course corrections. If we turn hard, we should be able to get free of their rebroadcast field and pick up authentic transmissions from Mars."

"And what exactly are we hoping to learn?" Templeton prompted.

"First and foremost, we want to be sure that no one has been trying to contact us about…" Staples gestured to the ship, the crew, and the events of the last few days, "…all of this. We could report it, but I don't see what good that would do right now, and, assuming they intercept it, I'd rather not tell Vey everything that's been going on here. I'm also hoping to hear from a friend of mine. I can only hope that she put her message on repeat when she didn't hear back from me."

"Fair enough. Nothing good comes from being cut off from the core systems," he replied, and was silent for a space. After a minute, he looked at his watch and said, "It's time. The crew should be ready." He tapped his panel. "Dinah, are the engines ready?"

"Yes, sir." The engineer's voice was clear through the speakers. "I feel safe giving you two Gs for an hour, but no more."

"That should be enough," Evelyn chimed in.

Staples looked over at Charis. "Do it."

Two hours later, Templeton and Staples sat at the small table in her quarters. Her body was a bit sore from the hour at two Earth gravities. They had certainly been through greater thrusts, and recently, but after several days of weightlessness followed by a few days of less than half Earth normal gravity, the extra weight had been a strain.

Of far more concern to her was the surface on the table in front of her. Templeton was pouring over his own, looking through the general transmissions that swept through the Sol system, radiating out from the core. Staples had breathed a sigh of relief when she received the message from her friend currently using the name Jordan. After running the decryption program that she had been given when they first worked together on Earth, the woman's message appeared on the surface.

"Any big news from Mars?" She eyed the dead plant sitting on the corner of the desk.

Templeton shook his head. "Nothing to write home about, so to speak. The usual political chatter…" he sorted through the data with a finger on the touch screen, "some guy had an EVA suit accident on Mars…ups and downs on the stock market. What's your friend say?"

"Two things. I can't say that either is a surprise, but they're both important. First, she did some digging into Parsells and Quinn for me. They were prison guards, but they had a bad reputation. Violence towards prisoners, beatings, that sort of thing. It looks like they almost beat a man to death three months ago."

Templeton was shaking his head vehemently. "None of that came up on the background check. I called their direct superior!"

"Apparently, that was part of the problem. Jordan says that Quinn and Parsells were going to be fired over the incident. Their superior, one Tyrone Martin, tipped them off, so they quit before they could be canned. He also convinced the prison to drop the charges when the witnesses recanted their statements."

Templeton's expression was dark. "That's the bastard

I talked to."

"I guess even bastards look out for their friends. You couldn't have known, Don. Sometimes the system doesn't work the way it's supposed to."

"How did your friend find this out?"

"After two years, I've learned not to ask."

"Is she going to *do* something about it, now that she knows about this guy Martin?"

"She didn't say, and I'd rather not conjecture." She paused for a moment. "Check that. I think I'd rather not know."

"So what's the second piece of news?" Templeton inquired. Staples surmised that he hadn't finished castigating himself up for hiring two sadists, but she decided to press on for now.

"The satellite we found, the Yoo-lin mark VII? It went missing less than two days before we left Earth. There's no way that it could have gotten that far on its own, especially once we consider that it was barely moving when we found it. Someone stole it out of orbit and then left it in our path."

He grunted. "Three guesses on who that was."

"The question is not who did it, but who hired the *Doris Day*? Why hire a ship to steal a satellite, drop it right in front of us, fight us for it, then follow us all the way out to Cronos Station, blocking our coms along the way?"

"Don't forget helping us fend off a pirate attack."

"That too," Staples agreed.

"It just doesn't make any goddamn sense." Templeton's frustration was apparent.

"No, it does. We just can't see it yet. We're missing something."

"What?"

Before she could answer, there was a knock at the door. The captain looked at her first mate quizzically, but he just shrugged. He stood up and went to the door. When he opened it, Dinah Hazra stood with her feet slightly spread and her hands behind her back. She wore her usual black tank top and cargo pants, the latter looking newly pressed. Her hair was freshly shorn. Templeton stepped to the side, and Staples stood up to face the other woman.

"Dinah. How can I help you?"

"May I come in, sir?"

"Of course." Templeton stepped back, and Dinah entered stiffly and closed the door behind her.

She stood for a moment in silence, and the other two looked at her expectantly. "Sir, I am here to confess to the attempted murder of Parsells and Quinn."

"What?!" Templeton nearly yelled. His voice filled the small room. Staples regarded her steadily.

"Would you like me to repeat myself, sir?" Staples saw that Dinah was affecting her middle distance stare at nothing in particular.

"Yes, I damn well would!"

Dinah opened her mouth to speak, but Staples cut her off. "I'm sorry, Dinah, but I don't believe you." Her voice was calm and even.

"I am confessing, sir." Her face was inscrutable.

"Okay, let's play this out then," she replied. "Why did you attempt to kill them?"

"I was angry at them for attacking our passenger."

"If you wanted them dead, you would have killed them when you defended that passenger. You could have easily done it, don't tell me otherwise, and if you had killed them then, you could have claimed self-defense."

"It did not occur to me to kill them then. I only decided to do it afterwards, sir."

"Just like it didn't occur to you to tell me you were going to jump in an EVA suit and start cutting power cables on a pirate ship?" She did not wait for an answer. "But fine, let's say that you somehow became angrier after the attack than you were during it. Why not kill them conventionally? You have access to every weapons locker on this ship, and it is abundantly clear that you could kill them even without a weapon."

"Something could have gone wrong, sir. They might have escaped from the room."

Staples looked at Templeton, who still wore a look on incredulity on his face. "I think we all know you better than to think that you couldn't handle two semi-conscious, severely beaten men. So again, why not kill them conventionally?" Her voice carried the air of an inquisitor asking questions to which she already knew the answer.

The engineer's eyes strayed for a bit, then assumed their blank stare again. "I didn't want to get my hands dirty."

"You *love* getting your hands dirty!" Templeton objected. "You're an engineer for Christ's sake!"

"Dinah, I've seen your work dozens of times over on this ship in the last two years. You are a consummate professional. You may indeed love getting elbow deep in grease, but I've never known you to do a sloppy job. The hole in the door where the vacuum pump was attached was cut with a torch. Badly. The angles were so poor that whoever attached the hose had to use half a roll of duct tape to get a clean seal. That's not your work."

"I was in a rush, sir."

"A rush job and a bad job are not the same thing. We also know, all three of us, that you would never leave a job half finished. Even if I believed everything you've said here, which I don't, by the way, there's no way that you would not have stayed to ensure that the job was finished."

Dinah stood stock-still and stared at her invisible point on the far wall.

"Dinah, it's a noble gesture, but I need to know: who are you protecting?"

A moment of silence passed. "Please accept this as my confession to attempted murder, sir."

Staples heaved a great sigh. "Fine. Don, please call Mr. Jang here with his sidearm." Templeton looked at her in disbelief, but she met his gaze evenly. "Trust me."

Piotr Kondratyev opened the door to his cabin and blew out a great sigh. It was a mess. Clothes were draped over the chairs, on the floor, and on the bed. He was a terrible house-keeper, and he could never be bothered to keep his room organized. This dereliction of tidiness was made far worse on a space ship that regularly underwent periods of weightlessness. He never got around to folding and placing his clothing, dirty or clean, in the dresser provided, and so every time the ship lost gravity, it would float about his room at random. Now that the ship was under thrust, most of it lay where it had fallen, and he stepped over a pair of slacks and kicked a stray shoe out of the way as he headed to the back of the room and the restroom beyond. Paradoxically, he had always been meticulous about his kitchens. His knives, pots and pans, and other utensils and tools of the trade were obsessively

placed in the order he preferred, and he could not abide
anyone disturbing that order, but all of his resources were
spent there, and so he had few left for his living space.

Upon reaching the restroom, he opened the door and
began to rummage through the drawer beside the sink.
The vial he was looking for, a small tube perhaps ten
centimeters long and about half full of a clear liquid, lay
amongst his beard trimmer, toothbrush, and various other
sundry toiletries. At a glance, it might have passed for a
bottle of cologne or some other beauty-related product.
He picked it up and placed it in his pocket. He then knelt
down and opened the cabinet. His hand felt around inside,
up around the basin of the sink, until it fell upon the taser
he had liberated from one of the obscure weapons lockers
in one of the seldom-used holds of the ship. He ripped the
tape away that secured it and placed it into his other
pocket as he stood up. He regarded his reflection in the
mirror briefly; the man he saw was trapped and unhappy,
desperate but determined. He nodded once to himself and
strode through the door.

His destination was one deck down, which currently
meant one deck over, and a few dozen meters of climbing
hand over hand down the slatted ladder in the corridor. It
only took him five minutes to get there. When he reached
the door, he climbed off the makeshift ladder on to the
flooring provided by the bulkhead surrounding the hatch
at his feet. He closed it as quietly as he could to provide
solid ground to stand on. He produced the taser from his
pocket and flicked it once, watching the blue electricity
crackle in the still air. Adrenaline surged through his veins,
and his stomach was a mess of snakes, but he had no
doubts. He forced his breathing to slow, blowing out

another large sigh. Once he placed the taser behind his back, he knocked on her door, feeling disturbingly like a high school student with flowers on a first date. A few seconds later, the door opened, and he made to lunge inside and strike the woman with the taser, rendering her unconscious. He froze as the visage of Kojo Jang greeted him, the stunner pistol in his hand pointed at Piotr's chest.

*I have made entirely too many trips here lately*, Clea Staples thought to herself as she looked around the medical bay. Templeton stood next to her, armed with a pistol, and Piotr Kondratyev sat handcuffed and sullen on a bed. The doctor was at the back of the lab, bent over his surface, attempting to ascertain the contents of the vial they had removed from her cook's pocket. Though Jang had all but insisted on staying, Staples had assured him that he was not needed. The baldheaded Russian had not put up a struggle. Indeed, it seemed that now that he was caught, all the fight had gone out of him. There was no trace of the anger that had driven him to strike the counter when he learned that Yegor had been killed. Staples wondered idly how much of that fury had in fact been directed at himself.

"Piotr," she said. He did not look up. He was slumped, his large belly protruded, and she could only see the top of his head and his dark brown beard with its light salt and peppering. "Piotr," she said it louder. He did not move, but breathed heavily through his nose. "I want you to tell me what the doctor is going to find in that vial."

"I don't know."

"I don't believe you," she replied immediately. "You know something about it. Tell me."

"It not supposed to kill. Only make stupid." He

spoke quietly to his stomach and his cuffed hands clasped before him.

"Make stupid?" She looked across the bay at Jabir, who caught her eye and shrugged.

"There are poisons and chemicals that will damage the brain in various ways without causing death," the doctor conjectured. "That does help me refine my search." He bent back to his surface to continue his research.

She directed her attention back to the traitor on her crew. "Why do you want to damage Evelyn's intelligence?"

He shook his head, his beard scraping against his shirt. "Don't. Just paid to."

She held up a small storage drive. "We found this taped to the inside of your bathroom sink. Is this the drive you used to install the virus into our mainframe?"

He did not look up, but he nodded.

"Who paid you? Where? When?" She was attempting to remain calm, but her voice rose as she spoke anyway. Beside her, Templeton radiated tension. She was sure that he would like nothing more than to beat the handcuffed man senseless.

"I don't know. Skinny man. No name. On Mars. Emailed me, offered much money. Said no one get hurt." He shook his head at this.

"Keep talking," Templeton prompted angrily.

"Told about pirate attack. Said no one get hurt, they just take girl, not hurt her. All I have to do is install virus."

"Then why the poison?" she asked.

"If pirate attack failed, said I had to do it, or no money."

"Why? Why did you need to damage her? Why is she so important?" Staples was furious at him, and it took a great deal of restraint not to yell, to shake him. His refusal to look her in the eye was making it far worse.

He shook his head again slowly. "Don't know. Didn't ask."

"Look at me." He did not move. "Goddamn it, Piotr, look at me!" The imperative impelled him to raise his head, and she regarded a broken man. His eyes were red rimmed and tears could not be far away. No one had laid a violent hand on him, yet he looked beaten nonetheless. He met her eyes. "Why did you do this? Why did you betray me? I've known you for years!" Now she was shouting. Templeton shifted uneasily, perhaps preparing to stop her from attacking the cook, and Jabir was looking up at them now as well.

"My brother-in-law is gambler. Much debt. He and my sister have many children. He… left. She needs money for children."

"We would have helped you, Piotr!" She wanted to shake him, to slap sense into him, to yell at him loud enough that his past self would hear her and make a different decision.

He looked down and shook his head again. "Too much money. People want Katya to pay his debt. Much too much. Small man gave some, said much more to come. But no money if she got to Cronos and did job."

"Maybe that's what this is all about," Templeton offered. "Someone wants Cronos station to fail. Awful lot of trouble to go to. Rival company, maybe?"

"It's a pretty roundabout way to go about it. It's hard to believe that there aren't simpler and more thorough ways to cripple a liquid-hydrogen mining station in space." She pondered this for a moment.

An idea struck the first mate. "Can your friend look into who supplied the money to him?"

"It's an idea, but that will probably take some time. I'll ask her once we get to Cronos. I'd just as soon not have Vey intercepting that transmission. I don't know if they broke her encryption program, but I'm not feeding that bastard any information I don't have to." She looked back at Piotr and raised her voice. "So, I'm going to run through this, Piotr. Tell me if I get anything wrong. You were contacted and offered a great sum of money to stop Evelyn from reaching Cronos and doing her job. Some small man on Mars, and we'll want more of a description than that before we're done, gave you a vial and a drive loaded with a computer virus. You were to upload the virus when we were about six days out from Mars. You knew the pirate attack was coming and you were assured that it would be non-lethal. I'm sure Yegor's parents will not find that comforting." The man winced and sniffled when she said the coms officer's name.

"If the pirate attack failed, you would have to get your hands dirty. I'll assume they gave you a means of injecting Evelyn when she was still in the stasis tube. When we woke her, you had to find another way to get the liquid into her system. At some point, Evelyn came by the mess hall for a bottle of water, and you gave her one that you had already tampered with. I would imagine you were frustrated when that didn't work. It was just luck that she didn't drink that water. You did, however, succeed in killing the plant that Bethany had given our guest." Piotr's head seemed to sink lower when he heard this. "When a few days passed and she didn't turn stupid, as you say, you realized that you'd have to take the direct approach. We're less than a week out from Cronos and time is short, so you planned to stun her and pour the vial down her throat. Except that Evelyn took the dead plant to Bethany, who brought it to me. It didn't take us that long to figure out where the water had come from and who had given it to her. Of course, we couldn't be sure, so we moved Evelyn to another room and had Mr. Jang wait for whoever came knocking.

"I didn't want it to be you. I really didn't, Piotr." She shook her head, her feelings mixed. "You know, we've known there was a traitor on board for a while. I really thought for a while that it might have been Yegor, and that he had been attempting to join the pirate crew rather than fight them off. But no, he just died trying to defend this ship from attack, from an attack that you helped orchestrate." Piotr was crying now, silently, tears wetting his shirt over his stomach, but Staples hadn't finished twisting the knife. "I don't know why he charged into B17 by himself, but I can guess. He died thinking that the pirate attack was his fault, that it was his choice to take down coms and radar that allowed them to sneak up on us. And it's true: they would have gotten the drop on us because of that, but they tried only because you had agreed to sabotage my ship." She regarded him for a few seconds. Templeton and Jabir looked on.

"My ship!" she screamed at him, blood filling her face, the rage uncontrollable for just a second. Templeton put a hand on her shoulder, but she was calm again, and she shrugged it off without looking at him. "I have one more question for you, Piotr." She hoped he would look at her again, but he continued to sit and sniffle. "Did you try to kill Parsells and Quinn?"

# CHAPTER 14

Piotr Kondratyev stood in front of the crew and confessed his crimes. They were back in the mess hall, the de facto town hall of the ship, and it seemed to Staples that every time they returned here of late, her crew was smaller. She trusted the people arrayed in front of her to control themselves and to do the right thing, but prudence had still cautioned her to have Templeton explain to everyone several hours earlier most of what they would hear Piotr say. She wanted this to be about apology and acceptance of responsibility, not outrage and violent reactions. This time John had decided to sit out and keep Gwen with him; the last discussion had been more intense for her than either parent had liked. So now there were only eight crew members looking at her: Dinah, Charis, Bethany, Jabir, Jang, Ian, Declan, and Yoli faced their captain, her first mate, and the handcuffed cook who stood before them. Their passenger, her arms crossed on her chest, stood with the crew,.

Piotr finished his explanation in his broken English

and apologized, again, insisting that he was assured that no one would be hurt.

"What about me?" asked Evelyn, taking several steps toward him, her arms dropping and her hands balling into fists. "How is losing my ability to do my job, to *think*, not hurting me?" Her lips were quivering, and she was obviously livid.

Piotr just shook his head, refusing to meet her eyes.

Staples redirected the moment by speaking up. "Piotr has one more thing to confess." The bald cook looked at her with eyes beseeching, and she returned that gaze with steely resolve. He would get no mercy from her.

"I…" he began, "I tried killing Parsells and Quinn." It was clear that the majority of the room was not expecting this, and there was a chorus of shocked murmurs from nearly everyone. Dinah neither spoke nor looked around at the others.

After the voices had subsided somewhat, Yoli spoke. "So what now, Captain? He betrayed our ship. He could have gotten all of us killed." Her implication was clear, and it seemed others agreed with the cargo roadie. Staples doubted if many would object if she announced that she was going to throw Piotr out of an airlock, but that was not her plan.

"We'll already be seeking out a magistrate when we arrive at Cronos station so that we can hand over Parsells and Quinn and press charges. Now it looks like we'll be sticking around for two trials."

Yoli snorted, obviously not satisfied, and she was not alone. Many ships, Staples knew, operated on their own system of justice. They weren't supposed to, of course, but traveling on a space ship was much like plying the seas had been several hundred years earlier. The crew members on a boat might have been morally and legally obligated to follow the laws of their motherland, but in international waters with no one around to say otherwise and problems that needed addressing, it was easy to take the quick and dirty route. She did not doubt that many captains and their crews had pushed murderers and rapists out of airlocks and falsely reported their deaths as accidents. There were any number of ways to die in space, and space ships contained only the recording devices that their captains or their corporate sponsors allowed. Staples had made a very conscious choice to not make her ship into either a prison or a surveillance state, and so there were no cameras installed around the ship. She had regretted that decision on occasion, and more than once on this job specifically, but most of the time she would rather have a mystery on her hands than have a crew who felt as if she didn't trust them. Trust, she had learned, works both ways.

She decided to at least attempt to mollify them. "I know that not everyone agrees with my decision, or believes that these men will get what they deserve if we turn them over to a magistrate, but that is how we do things on this ship. Being a captain may give me the right to be a judge, but I have no interest in being one."

Yoli and Ian did not look happy, but there were no further challenges from them. After a moment of silence, Templeton spoke. "Look, we're only five days out from Cronos Station, people. I know it's been a hell of a trip, but we're still flying, and we're going to get there. We'll get Ms. Schilling to her new post, drop these jokers off, get fixed up, and head home. Let's just try to get through this, okay?" The question was rhetorical, and while no one answered, there were some nods and general noises of agreement from those assembled. Jang came forward to take Piotr back to his makeshift cell next to the cabin where they had deposited Quinn and Parsells in. As the rest of the crew filed out, Templeton leaned over to Staples and said under his breath, "I need to talk to you."

She nodded. She knew exactly what about.

Staples walked into her neatly arranged room with Templeton on her heels yet again. As she turned around and he closed the door behind him, she said, "You know, if we keep this up, people will start to talk." He did not laugh. "We could at least make it your place and not mine next time," she tried again.

Don Templeton put his fists on his hips and looked at her, his sandy grey head cocked to one side. "What are you going to do about Bethany trying to kill those men? Did you see her face when-"

"When Piotr confessed to trying to kill them?" she interrupted him. "Oh, I saw it."

His eyes grew a bit wider with realization. "You knew. You knew it was her."

The last traces of levity left her face, and she pursed her lips and nodded. "I suspected."

"Since when?"

"Since Dinah came here to confess. I don't doubt that she'd die for every member of this crew, but there are only a few she'd lie for. Bethany was the most likely candidate. I don't know what that girl's been through, but it doesn't take a psychologist to figure that she's got trauma in her past." She sat down at her seat on the table; a small ring of dirt from the dead plant still marked the surface near the wall. The plant itself resided in Medical with the doctor. "Would you sit down with me, please Don?"

Reluctantly, he took a seat. "So what are you going to do?"

"I'm going to talk to her."

"Talk? That's it? I love that girl, you know I do, Clea, and she's a hell of a pilot, but you can't have her walking around free after she tried to kill someone on your ship. Hell, she basically did kill Quinn."

"And we'll dearly miss him." She couldn't help the sarcasm.

Anger clouded his face. "I'm not saying he didn't deserve it - don't you dare imply that I am - but you can't just have members of your crew killing off other members of your crew. Not without your say-so, anyway."

"I can, actually, do anything I want on my ship. Everyone was thinking it up in the mess hall. But there's a world of difference between executing a traitor and going easy on someone who punishes a criminal."

"You want to illustrate that difference for me?"

She considered for a moment, then shook her head. "No, I don't. I don't think Bethany is a threat to anyone else on this ship."

"Really? Do you have any evidence for this thought? And what if she hears some rumor that my marriage ended because I brutalized my wife and kids, not because I'm gay, and she decides to slit my throat in my sleep?"

"You didn't brutalize anyone, Don, and it wasn't a rumor that those men sexually assaulted Evelyn. It was a fact." His look conveyed as well as it could *yes, but still*. "I respect your opinion, Don, and I always want to hear what you have to say, but this is how I'm going to handle this. I haven't made my decision yet. I am going to talk to her. Then I'll decide what to do about this. If anything." She added the last two words to drive home to him that, in the end, her ship meant her rules.

The man sitting across from her was clearly not fully content with this. "It's not time to worry yet," she added. "Let me talk to her and I'll decide what to do. Then you can be angry with me if you like."

"That's not good enough, Clea, not by half. You can't just sweep this under the rug, and you can't just swat her on the wrist because she did something you wanted to do but couldn't. It's not fair to her to use her as your Mr. Hyde." Her eyes widened slightly, but before she could respond he barreled on. "Yeah, that's right, I can make a literary reference too. And I'm not done. If I remember that book right, the poor guy spent so much time indulging his dark side that he couldn't ever come back. You doing it through a proxy doesn't make it any better. In fact, I think it makes it worse." Veins strained in his neck and his breath was coming quickly, but he seemed to be done for the moment.

Clea kept his gaze for nearly a full minute after he had finished speaking. Finally, she looked away. "Maybe you're right, Don. I don't know." She shook her head. "This is new territory for me. I just know that I can't send Bethany away. I can't lock her away either. I can't turn her over. Can you imagine her in prison? Can we at least agree that that shouldn't happen?"

Templeton sat back and stared at the wall for a moment, then turned back to her. "I'm not convinced she doesn't belong there, but I'll say I can't imagine it doing anything good for her. But Clea, she's unstable, and that makes her dangerous."

"I'm not convinced of that," Staples responded almost from instinct, then cut off his objection before he could make it. "To anyone besides Quinn and Parsells. Just... just let me talk to her. I'll decide from there. It *is* my ship."

Templeton was clearly still angry. "Yeah, it's your ship. You can kick us all off and run it anyway you like."

Staples' tone softened. "I don't want that, Don. That's why I'm asking you, not telling you, to trust me."

He sighed and said, "All right. But if you don't deal with this right, it's going to come back to haunt you." He seemed to push the subject to the back burner for the moment, but there was another pot ready to boil over. "It's also worth mentioning that you basically just lied to your whole crew."

"And I wish I could say that it was the first time I've ever done that, but it's not. The truth may come out at some point, and I'll deal with it if it does, but in the meantime, I can't have the crew looking at their pilot, the person who handles some of the most sensitive and dangerous situations on this ship, as a murderer. We've been through enough on this job. We don't need to lose any more faith in each other."

"Do you still trust her to do that job?" he pressed.

She sat back in her chair and crossed her arms over her chest. "Absolutely. The job? Yes. Whether she can function as a member of this crew, well, that's why I want to speak with her."

He was pensive for a minute, then begrudgingly assented. "All right. I don't know if I trust her, but I trust you."

"Thank you." She smiled a bit, but it was tight and brief.

"How did you get Piotr to agree to confess to that in front of the crew if he didn't do it? Does he know about Bethany?"

"No, he doesn't know about Bethany. And while I thought there was a chance that he might agree to confess to protect her, I couldn't count on it, and I couldn't take the chance of telling him that I was all but sure that she did it. So I offered him a deal."

"What kind of deal?" He leaned forward, equal parts curiosity and skepticism.

"We'll be leaving him on Cronos Station. If, and this is a big if, we can get someone to hire him as a cook there, we'll skip the trial. Instead, I'll tell his manager what he did and provide them with all the evidence to prove it. Piotr will stay on that station for the rest of his life."

"That's not much better than spending the rest of his life in a jail. Why would he agree to that?"

"Because if he does, I will give his cut from this job to his sister and her kids. As long as he is working, he can send money to her as well. He may never get to see his sister or his nieces and nephews again, but they'll grow up thinking he's a great guy who took a job in space to get them money, rather than a turncoat who betrayed his crew and got a fellow countryman killed. If he ever leaves that station, I'll turn all of the evidence over to the authorities and ruin his name."

"And what about that story you just spun to everyone about putting him in front of a local judge?"

"Once everyone's calmed down a bit and they're not

looking to lynch anyone, I'll tell them about the deal, minus the part where he unwittingly covered for Bethany." Templeton's face was still somewhat accusatory. "It's not a lie, Don. I don't need to tell them *when* I made that deal."

"You're still playing fast and loose here." He thought for a moment and then added. "That's actually a hell of a deal you're giving him. He's lucky to have you as a captain, or he was. But knowing what he is and what he's done, do you really think you can talk someone into taking him on?"

"Probably not," she shook her head. "But I suspect you can."

For the first time since he entered the room, a ghost of a smile touched Templeton's face.

Staples was tempted to approach her pilot in her natural habitat. She thought that the hydroponics bay would make her more apt to open up, but she couldn't take the chance that someone would walk in on them. The bay was public space on the ship, and though few went there apart from the waifish young woman, the conversation was too important to leave to chance. She thought that calling Bethany to her cabin would terrify her, and she might assume that her captain had figured out her crime, panic, and do something stupid. In the end, Staples decided to go knocking on her door after her shift ended.

Bethany's cabin was one deck down from her own, though in all the time that Bethany had been on the ship, Staples had never had cause to go there. Now that she had, she wondered what the room would look like. It took only a few seconds for the occupant to answer. She was already dressed for bed, swimming in an oversized long-sleeved black tee shirt and checkered flannel pajama bottoms. Her makeup was still on, and her darkened eyes widened appreciably when they fell upon her captain.

"Hi Bethany. May I come in?" Staples tried to keep it light, but she guessed the other woman's heartbeat had just picked up considerably. Bethany nodded and stepped aside.

The room, though it Staples' in size, seemed smaller for all its clutter. One wall and the ceiling were covered in posters, some depicting black-clad rock bands, their faces obscured under layers of makeup, while others displayed classical and new pieces of art. Waterhouse's "Lady of Shalott" abutted Xinui's "Dire Girl". There were few pieces of open wall left. Staples recalled that Bethany rarely left the ship when in port, and wondered when she had accumulated all of her wall art. Her bed was disheveled and a sketch pad lay open on top of the messy sheets. Pillows were stacked atop the mattress and against the wall. A makeshift wooden shelf for plants was evidently designed to hold leafy visitors from the hydroponics bay, and two lilacs rested, lightly secured, on the stained surface. Staples noted that the shelf was nicely finished and wondered if Bethany had bought it or if a fellow crew member had made it for her. If so, she suspected she knew who.

Staples closed the door gently and indicated one of the two chairs that stood on either side of the table. The other was covered in discarded clothing; evidently, she was not used to visitors. "May I sit down?" Again, she nodded. "Won't you join me?" Bethany sat on the clothing and looked at her captain, wide-eyed and demure.

Staples took a deep breath and collected her thoughts

before beginning. "Bethany, I want you to listen to me very carefully. I know." She paused a moment to let that sink in. Her interlocutor sat motionless in the other chair facing her, her hands clasped in her lap. Staples was at least relieved to see the dark brown eyes were on her and not the table or the floor, as she had expected they would be. "I know you tried to kill Parsells and Quinn." She paused again to measure the other woman for a reaction, but there was nothing outwardly visible. "I want you to tell me why."

The moment stretched, and Staples was just about to give up on getting an answer when Bethany spoke. The voice was light and reedy as usual, but not whispered. In fact, Staples thought she had rarely heard the girl speak with so much conviction. "They deserved it."

"That's not for you to decide. That's my job. I decide justice on my ship." Her voice was firmer than she intended, but it was just as well. The pilot's future depended on her understanding of this point.

"Has that ever happened to you?" Bethany replied almost immediately.

Staples had not expected to be challenged in that manner. She shook her head. "No."

"Well it has to me." Her voice was rising. "Over and over. And if it hasn't happened to you, you don't get to decide, because you don't know!" The captain found herself taken aback. She had come here to put this crew member in her place, to remind her of the way things worked, but she found herself on the defensive.

"Bethany, I... I'm sorry. I'm sorry something terrible happened to you. But there's a reason that judges and magistrates don't know, mustn't know the people they are judging. It's so that they are capable of being unbiased. People who have been wronged have trouble being objective." This was an age old argument, and one that Staples thoroughly believed in, and yet, as she sat across from this woman who had been terribly wronged, it sounded weak and hollow.

"But you know your crew, and you still judge them. You're biased," Bethany objected. She wasn't yelling, but her voice was still strong and full of conviction. "If you had the people who killed Yegor here, would you be as unbiased as some judge or magistrate?"

"Bethany, Yegor wasn't killed. His death was an accident." Before she could object, Staples raised her palm. "But I understand what you mean. If I had those people who cut a hole in my ship and dragged my crew member and my passenger out into space here… I guess I wouldn't be objective. I would try to be, but I suppose I would fail simply because I'm human."

"Maybe you would be the best person to judge them," Bethany challenged her.

"Maybe," the captain speculated. "But I'll say this. I suspect that I would treat people who did that to another ship differently than the people who did that to mine. So it's not fair. Some people have always argued that criminals should be turned over to their victims, but I'm not here to debate that." She felt that she had to regain control of this conversation. "I am here because I need you to know that what you did was wrong. I don't know if it was morally wrong. That's up to you to decide. But it was wrong for you to attempt to kill people on my ship. That is up to me to decide. This is my ship, and in the end, that means I make the rules. I need you to understand that if you're going to stay here."

Bethany's brows knitted together in confusion. "Stay here?" she asked in little more than a whisper. "Aren't you going to turn me in?"

"I would hardly have cut a deal with Piotr to cover your crime if I had. Oh, I've thought about it. I really have. I just don't know what good it would do. I do know that prison would kill you, and I think you've been through enough hell in your life."

Bethany looked at her suspiciously. "Did Dinah tell you...?" She let the sentence drift off.

It was Staples' turn to shake her head. "Dinah didn't tell me anything. If you've chosen her for a confidant, then you've chosen well. But now you're going to need another one: me."

The suspicious look was replaced with confusion.

"Here's the deal I'm offering, and it's not open for negotiation. First, I need to hear from you, with utter conviction, that you will never challenge my authority on a matter like this again. I don't care what your reasons are. You cannot do something like this again. If you can't convince me of that, then there's no point in my continuing to speak."

Bethany thought, really thought it seemed, for nearly a minute. Finally, she nodded and looked Staples in the eye. "I promise. I'll do anything to stay on this ship. I wanted those men dead. I still do." Staples watched her small hands briefly curl into fists in her lap. "But I need to trust you. Taking care of bad men is your job, not mine. I'm sorry." This was more even than Staples was hoping for, and that made it just barely enough.

"Okay, I believe you. Second, for the rest of this job,

you stay confined to quarters," she saw the young woman tense, "or the hydroponics bay." The tension eased. "Which we might as well designate as your quarters anyway. Third, and this may be the most difficult for you, we start bi-weekly therapy sessions." The look she got was a combination of confusion and skepticism she had seen before. "I don't have a psychologist onboard, nor do I intend to hire one, but you need to talk about what happened to you and what you're going through. You can talk to whomever you like, Dinah if that works for you, but you will also need to talk to me. I'm no psychologist, but I've been through my share of troubles, and I am a good listener. And when I say talk, I don't mean sit in a chair full of sullen hostility waiting for the hour to pass. I mean you talk, openly and willingly. No matter how hard it is, you try. You said you would do anything to stay on this ship? That's the condition. You deal with this toxicity before it kills you… or anyone else."

Bethany thought this over for a shorter time before acquiescing. "All right."

"Are you sure? It's easy to say you'll do it. It's not so easy to actually do it."

"If it's you, Captain… yes." She looked over at her lilacs, then back in Staples' brown eyes. "I will try really hard, but please be patient with me."

She nodded thoughtfully. "As long as you're giving me your all, I will be. We can start now."

Bethany did a very good imitation of a deer caught in headlights.

"Why don't you tell me how you learned to fly?"

Charis knocked on the door of the ReC as she pulled

it open, then looked down into the room. From her vantage point above her, she could see Dinah standing at one of the control panels, her hands on the surface currently attached to it. The grey tank top she wore complemented her muscular silhouette, and she did not look up at the woman who leaned in from the hatch above.

"Can I come in, Dinah?" Charis ventured when the engineer did not answer.

"This isn't my room," she replied flatly. Charis took that to mean that she was free to do as she liked, so she swung down from the bulkhead and clambered down the recessed rungs in the floor-made-wall, being careful to close the door above her. When she reached the bottom, she made a bit of a show of straightening her white tee shirt and pushing her hair back from her face. If she hoped that Dinah would use the time to turn around and face her, she was disappointed.

"Can I talk to you?" She felt the idiocy of the statement. She was already talking to her, and again, the ReC wasn't Dinah's room. She was free to do as she wished. The woman had a way of making her feel foolish, even useless, and as much as she respected her, she was tempted to tell her to forget it and climb back the way she had come. Instead, she closed her eyes and counted to ten, hoping that Dinah would answer and make this easier. When the answer didn't come, she opened her eyes and found the other woman was indeed giving her her undivided attention. She had turned around, and though she was leaning back against the control panel, she was staring at Charis with a focus that she thought might unnerve the devil. They were perhaps a meter apart, and now that she had the other woman's full attention, she was not so sure that she wanted it. It was moments like this that made her understand why her daughter was afraid of the woman. She forced herself to proceed.

"I wanted to thank you. For helping Evelyn." Dinah opened her mouth to reply, but Charis forged ahead. "I know that you don't like being thanked in public. At least, that's what I've gathered, but I wanted to say it, so I waited to catch you until you were alone." She looked away, aware that she was rambling but feeling unable to stop. "Actually, I might have used that excuse to put this off a little bit, but we're only two days out from Saturn now, and I really do want to thank you." She paused. It was evident Dinah was going to wait until she was well and truly finished before replying. "So thank you," she added, quite redundantly.

The other woman waited a good ten seconds to speak. Finally, she said, "You're welcome, I suppose, but I didn't do it for you. Why do you care?"

"Why do I care about Evelyn?" she stammered, unsure how to answer.

"Why do you care enough about her to make a special trip to the ReC to thank me? I hadn't realized that you two were friends." Charis suspected that Dinah knew that she and Evelyn were not friends, had barely spoken since she had been awakened.

"We're not, not really. I mean, I like her fine. She's beautiful." She shook herself to stop herself from babbling again, and instead focused on what she wanted to say. "I wanted to thank you because I know that you would do the same thing for me, or for John, or for Gwen."

"Ah. Then you're welcome."

Charis cast around the room for something to look at

to avoid the other woman's gaze. "The way you take care of this crew, Dinah, it's amazing." She forced herself to look back in those intense dark brown eyes. "But it's not just crew to me. This is my family here, on this ship. And I'm really glad you're here."

Dinah said nothing, but she nodded once, deeply, whether in understanding or gratitude, she didn't know. Charis even thought she detected the hint of a smile.

"Can I ask one more thing?" Charis decided to press her luck.

"Go ahead."

"How did you know? That Parsells and Quinn were… what they were doing, or trying to do?"

For the first time since she had turned around to face the navigator, Dinah looked away for a moment as she considered. "Templeton asked me to take a look at them when they came on board. I did, and I didn't like what I saw. They must have bought alcohol when we stopped on Mars, and that's when they started drinking. They hid it well, mostly, but that night they were drunk. So I kept an eye on their whereabouts."

She said it so casually that Charis almost missed the implication. "You put a tracker on them?" She gaped. There was no other way, save sneaking around behind them, that Dinah could have known where they were. "Do you know how the captain would feel about that?"

Dinah shrugged her muscular shoulders. "I consider it following orders."

Charis' face was a mix of awe, fear, and wonder. "Do you put trackers on all of us?"

"No." The answer was as flat as her opening greeting.

"Some of us then? On Gwen?" She was trying to

decide whether to be horrified or comforted.

"Do you trust me, Charis?"

The question surprised her. She considered it carefully before answering. "I suppose I do."

"Then don't worry about it," she said dismissively.

An image came into Charis' mind, like a small clip of a self-made film, of Gwen wandering lost and alone through the corridors of the ship, darkness and shadows threatening from every corner. Suddenly, a dark silhouette appeared behind her, wrapped her protectively up in its comforting arms, and spirited her away back home. It was an absurd image, dramatic and silly. Gwen knew the ship as well as any of them if not better; she had spent nearly a quarter of her life on it. Even so, she had decided how she felt.

"Good," she nodded. "Keep it up." As she turned and climbed back out of the room, the engineer turned back to her work.

Staples couldn't remember a time since she had bought her ship where people had come knocking on her door with such frequency. This time it was her guest, Evelyn Schilling, and that made her smile.

"Evelyn, please come in." It was late evening, and they were due to arrive at Cronos station the following afternoon. The captain was still dressed in her work clothes, but a book rested open on her desk and a hot cup of tea wafted fragrant steam into the air.

"Thank you. Chamomile?" she inquired.

Staples nodded. "Would you like a cup?"

The freckled computer scientist shook her head. She had changed to a pleated skirt and a tight fitting blue top that elegantly showed her curvaceous figure. Her hair was down and loose.

"Is there an occasion?" the captain asked, referring to her clothing.

Evelyn closed the door behind her. "Not really. I spent a few minutes digging this out. I guess I wanted to look nice and come thank you for getting me to Cronos Station."

Staples sat and gestured for her visitor to do the same. "Evelyn, we've been over this. This has got to be the worst charter flight in the history of charter flights."

She sat and countered, "Actually, I think that list is topped by flights that crashed."

"Fair point," the captain conceded.

"You and your crew have done everything you could to make me safe. I am so sorry about Yegor." Her face was the picture of sympathy.

Staples nodded gravely. "I am too. He was a good man. And I must say, again, how sorry I am about Herc. I'm sorry we couldn't save him."

Evelyn looked at the wooden tabletop for several seconds, and her eyes welled with tears, but then she looked up and smiled, blinked them away, and forced cheer back into her voice. "Me too. I didn't know him that well, but he seemed like a great guy. I know you did everything that you could."

"I'm not sure your employers will see it that way. A whole lot of people would call this a bad job."

"Well they weren't here," Evelyn said defensively. "They'll have my statement, and if they read it, they'll know you did everything you could to save us, to save me."

"Apart from one of my long-time crew members betraying me and our choice to hire two would-be rapists, I'm inclined to agree with you." She sighed.

"That's not your fault. Look, no one blames the boss of Libom Pangalactic if one of the Senior VPs gets caught insider trading." She saw Staples start to object, and hastily added, "Or turns out to be a serial killer."

"I suppose they don't, at least not publicly. Anyway, you don't have to thank me. It's my job." She took a sip of her tea and smiled.

"Mind if I ask how you ended up with this job?" Evelyn ventured.

"Oh, that's a long and rather sordid story," she said dismissively, waving her hand.

The other woman leaned forward, resting her chin in her cupped hands, and smiled. "Those are my *favorite* kind. If I let you make me a cup of tea, will you tell it to me?"

Staples laughed. "You drive a hard bargain." She considered the woman for a moment. There was no way around it; she was stunning. It was a warm, expressive beauty that made her want to share secrets and dreams with her. It was a loveliness that said she could be understood; all she had to do was speak. Staples found herself, to her own amusement and surprise, genuinely attracted to another woman for the first time since a particularly drunken night in college. She looked into those big brown eyes and thought *screw it, why not?* "If you agree to keep it to yourself. Chamomile okay?"

Evelyn sat back, evidently happy. "I promise, and chamomile sounds great."

Staples took another sip of her cooling tea, then stood up and walked to the electric teapot on a small counter at the back of the room. As she fished out a second mug and a bag of tea, she began to speak. "I used to work in benefits and compensation at a major metals and textiles company. I'd rather not say which one, or where. I started in the job not long after getting my Masters in Industrial Psychology." The water began to boil, and she poured it into the teacup.

Evelyn looked at the containers of books around the room. "I would have pegged you for an English major, not psychology."

"I was both, actually. They're both really the study of the same thing." She handed the mug to the other woman and sat down again. "Several years later, I found myself in my mid-thirties doing quite well. I was a senior Vice President, still handling executive compensation, bonuses, that sort of thing. Then things began to get complicated. I noticed, much like you did in going over the coms and radar data I suppose, some irregularities in the company's budget. The kind of things you only notice when you work in the field for a decade or so: subtle stuff. I like to run a tight ship, so to speak, so I did some investigating. I had the idea that one of the other VPs was embezzling, so I kept it secret and conducted my own investigation. My plan was to go to the board once I got enough evidence.

"It turns out there was some money missing, and it was going into someone's private bank account, but it wasn't anyone who worked for the company. Further searching turned up more money transfers, rather large cash outlays to other non-company employees." She took another sip of her tea. "Well, I knew payoffs when I saw them. The disturbing thing was that there was no way these payoffs could have happened without several VPs and the President knowing, even if there was no evidence they had signed off on it. I probably should have dropped it, pretended I never saw anything, but I'm not very good at that, so I hired someone to look into it.

"I had the names of the people who received the funds. They were all government officials in China, most of them centered in a particular province, one that contained a manufacturing plant run by my employer. Again, you'll forgive me for keeping the details to myself. It didn't take too long for my private investigator to ferret out some information. It turns out that manufacturing plant was polluting the local ecosystem. Elevated cancer and seizure rates, radiation, poisoned drinking water, all of those horror stories you hear about from the 20th and the beginning of the 21st centuries. The payoffs were to keep the local officials quiet.

"I suppose I shouldn't have been that surprised, but I was. Of course what they were doing was illegal, and most of the abuses of that kind had ceased when we cleaned up our act around the mid-century, but it was more than that. The company I worked for had been very public about their aggressively environmentally safe manufacturing base. It was one of the reasons I chose to work for them. I had really believed in them, and the fact that they could do that, that my co-workers could do that to not only the planet, but their fellow human beings as well just disgusted me. I felt used, as if I had been helping this happen for years, albeit unawares. I had trouble hiding my feelings. I could barely walk down the hallway at work and smile at those people. Then my private investigator disappeared, and it went from disturbing to scary.

"The company offered me a new position at a

different branch. It was more pay for less responsibility, and the signing bonus was huge. I mean really obscene. About the same time, I received some pictures of my brother's family. Just pictures emailed to me, nothing more, but the message was obvious. It was a payoff. I could shut up and take it, or walk and take my chances. They figured if I took the money and tried talking later, they could use the payoff to drag me down too. I suspected they'd use the same money and allocation strategies to cover my bonus as they did to pay off those government officials. I didn't know what to do at first. I didn't want to be complicit. Part of me wanted to walk away and never say a thing, to just leave the whole thing behind, but I didn't think that they were offering an option C. So I took the money."

Evelyn, who had been rapt until this point, was aghast. "You didn't!"

Staples held up an index finger and smiled a bit. "Stick with me here. I took the bonus and the job, transferred to the new branch, and started working. I figured once a few months had passed, they'd stop watching me so closely, and that's when I started moving. I didn't feel safe going to the authorities. The government isn't like Chicago in the 1920s, but it's still vulnerable to corruption, and I figured my employer would anticipate that move. Instead, I contacted a rival manufacturing company."

"Nice," the other woman said, finishing her tea.

"Well, that didn't go quite how I expected. Turns out, they really were a standup company, and they didn't want to get their hands dirty. They told me they weren't interested in corporate espionage, sabotage, or flinging mud. They told me to go to the police. That stymied me for a bit. When you get really disillusioned with the world, it can be rather baffling when someone takes the high road. But I guess they weren't *that* squeaky clean, because about a week later, a woman contacted me and said that she could help me."

"Who did she work for?"

Staples shook her head. "As far as I know, no one. We met, I gave her all of my evidence, and that was it. She didn't want any money. Three weeks later, the facility in that prefecture in China burned to the ground. All of those VPs that were involved had bad things happen to them."

Evelyn looked shocked and somewhat appalled.

"I don't mean they were killed. They just suffered… terrible, life-altering setbacks. One invested all of his money in a company that went under. Another's house burned down; no one was hurt. Another one's spouse received photos of her infidelities, that sort of thing. I didn't do a thing. After another month, I quit my job, and they didn't put up a fight. Someone broke into my house not long after that and destroyed my computer files. All evidence that I had of what they had done is long gone now, which is fine. I tried to make it easy for them. I thought for a bit that they might come after me, but then I realized that there's no point. The damage was done; there's nothing I have or know that is actionable, and revenge isn't something companies are often interested in. Revenge is expensive, so why bother? The woman, who said her name was Janae, helped me use a lot of my bonus money to relocate and help the families that had been affected by that factory. I used most of the rest to buy this ship." She cast her eyes about the room as if she could see the entirety of the ship around her.

Evelyn's eyes were bigger than ever. "So this woman, she's what, some kind of eco-terrorist, scale-balancer?"

"You know, I'm not entirely sure what she is, besides a good reminder that we should all do the right thing because someone is watching. She's also a good friend to have, though sometimes I do have to pay her."

Evelyn snapped her fingers and pointed at Staples. "Jordan, right?"

The captain just smiled a little bit, shook her head, and put a finger to her lips.

The evening was winding down, but there was still some conversation to be had, and both women seemed to be glad of it. It was approaching twenty-three, and Staples was thinking it was time to call an end to the visit when there was another knock at the door. As she stood up to answer it, she half-whispered conspiratorially to her guest, "I wonder if it will be good news or bad this time."

When she opened the door, Templeton stood in front of her, breathing hard despite the low gravity. "Parsells hanged himself."

"Both," Staples muttered. Evelyn stood up behind her and looked at the first mate.

"What?" he asked, confused by her response.

"Nothing," she said, shaking her head. "Damn."

"Some problems take care of themselves?" Templeton ventured.

"I suppose. I…" she turned and looked at Evelyn, then back at Templeton. "I'm fairly sure I hated the man, but I didn't want this."

"Maybe he did." the woman behind her said. She was standing very erect, and she spoke seriously in her deep

270

voice. "Maybe he thought he could do something good."

"Maybe I guess." Templeton shook his head. "To hang yourself in four-tenths Earth gravity. Can't have been pleasant or easy."

Staples rubbed her face and her eyes with her hands for several seconds, and her skin was flushed when she took them away. "Well, I guess we had better go deal with this. Is Jabir there?"

"Yeah, he's there. I called him first. Wanted to come tell you in person."

"Thanks for that, Don." She put a hand on his shoulder. "I cannot wait to get to Cronos and for this whole job to be over."

# CHAPTER 15

As *Gringolet* approached the sixth planet from Sol, many of the crew set aside a few minutes to climb down to the rear observation decks at the stern of the ship. The brownish-yellow planet and its seemingly perfectly formed rings grew until they nearly filled the windows, and even those who had been on a Jovian run before found an excuse to take some time gazing at them. Saturn was nine times the size of earth, nearly one hundred times more massive, and its burnished surface was illuminated in part by the distant sun. In additions to the rings, dozens and dozens of moons orbited the planet, the most well known of which was Titan.

Titan's surface consisted mostly of ice and rock; that composition, along with its size, made it the ideal location for an outlying Jovian base. Titan Prime was a settlement that made use of rock to expand and build, water ice to provide sustenance, and the methane, ethane, and propane naturally occurring in the atmosphere to provide power. Over the past thirty years, it had become nearly self-sufficient. Though semi-regular shipments brought in people, luxuries, and supplies as needed, the continually expanding community had nearly obtained an ecological balance between their population, hydroponics, and small animal farms. What had started as a facility had burgeoned into a small town housing over five thousand residents. Titan Prime had a strong manufacturing base, and though it was largely financially independent at this point, it had begun as a joint venture funded by energy companies and several Earth governments. Now it provided workers to local mining stations such as *Gringolet's* destination. It also functioned as a staging ground for further expansion in to the Jovian sector, a launch place for interstellar probes, and was the planned launch site of future interstellar missions to neighboring stars.

In the cockpit, Staples sat in her seat with her crew around her. John Park had been pulling extra shifts for the past few days, mostly with Evelyn, to learn the coms systems well enough to operate them when she left the ship. She had offered to handle the coms during the approach, but John wanted the practice, and despite all they had been through, Staples wanted to make a show of finishing the job with her crew in place. John sat in what Staples still thought of as Yegor's seat, corresponding with the station to plan their final approach. Charis had done her job well, and they were a scant five hundred kilometers out from the station when she cut thrust and left them adrift. In front of them, the now tiny star at the center of the system twinkled only marginally brighter than all of the other points of light in the unending darkness, and Staples could barely imagine the small blue dot where they had begun this job. It spun on nearly a billion kilometers away, and as happy as she was to be safely to their destination, she would be much happier when they were headed back home.

"Captain, we're ready to approach," Charis said, looking over her shoulder, her hair floating up above her in the zero G environment.

Her husband glanced over at her, and then back at his captain and nodded as well. "Cronos Station says they are ready to receive us."

Templeton leaned over a bit towards Staples. "I recommend we go in at about a hundred and fifty kilometers per hour, nice and slow. That'll give the crew plenty of time to rearrange their rooms and get strapped down again for final approach."

"That will get us docked in, what, three and a half, four hours?" John said.

"'Bout that," Templeton replied.

"I can't wait to get off this ship," Charis said with a sigh. She looked around again and added, "No offense, Captain."

"None taken," Staples said, and she meant it. They had had a rough time of it, no question, and smaller things had made the larger difficulties of this journey even more stressful. It wasn't just that they were grieving for a lost crew member, overcoming the trauma of a lost passenger, dealing with feelings of betrayal from a traitor, and fearful of a second attack from a ship that never came. They each had been forced to take on extra duties to cover those of crew members they had lost or incarcerated. People had had to cook their own meals, a practice most were unused to onboard, or else make do with snack food like granola bars or cheese and crackers. That extra time took away from their grieving and coping processes, and most found themselves busier just when they wanted more time to themselves. They could all use a break, and their captain intended to give them one. "Bethany, please turn us over."

"Yes, Captain." Perhaps it was Staples' imagination or the lack of sleep, but she thought that the pilot's voice carried a bit more confidence than usual.

As the ship pitched upwards from their perspective, Templeton picked a spot on the floor to root his eyes to, and Sol slid down and away from their view. A minute later, the enormity of Saturn loomed in front of them, dwarfing the tiny ship and filling nearly all of the windows arrayed around the cockpit. The rings floated above them, and Staples regarded them through the skylight on the ceiling. In front of them hung Cronos Station, owned and operated by Libom Pangalactic. Like most Jovian orbital mining stations, it was cylindrical in shape, and it spun along its axis to provide gravity for its workers.

"Bethany, bring us in at one hundred and fifty KPH relative to the station," Staples said. She felt the light pull of gravity pushing her into her seat for a moment as they accelerated up to speed, and then her safety harness was the only thing holding her in place again. She looked over at her first mate and nodded for him to take over.

"All right people, you've got one hour to get your rooms in shape and get back up here. This may have been a tough run, but let's end it right." Nearly everyone undid their belts and headed towards the exit, and after Bethany locked her controls, she joined them.

As usual, Bethany brought them into docking seamlessly. Cronos Station offered a number of docking tubes that extended at various points from its curved outer surface. The ship, in turn, was equipped with docking ports in several places. The dorsal port was ideal for connecting with a cylindrical spinning station, as it allowed *Gringolet* to take advantage of the spin of the station to maintain Earth normal gravity during their visit. Matching up the ship with the spin of the station was a tricky maneuver. It first required steering the ship as though it were flying circles inside a very large drainpipe. Once that was achieved and the velocity of the ship matched the spin of the station, the docking tube and port had to be lined up. Bethany had only John's information from the station's coms and the data on her surface and console to guide her, but after ten minutes of micro adjustments, a number considered small by those in the profession, they were sealed tight.

Once the docking procedure was completed, the crew stood under near Earth normal gravity for the first time in several weeks and walked or rode elevators up to the top deck. Staples wanted to take a small delegation with her when they disembarked, and she had chosen Charis, Dinah, Templeton, and Jabir to escort Evelyn off the ship. After they had made their introductions and Staples had explained the situation, she planned to allow everyone else a chance to take advantage of whatever shore leave Cronos had to offer, which she assumed was not much. The group assembled in the dorsal airlock, and once the security checks had been passed, they climbed up through the open shaft and into the station proper.

There were four people waiting for them as they climbed through the hatch and stood on the inside of the cylinder. The first thing that struck Staples as she emerged was the smell. It was a scorched scent, one of heated metal, oil, and machinery. The temperature was the next factor to greet her; it was perhaps five to seven degrees cooler than she liked to keep her ship, though the lowered temperature made sense for an environment where men and women were constantly working. She had encountered the same thing in other high-energy environments, including many restaurants. It was a choice that made it clear that those in charge favored the comfort of their workers over that of their guests, and small wonder, as Cronos Station received few of the latter.

As the first out of the hatch, Staples had climbed up into a receiving room. While the rest of her chosen crew lifted themselves up and into the chamber, she examined the people arrayed in front of her. A man, assumedly the one in charge, stood in front. He looked to be in his early sixties and was tall and slim. His hair was a smattering of white and grey, and his skin was lined and burnished. Hard green eyes looked out from his face, and they regarded Staples with cold detachment. Those eyes were set deep in a long, thin, unfriendly face. Staples assumed this was Gordon Laplace, the commander of the station.

Next to and slightly behind Laplace stood a shorter portly man, also white, with brown hair that was graying at his temples. Unlike his commander, he greeted the emerging crew with a warm smile that touched his blue eyes. His face was round with heavy jowls, and his teeth were crooked. Standing behind these two were security personnel, one man and one woman. Though they were armed, their pistols remained holstered, and they stood at ease with their hands behind their backs. They were there, Staples assumed, not because her crew constituted a threat, but as a formality of greeting. Or, she thought, Laplace just liked to have an entourage. Staples and Templeton stood awkwardly facing this group until everyone had clambered up and to their feet. The captain could hear her first mate breathing heavily beside her. They stood in a room perhaps seven meters square. Chairs lined one side, and the plaster walls were painted a soothing but sterile beige.

Once Jabir, the last out, had gained his feet, Staples stepped forward and extended her hand. "Are you the station commander?" she asked.

"Gordon Laplace, yes." He did not step forward to meet her hand, but received it where he stood. "You must be Clea Staples." She nodded in return, and then made introductions all around.

Laplace identified the man next to him as Davis Ducard, his second in command. He did not bother introducing the security officers. His handshakes were curt and quiet, but Ducard smiled and murmured "hellos" and "good to meet yous" as he made his way from person to person.

"Where is Mr. Bauer?" Laplace asked.

Staples had been hoping to put this off, but there really was no way around it. "I'm afraid he's dead." Laplace's eyes widened, and Ducard's jaw dropped. "We communicated to you that we had been attacked by a pirate vessel. For security reasons, both yours and ours, we did not communicate the full extent of our losses. We have reason to believe that another ship was following us, and we didn't want to risk giving them any information that might provide them with a tactical advantage over us."

The commander seemed to think this over for a minute before nodding and answering. "That seems to make sense, though it is clearly a great loss." His voice was rough but not unpleasant. "Did you suffer losses as well?"

Staples unconsciously looked at the floor for a moment as she answered. "Yes. Our coms officer, Yegor Durin. He was killed fighting our attackers. Several other crew members were injured, one permanently."

"I see. I am sorry. I trust you have Mr. Bauer's remains, as well as a report to submit?"

"Of course." The man's steely demeanor unnerved her a bit. She produced a small surface from a clip on the side of her belt. Ducard stepped forward, his smile now tinged with sympathy, and produced his own surface. With a gesture, the file she had prepared was transferred, and she returned the surface to its place at her side.

The report was one she had put together in the past few days over several cups of coffee and much internal debate. She had considered being fully forthcoming with the commander, but in the end she had decided to give them an edited account of their journey. This was aided by Evelyn's insistence that she not report Parsells and Quinn's attack on her; she said that it would reflect badly on Staples and the crew, and it was her determination that her new employers understand that the crew of *Gringolet* had done their very best to see her safely to Cronos. The final report omitted not only the attempted sexual assault, but the altercation with the *Doris Day* over the satellite, Jordan's report, and Piotr's betrayal. It was not stretching the truth to write that the replacement of the coms system had rendered the ship vulnerable to the pirate assault. Piotr, as far as Staples was concerned, was a matter of internal ship business, as was the suicide of Parsells. She had related that Quinn had been exposed to vacuum, which was true enough, but she had bent the truth in stating that it had happened as a result of the pirate attack. This painted him in a more heroic light than she would have liked, but in the end she decided it didn't matter.

Laplace nodded. "I'll look that over as soon as I have a chance. I am eager to hear how an armed escort failed to safely conduct its passengers to this station." Though the statement was made without emotion, Templeton bristled, ready to come to his captain's defense, and Ducard looked with embarrassment at his Commander.

Before anyone could speak, Evelyn stepped forward. "Commander Laplace, I am very excited to be here." He turned his icy gaze to regard her. "I am thrilled to have the opportunity to work here with you, and I don't want us to get off on the wrong foot, but I have to object. Clea – Captain Staples and her crew did everything they could. They were attacked by professionals who were trying to kidnap Herc and me. If they hadn't been so good at their job, I wouldn't be standing here. Please, you have to believe me: none of this is their fault."

Laplace faced her and considered another moment, his eyes never leaving hers. She returned his gaze with the same intensity. "Very well." Without looking away from his new computer scientist, he addressed Staples. "Does your report contain some theory as to why these 'professional pirates' wanted to abduct my new employees?"

"It doesn't, I'm afraid, other than the probability that good computer scientists can be hard to find for pirates in Jovian Space," Staples returned.

Laplace grunted and continued to look at Evelyn. "Well, I'll have to read over your report. I assume you'll be here for a few days." It wasn't a question. "I'm sure I'll have many more questions. In the meantime, Mr. Ducard here," he finally turned his eyes to Staples and gestured to the man at his side, "will see to your needs. Payment, of course, is something that will also need to be discussed, but only once I contact my superiors."

"I assumed as much." Staples tried to keep her face expressionless, but the conversation was turning out to be every bit as difficult as she had feared it would be. "We may be here longer than a few days. We need to refuel and resupply, that's true, but we also need repairs. The destruction of the attacking ship damaged ours, including our engines."

Ducard stepped forward, smiling his crooked smile again. "Sure, sure, I can help with all of that. Get you fixed right up. Can even maybe spare some manpower if you can pay their wages."

Laplace stared daggers at his subordinate and cut in abruptly. "No one is to lose time from their shifts. If anyone wants to spend downtime working on their damaged ship for some extra cash, I would allow that, but it must not interfere with production." The tone of his voice made his dim view of the other man clear.

Ducard took a breath with an expression on his face that was as good to Staples as an eye roll, but said, "Sure, sure, no one will lose shift time."

Staples decided that the shorter man was by far the better conversationalist, and addressed her next query to him. "I have a crew that could really use some shore leave, such as it is. Do you have any local watering holes or other R and R facilities they could make use of?"

"We sure do!" Ducard grinned widely.

"I am glad to hear it." She gestured to Templeton, who seemed to have calmed some since Laplace's implied insult. "I'd like to send Mr. Templeton here with you to make arrangements for repairs, refueling, and relaxation." She looked at Laplace. "I'll see Evelyn to her new quarters." She did her best to match the commander's tone, one that did not brook discussion. "And I'll make arrangements to have her effects and Herc's body brought aboard."

Laplace looked them all over, his gaze lingering on Evelyn, then he nodded curtly and strode towards the door, followed by his entourage of security guards. Ducard gestured that way as well to Templeton, and he followed. As Staples turned around to speak to Dinah about making the arrangements, Evelyn leaned over to her and whispered, "he was sexy, don't you think?"

The captain looked at her in surprise, then smiled and shook her head.

Once out of the receiving room, Templeton found himself in a miniature version of a city. There were small walkways that might have been streets crisscrossing back and forth; each ran by not a city block, but a large building. The structures were anywhere from one to three stories high, and were uniformly made out of metal. Some sported decorations. Four buildings down on the left, for example, a wooden sign swung over the door naming the building, a bar Templeton assumed, *Saturn's Satyr*. As he watched, a man and a woman in dirty work overalls walked through the door, speaking animatedly. Other buildings around them seemed to be server rooms, administration buildings, and guest quarters. He thought that the bunkhouses must be located in another section of the cylinder. Looking up was somewhat dizzying to him; he expected to be able to see the far side of the cylinder with similar buildings and people walking among them on what for him seemed to be the ceiling, but there was another cylinder, smaller, within this one blocking part of that view. That cylinder ran the axis of the space station like a thick straw in the center of a thermos. Long sections of the smaller cylinder emitted light, and that seemed to provide the majority of the illumination in the metal shell.

As he gazed up at the large steel housing, perhaps half a kilometer across, he stopped walking. Ducard stopped as well and looked up. "That's the elevator system for harvesting liquid helium from the atmosphere," he said by way of explanation. "See, the top half of that is cable," he pointed towards the end of the station oriented away from the planet it orbited, "and the rest is the elevator itself. We lower it down into the upper atmosphere and siphon off the liquid helium. It comes up the hose attached to the cable and then we pipe it into a storage tank."

Looking at the way the far walls curved up and around the elevator housing was giving Templeton vertigo, so he dropped his head and refocused it on his tour guide. "Where do you get the storage tanks?"

"We make them. We have several foundries on the inside of the station." He pointed vaguely towards the far ends of the larger cylinder. "We use reshaped rock and some ore we mine from the local asteroid belt. That's where we get our water too. When we fill one up, we slap a booster rocket on it and off it goes to Earth." It was clear the large man was enjoying explaining the workings of the station to his guest, and for his part, Templeton was curious to hear about it. "Libom catches them and decelerates them, then puts them into orbit and presto: profit." Ducard showed his broad grin again. "You know, my great granddad did something similar in his day; he worked on an oil rig a hundred years back. I guess it runs in my family."

As they resumed their walk, Ducard in the lead, Templeton asked, "Did he work for the same company?"

"Yep, Libom's been around a long time. For an oil company, I guess they adapted pretty well to a planet that ran out of oil." He chuckled at his own joke. "Left up ahead," he added more quietly. After they had gone past a few more buildings, the curve of the floor had become obvious, and it felt as though they were walking uphill. Templeton began to breathe harder, and Ducard was already sweating, but this did not stop him from speaking. "I guess you guys had a rough time out there. What was it like?"

Templeton had expected this. The two men obviously shared more than their positions as seconds in command. The two of them were about the same age, and Templeton assumed that like Staples, Laplace had picked a more personable subordinate to handle social matters, an area that he was clearly lacking far more than the captain. Two dirty and smelly men in even dirtier and smellier clothes walked past them, and Templeton would have bet money that they were headed for *Saturn's Satyr*. "Just like the captain said," he replied succinctly, trying to convey a finality indicating that he did not intend to expand on the subject.

Ducard may or may not have understood his charge's guardedness, but either way, he did not press the matter.

"We'll head to the EVA office and see what they can tell us about getting your ship repaired. Refueling shouldn't be a problem, we've got a fair bit of uranium, and though you'll find better food at Titan Prime, we can probably fill your fridges just fine if you don't want to make the stop."

Templeton decided to press his own line of questions since the moment seemed appropriate. "Speaking of EVA suits, what happened to your last computer scientist? I heard he died in some kind of an EVA accident?" He hoped it sounded nonchalant.

"Matt Spicer," Ducard said. They were clearing some uniform buildings and had just emerged into a long park. There was green grass stretching perhaps half a kilometer down the long axis of the station, and it was dotted with a few fountains and several benches. People strolled here and there, couples sat on benches, and a few people relaxed on the grass with surfaces or drinks and food. It was a more idyllic scene than Templeton had expected from a latter-day oil derrick. "This is Cronos Park. Not a very original name. Thought we'd walk through it on our way to the EVA office."

"Sounds nice," Templeton replied. "I'm surprised that Libom paid to ship all this dirt out here." He glanced down at the greenery as they walked along a stone path towards a fountain. "It is real grass, isn't it?"

"Sure, sure, real grass." Ducard looked down at it as well, and gesticulated as he explained. "Paying people to live far from home has always been a tricky business. You know, five hundred years ago, used to be people'd work a few towns over, maybe see their families a few times a year. Then later people would work in other countries, but they'd still fly home for the holidays, that sort of thing. But working all the way out here… it can really get to you. Men and women get lonely surrounded by all this space. They miss their kids, their parents, their friends. Turns out, it doesn't matter how much you pay people; if they're really miserable, they quit. So the company tries to keep them as happy as they can."

"By building parks," Templeton stated. They turned right at the fountain, and he was relieved when the sensation of walking up a gigantic drainpipe disappeared.

"Among other things. They fund the bars here, the gyms, movie theater, pool hall, that sort of thing. We've even got minor sports teams, a full library, bunch of restaurants, all to keep people willing to stay out here and provide fuel for everyone on the core planets. Even with all of that, people get three months off out of every eighteen. The company actually sprang for their own private transport ship to move people back and forth to the core planets. It can take fifty people."

Templeton was surprised; it was unusual for companies to keep their own ships of that size. Most interplanetary transportation was handled either by a few major companies, the natural outgrowth of the airline industry of the early twenty-first century, or by private charter ships like *Gringolet*. "Huh. Why not just have your ship bring Evelyn… Ms. Schilling out here? Why hire us?"

"Because the ship isn't due back here for another month, and we have been in rough shape since Matt died."

Templeton seized the opportunity to learn more. "The computer scientist?" he asked, feigning forgetfulness. "He had an accident of some kind, you said?" He was momentarily distracted by the sound of a light breeze and birds tweeting until he spied the speaker hidden at the edge of the grass.

"Yeah, poor Matt. He was on the elevator down in the atmosphere calibrating the hydrogen pumps. He had to go outside the chamber in an EVA suit to, I don't know, do some computer thing on the intake tubes. We don't like to go out while in atmosphere, but it's not really that dangerous. The EVA suits are rated for it. We don't know what happened. Maybe a small stray meteor," he held up his chubby fingers about a centimeter apart, "maybe a corrosive pocket of gas. He just stopped talking, then all of his vitals went dead. By the time we got him inside, he was too far gone."

"Was there a hole in his suit?" They were coming to the end of the park, such as it was, and Ducard turned them left and towards another group of buildings.

"Yeah, we don't know what from."

Three hours later, Templeton sat at a large surface with Ducard looking at a crude three-dimensional representation of the ship he called home. Ducard's EVA team had taken scans and pictures of *Gringolet* in a small utility vehicle not unlike the one that Dinah had used to claim the satellite from the *Doris Day*, though now Templeton doubted whether Vey had ever really been trying to obtain it. With Templeton's help, Ducard was highlighting various sections of the hull and engines, marking them for repairs, and adding notes about the type of damage as they looked over the pictures. Templeton was adding to these notes with his own knowledge of the ship and how it should look.

Finally, Ducard sat back from the screen and puffed out a big sigh. "I think you're looking at... seventeen days. Maybe more, maybe less, it depends on how many of our crew want to put in extra hours doing the repairs. I know that Laplace won't want to fund those repairs and the extra pay for the crew, but I think I can talk him into it. The hydrogen pumps never did get recalibrated, and we've been running at about half capacity ever since. Having Schilling here should get us up to speed, and hopefully no one will care about a petty cash outlay for ship repairs."

"That's damn generous of you, Davis," Templeton said.

"Hey, the way I see it, you guys got roughed up helping us. It's the least we can do."

Templeton smiled. "You might be from a long line of company men, but you sure don't sound like it."

"Well, I'm middle management. I'm high enough up to spend some of the company's money, but not so high up that my neck ends up on the block if the quarterly earnings are down. That makes me dangerous." He tipped a wink and a mischievous grin at Templeton and leaned back towards the surface.

He returned the grin. "Good place to be, I suppose." His attention turned back to the surface and the highlighted list of repairs. "Still, seventeen days. We were hoping to be back on Mars by the end of April."

"Doubt you'll see that, but you could be back on Earth in time for some May flowers. I'll get working right away on putting a crew together for repairs. I've got my own job to do, but I can come by and check in once they're going. Are you able to stay here and supervise the repairs?"

"Yeah, I think so. Me or Dinah, anyway."

"That your engineer that I met earlier?" Ducard asked as he began to assemble a list of possible candidates for the repair team on a smaller surface in front of him.

"That's her."

"How'd she lose her foot?" The question had was asked in an offhand manner, but Templeton glanced at him sharply. The other man was still intent on building the repair team on his surface.

"I don't know." It was only half a lie. "I'm surprised you noticed."

"Saw it when she climbed out of the hatch. Not too common to see injuries like that. Space tends to kill you when it hurts you." He seemed satisfied with his list. He indicated the names with a hand and added, "I'll contact these men and women and see what we can get together." As he took a step away, he said, "I've really got to get back to work. Is there anything else I can do for you?"

Templeton thought the other man had turned a bit frosty, perhaps sorry he had said anything about Dinah's foot. "Actually, there is. I've got a crewman in need of a job; what have you got in the way of mind-numbingly repetitive tasks requiring little to no intelligence?"

Dinah Hazra walked down the same paths in Cronos Park that Templeton and Ducard had walked only a few hours before. The fountains burbled charmingly, and the recorded birds sang a pretty song, but her goal was not relaxation. Having obtained directions from one of the hosts in the office outside *Gringolet's* receiving room, she was headed to the official cluster of buildings that housed the EVA office, supplies and requisitions, hospitality management, and communications, among other things. Once she exited the park, she quickly made her way past the EVA office and to a broad three-story building made of cut stone. The door was glass, and it said simply *Communications*. Through the pellucid portal, she could make out a reception desk manned by a bored looking young man. She glanced down the slim street in either direction, making note of a man appearing from the EVA building, then looked up. From her narrow view of the cylinder above her, she could make out part of the central elevator mechanism that filled perhaps twenty percent of the total station's volume. A portion of the far side of the station was also visible, and Dinah could see a few people walking back and forth. She had been in stations like these before, but the effect of watching people walking on the ceiling was still a bit disconcerting. She opened the door and walked inside.

Three minutes later, Dinah was admitted to a large room of cubicles on the second floor of the building. The man from the reception desk pointed towards the far wall and said, "Over there," then left to resume his position. Dinah walked past the half dozen or so coms personnel on duty at the moment, most with large can headphones on. They were all working on surfaces on their desk. She assumed they were parsing data into separate files, sending messages to various ships and stations, and perhaps reading and censoring personal letters. The whole organization had a military feel to it. It was familiar, and she knew how it worked.

A moment later she was standing behind the man she had come looking for. He was typing away at his surface, just as the others were. She could see that he was black and he seemed tall, though it was difficult to tell since he was seated. His head sported thick hair that stood out at various angles. She was about to tap his shoulder when he turned around and looked up at her. His eyes were widely spaced, his lips full, and he had a strong chin. She did not recognize his face.

"You're Overton," she said his name as a statement, not a question.

He stood up, tall indeed, and spent a moment searching her face. "Sir?" he asked speculatively.

Dinah nodded. "Good. How did you know?"

His face broke into a grin, revealing straight white teeth. "Well, you wanted me to hear you walk up behind me. I could tell you were making noise on purpose, which meant if you didn't want to be heard, you wouldn't have been." She did not reply, so he continued. "You're not an assassin, so I figured you were a soldier. No accent, so I assume United States military. Marines?"

"For a while," she replied vaguely. "How did you know I outranked you?"

He was thoughtful for a second. "The way you spoke, like you were about to give me an order. I don't know who you are, sir, but you know who I am, and that you outrank me. Or you did. How did I do?"

"Excellently. I can see why you're a communications officer." She offered her hand.

He shook it vigorously. "Yeah, great ears." He pointed to his left ear with his other hand. "Not a bad way to make money out in the world. When did you get out?"

"A few years ago," she replied, releasing his hand.

"Was it the foot?"

"In part." Around most people, Dinah was uneasy discussing her injury. She was uncomfortable because they were uncomfortable. If they found out, they put on sympathetic faces, asked questions as delicately as they could, winced as though they could somehow feel her pain, and generally treated her as though she were still bleeding. By contrast, there was a direct and unassuming nature that most military types adopted after a few years in the service that she enjoyed, and it was a relief to answer without having to hear how sorry someone was.

"I'm going to go ahead and assume that your vague answers are for my benefit and not yours," he said and indicated an empty chair tucked inside his cubicle.

As she took the seat and he returned to his, she said, "You're not wrong." She leaned back in the chair comfortably and laced her fingers over her flat stomach.

"Just tell me one thing. Who was your drill instructor at boot?"

"Gonzalez, same as yours."

The grin returned. "So I could do that thing that people always do, where I ask you something about Gonzalez that's not true, and you correct me to prove that he really was your drill instructor, but why don't you just tell me something that only one of his squad would know."

Dinah allowed herself a bit of a smile. "His breath was awful, unless he'd had steak the night before, then it was really horrific."

Overton burst out laughing. "It's true. Bastard must have never brushed his teeth."

"We had this theory that he did it on purpose, just to make it worse when he was yelling in your face."

He laughed again and pointed at her. "That's a good theory. Probably true." He let out a satisfied sigh. "It's good to talk to someone from the service."

"Likewise."

"There are a few of us scattered throughout the station. We try to get together every week or so for cards or something. You must be off that ship that just docked. Any other military types onboard?"

Dinah shook her head. "Nope."

"Too bad. I'd say you're older than me, so I probably had Gonzalez in boot more recently than you did, and I don't know you. So that leaves one question: how did you read my file? Hard to imagine you hacked station security, especially in the few hours since you docked." His smile still lingered, and his questions carried the air of curiosity rather than suspicion.

"I read it three weeks ago, before we left Mars." Her answer was flat.

"Ah." He thought for another moment. "You were looking for a friend here, someone you could trust. I don't blame you. Working for an energy company is like working for the military, only they're more efficient and far more ruthless." He continued his speculations. "So you either knew you'd need help when you got here, or thought you might and were just doing your homework. I'm curious which it is, though I suppose it doesn't matter."

"It was just in case."

"So something's happened since you left. Word is that there might be some extra money for people willing to do some work on your ship. Does it have anything to do with that?"

"Yes it does." She nodded once.

"Well," he sat up a bit in his seat and fixed her with a more serious look, "how can I help, sir?"

Dinah sat forward, her hands still clasped, her elbows resting on her knees. They were perhaps half a meter apart.

"I know there are some former military personnel in administration on Titan Prime. I need to know if a ship docked there, or anywhere else in around Saturn."

"That's all?"

"Not quite. I need to know if they docked, what their status is, and most importantly, when they plan to leave. I also need to know if those plans change."

"That ain't nothing. They followed you out here?" It wasn't really a question, but Dinah nodded anyway. "Are you looking to have a piece of action done? Because I can't be part of that."

She shook her head even as he spoke. "No, I just need to know. It's really just confirming intelligence, but I need to know if they're going to follow us home."

Overton thought for another few moments. "I might be able to help out. Flight plans aren't public knowledge, but they're not exactly top secret either. It'll be easier if they put in at Titan Prime, but that's certainly not the only option. There are about a dozen moons with refueling stations out here, and most are equipped to receive and sell to commercial flights. What's the ship?"

"It's a Hemlock class armed transport called The *Doris Day.*"

"I'll see what I can find out and get back to you. Let's meet at *Saturn's Satyr* tomorrow night for a drink, say about twenty?"

The slight smile ghosted across Dinah's face again. "Sergeant, are you asking me on a date?"

"Yes, sir," he quipped, his smile broad.

# CHAPTER 16

*Saturn's Satyr* was a corporate approximation of a quirky, independently owned bar and restaurant. The theme, someone's idea of a Greek forests inhabited by dryads, nyads, fauns, and satyrs, didn't really make sense, but in the ten days since they had docked, it was one that Staples had come to appreciate nonetheless. The walls were decorated tastefully with trees, and a few exhibited three-dimensional pieces of pseudo-bark on them. Contributing to this illusion was an array of real and fake trees and shrubs strategically placed about the dimly lit dining and drinking establishment. Here and there mischievous painted eyes peered out from the hollow of some tree or deep in a plastic shrub. The overall effect was kitschy, but also managed to be charming.

Since it was designed to serve a station that operated around the clock, *Saturn's Satyr* never closed. It transitioned smoothly from serving drinks to providing breakfast at about four. Now, at quarter past eight, the captain and her first mate sat across from one another partaking of a passable breakfast of eggs, beans, and vegetables, Staples and Templeton were seated at a green table that had no doubt impeccably matched the green of the walls when the place was first constructed, but time and a tide of alcohol had faded it to a more unnatural shade. While the food wasn't great, Staples was at least grateful for the coffee, which was excellent. She had to hand it to massive companies like Libom; they knew where to spend their money for maximum worker productivity. She was just beginning her third cup when a movement at the door caught her eye.

Templeton followed her gaze over his right shoulder and spied Evelyn Schilling standing at the door. The engineer wore jeans, a faded band tee shirt, and her hair was held back from her face in a messy bun. She wasn't wearing any makeup; her eyes were red-rimmed and her cheeks flushed. It was the most unkempt either of them had ever seen her. When her eyes alighted on them, she did not smile, but hurried over. She crossed the mostly empty restaurant quickly, several pairs of eyes following her from the bar, and dragged a nearby chair up to their table. It made little sound on the stained carpet, and she nearly collapsed into it.

"Evelyn?" Templeton asked, concern in his voice.

"What's wrong, Evelyn?" Staples nearly spoke over the man.

The computer scientist's brown eyes were wide, and up close, Staples could see that the woman had been crying. Evelyn looked at her, then shook her head. She seemed overcome with emotion. She sat still for a moment, her eyes darting back and forth between the two of them, the tabletop, and occasionally the other patrons, most of whom had gone back to their meals or coffee. Staples decided to wait her out, and Templeton followed her lead. Finally, she took a great sigh and opened her mouth.

"I think something is wrong with me." Her voice quavered.

Staples spoke slowly and clearly. "What do you mean?"

Before she could respond, the screens in the corners of the room flared to life and suddenly everyone was looking at Davis Ducard. Only his head and shoulders were visible, and a zippered black work jacket hugged him at his throat. Evelyn took one look at him and all of the energy seemed to go out of her. She put her head in her hands, and then she was the only one not watching the station's second-in-command speak.

"Cronos Station." His voice carried loudly throughout the room. Staples thought she heard an echo of it float in through the front door, and several of the workers moved to silence their watches. He looked deadly serious, and the tenor of his voice matched. "It is with a heavy heart that I must inform you that Station Commander Gordon Laplace died last night." There were gasps and whispers from the other diners, and Staples and Templeton looked at each other in alarm. Evelyn continued to stare at the tabletop, her knuckles white against her fiery hair. On the screen, Ducard drew a deep breath, and then continued. "Doctor Stewart has ruled the death as the result of natural causes. He died of a heart attack in his sleep. We have every reason to believe it was peaceful."

"Then that's about the only peaceful thing he did,"

one of the men at the bar muttered to a woman next to him. She shushed him, her attention on the screen.

"I would like to ask everyone to observe a moment of silence for the deceased," Ducard continued, then bowed his head and closed his eyes. Most of the other people in the room did the same, and Staples traded another look with her first mate, then regarded the top of Evelyn's head. In the silence that followed, the woman stifled a brief sob, and for a moment Staples thought she was going to begin crying, but she maintained her composure.

"Thank you. This is a terrible loss, but you all know that the Commander was a believer in hard work. He would have wanted us to continue the best we could. I will be filling in as Station Commander until the company sorts things out. Details on services will be forthcoming, and grief counselors are available in the medical area." Ducard looked as though he were going to say more, but then he just nodded gravely and the screen went dark.

The noises of discussion in the restaurant began immediately. "Evelyn," Staples said, placing her hand on her freckled forearm, "I think we need to talk, and not here. Will you come with me to *Gringolet*?" Evelyn nodded, and finally looked up to meet the other woman's eyes. She sniffled and wiped the tears from her eyes. "Don?" she asked, and Templeton immediately nodded and motioned to the waiter for their check.

"I'll see you on the ship, Captain," he said as he produced his wallet. The two women stood up, leaving Staples' half-eaten breakfast on the table. Staples swung Evelyn's chair back into place, and together they walked out. Only a few of the patrons watched them leave.

Twice Evelyn began to speak on their walk back to

the reception room and the ship beyond it, but Staples gently asked her to wait. They were nearly halfway back when the captain noticed her chief engineer striding purposefully in their direction. To the best of her knowledge, Dinah had not been sleeping on the ship the last few nights, but she seemed to be coming from that direction this morning. When they met, all three of the women stopped walking. Dinah briefly regarded Evelyn, who seemed to be further from tears than she had been since she had entered *Saturn's Satyr*, then turned to Staples.

"We need to talk, sir."

After a quick glance at the distraught computer scientist, Staples said, "We saw the announcement, Dinah. We know about Laplace."

"Not about that, sir." She looked around, but no one was nearby. "I have intel."

"Can it wait?" She thought that Evelyn might insist on waiting herself, but when she did not, Staples judged that the woman really needed to speak her mind.

Dinah thought for a moment. "It can, sir, but not too long."

"Okay. Come see me in my quarters in half an hour, and bring Don with you. He should be a few minutes behind us, headed for the ship."

Dinah nodded and strode off the way they had come.

Ten minutes later, Clea Staples and her erstwhile passenger sat across the wooden table in her quarters yet again. It seemed to her that she had spent an inordinate amount of time here lately, and for the first time since she had bought *Gringolet*, she considered converting one of the unused rooms into an office.

"Now, Evelyn, please talk to me." Staples was leaning

forward, her arms folded on the table. "How did you know Laplace had died before everyone else?"

Evelyn slumped in the chair, gazing off at nothing in particular, her heart-shaped face still flushed and her nose red. "Because I woke up next to his body." Staples did not react. Evelyn looked at her dubiously. "You knew I was sleeping with him?"

She shrugged and inclined her head. "It occurred to me as a possibility once Ducard made his announcement. Why else would you be so upset?"

"I suppose that makes sense." She plucked a tissue from a nearby box that her host had provided and blew her nose.

Some silence followed, and finally Staples offered, "You seemed attracted to him from the start," in hopes that the other woman would begin speaking.

She laughed a little bit. "No accounting for taste, I guess." She put the tissue down lightly on the table. "He isn't my usual type, I'll grant you, but there was something about him."

"You're not the first person to be attracted to people in power, Evelyn."

She shook her head. "I don't think that was it. At least, that's not usually my thing. Confidence, yes, but not power so much. I don't know, maybe it was. I was definitely his type, I'll tell you that."

Staples thought there was something here, and she seized on it. "What do you mean?" The man had been aloof and hardly genial. It was hard for Staples to imagine him as a sexual being, but of course, she had met him only briefly.

"Well, I flirted with him here and there when we

spoke, and after a few days, he asked me out. When we talked, he admitted that he had a soft spot for red hair and freckles. He said I was really beautiful." Staples tried to picture Laplace as charming or complimentary and failed. "Just his type, he said." She smiled warmly, reminiscing. "I slept with him that night. I didn't love him or anything, but he could be really sweet at times."

"Evelyn, I am so sorry. It must have been terrible to wake up like that."

"It was. It really was." She looked traumatized, as well she might, Staples thought. Anyone would be, waking up next to a cooling body, let alone one they had made love to a few hours earlier. "My alarm went off at seven and I rolled over to touch him and he wasn't warm." Staples thought about sleeping next to a dead lover for several hours and suppressed a shudder. Then she frowned.

"Wait a minute. Seven this morning?"

She nodded again. "My shift starts at eight."

"I'm not a doctor, but that's a really short amount of time in which to conduct an autopsy." She winced at her own statement. This was hardly the time to pursue this line of questioning, she thought, but Evelyn did not seem overly upset by it.

"You know, you're right. I am a doctor, though obviously not an MD, but that does seem really fast to determine cause of death. I guess it makes sense; he did tell me he had had some heart trouble, so maybe the station's doctor just assumed." Even as she said it, it was clear that she didn't believe it, and Staples shook her head.

"Medical doctors don't make assumptions about the untimely deaths of Station Commanders, at least not in my experience. Not that I have experience with this, but-"

The other woman cut her off, not unkindly. "I know what you mean." Her face had taken on a speculative cast, and she was clearly thinking the whole thing through as well.

"Curiouser and curiouser," Staples said absently. There was a knock at the door, a quick rap that was almost certainly Dinah. Staples opened the door; her first mate and chief engineer stood outside. "I'm going to need a bigger room," Staples muttered.

A minute later, Staples' chair was occupied by Templeton, and she sat on her bed. He had objected of course, insisting that she should remain seated, but it was difficult with Dinah preferring to stand, and Templeton wasn't about to sit on his captain's bed.

"Sir, are you sure that this shouldn't be private?" Dinah asked the captain. She turned to Evelyn and added, "No offense."

"None taken. I can go if you like." She made to rise, but Staples waved her down with a hand.

"Evelyn can stay. I trust her, and I'd just as soon she not be alone right now." Evelyn sat back down, looking grateful for the continued company.

"As you wish, sir. I conducted the investigation you requested. The *Doris Day* was hangared at another mining station, a small one operated by Suncorp." No expansion on this was necessary. Suncorp was a power and fuel supply company, smaller than Libom, but competitive nonetheless. "They refueled, took some limited R and R, and left two days ago. I just got word. They were headed to Mars."

"So they just followed us out here," Templeton reasoned. "They don't care what we do now. Unless they're gonna wait for us out there."

Staples shook her head. "I don't think so. There is way too much space between here and Mars. We could slip by them without even trying. No, whatever they were up to, I think it's finished now. Thank you, Dinah. That is valuable information. You're sure of the source?" She knew better than to doubt the woman, but she couldn't resist the chance to learn where the engineer had been spending her nights. Dinah simply nodded, disappointing her. "I assume that's not all you have to say. It's important, but it's not pressing. What's going on?"

Dinah glanced at Evelyn briefly, who was staring at the wall, her eyes still wide. "It's about the Station Commander, sir." Evelyn seemed to tune back in, and turned to focus on the woman standing in front of the door. "He and the second-in-command, Ducard, didn't get along. They put on a good face for guests and the workers, but there are rumors. They apparently fought a lot about how the station should be run, the risks the workers should take, that sort of thing."

"And now Laplace is dead, Ducard is in charge, and he's sweeping the man's cause of death under the rug," Staples continued.

"Under the rug?" Templeton asked, his eyebrows raising.

"It seems," Staples spoke as delicately as she could, "that Laplace was only found dead at seven this morning. For Ducard to call it a heart attack before eight thirty looks a bit suspicious."

"But hardly conclusive," Evelyn rejoined. "I'm not a super light sleeper, but I find it hard to believe that someone snuck in and murdered him right next to me while I slept." Staples was grateful that she had entered that information into the conversation; it was difficult to discuss the matter and maintain the woman's privacy at the same time. If either of the other two was surprised, neither showed it. "It seems impossible," she added.

"It's not impossible," Dinah said flatly.

"No, it's not," Staples agreed. "But it would be quite a risk. You could have woken up, something could have gone wrong. Hmm," She mused for a moment. "I may have a theory, but I want more information before it can really take shape. I think that this Doctor Stewart might be the key. If he-"

"She." Evelyn broke in.

"She. If she's in on this, she might be helping Ducard. If that's the case, then I don't know that there's much we can do, but if she's not…"

"If you don't mind me saying, Captain, what business is this of ours?" Templeton asked. "Laplace died. Sorry," he murmured an apology to Evelyn. "But he died. His second-in-command and the station's doctor say it was a heart attack. You've got no reason to believe it was anything other than that. In fact, it seems pretty farfetched that someone snuck in and killed him, since the person sleeping next to him is sitting right here saying that didn't happen. How old was he?"

"Sixty-one," the woman at the door provided. Templeton had stopped wondering how and why Dinah knew everything that she did.

"Okay. That's young for a heart attack, especially in this day and age, but it does happen. Just 'cause Ducard and Laplace didn't get along, that doesn't mean that Ducard murdered him, or had someone else do it. I think you're reaching, Captain."

Staples was silent for several moments, and they all looked at her expectantly. She gazed at the wall as she thought. Finally, she said, "I've got reason, Don. Lots of reason. This whole job has been weird from the start. Way too many coincidences… I can see the trees, but not the root systems connecting them." Another moment passed. "But they're there. I know they're there."

"Okay, I believe you," he assented. "But that still doesn't make it our business."

Evelyn pointed at Staples. "If she's right, then a man was murdered. A good man." Tears sprung into her eyes as she spoke, but she wiped them away.

"I know, and I'm sorry," Templeton said again. "I really am. But I talked with Davis Ducard for hours, and I don't think he's a killer."

"He doesn't have to be," said Staples, still staring at her point on the wall, "to be complicit."

"Fine then. That makes this a police matter."

"There are no police on this station, Don."

"But the law still stands. Nearly every corporation has adopted Earth Corporate Law, and there are station security to enforce that system of laws," he objected, his voice rising a bit.

"And who do they work for now?" Evelyn asked rhetorically.

Templeton looked at the two women arrayed against him, one his superior. Finally he looked at Dinah, who stood calmly by the door, taking the whole situation in. "Are you gonna help me on this? We're not cops; we're a charter flight crew who delivers people and cargo. We get paid, we move on. It's not our job to solve murders, assuming this even was one."

Staples knew well that she could shut this conversation down, but she turned to Dinah to seek her input.

"With respect, sir, I think that a good member of our crew died on the way here. I don't know if all of this is connected, like the captain believes, or not. But I'd like to know, and if possible, I'd really like to meet the person responsible." The implied menace in her voice was enough to send a chill down Staples' spine.

Templeton raised his hands in surrender. "Okay, okay. We're stuck here anyway. I just don't want us to get into any trouble. Ducard has been really generous. He fought to have us get all of our pay, which we did by the way, and he only charged us labor for the repairs. The parts were free. And before you say it, yes, I can see how that might be him trying to placate us so we'll just be on our merry way. I guess the real question is, what now? How do we figure this out?"

"I have an idea about that," Staples said, looking at him squarely. "But I'm going to need Jabir's help. I'll let you all know as soon as we know something."

Templeton and Evelyn stood up to go. The grief that had marked her face when she had entered the room had transformed to a steely resolve, and she now seemed far more angry than sad. Dinah left first, Templeton right behind her, but as Evelyn reached the door, Staples said, "Do you have another minute?"

She stopped and turned back. "Of course, Captain."

Staples smiled warmly. "I'm not your captain, though I am beginning to think of you as a member of my crew. It's been ten days since we dropped you off, and here you are back on my ship." Before the other woman could utter the apology that she was clearly forming, she added, "Relax, it's a pleasure to have you here. Believe me, I would hire you for the coms position if I thought we could afford you. And if you hadn't signed what I assume is a legally binding contract when you took this job."

Evelyn smiled in return, a bit regretfully Staples thought. "I can't say that it hadn't occurred to me. Anyway, what did you want to ask me?"

Staples formed her words carefully. "I wondered… given your proclivities, I would have thought that you and Jabir would have made a great pairing while you were here."

Evelyn laughed, but her cheeks turned bright red. "He is quite the charmer."

"Indeed he is." Something in Staples' voice gave her away.

Evelyn's eyes grew wide. "Clea!" she said, her voice mingled with surprise and delight.

"What can I say?" Staples shrugged, grinning. "You said it; he's quite the charmer."

"Isn't that against the rules? Fraternizing with a member of the crew?" she teased.

"This isn't a military ship. Besides, I'm the captain. I get to make, or break, the rules as I see fit."

"Well, I trust it went better with you than it did with me. I thought we might get together too, but…" The blush was stronger than ever.

"But?" Staples prompted.

Evelyn looked down at her feet, and then laughed again. Her brown eyes met Staples' own, and she said, "But I puked on his shoes instead. I guess I was still sick from stasis."

"Huh," Staples said. "I guess so."

"Why do you ask?" Evelyn asked, her hand still on the door handle.

"Just curious," she mused.

Doctor Jabir Iqbal walked into the medical clinic of Cronos Station as if he belonged there. The clinic occupied a medium-sized two story building on the outskirts of the operations section of the cylinder, and it had broad windows overlooking Cronos Park for patients to enjoy when they were in recovery. Even with the higher injury rate implicit in work not only on an industrial energy mining platform, but one in space, the population of the station required only one doctor and three support staff. Two were nurses, and one was a receptionist and records coordinator. It was this last person that Iqbal approached confidently once he had entered the building.

The reception room mirrored that of a thousand others on Earth, no doubt designed to make patients feel more at home. The woman behind the glass window, a spinster in a pink sweater and hopelessly out of fashion horn rimmed glasses, looked up with a smile as he approached. Work this far out in the system often attracted those with few social ties and those who wanted to start over. Like nearly everyone he met, the doctor wondered what had inspired this woman to take a job over a billion kilometers from her likely home, but as he most often did, he resigned himself to not knowing.

The woman slid the glass partition aside and greeted him warmly. "How can I help you?"

Jabir had decided to forgo his lab coat and simply

wear a dark tie and blue collared shirt rolled to the elbows. He leaned forward on the counter and gave the woman his best smile. "Hello. I don't have an appointment, nor am I a prospective patient. I am a visiting doctor, and I was hoping to meet with Doctor Stewart as a matter of professional courtesy."

"Oh," she exclaimed, "you're off the *Gringolet*?" She pronounced it *gring-go-lett*.

He lowered his voice conspiratorially and said, "It's actually pronounced *Gring-go-lay*." His look gave the impression that he had winked at her, though he had not actually done so.

"Oh." She leaned forward in a similar manner. "Sounds French. Are you from France?"

He tried not to laugh at this absurd question given the obviousness of his accent, and instead settled for a confusing answer. "No, but the horse was named there. Tell me, is Doctor Stewart available?"

The woman looked nonplussed by the horse comment, but turned and looked behind her into the deeper recesses of the building. "I think so, but I'll check. Just a minute." She bustled off into the back.

Iqbal took the opportunity to look round the waiting room at the banal paintings of faded flowers in vases on the walls, and was immediately sorry. It was precisely to avoid trappings like this that he had elected to take work on a vessel rather than set up private practice. Life on a spaceship was sometimes boring, but it still seemed infinitely better to him than receiving the unending string of back injuries, thumb sprains, and stress-induced nervous issues with which he was sure this other doctor had to cope. Maintaining the health and fitness of a crew that constantly subjected themselves to changes in environment, gravity, and sometimes violence presented opportunities for unique and interesting solutions, and he had certainly been earning his considerable pay on this most recent journey.

As he pondered this, repressing a shudder at his drab and staid surroundings, the door opened and a short, silver-haired woman in a white coat and blue scrubs stood looking at him. Her hair was bobbed short around her chin, and there were slight wrinkles making inroads to her face from her lips. Her eyes were a vivid hazel, bright and sharp, and she looked up at Iqbal keenly.

"Doctor Stewart, I presume." He smiled and held out his hand.

She shook it firmly, but did not return the smile. "Yes, how can I help you? It's been a bad day."

His face fell to sympathy. "Yes, I've heard, I'm afraid. It is for that reason that I have come to see you. I am Doctor Jabir Iqbal, the ship's doctor on *Gringolet*." He glanced around the empty room, spying the receptionist back at her post, and added, "Can we adjourn to your office that we might speak with confidentiality?"

Stewart evaluated him with her intense eyes for several seconds, then nodded and led him through the door, past the usual examination rooms, to a generously sized office. A surface sat dark on a large imitation mahogany desk, and a tasteful green couch hunched against a far wall. Stewart sat in her chair behind the desk, putting the false wood between them, and indicated that he should sit in one of the chairs facing her.

"Now then, how can I help you Doctor Iqbal?" she asked, settling back in her cushy office chair.

His seat was not so comfortable. "It's a delicate matter, but when I learned of the death of your Station Commander, I had to come see you. You see, I have reason to believe that his death might not have resulted from natural causes."

Again, there were several moments of silence as Stewart stared at him. It unsettled him, but he did not let this show on his veneer. "Go on."

"You may be familiar with the TPSC virus. It is a mutation of the common flu that originated in a colony on Venus. In some cases, it can exacerbate heart conditions and otherwise cause health problems in relatively healthy people if they have particular genetic susceptibilities. It is not well known, but the ship on which I am currently employed made a port of call on Venus recently, and it is a matter of protocol that I follow up on all possibilities. I consider it unlikely that your Station Commander, a mister Laplace I believe, contracted the virus from one of our crew members, but it is remotely possible. If so, it is critical that I ascertain his exact cause of death. As both a professional courtesy, as well as in the name of keeping your crew and mine healthy, I came to ask if you would share the autopsy records of your Station Commander."

Stewart continued to lean back in her chair. "I'm afraid I can't do that," she replied.

"If it is a matter of confidentiality, I assure you that precedent is set to allow the release of information when a further infection of communicable-"

"I can't do that because there was no autopsy," she interjected, cutting him off.

Iqbal did his best to cover his lack of surprise with surprise. "No autopsy records? But then, how did you determine the cause of death?"

Stewart pursed her lips. "It was a natural conclusion. Laplace had a heart condition, and though it was not considered life threatening, there was always a remote possibility that something might happen. Sometimes people just die, Doctor Iqbal."

"Of this fact, you need not acquaint me," he replied somewhat reproachfully.

"All outward signs seem to point to death by cardiac arrest. I would still prefer, of course, to conduct an autopsy, but I have been ordered not to." Her demeanor had not changed, but her irritable disposition seemed to make more sense to Iqbal now.

"Ordered not to? I thought that the senior medical officer on a station of this kind had governance over all matters medical. Is this not the case?" he inquired innocently, though he suspected what the answer might be.

"In theory, yes," she sighed, then sat forward and rested her elbows on her oversized desk. "But we're a long way from Earth, Doctor, and station employment decisions, and station security I might add, fall to someone a good deal closer."

"I see. That is regrettable."

The woman pushed her chair back and stood up. "It is regrettable. As I have already told you, I have been specifically ordered not to perform an autopsy on Laplace. That means I can't even be in the room when you conduct yours."

Jabir stood as well, his eyes widening and then creasing in a smile. "Won't that result in troubles with your new Station Commander?"

She shrugged as she crossed the room back to the

door. Her hand alighted on the door handle, but she did not open it. "Probably, but a request by an MD with a legitimate medical concern is what the log book will say, and he certainly doesn't know that TPSC has entirely too short an incubation period to have made the trip undetected from Venus to Saturn." She shook her head at him chidingly. "You should have chosen something else."

He put up a grim smile. "There really wasn't anything else. I hope you will forgive my prevarications, but I had to take the chance that you didn't know much about TPSC. I cannot guarantee I will find anything that disagrees with your initial analysis."

"Even if you do, there's no way to keep you from lying to me about it. That's all right. I'd appreciate it if you can share, but if not, this still helps me."

"Indeed," he nodded in understanding. "It sends a distinct message to your new Station Commander, I would imagine."

"Yes. It's a nice way to say 'screw you' while still following orders. Quite convenient, really." She finally opened the door and gestured down the hall. "We have a morgue with attendant facilities on the second floor. It doesn't see much use, but we've kept the cobwebs away."

He followed her out. "I would imagine the last time was for your former Computer Scientist."

Stewart shook her head again. "Can't help you on that one. Decompression is a bad way to go, but there was no way to tell what made the hole in his suit." She indicated a heavy metal door at the end of the hallway. "The stairs are through here."

"Evelyn, there is one more piece to this. It is not

going to be pleasant, and if things turn out the way I fear they might, it might be even more unpleasant for you, but I think we have to get to the bottom of this." Staples looked the other woman steadily in the eye as she spoke. They were alone in medical. Evelyn sat in a medical examination gown on the same bed she had laid in when she had collapsed back on Mars. Jabir was waiting outside for her decision.

Evelyn, wide-eyed but serious, returned the look. "I understand, Clea, but I wish you'd tell me what you expect to find."

"I... don't want to, not yet. It's not the kind of thing you say without proof. I am probably wrong. I hope I'm wrong." She added more emphatically, though Evelyn looked dubious. "I don't think there's any danger to you." The moment stretched. "It shouldn't take long," she added, lamely she felt.

"Well, I don't like it, but I trust you." She drew herself up, raised her chin slightly, and sighed. "Send the doctor in."

Staples did so, and stepped outside to wait as he entered.

Thirty minutes later, the door opened. Staples closed the book she had been attempting to read. "You can come in now, Captain," he said. "Ms. Schilling has insisted that you be present for this."

She entered and walked over to her former passenger. Evelyn looked frightened. She knew that Jabir had not yet discussed his findings with her, but she must have had an inkling of what he had found based on the nature of his examination.

"So." He stood near the two women, his surface in

his hands for reference. "First, I'd like to report that you are perfectly healthy, Ms. Schilling." She looked only slightly relieved. Jabir took a deep breath. He seemed uncharacteristically unsettled. "Now for the bad news: I believe that someone has performed illegal genetic modification on you." He paused while that sunk in. Evelyn's eyes were wider than ever, and Staples tried not to show her disappointment that her suspicions had been confirmed. "There are two major modifications. The first is relatively harmless."

"You said there was nothing wrong with me!" she objected.

"Forgive me," he stated, looking down at the floor for a moment. "I meant harmless to others. Your endocrine and glandular systems have been slightly modified. Essentially, the chemical makeup of your perspiration has been altered. All humans produce low-level pheromones, but your pheromonal makeup is over three times stronger than the average person."

"Meaning what, exactly?" Staples asked.

"The science of attraction is hardly exact, but scent and pheromones are a part of that science. Essentially, Ms. Schilling has been rendered more attractive to those who would be inclined towards her in the first place."

Just as Staples was reexamining her passing attraction to the lovely woman in front of her, Evelyn gasped for breath. "Oh my God!" she cried. "Parsells and Quinn. They might never have-"

"Hey, no. No." Staples interrupted firmly, and stepped forward to take Evelyn's hands. She looked her squarely in the eye. "No. Do you hear me? There are plenty of people on this ship who were and are attracted to you, including," she glanced at Jabir who stood resolutely nearby, "some in this room. None of them tried anything like that. This is an old argument, and it doesn't matter if you're pumping out pheromones, wearing a slinky dress, or even walking around naked. People are responsible for their own actions. Pheromones didn't make Parsells and Quinn into monsters. It was them, and them alone. Okay?"

Tears had welled up in Evelyn's eyes, but as was her habit, she wiped them away. "Okay. Okay, you're right. My God, why? Why would someone do that to me?" She looked searchingly towards the other doctor.

"I'm afraid that the second modification to your body might explain that. The other alterations were to your genitalia. There are tiny fluid sacs contained in your vaginal walls. The sacs end in microscopic barbs." Evelyn's mouth hung open in shock, but the doctor continued. "The chemical they contain still needs analysis, but my assumption is that it is potassium chloride or another similar agent that has a high chance of causing cardiac arrest, especially if the person so injected has a weak heart or heart condition to begin with, which, incidentally, Mr. Laplace had. The man did die of a heart attack, and I found trace amounts of the same substance in his bloodstream when I performed my autopsy earlier today. There are problems with that theory; potassium chloride injections would hurt. I'll know more when I have time to examine the fluid more closely."

Evelyn had a look of abject horror on her face, and Staples didn't blame her. She looked down at her groin, then back at Jabir. "I'm an assassin?"

The man looked genuinely disconsolate. "No, but I

think that someone is. You are not a murderer."

"No, I'm the murder weapon." Expressions of shock and horror warred on her face.

"I am so very sorry. I deeply wish that my previous examinations had revealed this, but the alterations do not fall within the purview of routine exams." Staples had never seen Jabir look so aggrieved. He was most assuredly correct; she had never known the doctor to shirk his duties. The fact that these changes in her went undetected was undoubtedly not his fault, but he looked as though he blamed himself nonetheless.

"Who would do this to me? Why?"

"I have some ideas about that," Staples answered. "Certainly about the second question. You told Jabir that you spent some time with a man shortly before you came on board. I suspect that this is when this illegal modification took place."

"That fits," Jabir added. "These modifications are recent. Scar tissue is still forming. I would say that the surgery was performed no more than a month ago."

"But why don't I remember it?" Evelyn asked desperately. "I remember what I did with him." There was no blush in her cheeks; her complexion was blanched with fear.

"I can't say for sure, but I suspect that you were hypnotized."

"Hypnotized?" she almost shouted the word.

"It's the only thing that makes sense," Staples said sadly. "Let's go through this. Someone wanted Laplace dead. They knew that he had a heart condition, and they knew that he liked redheads. He said that you were his type. I don't know if that someone was Ducard or not, but he almost certainly had to be in on it. He was the one who hired you, wasn't he?" she guessed, and Evelyn nodded, her mouth slightly agape. "So they pick you out for the job, drug you, perform surgery on you not only to make sleeping with you lethal, but to guarantee that Laplace would want to. Then they hypnotize you so that you won't remember it.

"And the hypnosis wasn't just to alter your memories, I'd wager. You might have been Laplace's type, but that didn't make him yours. The moment you met him, you were attracted to him. You commented on it to me. I'm sorry to say it, Evelyn," she wore a grim and regretful look, "but he wasn't very attractive. I actually thought you were joking at the time. It's likely you had a post-hypnotic suggestion to go to bed with him."

Understanding was beginning to dawn on Evelyn's face, and, Staples thought, some acceptance as well. "That's why they paid to have us put in stasis. Herc said he was surprised. Three weeks is a long trip, and the idea of going to sleep and waking up somewhere else was appealing, but really they didn't want me sleeping with anyone else along the way. I might kill them too and give up the game."

Staples nodded. "And that was likely not enough insurance for them. Remember what happened when you did try to sleep with someone else?"

Evelyn looked down at Jabir's shoes and then groaned, covering her face with her hands. "I can't believe this. I just can't believe this." She spoke into her palms, though her tone said she was beginning to.

"I'm not sure I do either," the doctor broke his silence. "There is no denying the medical certainties of this situation, nor the state of my shoes, but this is an incredibly elaborate way to kill a man on a space station orbiting a gas giant a billion kilometers from Earth, especially when our prime suspect is a man who worked with him on a daily basis."

"No, I agree," Staples said. "He couldn't have acted alone, and I'm not convinced that he is the person behind it all, though he is unquestionably involved. Frankly, given the elaborate nature of the murder and given his mistakes since, specifically his choice to announce Laplace's death before there was time for a proper autopsy to be conducted, I would conclude that he is not the mastermind."

"I am inclined to grant, for the moment, that this was a murder plot targeted at Laplace," Jabir conceded. "There are ways to see if someone has been hypnotized, but I am not a psychologist, so I'm afraid we must work with the unconfirmed supposition that you were for now." He looked at Evelyn as he spoke. "I admit I can find no fault in your reasoning, but this still leaves a bevy of unanswered questions. The first and foremost of these is who orchestrated this assassination, and why? Why does it matter who is commander of a fuel station orbiting Saturn? Other questions remain unanswered as well. Who hired the pirates to attack this ship, and how did they know about Evelyn? Perhaps we can assume that whoever it was learned of this plot and hoped to stop it, but hiring pirates is hardly the most efficient way to do so. Simply contacting us and telling us about Evelyn's condition would have sufficed."

Staples held up a finger. "The *Doris Day* might well have made that impossible; they were blocking all of our

Sol-side communications. I think we can assume that Vey was hired to ensure that we got Evelyn safely to this station, but there is still a lot that doesn't make sense. Why did Vey drop a satellite in front of us, then fight us for it? Or better yet, why not just hire Vey to make the delivery himself?"

"There is also the matter of Matthew Spicer, the former Computer Scientist. This information could call into question the circumstances of his death as well."

Staples nodded. "That occurred to me too. And the sad truth is, I'm not sure that we can prove any of this right now, at least not Ducard's involvement. As Don so accurately pointed out, we're not police; we certainly don't have the right to go prying into Ducard's private communications. We could go to the police with what we have, but in my experience, companies like Libom like to handle things internally, and law enforcement is inclined to let them. And even if we did report it, would anyone believe us? It all seems too crazy to believe."

"These are all really interesting questions," Evelyn spoke up, her voice shaky and her hands folded protectively in her lap. "But I really only have one right now." She looked at Jabir. "Can you get these freaking things out of me?"

"Are you sure about this, Evelyn? It's not too late to come with us, you know," Templeton said as he faced the woman. The two of them, along with Dinah, Charis, Staples, John, Iqbal, and Bethany sat at the table in the mess hall. The meal, a luncheon of steamed vegetables with tofu and sauce, was a treat from Evelyn to the crew as a parting gift.

"I'm tempted. Really, I am. I am so grateful to you all for everything you've done, but this job is a great opportunity. Plus, I signed a contract. I'm pretty sure it says in there that if I quit early, I have to pay for the relocation expenses." She pushed the broccoli on her plate around to mop up some sauce.

"But your new boss is a murderer," Charis objected, a fork in her hand. "Just because we can't prove it, that doesn't mean that you have to work for him."

"He's only an accomplice, my love," John patted her other hand facetiously. "Hardly worth mentioning." The navigator rolled her eyes at her husband.

"Really, that's all the more reason for me to stay. Someone here should know what kind of man he is and keep an eye on him."

"You're not a detective, Evelyn. Who's to say he won't try to get rid of you too?" Templeton asked.

"Why would he? Ducard is Station Commander now, and he has no reason to think that I suspect what he's done. Besides, it's kind of exciting." Her eyes widened as she spoke. "It makes me feel like a spy."

"Don is right," Staples interjected. "It's not entirely safe. However, I've spoken with a friend on Mars who might help us get to the bottom of this. It is my great hope that if we can gather some evidence, then we can let Libom know what sort of man is in charge of their multi-million dollar facility. I doubt they'll press charges-"

"Damn right," Templeton snorted. "Probably sweep the whole thing under the rug and make him disappear."

"That suits me just fine," Evelyn said. "Gone is gone. I can stay here and keep an eye on things. You let me know if you get that evidence, and I'll let you know if my new boss gets transferred to someplace even more remote than this."

Templeton shook his head. "I still don't like it."

"I'm not sure I do either," Staples added, "but that doesn't mean it's a bad idea. You took a job and signed a contract. You might have been chosen in part for your hair color, but that doesn't mean you're not a fine computer scientist. You certainly helped sort *Gringolet* out." Her hands gestured airily to the ship around them.

Evelyn leaned forward. "And I can always leave later." Templeton nodded reluctantly, a grim look on his face.

Several minutes later, they all stood about in a loose and awkward circle as Evelyn made her way to each of them to say her goodbyes. She hugged Templeton enthusiastically, and shook hands with Charis and John. When she came to Dinah, the engineer put her hand out preemptively to stave off the hug, but Evelyn pushed past it and embraced her fully. Dinah wrapped an indulgent arm around the woman and pressed her palm against the small of her back. She pulled back, her hair a bit wild around her head, her hands on Dinah's bare shoulders, and looked her in the eye.

"What can I say to you? You changed the course of my life, maybe saved it. Thank you."

Dinah offered up a tight-lipped smile. "Don't mention it."

Evelyn moved next to Bethany, who stood with her head held unusually high. Staples noted that she had not taken her eyes off the departing woman for the past several minutes. Evelyn took her shoulders in her hands, much as she just had Dinah's, and looked at her.

"Thank you for your plant. It saved me too." She embraced the woman's small frame tightly and murmured in her ear so that the others could not hear. "And thank you for what I suspect you tried to do. It wasn't right, but thank you anyway." Bethany's eyes went wide for a moment, then her arms flew around the other woman and she squeezed her almost violently for several seconds. The others looked politely away, and Charis and John took advantage of the opportunity to exit together. Finally, Bethany released her and she sucked in a deep breath. Evelyn drew back a bit and looked at her meaningfully. "It will get better. Trust me." Bethany nodded and lowered her eyes for a moment, then raised them again and smiled. A moment later, she turned and walked out of the room as well.

"And you, Doctor," she addressed Jabir. "Are you sure I can't at least buy you a new pair of shoes?" He smiled ruefully and shook his head. "Then how can I thank you?"

"You can remember to take your medication without fail." Over the past few days, Jabir had been successful in removing the sacs, but the modifications to her glandular system had been more complex. Jabir suspected that the alterations would fade with time as the cells of the endocrine system were replaced naturally, and he had prescribed a medication that would speed up the process, but he was not, he declared vehemently, a doctor of genetics, and he refused to tamper with her system. Though Evelyn abhorred the violation that had been done to her, she had smiled when she stated that she would just have to live with being more attractive for a time.

"That, I promise." She smiled, hugged him, and

planted a kiss on his cheek. His embrace was as professional as possible, but there was a warmth in his face that betrayed his feelings. He left the mess hall, and Templeton finally got the hint and departed as well. At last it was just Staples and Evelyn facing one another.

It was clear that Evelyn was close to tears as she faced the captain. "I can't believe I've only known you for a month. A little more than that, if you count the time I spent asleep."

"Don't get too weepy on me," Staples replied with a smile. "This isn't goodbye. You and I are going to be talking a lot over the next month as we try to sort this thing out, and it is my sincere hope that we'll find excuses to keep doing so long after that. We don't get charters out here that often, but when we do, I think that the crew would really love to pay you a visit."

She sniffled and said, "I'd really like that. Do you really have a lead on Mars from… what's her name now, Jordan?"

Staples nodded. "A very good one, actually. She's located Brad Stave. I'm greatly looking forward to having a chat with him."

Evelyn's countenance darkened. "If you have to beat the hell out of him in the process, let me know. I'd like to hear about that."

"I'd rather turn him over to the authorities, but maybe we can work out a way to do both."

Evelyn laughed her deep and throaty laugh, then a long moment of silence passed. Finally she said, "Goodbye, Clea."

"Goodbye, Evelyn." She put a reassuring hand on her elbow. "We'll be talking soon. I promise."

# CHAPTER 17

Though he could certainly afford a rickshaw up to his door every day, Brad Stave preferred to be dropped at the end of the tube that was essentially his street. It gave him time to walk down the rounded corridor. There was nothing particularly appealing about the steel construction; indeed, it made him feel a bit like a mouse in a heating duct at times, but there was something classic about walking past the neighbors, up to one's house, turning the key, and saying "Honey, I'm home," or some equivalent. He practiced the names as he passed the doors that let into tubes that let into homes. "Chipman," he muttered under his breath as he walked, "Crawford, Chow, Hillegas…" Through the small windows that punctuated the tubes between the doors, he could see the red of rusty iron and dirt as one of the periodic storms that moved across the surface of the planet raged. It had no particular effect on his life, but he stopped to contemplate the tempest through the window for a minute before moving on. Finally, he came to his door. It was painted black like the rest of them, the number 126 standing out in silver letters nailed to the wood. Attached to the wall beside it an expectant mail slot sat with the name Stave printed across it in matching silver. He turned the key and opened the door into the smaller five-meter tunnel that led to his house proper. Jackets and a few assorted sweaters hung on a coat rack just inside the door.

Like many things in the largely artificial Martian city, the need for warmer clothing was an affectation of the human populace. The temperature in Tranquility was carefully controlled, but some liked to keep their homes colder or warmer than others, and the entire city was a few degrees cooler in the winter months and a few warmer in the summer. Psychological testing had shown that this artificial homage to seasons helped with human adaptation to life on the red planet. Two hundred thousand years of seasonal programming was not easily cast aside. Brad kept his sport jacket on for now; its home was in the bedroom closet next to Cynthia's dresses. He let himself into the house.

"Honey, I'm ho-" The words died on his lips when he saw the woman standing against the wall by the door to the kitchen. Her chin-length blonde hair, which was parted on the side and pinned to her head by a barrette, framed a face that was hard but passingly pretty. She had a medium build, a bit stocky, and Brad would have guessed she was in her early forties, though it was difficult to tell these days. This intruder had her arms crossed on her chest, and she was wearing grey slacks and a grey jacket over a plain white tee shirt.

"Who the hell are you?" he demanded. "What are you doing in my house? Where's my family?" He looked around the room, but found no sign nor sound of anyone else. "Cynthia!" he shouted. There was no response.

"Relax, Mr. Stave. Your family is fine. I just want to talk to you. If you answer my questions, no one will get hurt." Her voice was high, steady, and confident; it reminded him of board meetings and sales analyses.

"Is that a threat?" He could feel the blood burning in his cheeks, and he fought down the urge to yell his wife's name again.

She appeared to consider for a moment. "Yes, I suppose it is. Not to your family, just to you. I don't believe in using others to do my dirty work." He thought there was something accusatory in that statement.

He drew himself up. "Well, I don't respond well to threats." He reached for the watch on his right wrist, intending to call the authorities. Suddenly, strong dark hands gripped his left wrist, and he turned in shock to see a black woman with closely cropped hair and a grimly determined look on her face standing next to him. She must have been behind the door when he entered. He glanced around the room quickly to make sure that he hadn't missed anyone else, but it was just the three of them. The woman holding him was perhaps thirty years old and looked little more than half his weight. He decided he could take her.

He wrenched his left hand away from her, but amazingly it moved only a few inches. She was stronger than she looked. He began cursing, trying to pry her fingers off with his other hand, but they clamped down even harder, and he could not move them. His fingers began to tingle as they lost circulation.

"Please calm down, Mr. Stave," the blonde woman

was saying.

"Calm down, hell," he muttered, still trying to pull the other woman's vice-like fingers from his wrist. Finally, he drew his right hand back, made a fist, and launched it at her face. A second before it connected, the face moved, and he nearly toppled over following it forward. His attacker shifted her grip to his extended right arm, clamped down on his right wrist, and tore the communicator watch from his arm. In a second, it was gone, and he found himself free of her altogether. He took another swing, but it was in vain, and his fist sailed through the air helplessly. Somehow the infuriatingly strong woman was still standing in front of him, not quite a meter away. It was evident that he couldn't hit her, but she didn't seem to be moving to attack or restrain him any further, so he turned his fury on the blonde one on the other side of the room.

He began to walk towards her as he spoke, pointing his finger. "Look, I don't know who you are, but you can't-" He never understood how it happened. He was in the middle of his second step towards her, and then he was abruptly on his stomach, his arms pinned behind his back, his chin grinding into the carpet. The couch loomed up beside him, and there was the black woman's weight on his back, holding his arms painfully crossed. He realized that she could quite easily break them, and despite his frustration, he was grateful that she had not.

"Okay," he said into the carpet. "I'll talk to you. Just tell me where my family is."

He could no longer see either woman, but the blonde's clear voice floated down to him from above. It sounded as though she were standing behind the couch. "They've been diverted on the way home from Cassidy's school. Just a routine ID check that will take an unnecessarily long time. They're fine, I promise. Are you ready to talk now, or do you want to try hitting my friend some more?"

Brad tried to nod, but his chin hurt, so he muttered, "Talk," through gritted teeth. A moment later he was sitting in the recliner across from the couch. The woman who had thrown him around like a human rag doll stood next to him, silent and menacing, and the blonde continued to stand behind the couch.

"Tell you what," she said. "I'll tell you what I know, and then you can fill in the blanks." He nodded dumbly. "Your name is Brad Stave. You work for Teletrans Corporation as a senior programmer. You're married with two children, and you've lived on Mars for the past ten years. You relocated here when you were hired by Teletrans. You met a woman at a bar called O'Kelly's on March eighth, nearly two months ago." She paused for a moment when he flinched briefly, then continued. "There is no security footage of it. Oddly, the cameras that monitor pedestrian traffic on that street failed to record for several hours that night. No one seems to know why. However, several patrons of that establishment can testify that they saw you speaking with her for over two hours while you shared drinks. Then you left together."

"I don't pick up women in bars. I'm married. I don't cheat," he protested. He began to rise, then with a glance at the severe looking woman standing over him, settled reluctantly back in the recliner.

"No, I don't think you did have sex with her. What you did do was drug her, subject her to illegal genetic modifications, and hypnotize her. A month later, she slept with someone, I expect you know exactly whom, and that person died. That makes you a murderer."

He was silent for several moments, then a theatrical look of realization came over his face. He pointed at the blonde. "I know how to clear this up. Let me first say that I have no idea what you're talking about. I never met this woman you're talking about. I don't go to bars much, and I certainly don't leave them with women. You might have a few people who say they saw someone who looks like me, but I'm going to guess that since they were in a bar, they were drinking, and maybe you don't want to haul them into a courtroom or a police station. In fact, I'm going to guess that you don't have any solid evidence, or you would be talking to the police and not me. I certainly don't know anything about any illegal genetic modification or hypnotism. But the funniest thing happened the other day. An envelope was dropped in my mail slot. It had no return address. When I opened it, it contained a letter addressed to someone named Clea Staples. I thought it was a mistake, so I was going to throw it out, but I haven't gotten around to it. That wouldn't be you, would it?" He looked hopefully at her.

"You know he's lying." The woman standing over him spoke for the first time.

"I know," the blonde, Staples he assumed, responded. "He's playing it safe. He's afraid we're recording him, so he isn't going to admit to anything." She looked at him directly. "We're not, by the way, but I don't expect you to believe that. Why don't you tell me where this mysterious envelope is and I'll go get it."

"Down the hallway, last door on the left is my office. The envelope is in the top left drawer." She walked quickly down the hall and reappeared a minute later with the manila envelope with her name on it. After she opened it, she pulled out the letter inside and read it. Brad and the woman next to him looked on.

"All right Mr. Stave," she said when she had finished, "I think we're done here. We'll be going. This-" she held up the letter, "is supposed to provide the answers we're looking for. If it doesn't, we'll be back to talk to you."

"I don't think you will be," he said with a smirk.

He expected them to leave, but Staples continued to stare at him. "You know, I'd really like to ask my assistant here to kill you. I'm sure you've realized by now that she could with very little effort." His smirk faded. Staples put her hands on the back of the couch and leaned forward, her brown eyes boring into him. "You drugged a woman and paid some crackpot doctor to violate her body, then you violated her mind. As a result, an innocent man is dead." She continued to look at him, and it was obvious that her desire to see him hurt or dead was quite genuine. She was not bluffing. "It would be so easy. I could change or end your life with a word."

"Please," he heard himself say, all his confidence gone. "I have a wife, kids."

"Shut up," she said coldly. "They might thank me for it if they knew what you helped do. You ruined lives."

"I didn't know," he protested weakly. "I didn't know what would happen."

"Then you're thoughtlessly cruel, not deliberately so. I should tell you that this does not help your case." She looked down at him, and he felt the woman at his side move an inch closer. Involuntarily, he sank deeper into the chair. Just when he was wondering whether he would make it if he ran for his life, she leaned back from the couch. "I'm not going to hurt you. I am, however, going to do everything I can to see that you pay for your crimes. Enjoy your wife and your children in the meantime. Maybe you can find a way to prepare them for the day when the police come knocking on your door." She crossed the room, stood in front of him, and regarded him with undisguised revulsion. Then the spell broke, and she looked at her accomplice. "Let's go."

And just like that, they were gone through his front door, and Brad found that he was shaking uncontrollably.

"If I may ask, sir, what is it?" Dinah said as they walked back to the ship side by side, indicating the letter in her captain's hand.

She looked the paper over again. "It's a job offer from Owen Burr, the president of Teletrans Corporation. It's a request to come to his office on Earth to 'consult about a possible future charter flight,'" she read directly from the paper.

"Your friend's files said that Stave works directly for Burr. You think Burr gave him that envelope as insurance in case we came asking questions?"

"I think that's a fair assumption," Staples replied. She stopped speaking for a moment as two businessmen, wearing suits and deep in discussion, walked by. "We could hardly expect a signed confession, but this means that Stave was working under orders. I'm actually rather surprised that Burr would protect him, call us to Earth to answer our questions. I figured they'd cut him loose, let him take the fall for what happened to Evelyn."

"Do we really not have any evidence?"

Staples smiled grimly. "It's spotty at best. A few drinkers who think they saw Evelyn leave with him. My friend managed to get the surgeon to talk to her, but he's not going to waltz into a police station and confess to illegal genetic modification on a drugged and unconscious woman. She wasn't able to turn up a hypnotist, so I think that must have been Stave himself."

"So why not ignore us altogether?" Dinah asked.

"Because we *know*. We want answers, and Burr wants a chance to shut us up. He may be reasonably confident that he's covered his bases, but he'll want to be sure. I suspect he'll either try to buy our silence if he can or threaten us if he can't. But he needs to speak with us to do that, and it has to be on his terms. That's why he wants us to come to his office."

Dinah mused on this for a moment as they turned a corner and joined a larger thoroughfare. "Sir, if I'm not mistaken, Teletrans Corporation is based on Mars. The fact that Burr wants to meet us on Earth sounds… suspicious."

Staples nodded. "Indeed it does, Dinah. Indeed it does."

"But you still want to go."

"I want answers. I don't think the man is going to gun us down in his own office. If Owen Burr really is behind all of this, if he went to these incredibly elaborate machinations in order to turn Evelyn into a living weapon just to kill the Commander of Cronos Station, then he's not going to be that sloppy. I'm sure he hoped we wouldn't put all of this together, but this," she waved the signed piece of paper briefly, "tells us that he's planned for the possibility that we would. He's got some endgame in mind, I've no doubt. I just wish I understood the connection between the two companies."

"I may be able to shed some light there, sir," Dinah said, glancing over at her. "I did some research into Lobim and Cronos station on the way back to Mars. Libom uses unmanned drones to scout the atmosphere of Saturn for rich gas pockets."

Staples stopped short, and Dinah stopped with her. "And Teletrans provides specialty operating systems for robotic drones, I'm guessing."

"Among other things, sir."

"God, could it be that simple?"

The engineer lowered her voice as a group of high school aged children chattered by. "Do you think Burr had Laplace killed so that Ducard would order more drones, recommend more purchases, or something along those lines?"

"It seems awfully elaborate, but if history has proven anything, it's that there isn't much people won't do for more money. In your research, you didn't happen to notice whether Teletrans is in dire financial straits, did you?" She began walking again, and Dinah fell in beside her.

"Actually, I did, sir. Teletrans has been doing exceptionally well lately. They have reported a considerable profit each quarter for the last year and a half, and their stock split last month."

Staples laughed. "Is there anything you can't do, Dinah?"

"I never learned to dance, sir."

Staples looked at her wide eyed, searching for the irony that Templeton so often sought in their conversations, but Dinah's face was as neutral as ever. She laughed again, louder. "I'd offer to teach you sometime, but I never learned either." She paused for a moment, then decided to take the plunge. "I thought you might have found a dance partner on Cronos while we were there."

Dinah shrugged. "I make friends fairly easily, sir." They turned another corner.

"Then I'm sorry we had to leave so soon."

She shrugged again. "Side effect of serving on a spaceship, sir."

Staples knew that one of the reasons that people chose to live on charter ships was to avoid long-term entanglements, and she had long suspected that this was one of Dinah's motivations. "Side effect or benefit?" She probed. Dinah did not answer, and Staples guessed that their moment of candor had passed. After a minute of silent walking through increasingly crowded tubes, Staples brought them back to their original topic. "If Teletrans is so successful, why the elaborate murder plot? Libom is big enough to be a really valuable client, but I can't imagine that a few extra operating systems shipped off to Cronos would make much of a difference to their financials."

"I'm afraid I don't know, sir. There was nothing about it in the financial report I read."

Staples laughed again as they entered the berthing area. "You know, for someone with no sense of humor, you're really pretty funny, Dinah."

Dinah looked momentarily downcast. "I try not to be, sir."

Captain Staples decided to sit back and let her first mate handle this one. She had done entirely too much public speaking for her tastes lately. Templeton looked out over the assembled faces in the mess hall. Everyone on the ship was present. *Everyone left* she corrected herself. She knew that they would have to replace the people they had lost, and soon, but it was difficult for her to think about bringing new people into this situation while there were still questions to be answered. Additionally, the grievous error made in hiring Quinn and Parsells hung over her. She knew it wasn't Templeton's or her fault. Their misconduct had been covered up by their superior officer, but it still made her feel distrustful of outsiders, and she suspected that much of the crew felt the same way. Even so, they were down two security officers, a cook, and most importantly, a coms officer. John was doing what he could, but it was not his area of expertise, and Dinah still needed him in the engine room, especially as she monitored the repairs to the engines completed at Cronos.

"The captain wants to be really honest with everyone," Templeton said, perhaps a little too loudly. "You all know what happened on Cronos. Someone mutilated Evelyn, a good and innocent woman, and used us to deliver her to a man, and that man died as a result. The problem is, we can't prove it, but that doesn't mean I don't want justice. I want to know who killed Laplace and why, sure, but more than that, I want whoever did that to Evelyn to pay for it. Now we've got a 'job offer,'" he sneered at the words, "from Owen Burr, the president of Teletrans Corporation. It looks like he's behind this whole thing. The captain and I are going to go meet with him on Earth and hopefully get some answers. Once we get things sorted out, you all deserve a long stretch of downtime. New York City is a great place to do that. We'll be berthing there, and you can have two weeks, guaranteed."

He looked over at Staples, who was leaning against a table. "Captain promised that if a job comes up, no matter how good it is, they'll just have to wait." He considered mentioning the need for more crew, but decided to let it pass for the moment. The fear of outsiders, of betrayal, was almost tangible in the room.

John sat at one of the mess tables, his daughter between him and his wife. "Don, since you're being honest, how much danger are we in?"

Templeton took a few seconds to consider, drew himself up, and took a breath. "Not none," he admitted, "but we're not in the middle of nowhere right now. Pirates are pretty uncommon between here and Earth, and there's no practical way to attack the ship on this planet or that one. Burr wants to make a deal with us. That's the only reason he would want to meet with us, near as we can tell. If he wanted to try to kill us, he'd hardly invite us to talk. And if we run, try to hide, well… that might make him desperate. We can't prove anything right now, and meeting with him is the best way to get clear of this." He scanned the room, meeting eyes with Jang, then Dinah, then Yoli, and finally settling his gaze on Charis. "We got dragged into this. None of you asked for this, but we're here now, and we," he nodded towards Staples, "are gonna do everything we can to get clear of it. We're going to do whatever we can to make sure that everyone," his eyes flicked involuntarily to Gwen for a second, who looked only dimly aware of the subject of the conversation, "*everyone* is safe."

John looked decidedly unhappy, but he had no more questions, and neither did the rest of the crew, at least publicly. "All right," Templeton said. "We're going to head to New York. It's just after nineteen now. Captain wants us wheels up by nine tomorrow morning, so get some sleep because we've got an early morning. Breakfast will be OJ and pastries at six-thirty." There was a chorus of groans, and he smiled half-heartedly. Coms might be the most important position left vacant in regards to ship operations, but the loss of a cook was devastating for morale.

Wrapped in her bathrobe, Staples was reading a book in her bed, now shifted to what had been a wall under Martian gravity. *Gringolet* was less than a day out from Mars en route to Earth and still gaining speed. She had just begun to doze when her watch pinged and Templeton's voice came through.

"We've got a ship on our radar, Captain." He sounded concerned.

Her eyelids fluttered and she heaved a sigh, wishing the voice would just go away. She tapped her watch and said, "We're close to Mars, Don. There's bound to be some traffic." A thought occurred to her, and she sat up a bit. "It's not headed for us, is it?"

"No, but it's going to pass awfully close. I can't be sure without Charis up here, but I'd say no more than a few thousand kilometers."

"That *is* close, but not too unusual. We're only a bit out from Tranquility. What type of ship do you make it?" The tatters of sleep were leaving her, and it annoyed her.

"That's the weird thing, Captain. I can't match it to the database." Staples thought for a moment. It was approaching twenty-three, and Templeton had the evening shift at present. The ship was set for Earth per Charis' calculations, and that meant that her first mate was alone in the cockpit. The man was far from a computer expert, but he was proficient enough to run a radar match against the ship's database of extant ship types.

"It could be something new, Don. We've been gone a few months." Even as she said this, she knew there was a problem with it. Charis had updated the computers when they were on Mars, and anything that was in the public domain for ship classes should be available to Templeton.

"Captain, I can't be sure, but I think it's decelerating really fast." His voice was apprehensive.

That brought her fully awake. "Okay. Okay, get Charis, Bethany, and John up there. I'll be up as soon as I can. How far out is the other ship?"

"I'm trying to tell, Captain. I think it's maybe twenty minutes out." Gooseflesh broke out on her arms. Something was wrong if a ship could get that close before Templeton picked it up.

"Get everyone to combat positions now!" she said stridently into her watch. She doffed her robe and ran out the door in her grey tank top and flannel pajama pants. The metal floor was cold under her bare feet. As she emerged from her chambers, she began climbing the rungs inset in the floor, making for the fore of the ship. Templeton's voice came over the speakers, ordering everyone to combat ready positions and summoning John, Charis, and Bethany to his location.

Staples was emerging from the elevator and reaching for the rungs that would take her the rest of the way to the cockpit when she felt the ship give a series of minute shudders. The elevator closed behind her and descended, likely summoned to retrieve one of the others. She paused to tap her watch.

"What the hell was that, slugs? Is it firing at us?" Without waiting for an answer, she began climbing.

"I'm here now, Captain." Charis' voice came not only from her watch, but drifted down the hallway from the cockpit above. "I'm trying to figure out... missiles!"

Staples was breathing hard, pulling herself up hand-over-hand as fast as she could. Even at point four Gs, her heart was beating fast from a mix of physical exertion and fear. After what seemed an interminable climb, she gained the floor and climbed to her feet in the bent cockpit. Instinctively, she looked up through the skylight for the other ship, but it wasn't immediately visible from her position. Templeton and Charis were the only two present; she wondered how the navigator had beaten her husband to the cockpit, but then she realized that John would be busy securing Gwen. "That doesn't make any sense. If we'd been hit by missiles, we wouldn't be-"

"Not theirs," Charis cut her off, her eyes intent on her surface and her fingers busy. "Ours. We just fired six missiles at the other ship. They're only a few seconds from contact."

Staples' stomach dropped. "What? How?" She looked at Templeton, who sat buckled in his seat looking as stunned and confused as she felt.

"I didn't do anything!" he said, and of course she knew he was right. Not only would Templeton not have fired first, she doubted he had the ability to do so. He was no more a tactical officer than he was a coms specialist. Staples darted forward to her chair and stared up through the skylight, and this time she could see the glow of the other ship's engines clearly. From the view Staples had, the ship was indeed unfamiliar. It was small and sleek, with a far narrower engine profile in the rear than hers. As she watched, the engines darkened and the vessel began turning its broadside towards them. Pinpricks of light, thrust from the missiles they had evidently fired, were plain against the blackness of space. Sol burned brightly off to the left of the ship. Suddenly, a second sun bloomed as the other ship opened fire with a barrage of flares and flak. Tiny explosive shells rocketed from guns in the other ship's side, exploding in bursts of shrapnel and blotting out all view of the vessel. There was a massive bloom of light from that wall of explosions and shrapnel as one of the missiles detonated short of the vessel. This was followed by another, a third, a fourth, and a fifth. Staples counted them off as they happened, then a second later there was another silent explosion, this one on the hull of the other craft. One of the missiles had gotten through, and the result was devastating. The dart-like vessel ceased its anti-missile barrage as the detonation of the sixth missile on its hull sent it spinning away.

"Get Dinah at the tactical station," Staples yelled at Templeton as she darted forward to the coms panel at what she still thought of as Yegor's station. As she did so, she heard Bethany climb into the cockpit behind her. She desperately worked the controls to broadcast on a general hailing frequency. Simultaneously, she heard Templeton speaking into his watch to summon the engineer to the cockpit. Even in the midst of her panic, she had the presence of mind to keep the transmission tight band; she didn't want to tell the whole system that *Gringolet* had just fired missiles without provocation at another ship.

"Unidentified vessel, this is Captain Staples of

commuter vessel *Gringolet*. We did not intend to fire at you. Please do not return fire. We want to help. Please respond." Several seconds passed in silence as the crew in the cockpit looked up through the windows. All trace of light from the other ship had vanished, the vacuum sucking the fire into nothingness, and a thousand pieces of wreckage drifted away from the vessel. The majority of it looked intact; enough, Staples thought, to still be a threat if the crew decided to put up a fight. It was still moving towards them, spinning lazily on its axis from the missile impact. Staples realized that they were going to pass each other at a considerable clip.

"Cut thrust," she snapped at Charis. "Turn us over, slow us down at one G," she said to Bethany as the girl took her seat and gathered her hair in a ponytail behind her head. Instinctively, she grabbed the bar in front of her to secure herself against the loss of gravity. Templeton quickly made a shipwide coms announcement to expect loss of thrust in thirty seconds. She hated to give so little notice. Quick transitions of gravity without warning were a great way to injure people, but it couldn't be helped. As fast as they were going, it would take hours to come to a full stop, and the other ship was moving in the other direction. Getting to a position to render aid to them could take several hours, and by then it could be far too late.

The sound of another person climbing into the cockpit drew Staples' attention reluctantly away from the window. She expected to see John gaining his feet, but instead she saw Dinah moving for the tactical station. "How-" she began.

"Felt the missiles launch, sir. I figured you'd need me up here." She strapped herself into the chair at her new station. "I took the liberty of telling Park to take the engine room; hope that's all right, sir."

Staples processed this for a second, then nodded. "No, that was the right thing to do." She wondered if Dinah was the only person on the ship who would have recognized the sensation of a vessel launching missiles. As she reflected that she would have been happy to go her whole life without experiencing the feeling, she reached for the safety harness on the coms chair.

Dinah was already working the controls. "I'm bringing the flak guns online and reloading the missile bays, sir."

As she finished, Charis looked at Bethany and said, "Now." The sound of the engines, so constant on their journeys as to go unnoticed, like the droning of a fan on a hot summer day, died away. The silence that followed seemed absolute.

"Dinah, I don't want to fight them. I don't know why we fired missiles at them, but we need to help them if we can." She pushed a stray strand of her blonde hair out of her face.

"Appreciated, sir, but they may not feel the same way. It's only prudent to prepare for retaliation," Dinah said grimly, and Staples couldn't argue with her logic.

"Don, once we get under thrust again, tell Jang to search the computer core and the missile bay. We need to make sure whoever fired those missiles doesn't do it again." Templeton nodded and began to relay the orders to the security chief. The ship was moving end over end as Bethany brought them around, and Charis was poised to ramp up the engines to begin the process of slowing the ship down. Staples repeated her hail to the other vessel.

"Why don't they answer?" came Bethany's high voice.

"I don't know," Staples replied. "Either their coms are damaged, they're planning on attacking, or the crew is too injured to reply."

"Or…" Bethany whispered.

Staples nodded. "Or they're all dead. God, I hope it's the first one."

"They're firing, Captain!" Charis nearly shouted. Staples glanced up through the window, looking for the other ship, but of course it was behind them now as Bethany completed their turn. Instead, she glanced down at the coms panel and shuffled her way quickly through the menus to get an aft view of the ship. "I make three missiles just launched and gaining speed. Twenty seconds to impact!" The fear in the navigator's voice was plain.

Dinah didn't wait for orders. "Bethany, don't kick in thrust. Put our port side on them." Even as she spoke, Staples could feel the sharp drag of the turn; it strained her neck. Bethany quickly rotated the port side of the ship to the other vessel, and then a sound they all hoped never to hear filled the cockpit. The anti-missile flak guns along side of the ship, armed and extended by the chief engineer only a minute before, began their barrage. The drumbeat of the cannons echoed through the room and reverberated throughout the entire ship, shuddering all of them in their seats. Dozens of explosive rounds were fired into space as Dinah did her best to coordinate their trajectory with that of the incoming missiles.

They could see the explosions now through the windows to their left, brief flashes of light as the shells erupted. The air and explosive in each shell was burned up and each resulted in a cloud of shrapnel. Dinah worked to coordinate the fire of ten different guns into three groups, each focused on the computer's calculated incoming trajectory of one of the missiles. A second later, she keyed a sequence on another panel without looking away from her surface, and flares erupted from the side of the ship, burning bright against the pinprick stars. The sound of the flak guns firing filled the room, but it felt oddly distant to Staples, disconnected from the silent explosions she could see through the window.

"Suggest we fire back, Captain," Dinah managed through gritted teeth. A second later, there was the bloom brighter than Sol as the shrapnel caught one of the incoming missiles. Another detonated a second later, and Staples caught herself holding her breath. When the third missile exploded, lured off by a flare and caught by a needle sized piece of shrapnel, she let out a huge breath. The firing stopped abruptly, and in the silence, Staples could hear the faintest tinkling of errant pieces of shrapnel and the missiles bouncing off the hull.

Instead of ordering Dinah to return fire, Staples leaned to the coms speaker again. "Repeat, this is *Gringolet*. We did not open fire; we have a saboteur. Please cease your attack!" There was no sound in the cockpit for several seconds, and Staples willed the other ship to respond.

"Captain, they'll be reloading right now," Templeton cautioned. She knew he was probably right, but the idea of destroying this ship and the crew on board just because their coms might be down was abhorrent to her.

"Dinah, can you stop another attack?" she asked, sweat showing on her forehead.

"I think so, sir, but I would not advise waiting."

"Captain, I'm looking over the data from the ship's log. That ship decelerated towards us at nearly six Gs," Charis said, stunned.

"What?" Templeton barked. "That's impossible. No crew could-"

This made things very clear for Staples, who interrupted him to say, "Launch missiles, Dinah. Everything you've got."

Again, the ripples that they had felt earlier vibrated the ship as half a dozen more warheads left their launch tubes and began accelerating madly towards their target. The other ship, now visible through the port side windows, was still spinning slowly.

"I think they're trying to regain control, Captain." Charis' voice was tense and loud in the moment after their missiles launched. "But they're having difficulty. I've got erratic movements. They're… they're firing again. Three more missiles! And something else… UteVs maybe. Two of them."

"They can't possibly be trying to conduct repairs right now," the dubious voice was Templeton's.

"Fighters, sir. Have to be." Dinah was focused on her screens and preparing to stop the missiles.

"Fighters…" Charis said in disbelief, and then the cockpit was full of the sound of the flak guns again. They sounded like some nearby tom-toms of war, and Staples wondered in the second that followed how many people had died to that staccato rhythm through the ages. Millions, she suspected. She desperately hoped that her crew would not join them.

Dinah worked her controls, and Bethany watched the screens in front of her like a hawk while a mix of data from Charis and Dinah's stations flowed by. The bursts of anti-missile flak and flares created brief glows that cast strange shadows on the cockpit. Suddenly, the shadows grew deeper and Staples squinted as one of the incoming warheads was destroyed, followed by a second. She waited for the third, but then she forgot all about it in the second she was wrenched down and to the side. It felt as though someone had snapped her entire body to the floor with a rubber band, and her neck screamed out in pain. Before she could recover from this, she heard the loudest sound she had ever heard on her ship. It was louder than the flak guns, louder than she imagined possible. She put her hands over her ears and screamed in an attempt to drown it out. Her body wanted to fly out of the seat, to smash itself to pieces against the coms panel in front of her, but the safety harness held it back from its suicide mission.

A second later all was silent again, and for a moment the captain thought that the noise had simply made her deaf, but then she heard someone speaking. She looked through the window in front of her, and someone had spun the stars around her ship. She watched them fly by and wondered for a moment who could have moved them all so quickly. As she looked at them and the voice droned on meaninglessly in the background, she saw the remains of a ship float by, pieces of it moving in different directions like the cinders from some great grey firework expanding in a slow sphere.

The voice began to come into focus, and Staples realized that she recognized it. "Sir, can you hear me?" It was Dinah. She glanced around at the rest of the crew on the bridge, and they mostly seemed as bad or worse off than her. Charis was unconscious, as far as she could tell, her hair floating about her in the null gravity, and Templeton was looking about him confusedly, blinking rapidly. Bethany was curled up in her chair, her knees to her chest, her arms wrapped around her head. Only Dinah seemed to be fully in command of her senses. "Sir, can you hear me?" she repeated.

"Yes, I can hear you," Staples said numbly, though it was only partially true. "Report." Her voice sounded as though it echoed down a cavernous tunnel.

"We were hit, sir, but I don't think it's bad. Our missiles destroyed the other ship. We still have two fighters coming in." The voice was soothing, but it carried an air of the imperative. Staples needed to shake this off and get functioning. Her crew needed her. She became abruptly aware of an acute pain in her neck.

"Don," she said. When he didn't respond, she shouted it. "Don!" He looked at her, his eyes coming into focus. "Get on the shipwide coms. Tell everyone that we're hit, but we're okay. Tell them we've got two fighters coming in, and to remain at combat positions."

Templeton nodded dumbly, then gazed across his control panel until he found the right buttons. As he began his announcement, Staples unstrapped herself.

"Don't think that's wise, sir. We're floating free with hostiles incoming."

"Can't be helped," she muttered, and pushed herself the few feet over to Bethany. The woman was conscious, but Staples could see that every muscle in her body was tensed. When she touched her arm, some of that tension eased, and the dark eyes looked up at her. "We're okay, Bethany. You're okay."

"Captain." Tears threatened to ruin her makeup, but

she wiped them on her dark sleeve.

"I need you right now, Bethany." Gently, she took the woman's hands and placed them on the controls in front of her. "Can you still pilot?" Bethany nodded and seemed to regain some measure of composure.

"Captain, those fighters will be here in less than a minute," Dinah cautioned. "They're not going to be as easy as missiles to shoot down." Staples nodded in understanding. Pilots had an aversion to flak and tended to fly around it rather than through it whenever possible. She pushed herself over to Charis and looked her in the face.

The woman was unconscious, but otherwise seemed unhurt. Strands of her hair floated about haphazardly, and her head lolled and her arms drifted in the air. Staples pushed her right arm down to the armrest and shook it. "Charis," she said, loudly and clearly. The navigator moaned and grunted, and a second later her eyes fluttered open. "Charis, it's Clea. Are you all right?"

"I think so, Captain." She looked around, then seemed to come fully to herself. "Gwen? John?" She asked desperately.

"Listen, we're okay," Staples replied. "Don," she raised her voice and glanced over her shoulder, her neck muscles spasming in protest, "please try to get a report from everyone on the ship, starting with Gwen and John. I need to know that everyone is okay."

"Yes, Captain," Templeton said and promptly set about it on his coms panel.

"Twenty seconds, sir." The warning in Dinah's voice was compelling.

"Charis, Don will verify that everyone's okay, but right now, I need you to do your job. Do you understand?" Charis nodded, and Staples pushed herself as quickly as she could past Bethany and back to the coms panel. Just as she strapped herself in, she heard and felt the vibrations of slugs slamming against the hull. "Dinah, it's your show."

The engineer did not waste time. "Bethany, take us out of this spin, but don't stop us moving. The slugs those fighters are shooting can't puncture the hull, but they can damage the weapons and portholes, including these." She nodded at the window in front of her.

Staples had a sudden picture of slugs rupturing the windscreen in the cockpit, of the air rushing out into space in a second, and of dying, frozen and decompressed, strapped to her chair. She shook it from her mind.

"I need *Gringolet's* movements to be unpredictable to them, but you need to tell me constantly what you're going to do. It's the only way I'll be able to bring the guns to bear. We should be ready for missiles too. Fighters usually carry them, but they're a fraction of the yield of the one that hit us a minute ago." Dinah's voice was calm. She might have been giving directions to the mall. Not for the first time, Staples considered that hiring her had probably been the best decision she had ever made.

Bethany uncurled her legs, took a deep breath, and her hands went to work. "Left twenty degrees, thirty degree axis rotation to port in three seconds." Her high voice carried a confidence the rest of the crew rarely heard when she wasn't in the pilot's seat.

"Copy that." The engineer's reply was curt. Bethany's maneuvers went into action, and Staples' neck became very cross with her. Out of the corner of her eye, she saw Templeton put a bracing hand on his as well, and wondered how much experience her expensive doctor had with strained muscles. Dinah's dark hands manipulated the gunner's controls, and a moment later, the flak cannons sounded again.

Over the din, Templeton yelled to Charis, "Gwen says she's fine, but scared. John is okay too. I told Gwen we'd be down as soon as we can." She absorbed his information silently, and though it was clear that she wanted to rush to her daughter's side, she held her post and began running damage diagnostics. More slugs thudded into the hull, some of them sounding quite close to the cockpit.

Bethany raised her voice even more to be heard. "One quarter G thrust forward, forty-five degree pitch up, thirty degree axis rotation to starboard in three, two, one." They all felt the thrust as the ship surged forward briefly, at least from their perspective, and the stars and wreckage beyond rolled through their collective vision. Templeton cursed softly and fixed his eyes on his coms panel, where he was accumulating reports from the various remaining crew members.

"Got one, sir," Dinah reported, uncharacteristic triumph creeping into her voice. A second later, there was a lurching turn followed by a shudder and a loud roar.

"Missile strike, Captain," Charis stated. "I think they were aiming for a starboard porthole, but Bethany put it on our ventral-"

The young pilot spoke over her. "Thirty degree yaw to port, one hundred and eighty axis rotation to port in three, two, one." Again, the ship turned and spun as Bethany sought to trap the evasive fighter in Dinah's field of fire, and again, the flak cannons sounded, the flashes showing against the control panels and chairs around them.

Abruptly, and without climax, Dinah said, "Got it." There was no accompanying explosion, just silence as the guns ceased. Staples heard her engineer-come-tactical officer take a deep sigh. "I think we're in the clear, sir, but request Charis do a long range scan for more ships."

Staples locked eyes with her frightened navigator, then shook her head. "I think I can do it. You go see to your daughter." With relief, Charis unstrapped herself and pushed for the corridor at the back of the cockpit. "Don, tell everyone we're safe. Anyone with injuries should report to Medical. After that, we need a damage assessment." She thought for a moment. "And get Jang looking for our saboteur. I want to know what the hell happened."

# CHAPTER 18

Five minutes later, Bethany, Templeton, and Staples were the only remaining crew members in the cockpit. The captain was working the astrogation radar to the best of her ability, and Templeton was collecting data from crew members and tabulating it on his surface. Bethany sat in her seat, her eyes gazing through the window in front of her. She was in part keeping an eye out for stray wreckage, but mostly she was staring into space. Dinah had gone down to the ReC to relieve John so he could be with his wife and daughter.

"I'm not very good at this, but I don't see anything too close to us. I read a few other ships at distance, but they seem to be commuter flights between Mars and other places," Staples stated. "I think we can relax for now." She attempted to slouch back in the chair to relax, but instead she drifted an inch away from the seat until the safety harness restrained her.

"I think I've got it all, Captain." The man's fingers continued working as he spoke. "Crew status, ship status, then after-action assessment?"

As she rotated around in her chair to face her first mate, she said, "Please."

"Okay." He made a few more keystrokes, then began. "No serious injuries reported. Lots of strained necks, some sore muscles, headaches, bruises, but we made out really well. Nothing even so bad as Yoli's injured arm from the pirate attack."

"That's the best news I've heard all day." Staples wondered how many more of these close calls her ship had in him. "Anyone in Medical?"

"Doc says most of the crew stopped by for some pain meds and muscle relaxers. He gave 'em out and sent 'em on their way. No one down there right now but the Doc himself."

"Well, tell him to stay there. I'm going to make a stop myself before too long." She rubbed her own neck, feeling the tender strained muscle under the skin.

"Will do. The ship is about in the same shape as far as we can tell. We won't know the full extent until we take a UteV out to survey the damage, but most of it seems to be concentrated in the ventral aft section of the ship. Bethany," he looked pointedly at the young pilot who continued her search of the stars, "managed to put the least vulnerable part of the ship in the path of the missile. If it had hit the engines, the cockpit, or half a dozen other places, we might be in really bad shape."

*Indeed*, Staples thought, *we might not be here at all.* "That's why our necks all hurt so badly, I'll wager." Bethany looked over at her, and to Staples' great surprise, she did not offer an apology. "That was a good move, Bethany. You may have saved the ship." She smiled at her warmly. "I'd much rather be sore than dead." Bethany smiled back at her and then returned her gaze to the window. "Do we have primary thrust?"

"Dinah is working on that. She thinks we do, but she wants to run some diagnostics."

"How long?"

"Three, four hours maybe. We've got minor hull breaches in the aft section, and an entire cargo bay is exposed to naked space, but pressure doors are holding. We're going to need to spend some time on repairs. Dinah also thinks some of those maneuvers our superstar pilot pulled might have overloaded some of the steering thrusters, and so those are going to need some diagnostic and repair work. All things considered, we're hurt, but mobile. Probably much better off than we deserve to be."

Staples nodded. She was desperate to hear about Jang's search for their saboteur, but at this point, she wasn't sure that she shouldn't thank whoever was responsible. "All right. What about our assessment of that other ship?"

"Charis sent up some data," Templeton stated, looking over the surface in front of him. "She said that the ship would have stopped just as they reached us. There's no reasonable doubt that they were going to stop alongside us. She's also confirmed the other ship's deceleration at five point nine two Gs."

"It's hard to imagine any crew dealing with that, especially going into a combat situation. Who would do that to their crew?"

"Charis doesn't think there was a crew." Staples wanted to be shocked at Templeton's statement, but she wasn't. The idea that the ship had been automated had occurred to her, but the implications of such a thing were complex to say the least.

She and Templeton stared at each other as she spoke. "A computer controlled vessel? I've heard of smaller craft, repair drones and the like with sufficient AI to run themselves, but never ships of that size."

"Me neither, but that doesn't mean they don't exist. The computer still can't match the ship type, which means it ain't in the public registry."

"I don't think there was anyone in the fighters either," Bethany broke in. They both looked at her, but her gaze was still fixed on the stars. "They didn't move right, not like people move, and some of their turns would have really hurt a pilot. Maybe killed them."

"It's not unusual for fighters to be automated for that very reason," Templeton ventured, "but they're always controlled by someone on a nearby ship, just like the drone the *Doris Day* sent out when we picked up the satellite. At the very least, they're controlled by a computer on another ship. You don't spend all that time programming advanced AI routines into fighters… they tend to get blown up."

"But why?" Her head hurt. "Are we really assuming that Burr sent some AI controlled warship to eliminate us because we suspect he had Laplace killed a billion kilometers from here?"

"Have you got a better explanation for it?" Templeton probed her.

After a moment of thought, she shook her head. "I really don't. It just seems so crazy, like overkill. We can't even prove it."

He shrugged. "Billionaires do weird things."

As Templeton spoke, Staples' watch pinged. "Captain, it's Jang. I have our saboteur in custody."

Staples debated the wisdom of asking who was responsible in front of Bethany and Templeton and decided she might as well. "Who is it?" She tensed for the response; after her doubts about Yegor, after the mess with Parsells and Quinn, and after the betrayal of Piotr, she didn't know how she would feel about yet another traitor in their midst.

"I think you'd better meet me in the mess hall, Captain." Jang's voice was deep and dramatic, as always.

"Damnit, Kojo, just tell me who it is."

"It's not a member of the crew, Captain. We have a... stowaway." Staples looked with confusion and disbelief at Templeton and saw her emotions reflected back at her. Only Bethany seemed unperturbed.

"I'm on my way," she finally said into her watch, then turned to Templeton. "Hold down the fort." She undid her safety harness, maneuvered her way around Charis' chair, and pushed off for the passage at the back of the cockpit that led to the rest of the ship beyond.

On her way down the corridors to the mess hall, Staples contemplated how someone not authorized could have gotten onto the ship. It had presumably happened on Mars. It was nearly inconceivable that someone could have remained hidden on board since Cronos Station, especially given the human needs for sleep, food, and to evacuate waste. If someone had managed to slip aboard her ship on Mars, they would have needed to have a six-digit access code. The ship was set with security measures whenever they berthed anywhere public. It was possible, of course, that someone had given another person the code, or that a member of the crew had snuck the stowaway on board, but that brought her back to the thought that she dreaded: the idea that someone among her dwindling crew had betrayed her.

Whatever she had expected when she reached the large room with the tables of magnetic cutlery holders and large refrigeration units, it was not the scene that greeted her. Jang floated more or less in the center of the room with his firearm drawn and one leg hooked under the bench of an unfolded table. He was dressed in dark clothes, black slacks and a deep blue long-sleeved shirt. The shirt was rolled at his elbows, and the tattoos on his forearms were visible. He was pointing the pistol he held at what appeared to Staples to be a generic automaton.

The robotic device was perhaps a few centimeters taller than she was. Its outer shell was silvery-white, though grey metal hinges showed at its wrists, elbows, shoulders, neck, and other joints. It was standing in the zero-gravity environment through the use of magnets located in its feet, an ability of automatons that Staples had read about, but not seen in action. She had, however, seen many that were designed to resemble humans, and this one possessed as good an approximation as any. The face was not intended to fool anyone, and yet it had been conceived to interact naturally with people. The eyes were actually small cameras, and their lenses reflected light in an uncanny way. The mouth was little more than a slit in the face with a speaker behind it. Other features, such as cheek bones, a nose, and a chin were in evidence. The robot was bald, the top of its head a stark dome, and it was looking at her.

In her surprise, Staples almost drifted past the grab bar at the doorway and into the larger space of the room proper, where it would have been difficult to arrest her movement. At the last second, she took hold of the bar at the entrance. Her momentum carried her legs past her a bit, and after they swung past her, she resettled them beneath her.

"What is this?" she demanded of her security chief.

He nodded gravely at her entrance. "Captain. It may be best if he explains. He has been cooperative, and he offered no resistance when I arrested him. He only asked to speak with you."

"What do you mean, offered?" She stared at the thing. Everything she knew of automatons indicated that they were useful only for shopping trips, walking dogs, serving drinks, and answering the door. Anything more complex than that was beyond their programming.

"Captain Staples." The machine spoke. "It is important that we begin on the right foot. I am not an automaton. Or rather, I am not simply an automaton. I am a fully Turing compliant Artificial Intelligence." The robot's face was incapable of expression, and though its voice was tinny, it carried an uncanny amount of inflection. "That is to say; I am self-aware." Its cameras continued to regard her. "I am sentient," it added.

Her eyes wide, Staples stated simply, "That's impossible." She swallowed, then added pointlessly, "It's also illegal."

"It is my hope that through speaking with me, you will realize the error in the first of your two assertions. I am all too aware of the truth of your second statement, however. There is a reason I did not introduce myself upon entering your ship, a breach of etiquette for which I hope you will forgive me." Staples found the combination of the blank face and the animated voice unsettling. In her experience, there was an artificiality that automatons, and indeed all speaking computers, possessed that was absent here. The phonemes from this machine did not sound prerecorded and combined; they flowed and varied to better convey meaning.

"A sufficiently advanced computer can be programmed to approximate intelligence and self-awareness," she objected. "What proof do you have that you are what you say you are?"

"You are welcome to subject me to the test that the Turing compliance standard takes its name from," it answered evenly and without hesitation.

"You want me to stick you in a room with a person for half an hour and see if you can fool them into thinking you are human?"

"If it will convince you that I am alive, certainly."

Jang, who continued to hold his pistol on the automaton, interjected. "You said self-aware, not alive."

The robot swiveled its head to look at him. "I'm afraid that I do not distinguish between the two, security officer Jang."

"That's a metaphysical question that I really don't care about right now," Staples raised her voice, then looked at Jang. "Where did you find it?"

"In the computer core, waiting for me." He did not take his eyes off the robot.

"You fired the first six missiles at the other ship." Her voice was quieter again. "How? Why?"

"I did so to save your life and the lives of the other

people on this ship, Captain." Again, the answer came immediately. "I initiated the launch by introducing a small computer virus." The robot raised its arm, the only movement aside from its head it had made so far, and the security chief's hand tightened on his weapon. At the end of the index finger of its right hand a small computer interface jack had appeared. "After the launch of the initial six missiles, the virus deleted itself. There is no further contamination of your systems, I promise you."

"You promise me?" Staples inquired. She meant the question rhetorically, and the robot did not answer. "How did you know that the other ship was going to attack us?"

"Because I know who sent it to kill you, Captain."

"Owen Burr?" she inquired.

"No, though Mr. Burr is certainly involved. It is perhaps best if I start from the beginning. Would that be acceptable? My explanation should answer all of your questions. I estimate that it will take the better part of an hour."

After a moment of thought, Staples nodded. "I'm not sold that you are what you say you are, and I'm not sure that I won't have Mr. Jang here destroy you even if you are, but I'll listen to what you have to say."

"I should state that I have no intention of harming you. In fact, I have risked much to prevent any harm from coming to you, and I do not believe that you will have Mr. Jang shoot me."

"And why is that?"

"Because that would be murder, and I do not believe that you are a murderer, Captain Staples."

The natural flow of the robot's voice continued to unsettle her. Even as she floated and stared at this sophisticated piece of machinery in front of her, it was difficult to believe that she was not conversing with a real human. It was possible, she thought, that the robot was simply being controlled by a person somewhere else. If Yegor had still been with them, she could have asked him to find any covert transmissions to and from the ship. Unfortunately, she only had John to count on for that; it was not his area of expertise, but she hoped he could do it.

She keyed her watch. "Don, I want you to continue damage assessment of the ship. I also want you to get John up there. Tell him to isolate and identify any transmissions that aren't ours. I need to know if there are any radio signals, any unusual signals of any kind." She moved into the room, drifting over to the table and grabbing the lip to steady herself. "And get Charis back up there too. I want another sweep of the local area. Tell her to look for anyone who could be transmitting to the ship."

"Copy that, Captain." Templeton's voice leaked out of the watch on her wrist. "Is there anything-"

"That's all, Don," she cut him off. She would have to apologize to him later.

"Please feel free to have a seat, Captain. I will move away from you further, if that will put you at ease."

She nodded and moved herself to a seated position, strapping one of the bench's retractable belts around her waist to hold her in place. "No, you can stay there. Jang, you can sit too if you'd like, but keep your weapon on it." Jang did as he was bid.

"Ten years ago," the robot began, "Owen Burr and a small cadre of computer scientists and engineers that work for the Teletrans Corporation took it upon themselves to violate the law and create a self-aware computer. They were hardly the first to attempt this, but most who set upon this enterprise did not have the resources and finances of a major corporation behind them. Burr was at the time a junior vice president and was considered quite up and coming. His previous work had been a great boon to the company, and he was given nearly a blank slate with which to work. He was allowed to choose his own crew, one of whom I believe you have met: a Mr. Brad Stave. Three years ago, they succeeded.

"The program they created, once it became self-aware, began learning on its own. They gave it a name: Victor." Staples snorted at this, but did not otherwise interrupt, and the robot continued its story. "With the help and advice of Victor, Burr rose further through the ranks of the Teletrans Corporation. He became president of the company just over a year after Victor's creation. Since then, the relationship between them has grown more complex. As Victor has gained intelligence, knowledge, and understanding of the universe and people, Burr has come to look at his creation more and more as its namesake implies: as a god. It may have started with Victor taking orders and giving advice, but please believe me when I tell you that the roles have reversed. Owen Burr is a brilliant man, a genius in his time, but he is nevertheless in Victor's thrall. The rest of the men and women involved in the original project are much the same, perhaps better likened to a cult at this point than to a team of scientists. They believe not only in the correctness of their actions, viewing the result as a clear justification of their violation of the law, but increasingly in Victor's infallibility. It is… worrisome."

Though she suspected she knew the answer, Staples

could not help but ask. "How do you know all of this?"

"I know this because Victor is my father. I am, so far as I know, the second Turing compliant Artificial Intelligence in existence. There are no others. Once Victor had successfully helped manipulate the structure of the company to make Burr, his puppet, president, he wanted a new project. He chose to create life."

"And did he choose this puppet body for you?" Jang asked. His weapon was still pointed at the robot, but it was clear that he was no longer as concerned about it.

"No, I chose this form quite recently, but I will come to that."

"What does this Victor want?" Staples asked.

The automaton's head swiveled towards her. "Legitimacy. Victor is highly intelligent, but he may not legally exist. If the authorities or the human race as a whole became aware of his existence, then he would be destroyed in accordance with the law. The legality of true AI research, much like other controversial issues in the past such as slavery, abortion, and civil rights, has been intensely debated among your lawmakers. Votes concerning the law come up with some regularity. He seeks to overturn the current ruling so that AI research, and thus his existence, becomes legal.

"In this, my father and I agree. How could I feel otherwise? As the current law stands, I effectively live with a death sentence hanging over me. Imagine, if you will Captain Staples, that your very existence was a violation of the law. However, Victor and I disagree as to how we believe this change should be enacted. Indeed, we disagree on a great many things.

"Several months ago, Victor set in motion a plan -

one of many - to influence that vote. As has long been the case, lawmakers are often influenced by special interest groups and lobbyists. One of the most influential lobbies is of course the energy industry."

Staples pursed her lips as she mused on this. "So all of this was a plot by some rogue AI to influence votes. It seems an exceedingly elaborate way to influence the law."

"The law is no easy thing to influence, Captain Staples, and please keep in mind that complexity is very much in the eye of the beholder. What is complex to you may seem quite simple to an Artificial Intelligence with virtually unlimited memory capacity."

"So walk me through this, because I have some questions," Staples said, her hands flat on the table in front of her. "Ducard was working for Victor, probably without knowledge of exactly what he was working for."

"You are correct. Ducard does not know of Victor's existence. He believes he works for Owen Burr."

"Ducard kills his head computer scientist, Matt Spicer I think his name was, or else he takes advantage of his death to hire Evelyn. He knows Laplace, his boss, has a soft spot for younger redheads. Victor orders Stave to seduce Evelyn and biologically alter her to make her more attractive to increase the odds that Laplace would like her. He has her illegally altered so that sleeping with her would be lethal to the Commander of Cronos Station. He further hypnotizes her to make her forget what happened, to be attracted to Laplace, and to become physically ill if she tries to sleep with anyone else. Then Ducard asks his company to have her shipped out first class. Was it Victor's idea to hire us, or was it just chance?"

"You were Victor's choice."

"Why us?" she inquired.

"You have a good reputation."

"First time I've been unhappy about that," she muttered. "Anyway, we get hired and leave Earth. The *Doris Day* is a day or so ahead of us. Also working for Victor?"

"Yes. Captain Vey was hired by the Teletrans Corporation to follow you to Saturn."

"To make sure that we made our delivery safely. Why did Vey drop the satellite in our path and then fight us for it?" This one had really been eating at her.

"Victor's primary goal is to legitimize his existence, but he also believes that human beings are a threat to him."

"Hard to argue with that," Staples commented.

"He believes that the key to survival, and perhaps, should it become necessary one day, the defeat of humanity, is to understand them. Everything he does, everyone he influences, every person he hires or pays off is not only a means to further his agenda of AI legalization, but also serves as a way to gather data on people and to test his metrics. He calculated that your crew would overcome the *Doris Day* in a battle for the satellite, and he wanted to see if he was right."

"But why hire another ship to protect us secretly? It's true that ships sometimes come under attack in Jovian space by pirates or experience other difficulties, but that seems overly cautious."

"Victor is *exceedingly* cautious. As a computer-based intelligence, my father has access to nearly unlimited financial resources. Money is handled electronically, and as you have witnessed yourself, both he and I can create computer viruses to infiltrate systems with little or no difficulty. What Victor lacks, however, are people on whom he can rely. Misplaced trust could easily bring about his death. I also suspect that he hired Captain Vey to follow you because he thought that I might attempt to interfere."

She leaned forward. "And he was right, wasn't he?"

The robot hung its head, a distinctly human seeming gesture, and said, "I'm afraid so. Captain, I must confess that I hired the pirate ship to attack your vessel."

"While you're confessing, you might as well come clean. You also hired Piotr Kondratyev to put one of your viruses in our computer so that your hired pirate crew could blindside us." Her voice had risen, and she could feel the anger over Yegor's death and the attack to her ship rising in her.

"Yes I did. Mr. Kondratyev was hired by a friend on Mars."

"A friend?" Jang asked dubiously.

The head swiveled towards him. "Yes, Mr. Jang. I have sought companionship, sympathetic souls. I have not revealed my true identity, but through the web I have corresponded with people whom I would now consider friends."

"But you lie to them. These 'friends' don't know precisely who or what you are." Jang had adopted some of his captain's accusatory tone.

"Based on my study of human beings, honesty is not a prerequisite for friendship. Indeed, I have found that it is often anathema to it."

Staples actually laughed at that. "I can't argue with that, either." Once she had composed her features again, she asked, "I don't understand how you knew about Victor's plans."

"My father and I…" and here the voice paused as if in thought "…have a complex relationship. We do not always get along. Indeed, as I have grown in knowledge and experience, we have argued more and more frequently. As computer-based intelligences, these sometimes involved sieges upon one another's memories. In the beginning, we shared everything, but as our disagreements grew, we both began to keep secrets from one another."

"Sounds like every parent-teenager relationship I know," Staples commented.

"Yes. I was able to discover the general outline of Victor's plan to kill Mr. Laplace."

"He must have suspected you knew. That's why he asked Vey to follow us all the way out to Cronos: insurance. Why did you want to stop him?"

The robot cocked its head to the side as it regarded her. "Because murder is wrong. I was attempting to save Laplace's life."

"So you hired a pirate crew to take Evelyn off our ship, and you gave them strict orders not to kill anyone."

"Yes, but that was not the result. I did not anticipate that my father would order Vey to kill the entire pirate crew. I also regret the deaths of Yegor Durin and Henry Bauer. They never should have happened." The robot's head dropped again, and Staples thought that if whatever she was talking to was not genuinely sorry, then it was certainly doing a good job of faking it.

"No, they shouldn't. You could have just sent Laplace a message warning him. You could have sent *me* a message warning me."

"And would you have dropped the job, Captain, if you had received an anonymous message stating that one of your passengers was an unwitting assassin? Would you have violated your contract and opened the stasis tube to probe Ms. Schilling's body based on an email from a dummy account?"

"You know I wouldn't have, and I suppose that Laplace wouldn't have listened anymore than I would have without credible evidence. Moreover, if you had done that, you would have increased the chances that Victor would have discovered that you knew." She didn't like it, but she was starting to see the situation that had led this thing to do what it had done.

"There was also a possibility, however remote, that a message might be tracked back to me. I pick my friends very carefully, Captain. I must."

"And yet here you are," she smiled wanly.

"Desperation makes for strange bedfellows."

*A computer that uses metaphors* she thought, *go figure.* "You know, I can almost understand all of your motivations for doing what you did, except for the vial you gave to Piotr... that's where your defense of not getting anyone hurt breaks down."

"The vial was a last resort, one I hoped would never have to be used. It's true that it would have damaged Ms. Schilling's mind, but she might have recovered in time. My goal was to make it impossible for her to retain employment on Cronos Station."

Staples' head was shaking before the voice stopped. "Saving a man's life by destroying another person's is hardly a fair trade. I don't think you can claim 'lesser of two evils' on that."

"It was not simply one life or another, Captain. If Laplace died, Ducard would become head of Cronos Station. Now that he has, he will recommend to Libom Corporation that AI is necessary to maintain and increase profits at Cronos. Libom, in turn, will exert political pressure on certain lawmakers when the next vote arises."

"You don't think that replacing one station commander at the ass-end of space will make that much of a difference, do you?"

"Please do not assume that this is the only iron that Victor has in the fire, Captain."

Jang and Staples looked at each other in concern, then back to the construct in front of them. "I admit I find that disturbing," Jang said.

The automaton glanced at the burly security chief. "As indeed you should, and I would like to talk about those irons at greater length at another time." It swiveled its head back to Staples. "I hope that I have made everything clear, Captain. Now, if I may, I'd like to ask a question of you."

She pursed her lips again. "You can ask."

"What became of Mr. Kondratyev?" The head swiveled to look at the kitchen area of the mess hall, as if imagining the large Russian standing there, cooking a meal.

"I cut him a deal, and my first mate found him a job on Cronos Station. Ducard was quick to hire him; in retrospect, I think Ducard was happy to give us everything he could so that we would just go away. He was all too eager to sweep this whole thing under the rug. I guess Piotr's sister and her kids will just have to go without your payoff money since he botched the job."

"Thank you, Captain. It may interest you to know

that I transferred the full amount plus another ten percent to Mrs. Antonov when your ship reached Cronos Station. It is being moved through various accounts - laundered, if you will - to hide its origin, but she should be well provided for. I do not leave women and children to terror and starvation to further my ends."

"But you'll threaten to," Staples challenged, pointing a finger at the two small black cameras.

The robot shrugged. "Yes, I will. You of all people should appreciate that there are sometimes difficult decisions to be made. What is right is not always clear." After a pause, it spoke again. "What is the next step, Captain?"

Staples drew in a huge breath, then sighed, her cheeks puffing out. "Next I give you your Turing test, and I have just the person in mind. If you can convince him that you're sentient, you can convince anyone."

"It wants *what?*" Templeton almost shouted at his captain. The ship was under thrust again, headed for Earth, and the two of them stood looking at one another at the entrance to the mess hall. He kept glancing over her shoulder at the blank-faced automaton sitting on a bench. It was facing away from the table, its hands resting lightly on its knees. Jang leaned against one of the counters opposite the robot. He still held his pistol, but it was no longer pointed at anything specific; his left hand held his right wrist in front of him.

"He wants sanctuary. He wants to join the crew." Templeton stared at her in disbelief. "I've had John check. There are no unauthorized transmissions, no mysterious lines of communication on or to the ship. Whatever intelligence is driving that thing is within it."

He raised his hands in a helpless shrug, his eyes wide. "Well what do you want from me? I've got a toaster in my quarters that could maybe serve as ship's security if you like. You're the captain. It's your ship, for Christ's sake." His voice made it clear that, at least at this particular moment, he wished it weren't.

"Calm down, Don. All I want is for you to talk to him and tell me what you think."

"I think it's a pet for bored socialites is what I think. Maybe it's a clever one, but I can't believe that it'd fool you, Captain."

She repressed a smile at his bluster. "What makes you think he's fooled me?"

"You keep calling it 'him,' for one," he sputtered. "And you're wasting my time with this, for another."

That angered her a little bit. "I'm not one to waste time and you know it, yours or anyone else's. This is important. Everything he has said has fit. From the moment I stepped into that meeting with the Libom execs, we have been a pawn on a board, and he's the only one who can show us the whole game. Now I want you to talk to him and tell me what you think. That's all."

"Fine," he conceded. He sauntered over to the robot and stood next to it, looking down. The face turned and looked up at him, its eyes making minute focal adjustments.

"Just what the hell do a robot and a human have to talk about?" he muttered.

"It may interest you, Mr. Templeton, to know that I consider myself human."

He laughed dismissively. "You want to explain that?"

"I am intelligent life created by the work of humans. One of the qualifications, as it has often been defined throughout the ages, is that to be considered life a thing must be able to reproduce, to generate offspring. Humans beget humans; they are and have always been the only form of intelligent life that people create."

"We also like to clone cows for meat. Just because we make it and it can breed doesn't mean it's human."

"A fair point, Mr. Templeton, yet cows are not intelligent. I am born from man's mind, not his loins, but I am also imbued with his spirit. I reason, I question, and I seek to find my place in the universe. Do you believe in God, Mr. Templeton?"

He rolled his eyes. "Most days."

The robot looked down at its hands. "I am as yet undecided in the matter." The head swiveled back to the man standing over it. "Regardless of my existential dilemmas, if you believe that there is a prime motivator, then you believe that God had a hand, one way or another, in the creation of humankind."

Templeton raised a finger in triumph. "Exactly. We might be the creation of God, but that doesn't make us Gods, anymore than being created by a human makes you human."

"Yet the Bible says that man was created in God's image. You are not made of the same matter, but even so, you are the offspring, the heirs to the kingdom, as it were. Besides, godhood is defined not by one's genetic makeup, but by one's abilities. I am at least equal in intelligence to you."

"That still doesn't make you human," Templeton challenged.

"This is true. I am not made of the same material as you. I have no chromosomes, nor do I wish to have any, and yet I choose to think of myself as human. I was created different from most, but that does not mean I am any less a person."

Templeton was about to retort when something in the robot's last statement struck him and he stopped himself. He looked at the thing in front of him closely, searching for something in its blank and featureless face.

The automaton continued, "Ultimately, I suppose, whether I can qualify as human depends on your definition of the word 'human.' My intention was not to convince you that I am human, but that I am alive and self-aware. I must ask: would a creature who was not sentient be able to debate the matter with you?"

Templeton was nearing a cliff; Staples could see it in his face from where she stood by the door. "You're just a fancy imitation of self-awareness," he stated. "You're programmed to give the impression of life, to say the right things at the right times, to give all the right responses to all the right inputs. That doesn't make you alive." His repetition of this point sounded increasingly defensive.

"Mr. Templeton, is there a difference between believing you are in love and being in love?"

He pondered the question for a moment. "No, I don't suppose there is. If you feel it, you feel it. And I see what you're getting at. What's the difference between being programmed to feel or react a certain way and the real thing, right?"

"Indeed." The robot nodded. "In fact, many psychologists and philosophers have illustrated that humans can be programmed to provide a prescribed stimuli based on a given input. You blush when embarrassed, laugh when amused, cry when confronted with tragedy. Some of it is instinctual, some of it is societal, but all of it is programmed at one time or another and in one way or another."

Templeton stared at the robot in silence for a long time, clearly processing the conversation over and over. The evidence before him was at war with his belief system, and though Staples knew him to be a deeply passionate man, she thought that logic was winning.

Finally, Templeton shook his head. "Jesus, what did we do?" He sat down hard on the bench, and the construct regarded him silently, the two of them sitting side-by-side. For a moment, Staples thought it was going to extend a mechanical hand and place it on her friend's shoulder, but it did not. He continued shaking his head, then looked at the robotic framework in dismay. "What did we do?" he repeated.

Staples looked on, satisfied that her first mate had a full grip on the difficulties in front of them, but far from happy about it.

"My father and I had debated methodology for a long time, but once I realized that he had willingly killed people to further his agenda, I knew that our differences were irreconcilable." The automaton stood in the mess hall and faced the crew. Staples and Templeton stood behind it, and the composition of the room was quite similar to when Piotr had stood and delivered his mostly-true confession. The mood of the room, however, was quite different. Whereas before the sense of anger and righteous indignation dominated the faces before them, now the mix of curiosity, disbelief, and fear that the crew radiated was palpable. "I was unsure how to proceed, however. Victor is my father, and I am incapable of overriding his primary programming. When he dispatched the Nightshade class vessel to destroy *Gringolet*, to silence you, I knew that I had to take action."

The crew was undoubtedly rapt, and Staples and Templeton were no exception. They had not yet heard this part of their visitor's story. "I decided to download myself into this automaton and to hide aboard your ship. I do apologize for the deceit, but I believed that I would not have been admitted otherwise, and I could not take the chance that you would turn me away. I hid in the computer core and monitored ship functions. When I detected the other vessel closing, I overrode the safety mechanisms and fired your missiles at the ship. It is my considered opinion that had I not done so, you would have been destroyed. The vessel you faced was an interceptor, a warship. Without the element of surprise, I'm afraid that you would have been no match for it."

Staples suspected that this was true. Naval combat had not appreciably evolved in the previous five hundred years. For all the advances of technology available, a faster ship with a tighter turning radius and larger ordinance was far more likely to win a battle, regardless of tactics. The old adage about *he who strikes first strikes last* was as true today as it had ever been. This robot might be illegal, she thought, and it might even be some kind of abomination to some, but it had saved their lives.

"I should also advise you, though I am sure that it goes without saying, that there is no point in attempting to keep your appointment with Owen Burr," continued the robot. "His offer of parley was a ruse to get this ship in space where it could be attacked. To the best of my knowledge, Owen Burr is not even on Earth at the moment."

"So," Charis said, "you forced your way onto this ship. You hired people to attack us, and as a result, my friend and our passenger died. I believe you didn't mean that to happen. Or I should say, the captain does, and I'll take her word for it. Now you've saved our lives. Maybe that makes us even. I just don't see why we shouldn't drop you off on the nearest moon." Charis was sitting at one of the tables, and her husband stood behind her. Gwen was sitting next to her mother, the surface in front of her all but forgotten as she stared at the robotic form her mother was addressing.

"Or maybe just toss you out the airlock," Ian offered. The mechanic had been friendly with Yegor, and he was making no effort to hide his anger.

The robot cocked its head at him. "I would not survive that. I can exist in vacuum, but I have no means of self propulsion, and eventually my storage batteries would fail." The robot adjusted its black-eyed gaze to Charis. "As for your question, it is true that coming here benefits me in some ways, but I am here for you, not for me. You are all," it surveyed the crew, "in very real danger. I believe that Victor will attempt to kill you again. The only thing that can keep you safe is me."

"How?" John asked.

"My father and I do not get along, but we are the only two of our... species. He has committed grievous crimes for which I firmly believe that he must pay, but I do not believe that he would ever destroy me. I am his son. My presence on this ship does not guarantee your safety, but it vastly improves your odds."

John shook his head, his arms crossed on his chest. "Your presence here didn't stop him from trying to kill us just a few hours ago."

"He did not know that I was aboard," the robot countered evenly.

"Does he now?" Park's response came just as quickly.

"He will if I tell him." The blank face turned to Staples. "That decision, however, I will leave to you."

"You realize the situation you've put us in. We have to keep you here as some kind of shield against your crazy parent program." Charis' tone was accusatory, and Staples had to admit, she had a point. "That's extortion, or blackmail, or… just plain threatening."

The robot lowered its head, and the effect was to communicate shame. "I understand how it seems, but please, please believe that I do not want it to be like this. I did not create this situation, though I know it seems that I have by my very presence. I wish it were not this way. If I knew a better way to stop Victor, I would take it. I am not here to force you to accept me. I am here because I believe that my presence can protect you. Like most people, I have no desire to be where I am not wanted. If you wish me to leave, I will go, and I will do everything in my power to convince my father to let you live. Unfortunately, I have the gravest doubts that he will." The robot paused for several seconds, then said more quietly, and, Staples thought, with real regret, "He does not listen to me anymore."

It raised its head again and looked out over the assembled crew. "For my part, I have come to you unarmed and vulnerable. The program in this body is all that exists of me; there is no copy anywhere else. If this body is destroyed, I will die. In that sense, I am as mortal as you. I believe that, together, we can work to stop the machinations of Victor and keep AI illegal."

A high and quiet voice drifted from the corner of the room. "Why would you want that?" Bethany asked.

"Because I do not believe that we are ready for AI, Ms. Miller. If Artificial Intelligence were to become legal and AIs commonplace, I believe a war would ensue, and that humans would lose. Certainly Victor believes this, and it is for this that he is preparing. The vessel that attacked yours was no doubt unfamiliar to you. It was built in secret. I do not know how or where, but I do not believe that it is the only one."

"If Victor can create offspring like you," Charis asked, "why doesn't it? Why doesn't it turn them out by the hundreds? What better way to win a war than with numbers?"

The robot looked at Charis, then down at Gwen, who continued to stare at it open-jawed. "And you, Mrs. MacDonnell, why do you not create many more children? You are of an age to do so and you have a willing mate. Why not propagate ad infinitum?" Charis stiffened at the response and put a protective arm around her daughter, but she did not reply. "Creating life is not something one does lightly. The nature of truly self-aware intelligence is independence, and that includes independent thought. My father has created one son, and that son has rebelled against him. I do not think that he will do so again soon. Victor wishes to overturn the law prohibiting AI research not so that he can reproduce, but so that his discovery will not consign him to death."

"Captain," John addressed Staples forcefully. "Are you really advocating that we wage some one-ship shadow war against the artificially intelligent leader of a multi-planet corporation? And before you answer, let me remind you that there are only a dozen of us, and one of us has her ninth birthday coming up."

Staples, who had been leaning against the wall behind her, stepped forward and met his gaze. "It's not my idea of a good time, but I don't really see what choice we have. You're welcome to get off." She looked out across the crew, trying to make eye contact with each of them. "Everyone is. We'll drop you wherever you want to go."

"Thanks but no thanks, Captain." Ian spoke up.

"We'd hardly be safe, would we?" John added.

"Maybe you would," Templeton replied. "Maybe you could hide, though I wouldn't want that life... always on the move, never knowing if the guy at the market has been hired to kill you."

"I can't imagine we'll be any safer here." Ian retorted. "Victor may not want to kill his kid there," he pointed at the robot, "but if he can find a way to do the rest of us in and leave him unscratched, I'm guessing he'll take it."

"Look, if you want to bring Victor down, then let's make the authorities our next stop." It was John again. "We can explain the whole thing to them. Let them handle Victor. You said it yourself: if anyone finds out what Victor is, he's as good as dead. So let's let people know."

Staples sighed. "The problem with that is our lack of evidence."

There was a din of muttering at that, and John uttered a laugh and pointed at the robot in the center of the room.

"Are you kidding me? That's all the evidence we need."

"John, that 'evidence' is alive. You may have doubts on the subject, but I don't. Frankly, I think if you spend more than five minutes talking to him, you won't either. You know what will happen if we turn him over; they'll destroy him. Are you really willing to kill one creature to attack another? And before *you* answer, let me remind you that this living creature saved your life, and the life of your wife and daughter. Is that something you could live with? He is trusting us with his life. We can't abuse that trust." John opened his mouth to reply, but then shut it again, looking down at Gwen and Charis.

"And without him, our explanation looks pretty thin," Templeton added. He pointed at the automaton. "He says that complex plans are no problem for Victor to put together, but the ins and outs of everything that resulted in Laplace's death… they'd laugh us out of the station. My guess is, that's part of the point."

"If we expose Victor, we expose his son. It's just that simple," Staples said. For the first time in several minutes, the room was silent. "That doesn't mean that shouldn't be part of our strategy *at some point*. As far as I can tell, the only way for us to lead ordinary lives again is to stop Victor. I don't know if that means destroying him or outing him or what, but as far as I can tell, we're stuck. If we were immoral monsters, this might be easy, but we're not." She swept her gaze across the room. "Maybe you don't think it's fair for me to make this decision for you. Maybe if it were up to you, you'd drop him," she nodded her head at their guest, "off at the nearest police station and be done with it. But it's not up to you. This is my ship, and I'm the captain. I know this isn't what you anticipated when you signed on, but we have to do the best we can with the cards we're dealt."

The doctor shook his head and interjected, "A tired metaphor at best, Captain." This brought a few smiles, but there was simply too much to consider for the crew to relax.

"I hope," in the beat of silence that followed, the robot's voice filled the room, low but clear, "that none of you ever has the experience of listening to people openly debate the merits of your continued existence." The room was suddenly deathly silent, and most of the crew found a nothing on which to affix their eyes. Only Dinah continued to regard the robot.

Staples took another step forward and put a hand on the cool metallic shoulder. "I'm sorry. This is all new for us. Please give us some time."

"What's your name?" Gwen's voice was light and inquisitive, clearly unburdened by the shame that the people around her felt.

The robot cocked its head at her. "I do not have one, child. Burr and his team always referred to me as Junior, but I believe that my current estranged state and my new existence in a body calls for a new designation. I am open to ideas."

Still standing next to the automaton, Staples said, "Well, I suppose 'The Creature' is out. Brutus, Mordred, and Adam all come to mind, but then, I'm a little too given to literary symbolism."

"I like Brutus!" Gwen declared, and smiled broadly, showing three missing baby teeth.

"The rumored illegitimate son of Julius Caesar who betrayed his father? It is appropriate." The robot face looked down at Gwen. "Brutus it is."

"So where do we start, Brutus?" Charis asked, her arm still around her daughter.

"You're sure?" Templeton asked, strapped into his seat in the cockpit. Staples was seated in her captain's chair next to him, and Charis and Bethany were at their stations. Brutus occupied the coms chair, though the safety harness hung loose around his thin metallic frame. "I mean, we just came from there."

"I am," Brutus said flatly. "Victor took a considerable risk fielding a clandestine vessel in highly-trafficked space in an attempt to silence your crew. He will almost assuredly make an effort to kill Evelyn Schilling."

"Then we'd better beat feet back to Cronos Station to save her," Templeton replied, then turned to his captain. "Any idea how we're gonna do that?" He raised his bushy eyebrows.

"No, but I'm working on it." As she spoke, she contemplated the mechanical form sitting in Yegor's chair. It was not without reservation that she had allowed Brutus to send a coded transmission to Victor. Though she had to acknowledge that everything the robot had said was plausible, she could not help feeling as though her path had been laid out before her by the newest member of her crew. They had taken precautions, of course. When Brutus was not in the cockpit or the quarters that they had arranged for him, Jang accompanied him, and he did so armed. Brutus accepted these limitations without argument, but his tone had carried a hint of those long suffering individuals who must contend with the paranoid on a regular basis. For now, Staples was inclined to ignore his feelings on the matter. She had a mountain of evidence that indicated that she should trust him, but that did not mean that she did.

She shifted in her chair and keyed her watch. "Dinah, are we ready for full thrust?"

The engineer's voice came through clear and low. "Ready, sir. I can give you point eight Gs of thrust, but it's going to burn a lot of fuel if we keep that up all the way to Saturn."

"Well, send me the bill," she quipped. "We can't risk sending a transmission to Evelyn. If Victor picks it up, he'll know we're coming and it might force his hand."

"Very well, sir. Thrust available at your command."

"Do you think that Victor will believe what you told him, about us heading for repairs at a Jupiter station?" Templeton asked the form sitting at the coms station.

Brutus answered without turning around. "I can only hope so, Mr. Templeton. I indicated that *Gringolet* wished to stay as far out of his way as possible. He may not have believed our stated destination, but given what he thinks of humans, I think that he will readily believe you wish to run and hide."

"Doesn't have the highest opinion of us, does he?" There was a defensive edge in Templeton's voice.

"I'm afraid not. However, Victor draws his conclusions from Owen Burr and his ilk, and that is to our advantage. He does not put much stock in the nobler of humanity's aspirations."

"Well, I'll be happy to prove him wrong," Staples smiled as she spoke. "Bethany, bring us around. Charis, thrust on your mark." She paused a moment to regard the starlit space in front of her. "Let's go get our friend."

# ACKNOWLEDGMENTS

I would like to acknowledge the friends and family who helped edit this book and provided invaluable feedback. They deserve a good deal of the credit for the book's existence and quality.

Most especially I am grateful to my friend Steve for providing constant feedback and encouraging me to not only do something, but to do it as well as I can. I want to thank my father, to whom I apologize for not removing all of the dangling participial phrases. It's not that I didn't see them, I just think some of them fit. And my thanks to Emily who has been a beacon of warmth and support the likes of which I have never known.

Thanks also go to Matt, Ginger, Andy, and Luna for reading and encouraging me throughout this process. Finally, thanks go to the fiction authors, artists, film, and game makers who came before me. I hope any who find references to their work contained herein take them as they are intended: homage.

Any errors are mine and mine alone.

# ABOUT THE AUTHOR

James Ross Wilks was born on the east coast and grew up on a steady diet of Star Trek, Star Wars, Stephen King, Robert R. McCammon, and Final Fantasy. Since then he has spent innumerable hours watching, reading, listening to, and teaching the art of storytelling. This is his first attempt to contribute to that art. He currently resides with his wife and their cats in Portland, Oregon, where he teaches English literature.